W9-AWL-863

Trick

OF THE

MIND

Trick
OF THE
MIND

CASSANDRA CHAN

ST. MARTIN'S MINOTAUR ✖ NEW YORK

This is a work of fiction. All of the characters, organizations, and events portrayed in this novel are either products of the author's imagination or are used fictitiously.

www.minotaurbooks.com

ISBN-13: 978-0-312-36939-2
ISBN-10: 0-312-36939-5

First Edition: May 2008

10   9   8   7   6   5   4   3   2   1

To Jack and Mary Dodge,
for seeing me through the hard times
and providing so many of the good ones

ACKNOWLEDGMENTS

If often happens when one acquires roommates that one discovers hitherto unknown facets of their personalities. Sometimes these discoveries take the form of small, irritating habits, but I have been extraordinarily lucky in that Crissie has turned out to have a hidden talent for making up titles (something I am abysmal at), as well as being perfectly content to have the end of the book "spoiled" in the course of conversations about plot issues and whether or not clues are too obvious. So many thanks to Crissie Tucker (she also helped with the abbreviations in Gibbons's notebook).

I also owe fervent thanks to Paul Saccento for having had the good sense to marry Pat and for introducing her to me. Which leads to many thanks to Pat Saccento for sharing all her medical knowledge.

Chris West introduced me to the marvels of alexandrite gemstones and vetted some of the jewelry passages, and Jon Elliot once again came through with his extensive knowledge of London neighborhoods. A grateful author thanks them.

Then there are my usual helpers who correct all my mistakes: Linda Pankhurst, who fixes my British English, and Beth Knoche, who finds all my typos.

Lastly, but far from least, are those without whom this book would not exist: My editor, Kelley Ragland; her assistant, Matt Martz; and my wonderful agent, Jennifer Jackson, who soothes my anxieties and handles all the difficult bits so I don't have to.

Trick

OF THE

MIND

1

The Night

It was eleven o'clock when they finished dinner and spilled out into the Boulevard St. Germain in high spirits, Marla laughing and rather tipsy with the champagne she had drunk. The fine November rain was chilly and Phillip Bethancourt tucked his arm around his girlfriend while she demanded to know what the others were saying. Bethancourt, cocking an ear toward the rapid cross fire of French among their companions, answered, "They're still arguing about the nightclub. Let's get a taxi, shall we?"

In the end, three taxis were procured to transport the entire party to one or another of the several Parisian nightclubs under discussion. Bethancourt, gallantly ushering the ladies in, found himself separated from Marla when he finally slid into the back of the car and slammed shut the door. Jean-Louis, up front with the driver, was giving instructions, and Catrine was leaning forward to argue with him. Bethancourt settled back in his cramped corner, content to let the others decide their destination, and lit a cigarette while the taxi started off. In his pocket, his mobile phone began ringing and Bethancourt dug it out with some difficulty, given the tight confines of the backseat.

It proved to be Spencer Kendrick in one of the other taxis.

"Have you any idea where we're going?" he demanded.

"No," answered Bethancourt cheerfully.

"Well, ring me if we end up in different places."

"Righto," agreed Bethancourt, and rang off. Before attempting to return the phone to his pocket, he checked his messages, finding one left much earlier in the evening by his friend Jack Gibbons.

"Got an interesting one on," said Gibbons's voice. "I'd like to hear what you make of it. Ring me when you get a chance."

Eleven o'clock, reflected Bethancourt, meant ten in London, which in turn meant Gibbons should be at home, preparing for bed. Without much further thought, Bethancourt pressed the speed dial on his phone, half his attention on the conversation in the taxi, which still centered on the various merits of different clubs. Thus occupied, he started when the voice answering the phone was not that of his friend, but was instead the gravelly tones of Detective Chief Inspector Wallace Carmichael of New Scotland Yard. Unconsciously, Bethancourt sat up a little straighter.

"Sorry to trouble you, sir," he said at once. "It's Bethancourt here. I was just ringing Jack back, but I'm sure it can wait."

"Bethancourt?" said Carmichael. He sounded disappointed. "Where are you?"

"Paris, sir," answered Bethancourt, shifting to shield the phone from the sound of the nightclub discussion, which had suddenly increased in volume.

There was a slight pause while the chief inspector assimilated this.

"And you say Gibbons rang you earlier?" he asked.

"He left a message, sir. I've only just got it—I had hoped to catch him at home before he went to bed."

"Did he say anything? What time did he ring you?" demanded Carmichael.

Bethancourt was instantly uneasy. "It was about six thirty, sir," he replied. "And he only said he had an interesting case on and I should ring him back. Has something happened?"

"Too bloody right it has," growled Carmichael. "Sergeant Gibbons is on his way to hospital—he's been shot."

Someone was shouting at the taxi driver, and the car swerved suddenly, changing direction and toppling Bethancourt into the door. He clutched at the phone desperately.

"Bethancourt? Are you there?"

"Yes, sir," he managed. "Is Jack all right?"

"I don't know," said Carmichael, his voice angry. "He's still alive, at any rate, but they only found him half an hour ago. I'm just leaving for the hospital myself."

"I'll start back at once, sir," said Bethancourt. "If I leave now, I can be there by morning. The mobile number will reach me in the meantime."

The taxi was slowing; up ahead there were lights and people milling about on the sidewalk.

"I've got to ring off now," said Bethancourt. "I'll get under way as quick as I can."

It was raining in London, too. Carmichael tried to shield Gibbons's mobile as he gingerly pressed the off button with a gloved finger. Then he dropped it back into the plastic evidence bag, but hesitated as he started to hand it back to the scene-of-the-crime officer who had brought the ringing to his attention.

"Better keep it with you," he said. "If it rings again, answer it and let me know at once."

"Yes, sir," said the SOCKO, taking the bag. "You want the usual on it otherwise?"

Carmichael nodded curtly.

"Right, then."

Bag in hand, the officer turned away and Carmichael surveyed the scene with an irate eye, cursing the rain under his breath. Beneath the bus shelter, two SOCKOs knelt, taking samples of the spreading bloodstain as fast as they could, trying to shield the pavement with their bodies. Other officers were scrutinizing the sidewalk and street, though there was really no chance any evidence would remain. They would probably not even be trying if the victim had not been a fellow officer.

In any case, there was certainly nothing left here for Carmichael to do. He walked briskly back to his car, banging the door closed and starting the engine up with a jerk.

"Why the devil hasn't O'Leary rung up?" he muttered as he pulled away from the curb. He fumbled with his mobile as he squinted through the windscreen; his night sight was not what it was, and the reflection of the city lights in the raindrops did not help matters.

"Sergeant O'Leary!" he barked when his call was answered. "What's happening?"

"I don't know, sir." Detective Sergeant Chris O'Leary sounded frustrated. "They've whisked him away somewhere and all I know for certain is that he's not gone into the operating theater yet."

"Why the hell not?"

"I've been trying to find out, sir, but the doctors haven't come back out yet."

"Have you got his things?" asked Carmichael desperately. "They undestood his belongings would be wanted as evidence, didn't they?"

"Yes, sir," replied O'Leary. "One of the nurses brought everything out in plastic bags and I've got it all safe. Hodges is on his way here to take it all back to the lab."

"Thank God," muttered Carmichael.

"Sir," said O'Leary, his voice suddenly urgent, "I'll ring you back. I see one of the doctors."

The line went dead and Carmichael cursed as he flung aside his phone and concentrated on getting to the hospital as quickly as possible.

Bethancourt was engaged in the same enterprise, only at a much greater distance.

"I need a car," he told Spencer Kendrick as they stood outside the nightclub in the drizzle. "If I leave straightaway, I can make one of the late-night ferries and be in London before dawn."

"Take the hire car," responded Kendrick. "I've got the keys here somewhere."

"Do you want me to come with you?" asked Marla, striving to appear quite sober and responsible, and partially succeeding.

In truth, Bethancourt did not. "No need," he assured her, rather touched not only by the offer, but also by the fact that she was standing out in the rain without complaint.

"You know," Kendrick said, producing the car keys at last, "if you waited and took the first flight in the morning, you'd only be an hour or two later. You're not gaining much time by driving all night."

Bethancourt shot him a dry look. "I really don't think I could endure several hours of enforced idleness," he said.

"Well, no, I can see that," admitted Kendrick, handing over the keys. "The car's in the hotel garage," he added.

"Cheers," said Bethancourt. He stowed the keys in his jacket pocket and turned to kiss Marla good-bye.

"Be careful," she murmured. "I hope Jack's all right."

So did Bethancourt. Back in the taxi, he checked his watch, although he knew he could not possibly ring Carmichael back so soon; the chief inspector would not even have reached the hospital yet. So he leaned back with a sigh, unaware of his fingers drumming a tattoo on the car's upholstery. He was charged with adrenaline but had nowhere to expend it, his mind racing in a fruitless effort to understand what had happened.

At the hotel, he packed his bag hastily, cramming the clothes in anyhow, while the hotel staff fetched the car and searched out a ferry timetable for him. He ordered a large espresso to take away and sipped at it while he took the lift down, still impatient and trying to keep a tight rein on himself until he could at last be on his way.

The rain had stopped by the time he started out at a quarter past midnight, though the weather report on the radio said it was coming down heavily in Pas de Calais. He had a long way to go before he got so far. Lighting a cigarette, he concentrated on maneuvering his way out of Paris until at last he reached the Autoroute du Nord and could push the Volvo into fifth gear.

The hospital emergency room was awash with plainclothes policemen. Detective Sergeant Chris O'Leary, black-haired and only a couple of years older than his wounded colleague, still stood guard

5

over the polythene bags containing Gibbons's clothes and other belongings; apparently Hodges had not yet arrived to take them back to the forensics lab. Along the row of seats to O'Leary's left, Detective Inspector Hollings, who had been the first to respond to the call of an officer down in Walworth, sat with Detective Inspector Davies of the Arts Theft Division, for whom Gibbons had been working during the past few weeks. And hovering in the doorway, looking uneasy, was Detective Constable Jonathan Lemmy, Carmichael's own cross to bear during the current Scotland Yard rota.

Apart from Hollings, who had been on call, they were all dressed in casual clothing, but an air of officialdom seemed to cling to them, or perhaps it was the tension in their manner. Whatever the reason, the civilians in the waiting room had clustered together away from the policemen and from time to time cast curious glances toward them and their uniformed counterparts who stood guard at the doors.

O'Leary was the first to see Carmichael.

"Sir," he said urgently, crossing the room.

"What news?" asked Carmichael, lengthening his stride to meet the sergeant halfway. "Did you speak to the doctors?"

"Yes, sir," replied O'Leary. "I did try to ring you, sir."

"Never mind, Sergeant," said Carmichael impatiently. "What did they say? Is he still alive?"

O'Leary nodded, but his brow remained creased with anxiety. "They seem to think they can save him, though they haven't said as much," he replied. "He's not gone into surgery yet—they want to get him stabilized and his blood pressure up before they operate."

"How long will that take?" demanded Carmichael.

O'Leary spread his hands. "They didn't say. The surgeon," he added in an attempt to make up for this deficiency of information, "should be out to speak to us before they take him into OR."

Carmichael nodded brusquely. He knew he was taking his bad temper out on the sergeant, but at the moment he didn't care.

Hollings and Davies had risen and were waiting at his shoulder. He scowled and turned his attention to them.

"What case did you have him on, Davies?" he demanded.

Davies, a dapper man with a public-school accent, looked startled at Carmichael's accusatory tone, but was wise enough to reply mildly, "The Haverford robbery, Chief Inspector. Nothing out of the ordinary. Certainly nothing that could have led to this."

"Walworth isn't exactly the sort of neighborhood you'd look for clues about the Haverfords," put in Hollings and got the scowl transferred to himself for his trouble.

"Don't be an ass," snapped Carmichael. "Walworth is chock-full of stolen goods and people who fence them and you know it."

Hollings sighed. "Just trying to pour oil on troubled waters, sir."

"Keep your damned oil to yourself," muttered Carmichael, but he turned away as he said it so that the other men did not quite catch the words. No one asked him to repeat himself.

"Has anything turned up at the scene, sir?" ventured O'Leary.

"The bloody scene is washed out," said Carmichael, frustration and worry making his voice harsh. "The SOCKOs are salvaging what they can, but it won't be much."

Hollings cleared his throat. "I've put the local uniforms on to a house-to-house," he said. "And I've got DC Cummings down at Lambeth station—evidently there was a report of gunshots down there this evening, but they found nothing when they investigated."

Carmichael's eyebrows bristled. "And so they just toddled off to their beds with not a care in the world about the unexplained gunfire on their patch? Oh, that's brilliant, that is."

The others shifted uncomfortably.

"We're not yet certain what happened, sir," said Hollings. "I'm sure they did their best."

"Well, if their best didn't find the man who was bleeding to death on their patch, it obviously wasn't good enough, was it?"

Hollings sighed. "No, sir."

"Oh, never mind."

Carmichael turned away and tried to pull his thoughts together. Before this current rotation, Detective Sergeant Gibbons had been his blue-eyed boy, promoted to Sergeant unusually early, and Carmichael thought a lot of him. More than that, he liked the young man, and had come to admire the combination of intellect and hard work that had gained him his early promotion. Having him seriously wounded whilst under another officer's supervision was difficult for Carmichael to accept. He took a deep breath.

"Right then," he said. "We'll have to hope that when Gibbons comes to, he'll be able to identify his assailant. He was shot from the front, wasn't he?"

"Yes, sir," said Hollings. "At least, so the paramedics said. O'Leary here spoke to them when he arrived at the scene. They didn't beat him there by much."

"They were just examining him when I got there, sir," volunteered O'Leary. "I told you—he was shot in the stomach, they thought twice though they didn't rule out a third shot. The rain had washed a lot of the blood away, but from where we found his mobile phone, he had crawled a few yards before he passed out."

They were all silent, the searing picture of a bloody Sergeant Gibbons crawling on the pavement in the rain flashing into all their minds.

"I was wondering, sir," said Davies into the silence, his tone hesitant. "I was wondering about notifying Gibbons's people."

Carmichael was startled that he hadn't thought of this himself. He considered briefly, and then shook his head.

"There's nothing they can do," he said. "Aside, that is, from worrying themselves sick while they try to drive down here from Bedfordshire in the middle of the night. You're quite right to think of it, Davies, but I believe it would be kinder to send a car for them. With luck, we'll have better news to relay to them by the time it gets there . . ."

His voice trailed off, and they all avoided each other's eyes. Then Carmichael's mobile began to ring, relieving the tension, and the others stepped back to give him privacy to answer it, though they all watched him with eagle eyes, trying to discern every scrap of information they could from his words and expressions.

Only O'Leary, however, knew the name that Carmichael repeated in surprise.

"Bethancourt?" he said.

The rented Volvo sped along the A1, past Saint-Denis, heading out into the night along the rain-slick pavement of the motorway.

Bethancourt was normally an erratic driver, one more interested in what could be seen out of the car windows than in the road before him, but on this occasion he was fully concentrated on the highway and on putting as many miles behind him as quickly as possible. The traffic at this hour was not particularly heavy, even so close to Paris, and he was making excellent time, driving well past the limit allowed on the French motorways.

He checked his watch for the fifth time since he had set out, not wanting to ring Carmichael back before the chief inspector could reach the hospital and get some news of Gibbons's condition. Bethancourt had already allowed more than enough time for this, although he was not conscious of it. Deep down, he was dreading to hear his worst fears confirmed: that Gibbons had died.

"He must be there by now," he muttered to himself, and blindly reached for his mobile phone, lying on the passenger seat.

"Carmichael." The chief inspector answered at once, sounding distracted.

"It's Phillip Bethancourt, sir," said Bethancourt. "Is there any news about Jack?"

"Bethancourt?" Carmichael sounded surprised, as though he were trying to place the name. But in the next moment, a kinder tone came into his voice as he said, "He's still alive, lad. There's no real news yet—apparently they're trying to stabilize him before they take him in for surgery."

Bethancourt let out a long sigh of relief. "Thank you, sir," he said fervently. "I was rather afraid—well, never mind."

"We've all been worried," said Carmichael sympathetically. "We're just trying to sort out what happened here. You ring me a bit later and I may have more news."

"Thank you, sir," said Bethancourt. "Thank you very much. I'll do that."

Carmichael rang off and Bethancourt tossed the phone back into the passenger seat, very glad of this respite from his worst fears, even if it was only temporary.

He felt, he realized, guilty, as if he had let his friend down by being out of the country just when he was wanted. It was a wholly unreasonable feeling, but knowing that did not seem to improve his outlook.

"Idiot," he muttered to himself, and lit a cigarette, his fourth in the last hour. He had let his speed slacken a bit whilst he was speaking to Carmichael, but now he put his foot down again, cracking the window open to let out the smoke. The chill, damp air rushed in as the car sped up and the cigarette's ember glowed red.

Detective Sergeant O'Leary had retreated from the discussion of his superiors to resume his guard over the evidence bags. His position at the end of the row of chairs put him next to the double doors that separated the waiting room from the examination area, and so he was the first to see the two men in surgical scrubs emerge.

"Ah, there you are, Sergeant," said one, whom O'Leary recognized as the admitting doctor he had dealt with when he first arrived. "I've brought our surgeon, Mr. Wyber, out to explain the operation to you."

Wyber was a large man in his late forties with an abundance of dark gold hair, springing up from a hairline that was just beginning to recede. He smiled briefly, but O'Leary thought his eyes were cold.

"That your guv?" he asked, nodding toward Carmichael.

"Yes, sir," answered O'Leary, beckoning as Carmichael turned at the sound of the surgeon's voice. "How is Jack?"

"Still critical," replied the doctor. "But his blood pressure's coming up a bit."

Led by Carmichael, the other detectives came up, and O'Leary performed the introductions cursorily.

"The X rays are back," announced Wyber. "They confirm your man was shot twice, both bullets still lodged in the intestines. The first one went in at an angle and didn't do so very much damage all things considered, but the second penetrated deeply and the bowel will need to be resected in several places."

"But you think you can save him?" asked Carmichael.

"He has a good chance," replied Wyber. "If we can get him stabilized before surgery, he'll have a very good chance. But he's been badly wounded, Chief Inspector, there's no getting round that, and I won't know what kind of complications there may be until I open him up."

Carmichael nodded his understanding, but he was almost desperate for some kind of reassurance.

"Tell me this," he asked, "if everything goes as well as it possibly can, would he make a full recovery?"

"Oh, yes," said Wyber confidently. "In that case, a few months should see him put right. But we're not there yet."

"No, of course not," muttered Carmichael. "Is there any chance of speaking with him before the operation?"

Both doctors looked bemused at this idea.

"He's unconscious," said the doctor gently. "It would be unlikely that he should regain consciousness before his surgery."

"So he hasn't said anything?" put in Hollings. "Nothing about what happened?"

"No, I'm afraid not."

"He may not remember in any case," said Wyber, and all the detectives turned to stare at him. "Trauma victims often don't," he explained. "But," he added, forestalling their questions, "there's no telling for sure. Individual cases vary greatly. I've known some people to forget whole days, while others remember the most horrific things in every detail."

"We'll let you know when he's taken into the operating theatre," said the doctor, turning away. "I assure you, we'll do the very best we can for him."

"Yes, yes," said Carmichael automatically. "Thank you both."

They all looked at each other as the doctors left them.

"Well, that changes things," said Hollings, rubbing his chin. "If Gibbons can't remember who shot him . . ."

Carmichael was frowning. "There was always the possibility he hadn't seen his attacker clearly. But there's no denying I was hoping he would tell us who and why."

"If he's one of those who forget whole days, he may not have any idea why he was shot," put in Davies. "He may have forgotten the very thing he was shot for knowing."

Carmichael glared at him, and the inspector added hastily, "Not that he'll be one of those. I only meant . . ."

"We know what you meant, Grant," said Hollings wearily. "It's all right. And in any case, it was never sure Gibbons was shot for anything he's presently involved in. It might have been a revenge attack by some recently released criminal he helped put in jail."

"That is the first thing that came to my mind," admitted Davies. "I mean, considering what he'd been working on—there's just no violence connected with the case."

"Until now," muttered Carmichael under his breath, but in such a low voice no one but O'Leary, who was standing close beside him, heard.

"Chief Inspector?" asked Hollings.

"Never mind." Carmichael waved his own comment away. "Whether he remembers or not, we'll be able to track his movements better once forensics is done with his notebook. Meanwhile—"

He broke off, swinging round as another young man came into the waiting room. He was slight of build and fresh-faced, which combined to give an impression of a boy of about sixteen, although in fact he had reached his early twenties, and he was remarkably self-possessed for either age.

His eyes lit briefly on the policemen before traveling on to the bags containing Gibbons's clothes, which O'Leary still stood protectively over.

"Is that it then?" he asked, indicating the bags with his chin. "Mr. Hodges sent me," he added, although all of the policemen had recognized him at once as Guy Delford, their forensics department's latest genius and the apple of Ian Hodges's eye.

"That's it," affirmed Carmichael. "Where is Hodges?"

"Meeting me at the lab," answered Delford, moving to collect the bags. "He wanted to be there when the evidence from the scene arrived. We'll start work on it right away."

"Don't you want to know how our man is?" asked O'Leary, a little exasperated by this apparent detachment in the face of crisis.

"No!" For just a moment, Delford's brown eyes blazed. "No," he repeated more calmly. "I shouldn't be able to work properly if I heard he was dead. I like Sergeant Gibbons, you see."

This left them all speechless as Delford was already renowned amongst Scotland Yard detectives as not merely forgetful of names, but of actually being unable to tell one detective from another. In the ensuing silence, Delford lifted the plastic bags and carried them out into the hall, dodging around Constable Lemmy, who was still hovering in the doorway.

"The notebook," muttered Carmichael. "O'Leary, just run after him and say I want Gibbons's notebook back as soon as possible, will you?"

O'Leary left with alacrity, and in a moment they heard his voice echoing back from the hall.

Carmichael drew a deep sigh and turned to sit down at last, trying to think his way through this most difficult of investigations.

The rain had picked up again, drumming on the roof of the car and splattering against the windscreen. Bethancourt peered past the wipers in search of the junction with the A26. He had been on the road now for close to two hours and figured he was almost halfway to Calais. He was still hoping to make the three o'clock ferry, though he had had to slacken his speed somewhat in deference to the rain.

Apart from the steady sound of the downpour, it was quiet in the car, Bethancourt having long since lost patience with the vagaries of French radio and switched it off. In the silence, with the road ahead glittering wetly in the headlamps, he felt very much alone. He did not repent refusing Marla's company for the trip, but found he did miss the company of his dog, Cerberus, who normally accompanied him on a drive of any length. Cerberus, currently residing in kennels just outside of London, was a very well-behaved borzoi who would in all likelihood have curled up and fallen asleep in the backseat by now. But somehow Bethancourt was acutely aware of the dog's absence there. More than once, as his thoughts strayed, he found himself glancing into the back, only to find it empty.

Ahead a sign loomed up, glimpsed between the regular beat of the wipers: Béthune, Boulogne, Calais, Dunkerque it proclaimed.

"That's it then," murmured Bethancourt, shifting down to make the turn.

The evidence bags having safely arrived at the lab, Carmichael had sent O'Leary off to liaise with DC Cummings, who was conducting the house-to-house in Walworth. Hollings had volunteered to go look up the local bobby on duty in the neighborhood at the time of the shooting, and was currently at the Lambeth police station. And Davies had left to knock up the insurance investigator who had been working the Haverford robbery, though Davies clearly thought this a waste of time.

And he might be right at that, thought Carmichael glumly to himself. He suspected he had suggested it merely to leave no stone unturned rather than out of any real hope of a clue. Detective Inspector Davies, after all, had been with the Arts Theft Division for several years and presumably knew his own business. If he said there was no violence connected to the robbery of a fortune's worth of antique jewels, he was most likely correct.

That left Detective Constable Lemmy, who had stopped loitering in the doorway and taken a seat just inside it, in which he was now dozing. Sleeping, thought Carmichael wrathfully, was about the only thing Lemmy had shown any talent for since he had been visited on by the chief inspector.

His mobile rang and Carmichael pounced on it, hoping for a report from O'Leary. But it was his wife.

"How is Sergeant Gibbons, dear?" asked Dotty Carmichael, her voice without the faintest accusation despite the fact that Carmichael had promised to ring her with news and had completely forgotten.

"He's still alive," said Carmichael. "I'm sorry I haven't rung. I should have."

"I'm sure you've had a very busy night," said Dotty. "Do you know anything yet? Is Gibbons going to be all right?"

"I don't know," replied Carmichael. "They took him into surgery a half hour or so past, but I've not heard anything since. I suppose it's going well enough."

"Are you still at the hospital?" she asked.

"Yes. There didn't seem to be much point in leaving—I've got everyone out trying to find out what happened, but so far there's no one to interview, or even any suspects. And although the doctors said Gibbons wouldn't wake up, well, you never can tell, can you?"

"But surely someone else could have stayed," suggested Dotty.

"Well, yes," admitted Carmichael. "In fact, I've got some armed uniforms here just to be safe. But Gibbons doesn't know them."

"That's a good thought," she agreed. "He ought to have someone he knows there when he wakes up. Would you like me to come down and wait for him?"

Carmichael was startled. "Down here? You mean the hospital?"

"Well, yes, dear. That does seem most practical if one's waiting for somebody to come out of surgery."

She was teasing him now, gently, but teasing nonetheless. Despite himself, Carmichael smiled.

"Well, it's likely to be a long wait," he said.

"That's all right," she said. "I can't sleep anyway, not without knowing Sergeant Gibbons will be all right. And that way if you're called away, he'll still have someone who knows him there, won't he?"

"Yes," said Carmichael. "Yes, he will. If you truly want to, Dotty, I won't say no."

"Then I'll come down," she said firmly. "I should be there in forty-five minutes or so."

Bethancourt flicked his cigarette butt out the window, and took a drink from the bottle of Evian he had taken from the hotel. He badly wanted a coffee, but time was running on, and making the three o'clock ferry would be a close thing at this point.

He checked the time yet again and found it was past 2:30 A.M. A half hour ago he had reluctantly decided that ringing Carmichael on an hourly basis for updates would probably be overly onerous to a busy and distressed policeman who had work to do, but it had, by his calculations, been more than ninety minutes now; surely in that amount of time there should be news. He picked up the phone.

Unexpectedly, Carmichael sounded pleased to hear from him. "Bethancourt?" he said. "They've taken him into the operating theatre at last—not quite half an hour ago. I've left the hospital, but Mrs. Carmichael is there and will ring me the moment she hears anything."

"That's good news, sir," said Bethancourt, hoping it was.

"I wanted to ask you," continued Carmichael, "what time it was when he rang you this evening?"

"At six thirty-five," answered Bethancourt, wondering why this should matter.

"And when was the last time you spoke to him before that?"

"The day before yesterday," said Bethancourt. "I rang him to say I'd be back in London on Thursday."

"But he gave you no hint that anything was up?" asked Carmichael anxiously.

"Not especially," replied Bethancourt. "He told me about his transfer to Arts Theft and about how different it was from what he was used to, but nothing about any specific case. We talked about gambling."

"Gambling?" said Carmichael, sounding startled.

"I was in Monte Carlo at the time."

"Ah," said Carmichael, apparently dismissing this bit of information. "You said you're on your way back now?"

"Yes, sir," said Bethancourt. "I'm on the road as we speak—just passing Béthune. I'm hoping to make the three o'clock ferry."

"Good, good," said Carmichael. "Make sure you let me know once you're here."

"Of course, sir," said Bethancourt, wondering why Carmichael seemed so eager to speak with him, but forbearing to ask, given the chief inspector's distracted tone.

Carmichael rang off and Bethancourt tossed his phone back into the passenger seat thoughtfully. Carmichael often permitted Bethancourt to look in on Gibbons's investigations, this having been mandated by the chief commissioner of Scotland Yard, who happened to be an old school fellow of Bethancourt's father. But Bethancourt had always done his best to keep a low profile and certainly Carmichael had never sought out his thoughts before. Perhaps, thought Bethancourt, the chief inspector believed this shooting had to do with Gibbons's private life rather than his professional one, although Bethancourt had difficulty believing this could be true.

But it gave him something else to think about on the long drive north. Heretofore, his only thought had been to pray for his friend's life; he had given no thought at all as to why or how he had been shot. He mulled this over now as he lit yet another cigarette and let the car gather speed.

Hollings had at last managed to roust Constable Jacob Clarkson out of his no doubt well-deserved bed. Constable Clarkson was the local man in Lambeth who had been on duty that evening, and who, on hearing that a fellow officer had been shot, professed himself only too happy to return to the station to speak to Chief Inspector Carmichael about it. Clarkson was the salt of the earth, an experienced man who knew his patch like the back of his hand. He was also, however, one of those people who is not much good when awakened in the middle of the night, and although he did not actually fall asleep on the ride to the station, Hollings still thought it prudent to stop and procure the man a coffee before they arrived and had to face the chief inspector. Hollings had worked with Carmichael several times in the past and had generally found him to be an even-tempered man, but he could clearly see that was not the case tonight. Not that Hollings could blame him, but on the other hand, he didn't see why Constable Clarkson should suffer for it.

Carmichael had made it to the station well ahead of them, Clarkson living quite distant, out in Orpington, and was waiting impatiently. Hollings was very glad he had stopped for the coffee.

"There were reports of gunshots," Clarkson told them. "I reported it, but nearly everyone who had heard it thought it came from a different direction. I did look, sir. I'm mortal sorry I didn't find your man."

"But you didn't hear the shots yourself?" asked Carmichael.

"No, sir. Best I could figure, I was inside a shop at the time, sorting out a bit of trouble between the owner and one of his customers."

Carmichael waved this away. "We have your report, Constable," he said. "What I want is a blow-by-blow description. Here—show me where this shop is."

He slapped an open London A to Z onto the desk and Clarkson obligingly bent over it, yawning prodigiously. Carmichael scowled and Hollings, who was tolerably familiar with the area from a recent murder investigation, leaned in to point out where Gibbons had been found. Clarkson, it evolved, had been some distance away when the shots had been fired. He had already left the shop when he received word of the gunshots and the information that backup was en route to him from the station.

"It's that kind of neighborhood," he said with a shrug.

"But you didn't wait for your backup to arrive, did you?" said Carmichael.

"Well, no." Clarkson slurped at his coffee and blinked before realizing the chief inspector was waiting for more. "It didn't seem too likely that the gunman would still be about by the time I got there," he explained. "I mean, they hardly ever are. If you shoot someone, you don't wait about for the police, do you?"

Carmichael admitted this was so.

Clarkson traced his route on the map for them, and described the residents he had interviewed. They had all heard the shots, but none of them could pinpoint from whence the sound had come, nor did they report hearing any other signs of conflict.

"And that was a bit odd," said Clarkson. "Usually, there's some other disturbance connected with gunfire, like an argument, or at least the sound of a car speeding off. In any case, it didn't give us much to go on."

Backup having arrived, they had proceeded to take a look around the area, but had found nothing amiss, and given the wide divergence of opinion as to how many shots there had been, they had concluded that the noise might have been something else altogether. Clarkson had kept an eye out for the rest of his shift, but it had been an otherwise quiet evening and he had at last gone home, satisfied that nothing much was wrong in his district. He was more than chagrined to discover he had been quite wrong.

It was raining heavily in Calais, just as the radio had predicted. Bethancourt had been on the road for close on three hours and was beginning to feel it; he had missed rue Chevreul and had had to backtrack, but he had still managed to get onto the 3:15 A.M. ferry to Dover, if only just. The seas were heavy, not unusual for the Channel during a storm, but Bethancourt luckily had a strong stomach. He stretched and then lit a cigarette, leaning on the deck railing as the ferry pushed out into the sea, leaving Calais behind.

If Gibbons had not been shot, Bethancourt would likely still have been out at a nightclub at 3:15 A.M., thoroughly enjoying himself and in no way ready for bed. As it was, he felt dull and tired, and knew he was not thinking very clearly anymore. He had been going over in his mind all he knew of Gibbons's personal life, trying to find anything that could explain the attack on his friend, but he had come up with nothing. Gibbons's life was very much caught up in his work, the more so since he had had his heart broken last summer. He had not yet recovered sufficiently to be interested in dating, much less any kind of full-blown affair that might lead to jealousy and gunshots.

Bethancourt did not know all of Gibbons's other friends well, but he could not see any of the younger police detectives or, still less, Gibbons's old friends from Oxford, resorting to firearms. The other detectives, he concluded, might at least be accused of jealousy, since Gibbons was well ahead of his peers on their chosen career path.

With that absurd thought, he stubbed out his cigarette and abandoned the deck in favor of a comfortable chair inside. He had barely got himself settled, stretching out his legs and leaning his head back, before he fell fast asleep, worn out with worry and the tedium of the road.

Dotty Carmichael had come prepared for a long wait with a paperback romance novel, a pack of cards with which to play Patience if, as seemed likely, the book failed to hold her attention in the current circumstances, and a large thermos flask of tea. She had also brought a cushion from her sofa at home, an acknowledgment that at her age one could not sit for long on institutional chairs without becoming uncomfortable.

She did not anticipate having any difficulty in staying awake, despite the fact that she had not been up much past eleven since the birth of her second grandchild some three years ago, and in fact she did not feel in the least sleepy. She was the more nettled, therefore, to find that Detective Constable Lemmy was fast asleep. Carmichael had left him behind with orders to "see to Mrs. Carmichael," and Dotty could not help but feel Lemmy was not making much of a job of it. Over the last fortnight, she had heard any number of complaints from her husband about his new constable, and she had kept to herself the opinion that poor Detective Constable Lemmy's worst fault was to have supplanted the brilliant Sergeant Gibbons as her husband's assistant. As the night wore on, however, she was rapidly revising this estimation of the constable's character.

After about an hour, she decided to stretch her legs and find the WC. Lemmy was still asleep, sprawled across the row of chairs opposite her, so she told the uniformed men standing guard where she was going, instructing them to call her if the doctors should reappear. But when she returned, having worked the kink out of her hip, she found everything quiet and a glance at the uniformed men told her there was no news. She sat back down with a sigh, settling herself as comfortably as she could, and wishing that the waiting was over, whatever the outcome.

She poured herself another cup of tea, offering some to the policemen, but they declined, being well supplied with coffee by the nurses. So she dealt herself a hand of Patience, laying the cards out carefully on the little side table, grateful at least that the waiting room was not crowded with sneezing, coughing people. She had rather expected it would be at this time of year.

Just before four, Wyber reappeared, still in faultless scrubs but now looking rather tired. He glanced about the waiting room and, not seeing any of the plainclothes detectives who had greeted him before, looked a question at the uniformed policemen standing guard.

"This is Chief Inspector Carmichael's wife," said one of the men. "She knows DS Gibbons."

"How is he, Doctor?" she asked, rising and coming forward, steeling herself to hear the worst while hoping for the best.

"It went quite smoothly," Wyber told her. "I can't say he's entirely out of danger yet, but he came through the operation very well. A small section of bowel had to be removed, but that shouldn't bother him at all, and the other holes were reparable. Peritonitis is a concern at this point, but he's young and strong—I should say he has a good chance of coming through this."

Something in Dotty's chest suddenly relaxed, though she had not been aware of the constriction before, and she took her first deep breath in several hours.

"That's excellent news," she told the doctor, beaming at him. "May I sit with him? My husband wanted him to have someone there when he woke."

"He's still in recovery at the moment," replied Wyber, "but I'll tell them to let you know when he's moved into a room. He won't be waking for some little time yet in any case. Oh," he added as an afterthought, "the chief inspector wanted the bullets kept." He looked dubiously down at Dotty. "Do you, er . . ."

"No," said Dotty firmly.

"That would be Detective Constable Lemmy's job," said one of the policemen, and Dotty gave him a grateful glance. "Jake here will wake him."

Wyber nodded, looking somewhat askance at the spectacle of Lemmy stretched out across a row of chairs. "Yes, of course," he murmured. "I'll have my nurse bring them out."

"Thank you very much, Doctor," said Dotty. "My husband and I think a lot of Sergeant Gibbons and we appreciate your efforts ever so much."

"Not at all, not at all, Mrs. Carmichael. Pleased to be of service." And, with a little bow, Wyber withdrew.

Which left Dotty and the two policemen grinning foolishly at each other.

"Over the first hurdle," she said, and went to ring her husband with the news.

At just about that time, Bethancourt was driving off the ferry at Dover. His nap aboard ship had left him feeling blurry instead of rested, but at least he was once again in England, driving on the proper side of the road, and not much more than ninety minutes' drive from London.

And, best of all, within mobile phone range again. As he swung the Volvo onto the A2, bypassing Dover's city center, he reached for his phone, trepidation roiling his stomach as he waited for Carmichael to answer. He was all too conscious that he had been out of touch for well over an hour and that anything might have happened in that time.

"Carmichael here."

"It's Phillip Bethancourt again, sir," said Bethancourt, pressing the phone to his ear. It was absurd, but the reception had been better in Calais. "Have you heard anything?"

"I've just got the news," Carmichael replied, and he sounded pleased. "He's out of surgery and doing fine. He's still in critical condition, mind, but he's done well to make it this far."

"Thank God," said Bethancourt fervently. "Is he awake yet?"

"Not yet. They apparently expect that to take some little while. Where are you, lad?"

"In Dover. I've just come off the ferry."

"And you'll go straight through to the hospital?"

"I was planning to, yes."

"Good, good. I'll speak to you then—I should be back there by the time you arrive."

"I'll look forward to that, sir," said Bethancourt, and rang off.

He was beginning to feel more hopeful; that Gibbons had come through the operation was, he thought, a very good sign. And he himself was bound to make good time along the A2 at this hour; the only traffic consisted of a few early lorries speeding toward London with their deliveries. At this rate, he should be in town by half five, or six at the latest.

Ian Hodges, chief of Scotland Yard's forensics laboratory, had a raspy, unpleasant speaking voice, which was universally regarded by the Yard's detectives as music to their ears. Certainly Carmichael felt that way early that morning when he answered his phone and heard the familiar gruff tones.

"What have you got?" he asked eagerly.

"As far as we can make out from the times we've been given, Sergeant Gibbons was on the phone when he was shot," replied Hodges.

"On the phone?" The scene of the crime flashed into Carmichael's mind, the blood on the pavement washing away in the rain and the red stain left beneath the bus shelter. "Of course," he murmured. "He wasn't coming out of that house—he stopped there to use his phone and keep it out of the rain."

"Probably," grunted Hodges. "We're going to have some work to do to pull up all the data on the phone—it died on the way into the lab. All we managed to garner was the last number he rang."

"And what was that?" asked Carmichael eagerly.

Hodges seemed surprised. "It wasn't you, sir?"

"What? No, of course it wasn't me. Why do you say that?"

"Because it's your number," retorted Hodges.

"It can't have been," protested Carmichael. "I've had my mobile on all evening, ever since I left the office."

"Not your mobile," corrected Hodges. "Your office line. He rang it at nine fourteen this evening."

Carmichael cursed fluently. "I never thought to check," he admitted. "Let me know when you have anything else, will you, Hodges? I must check my voice mail at once."

"Right you are," agreed Hodges. "I'll ring you again as soon as I have any more."

"Thank you, Hodges. You're a godsend."

Hodges accepted this accolade with his usual insouciance and rang off, leaving Carmichael to meet the questioning eyes of Inspector Hollings and Sergeant O'Leary. They were all sitting in an interview room at Lambeth station, having sent Constable Clarkson off to continue his well-earned repose.

"Gibbons apparently left me a message," Carmichael told them, dialing. "I never once thought to check my own messages."

"I wonder if Davies has checked his," said Hollings.

"See that he does, will you?" said Carmichael, typing in a code. "Ah, here we go."

Gibbons's voice came over the line, sounding just as usual; it gave Carmichael a chill to hear it.

"Gibbons here, sir. Something rather strange has come up and I wonder if you could spare me a few minutes tomorrow morning. I'd very much like to talk it over with you if you have the time. I'll ring you again when I get into the office. Thanks."

Carmichael played it over again, and then let Hollings and O'Leary listen to it.

"He doesn't sound particularly upset," offered O'Leary.

"No, he doesn't, does he?" said Carmichael thoughtfully. "Really, he could have wanted anything at all. It wouldn't necessarily have to do with a case."

"I can't see why he would be ringing you about a case at all," said Hollings. "If he'd had some idea about the Haverford robbery, he would have rung Davies. Unless—" He paused, thinking it out. "Have you spoken to him about any of your own recent cases, sir?"

Carmichael shook his head. "I last spoke with him about a fortnight ago," he said. "I stopped in to make sure he was doing all right with Arts. It's a big change from homicide. I may have mentioned the case I was working on, but since I wrapped it up last Sunday, I can't think why he should ring me about it now. There's no doubt in the case—the killer confessed."

"So we're back to square one," said Hollings, exasperated.

"Jack himself may be able to fill us in," said O'Leary. "We can't know until he comes to himself."

"Mrs. Carmichael will ring me the moment he does," Carmichael assured them.

Dotty Carmichael was at that moment sitting by Gibbons's bedside in intensive care, having finally been allowed in to see him. There had been a stool, but the sister had done away with it and brought up a proper chair. Dotty liked the sister, who was a brisk, no-nonsense sort of person.

"He's stirring a bit," she had said. "We'll probably move him into a room in an hour or so if he continues on as he's going."

"He's doing all right then?" asked Dotty doubtfully. Gibbons looked terribly unwell to her eye.

"Quite all right," said the sister, who apparently did not share this outlook. "His blood pressure is holding up nicely. We're keeping a close eye on his temperature, but he's doing well so far."

Much gratified by this news, Dotty had nodded and taken her seat, making herself as comfortable as she could and hoping she would soon be moving to a hospital room where—she knew from long experience—they had cushioned armchairs.

The sister had said Gibbons was beginning to come out from under the anesthetic, but Dotty could see no sign of it. He lay very still, the only movement the shallow rise and fall of his chest, and she contemplated him anxiously. She felt she knew him well, having heard so much about him from her husband, though in fact she had met the sergeant only a handful of times. She knew what it would do to her husband if Gibbons should die or be permanently disabled and she clung to the sister's encouraging words while she waited, praying silently, for him to wake up.

Time was ticking down on the clock in Bethancourt's mind, while his lips moved in an echo of Dotty Carmichael's prayers. He was beginning to feel that he would make it to Gibbons's side before the drama finished playing itself out, however it might end. He did not suppose his presence would make any great difference, other than to make himself feel better, but having come so close, he was desperate not to fail at the last.

His brief leg on the M2 had flown by and he was back on the A2 again, just now reaching the outskirts of Greater London. Another half hour should, he thought, see him at the hospital. His London A to Z was back in his Chelsea flat, and he did not know the area well, so he was dependent on the hire car's GPS system, which he did not wholly trust. It seemed, for some reason, to think he should have turned off some miles ago.

His back ached and his long frame felt cramped and stiff from sitting so long behind the wheel, but he was buoyed by the thought that the long night was nearly over.

2

The Morning

Detective Inspector Jack Gibbons was asleep, his face very pale beneath the brown stubble on his cheeks, his red-brown hair looking dark in contrast. He was normally a slightly stocky, energetic man, but he looked thinner now and terribly vulnerable. A tube snaked across one wan cheek into his nose, intravenous fluid dripped into his arm, while a blood pressure cuff tightened and relaxed about his biceps. The machines and monitoring devices gave off a constant low hum in the quiet of the room.

Bethancourt's face was sober as he stood by the bedside, his skin bleached nearly as pale as his hair with fatigue, his tall, lean form stooped a little from the same cause. He had taken off his horn-rimmed glasses to rub at his eyes and they dangled from one hand as he regarded his friend silently.

Dotty Carmichael watched the pair from her chair in the corner of the room. It was she who had come out to vouch for Bethancourt with the uniformed guards at the door, despite never having met him before. But Carmichael had told her he was on his way, and she easily recognized the young man from his description, secretly amused to find that Bethancourt was somewhat taller than her husband had ever mentioned, topping the chief inspector by at least an inch.

In times past, Carmichael had also described Bethancourt as charming, though Dotty had understandably not seen much of that in the present circumstances. He had been scrupulously polite in a distant, public-school sort of way, and was clearly terribly anxious about Gibbons. He had been standing at the bedside for at least ten minutes now and showed no signs of moving.

But in this she was mistaken, for the next moment he stirred and, replacing his glasses, turned to smile at her sheepishly.

"You must excuse me," he said. "I'm afraid I've been terribly rude."

"Not at all," said Dotty. "They tell me," she added, "that he's doing quite well."

"Ah," said Bethancourt, glancing quickly back at Gibbons as if her words might magically have brought the bloom of health to his cheeks.

"I know," she said. "He doesn't look it."

Bethancourt sighed and sat down on the stool. "No," he agreed. "He looks—well, rather worse than I had thought. Has he woken at all?"

Dotty nodded. "Two or three times now, but very briefly. He seemed very confused, but the sister said that was the anesthetic and painkillers at work. I don't think he recognized me."

"It must be very disorienting," said Bethancourt. "Passing out somewhere and then waking up in a completely different place, I mean."

"Yes, indeed."

Bethancourt hesitated, and then said, "Do you know—was the damage very extensive?"

"Oh," said Dotty, "I wasn't thinking—of course you haven't had any details, have you? Apparently the damage wasn't as bad as it might have been, or so they say. The surgeon removed two bullets from the sergeant's abdomen and performed a bowel resection. He said it went smoothly."

"Two bullets?" Bethancourt looked alarmed. "He was shot twice?"

"Yes, I'm afraid so. Since he wasn't found right away, they're worried he may develop peritonitis. His temperature is up a little."

"God." Bethancourt rubbed at his face again. "I never thought anything like this would happen," he said, looking up. "Not to Jack."

"No," agreed Dotty. "One never does. And it doesn't happen often, thank God."

Bethancourt murmured agreement, turning back to look at Gibbons again.

And just then Gibbons stirred, frowned, and opened his eyes. Even their normal fierce blue color seemed to Bethancourt to be dimmed.

Bethancourt was on his feet in an instant, bending over the bed. "Jack?" he asked. "How are you feeling?"

"Phillip?" said Gibbons faintly, looking confused. "What are you doing here?"

"I came as soon as I heard," said Bethancourt, not at all certain Gibbons knew where "here" was. "How are you, old man?"

Gibbons blinked, as if he were having trouble focusing. "Is there anything to drink?" he asked. "I'm awfully thirsty."

"Yes, of course," said Bethancourt, looking round.

Dotty was before him, experience having taught her that this request would be coming in short order. She handed Bethancourt a cup with a few ice chips in it.

"They said only ice, no liquid," she murmured.

Bethancourt nodded and dropped a bit of ice into Gibbons's mouth. Gibbons looked vaguely startled, but sucked on the ice anyway while Bethancourt said, "I'm afraid that's all you're allowed. Does it help?"

Gibbons nodded, his eyelids already beginning to droop again. "Cheers," he mumbled, and fell back to sleep.

Bethancourt, left holding the ice, smiled down at him.

Gibbons had only the vaguest recollection of this incident when he woke again, half an hour later. He was first aware of feeling generally bruised and battered, and something hurt quite a lot, but he wasn't sure what it was. He blinked his eyes open sleepily and found himself in a hospital room.

"Jack?"

His vision seemed oddly blurred, and he squinted up to see

Bethancourt leaning over him with a cup in his hand. Unconsciously, he swallowed in preparation for speaking, and discovered that his throat was one of the things that was very sore indeed. Moreover, there seemed to be some kind of tube stuck down his gullet. That, together with the hospital room and the muddy, sick feeling in his head, began to ring alarm bells. Fear started to coalesce in the pit of his stomach.

"Phillip?" he ventured, and his earlier brief bout with consciousness came back to him. "I thought you were a dream," he muttered.

"Not a bit of it," said Bethancourt.

Gibbons closed his eyes again, squeezing them tight in order to take away the blurriness, and tried to think. He had some hazy notion that Bethancourt was out of town, but that clearly was wrong. And he did not remember being in hospital.

"I was going to work," he murmured, trying to bring himself up-to-date.

"What?" asked Bethancourt anxiously. "I couldn't make that out."

The inquiry interrupted Gibbons's tenuous train of thought and he cracked an eye open to glare at his friend, only to find the plastic cup waving dangerously close to his eye.

"More ice?" asked Bethancourt helpfully.

"Not in my eye," retorted Gibbons, batting feebly at the cup. He made an effort to push himself into a sitting position; the effort ended abruptly in a blinding flash of pain that made him gasp and close his eyes again. It was so severe that he was not even sure where exactly it had originated. Dimly, he heard Bethancourt saying, "Whoa. Take it easy there—I don't think you ought to be doing sit-ups just yet," while he struggled to conquer the fear that something was seriously wrong with him. He found himself panting a little and tried to slow his breathing.

"Was there an accident?" he whispered in a moment.

"That's right," replied Bethancourt in a soothing tone. "But the doctors say you're going to be fine."

The soothing tone struck a false note with Gibbons. Still, he did not imagine that Bethancourt would lie to him, even if the prognosis was less good.

"What happened?" he asked. "I can't remember anything."

"Well, you've had a bit of an operation," said Bethancourt. "That's why your tummy's so sore. But it went very smoothly, so they say, and they expect you to make a full recovery with time."

Gibbons felt greatly relieved to hear it, but even in his dazed state, it was not lost on him that Bethancourt had failed to mention why he had been brought to the hospital to begin with. He was beginning to feel quite put out with his friend.

"But why have I had an operation?" he demanded. "Did my appendix burst? Was I hit by a car?"

"Not exactly," said Bethancourt, dithering a bit. "In fact, you were, er, shot."

Gibbons could not have been more surprised.

"Shot?" he repeated incredulously. "With a gun you mean?"

Bethancourt nodded solemnly. "That's right. You were shot twice, as a matter of fact. But as I say, it wasn't half as bad as it might have been. Your intestines are a bit shorter than they were this morning, but other than that, all's well."

It seemed beyond belief.

"But who shot me?" he asked.

"No one's sure just at the moment," said Bethancourt. "But Carmichael's working hard on it, and he'll no doubt have an answer shortly." He cocked his head. "How do you feel?"

"Not very well," admitted Gibbons. He shifted cautiously, relieved to find a more gentle movement did not result in the same hideous pain. "Perhaps I *will* have—is that water?"

"Ice," corrected Bethancourt, eagerly fishing out a chip and adroitly slipping it into his friend's mouth before he could protest. "You can't have anything else yet."

Gibbons might have questioned this, but sucking on the ice brought the tube in this throat back to prominence.

"What is this?" he asked irritably, fumbling at his nose.

"Er . . ." said Bethancourt and glanced over his shoulder.

"I don't know either," said a woman's voice. "They said something about keeping his lungs clear, but I didn't quite understand."

Gibbons was startled to find someone else was in the room—normally he was a very observant man—and peered around Bethancourt. His eyes widened as they lit on Dotty.

"Oh, hello, Mrs. Carmichael," he said weakly.

"Hello, dear," said Dotty. "We've all been very worried about you. Wallace will be glad to hear you're awake."

"Is the chief inspector here, too?" asked Gibbons in a small voice.

"Yes indeed." Dotty smiled at him. "He just went out to take a call and will be right back. And he's sent a car for your parents—they should be here in not much longer," she added with a glance at the lightening sky out the window.

"But . . ." began Gibbons, and then let his voice trail off as he, too, looked out the window and realized how early it was. "It's not the same morning," he said starkly.

Dotty looked confused, as well she might, but Bethancourt seemed to understand what he meant.

"Ah," he said. "Is that the last thing you remember? Yesterday morning?"

"I—I don't know," answered Gibbons, frowning with the fruitless effort to put his memories in order. "I guess . . . what day is it now?"

"Wednesday morning," answered Bethancourt.

Gibbons shook his head. "I remember going to work on Tuesday," he said, but his tone was doubtful.

"Well, don't fret over it," said Dotty. "You'll never get better if you do that. You leave it to Wallace to sort out—he will, whether you fret or not."

"Right," said Bethancourt. "Do you want anything? I can call the nurse."

What Gibbons wanted was to think clearly, but that was obviously not an option. He felt unbearably weary, as if he had run a marathon and got a bad cramp in his belly at the end.

"I don't think so," he said uncertainly. "Where are we, anyway?"

"University College Hospital," answered Bethancourt. "They rushed you here from Walworth."

"Walworth?" This made no sense at all.

"Don't worry about it," said Bethancourt. "It's the best trauma center in London—they'll get you well."

Gibbons felt that there was something vaguely sinister in the way Bethancourt kept harping on his recovery, but his brain was beginning to shut down again and he could not reason it out.

"All right," he replied, though what he was agreeing to he could not have said. "I think perhaps I'll have another sleep now. I don't seem able to stay awake."

"That'll be the anesthetic," said Dotty comfortingly. "You'll feel more alert later."

It hardly seemed possible. As he drifted off into soft, painless darkness, he wondered if he would have to give up his job because of not being able to think straight.

Bethancourt and Dotty fell into a hushed silence, watching the regular rise and fall of Gibbons's chest, fruitlessly striving to determine any deviation from normal sleep. Neither of them had yet spoken when there was the sound of a heavy footstep behind them and Carmichael appeared in the doorway. The long night had left its mark on him and he looked older than Bethancourt remembered, the lines in his face more deeply etched, his eyes bleary. Even his eyebrows, those bristling harbingers of Carmichael's mood, seemed damped down.

"Ah, Bethancourt, you're here," he said, his voice a low rumble. Then he looked toward the bed as he came into the room to lay a hand on his wife's shoulder. "How is he?"

"He woke again," said Dotty. "He seemed less confused than before and he recognized Mr. Bethancourt."

"Good, good." Carmichael rubbed a hand over his face and sank down on the arm of Dotty's chair.

"You look all in, sir," said Bethancourt sympathetically.

"It's been a long night." Carmichael was staring blankly at his wounded junior. "I'm glad you've come, Bethancourt. We'll need to go over anything you might know that could contribute to this."

Bethancourt nodded. "Certainly, sir," he said.

But Carmichael made no move to begin this interrogation; he just sat on the arm of his wife's chair, gazing worriedly at Gibbons. And after a moment, Bethancourt's eyes also returned there, and they all sat, very quietly, watching the slight signs that told them Gibbons was alive.

Bethancourt stood blinking in the thin, early-morning sunlight on the street outside the hospital. The rain had apparently stopped for the moment, and he was dimly taking this fact in while he tugged his cigarette case out of his pocket and then patted himself down in a search for his lighter.

Gibbons's parents had arrived and Bethancourt and the Carmichaels had left to allow them some privacy with their son. Dotty had taken her husband off to put him to bed as, she said, he'd not have the sense to get any rest, left to himself. She had recommended that Bethancourt do the same thing and he had meekly promised to comply. But now he had the sensation of something forgotten at the back of his mind, which was trying to come out.

Nicotine seemed to help focus his thoughts. He blew out a stream of smoke and knew at once what he had forgotten: making some kind of arrangements for the Gibbonses' stay. It would have to be somewhere nearby, which eliminated his own flat in Chelsea and left him with a choice of hotels. Half a cigarette later, he had decided on the Montague on the Gardens as being very comfortable and barely ten minutes' walk away. After so many hours spent in the car, he felt he could use a brisk walk himself and accordingly set out down Gower Street, pitching his cigarette away as he walked.

The Montague was quiet at this hour and in this season, but the girl at the desk was immaculately turned out and greeted him with a bright smile.

"Checking in?" she inquired.

Bethancourt shook his head. "No," he answered. "I want to make arrangements for some friends. Have you any rooms looking out on the gardens available?"

The smile stayed in place, but her brown eyes looked slightly worried. "Those are our most popular rooms," she told him. "When were your friends thinking of staying with us?"

"Now," said Bethancourt, startling her. "Tonight," he clarified. "I imagine they'll be here for about a week, or possibly two if . . ." That sentence did not seem to lead anywhere he wanted to go, and he began again. "Their son's in hospital," he explained. "They've only just arrived this morning, and I don't want them to have to worry about anything."

"Of course," said the receptionist sympathetically. "I'm sure we can accommodate them. At University College Hospital, is he?"

"That's right. He's a policeman and he was shot last night."

She paused as she was turning to her computer, appalled.

"How dreadful," she said.

"They say he'll make a full recovery," added Bethancourt hastily, realizing he had been rather abrupt and, moreover, had probably said more than she wanted to know.

"Thank God for that," she said. "Still, his parents must be very worried. Let's just see what we can do for them . . ." She returned her attention to the computer. "We do have openings just at the moment—November is a slow time for us—but even so, most of the garden rooms are occupied. Well, there, we do have a couple of suites."

She lifted a questioning eyebrow at him, clearly unsure if this would be beyond the means of a policeman's parents.

"A suite would be lovely," Bethancourt assured her. "Just what's needed, in fact."

She hesitated, her hands poised over the keyboard.

"Er," she said. "We usually greet our guests in their suites with a glass of champagne, but under the circumstances, well . . ."

"Ah, yes," said Bethancourt. "You'd better cancel that. A nice tea tray would be more the thing, I think."

She nodded, relieved, and began to type.

"The tariff," she murmured discreetly, "would be two hundred sixty-five pounds per night."

"Fine, fine," said Bethancourt. "Book it in for a week, will you? Here's my card."

The receptionist seemed reassured by the sight of an American Express platinum card, and proceeded with the booking.

"Have you got a brochure or anything?" asked Bethancourt, looking about vaguely. "I want to leave it at the hospital for them so they'll know where to go. They don't know London at all well."

Now that the brochure was in his pocket and his credit card charged, Bethancourt walked back to the hospital and sought out the uniformed guards at Gibbons's door, who greeted him with nods of recognition.

"Did you want to go in, sir?" asked one. "The sergeant's parents are still with him just now."

Bethancourt shook his head. "I'll leave them in peace," he said. "I've booked a hotel for them."

"Good job, that," said the other policeman. "I dare say they'll be too frazzled to work it all out for themselves."

Bethancourt produced his brochure. "Do you think you could give this to them when they come out?" he asked. "Tell them the hotel's expecting them and everything's taken care of."

The policeman let out a low whistle. "Posh place," he said.

"Do you know where it is?" said Bethancourt. "Can you tell them how to get there?"

Both policemen peered at the brochure.

"Oh, I know the place," said one. "Across from the British Museum, right? And you needn't worry about their getting there—I've got twenty pounds from the chief inspector and instructions to put the Gibbonses in a taxi whenever they want to leave."

"Good, good," said Bethancourt. "I'll leave it with you, then."

He could not suppress a huge yawn as he turned away, and thought to himself that he should really get himself home and into bed. But once on the street, he hesitated. The thought of getting back into the Volvo was repugnant, and he was tired enough to want to indulge himself. So he hauled his suitcase out of the car and hailed a taxi, collapsing into its spacious back with relief.

The morning rush hour was in full swing and despite the taxi driver's best efforts it was some time before they reached Chelsea. By then Bethancourt was fast asleep and had to be wakened by the driver.

"Oh, right," he said, peering blearily at his home while he dug out his wallet. "Ta very much."

Upstairs, he let himself into his flat and was immediately struck by the silence and its air of disuse. Anyone, he thought to himself, would believe he had been gone months instead of just a few days. He kicked the suitcase into the hall, letting the front door close behind him, and realized that what he really missed was his dog. There was nothing so dismal as coming home and not being greeted by a joyful bark and a waving tail.

He wandered into the bedroom and stripped off the clothes he had been wearing for the past twelve hours, leaving them in a heap on the floor. His dressing gown was in his suitcase, so he wrapped a towel around his waist and padded out to the kitchen for a drink of water. Thirst quenched, he returned to the bedroom and stood for several moments contemplating his bed in the silence.

"It's no good," he muttered to himself at last. "I'll never sleep like this."

His mind made up, he moved rapidly, taking a fresh set of clothes out of the armoire in the corner and dressing without bothering too much with details like a belt or socks. He shrugged into a jacket and transferred his wallet and keys from the discarded clothing on the floor into his pockets. Then he left the flat.

Twenty minutes later found him in his own gray Jaguar with yet another takeaway coffee in his hand, wending his way down Kings Road. He crossed the Thames at Putney and in short order was speeding along the A3 toward Surrey and the house outside of Oxshott where the Spoiled Rotten Pets Agency had arranged for his dog to be boarded while his master was out of town.

He was a day early and Mrs. Carter was understandably surprised to see him when she opened her door to his knock.

"I wasn't expecting you until tomorrow afternoon," she said.

"I know," answered Bethancourt apologetically. "There was a change of plans."

"Well, come on through," she said, ushering him in. "Cerberus is in the back garden. I'm afraid," she added, "I'll still have to charge you for the Thursday. It's the agency's rules, you know."

"That's all right," said Bethancourt, following her through the house.

There was a terrace at the back of the house, looking out on a wide expanse of lawn and trees. Cerberus had sensed his owner's arrival and began to bark as they reached the back door.

"He'll be so glad to see you," said Mrs. Carter, opening the door.

With a great *woof*, the Borzoi surged in, leaping up to plant his paws on Bethancourt's shoulders. Expecting this, Bethancourt had braced himself, but his weariness had apparently affected his balance and he only held himself upright for a moment before collapsing backward on the floor.

"Oh, dear, Mr. Bethancourt, are you all right?" asked Mrs. Carter.

"Yes," said Bethancourt with a laugh, making a grab for his glasses, which Cerberus's energetic licking had just dislodged from his face. "Yes, Mrs. Carter, I'm fine. In fact, it's the best I've been all day."

3

Rude Awakening

*G*ibbons was having a bad day. He supposed that was only to be expected after having been shot, but it did not make it any less aggravating.

He had at last come fully and horribly awake at a little after ten o'clock and found Bethancourt and Carmichael gone and his parents in their place. Gibbons was fond of his parents, and it was certainly nice to be coddled considering the way he felt, but they had no information at all. And although his brain still seemed appallingly muzzy, his thoughts had cleared enough to leave him impatient for an explanation as to what had happened to him.

Try as he might, he could remember nothing after getting on the tube to go to work on Tuesday morning. According to his much-distressed parents, he had not been shot until late Tuesday evening, so he could not understand why he did not remember the earlier part of the day.

The nurse who came in to check on him shrugged when asked about this.

"The brain does odd things sometimes," she said sympathetically. "There's really no telling why some people remember less than others."

"There," said his father, "that's just what I've been telling you. You must stop fretting about it."

"But what did I *do* all day?" demanded Gibbons.

His mother spread her hands. "We don't know, dear. I'm sure the chief inspector has some idea."

Gibbons muttered something unflattering about people who disappeared just when they were wanted.

"Really, Jack," said his mother reprovingly. "You must remember that the chief inspector was up all night investigating this incident. I'm sure he'll be back as soon as he gets some rest."

Gibbons, however, was not in a mood to consider other people. Once, when he was about ten, he had come down with bronchitis that turned into pneumonia. He remembered it vividly as it stood in his mind as the worst he had ever felt, and he was accustomed to judge all other ills by this benchmark, in comparison with which they usually paled. It had not occurred to him that he could actually feel worse than he had then, and he very much resented the discovery that bronchitis was a walk in the park when contrasted with being shot.

By lunchtime when Detective Inspector Davies arrived to visit, Gibbons was nearly overcome with frustration. It was lucky that he had not worked under Davies long and as a result felt a certain amount of deference was due his superior even under these circumstances or he might have exploded at the man. As it was, he brushed aside Davies's inquiries as to how he was feeling, and demanded to know what he had spent Tuesday doing.

Davies was an undemonstrative man, quiet in manner and slight in build with well-cut graying hair. He looked sympathetic at Gibbons's plea for information.

"Can't remember?" he asked. "They warned us you might not. Where do you leave off?"

"The morning," answered Gibbons, feeling somehow embarrassed that he could not recollect more. "I remember getting on the tube to come to work. I got a seat and was reading the paper, and then everything goes blank. I've no memory of arriving at Victoria, or going into the Yard, or anything."

The frustration was clear to be heard in his voice, and Davies nodded.

"It must be very unsettling," he said kindly. "Well, I can tell you some of what you did, though we're all still in the dark as to how you actually came to be attacked. Let's see . . ." He shifted in the chair, smoothing his tie while he marshaled his thoughts. During their short acquaintance, Gibbons had already come to envy Davies's ties, and he relieved some of his feelings now by glaring at the exquisite blue silk the inspector was currently sporting. In fact, Davies was far better turned out than anyone deserved to be after staying up all night and getting a bare four hours' sleep.

"You got to the Yard sometime before I did," Davies continued. "We met up shortly after nine and went to find out about Miss Haverford's will—quite the usual meeting with a family solicitor. Then I sent you off with Colin James to interview the Colemans." He paused and looked anxious. "You remember Colin? And the Colemans?"

Gibbons was indignant. "Yes, sir," he said. "It's not my whole brain that's gone on holiday."

"Good, good. Well, you interviewed them—you wrote a report on that, I'll bring it by later so you can look at it—and then presumably you stopped for lunch somewhere. Colin may know about that, but I couldn't find him last night. In fact, I'm just on my way to see him now."

Gibbons considered this. He was, oddly, aware of having a certain warmth of feeling toward Colin James, which his very brief acquaintance with the man did not wholly explain. Presumably something in their encounter yesterday had impressed him favorably. But he could remember nothing about it.

"You got back to the Yard by about four," continued Davies, unaware of this inner turmoil, "and wrote that report I spoke of, and I assume you did some other work from your desk." Davies gave a little shrug. "After that we don't know. Only that you ended up in Walworth at nine fifteen, and left a message for Chief Inspector Carmichael just before you were attacked."

It was all too much. Gibbons bit his lip and looked away while he brought himself under control and tried to sort through this new information. In a moment he asked, "What did I ring Carmichael about?"

If Davies was disturbed by the fact that Gibbons had telephoned the chief inspector rather than himself, he gave no sign of it.

"You didn't say," he answered. "You just asked if he would have a moment to speak to you in the morning."

Gibbons frowned. "That seems odd."

"Well, I think it shows that whatever you wanted, you didn't feel it was urgent," offered Davies.

"But it almost seems as if it couldn't have been about the Haverford case," said Gibbons. "If I'd found out anything about that, I would have rung you, not Carmichael. And yet I can't think of any other reason I would have wanted to talk to him."

"Perhaps it was a personal problem?" suggested Davies. "Something you wanted an older man's perspective on? It seems to me the chief inspector would be a logical choice for something like that."

"Maybe." But Gibbons looked unconvinced.

"Well," said Davies with a glance at his watch, "I'm afraid I must be going or I'll be late meeting Colin. I'll stop back later to tell you what, if anything, I find out and I'll bring by that report of yours."

"Thank you, sir," said Gibbons. "It's very good of you to take the trouble."

Davies smiled. "No trouble at all, Sergeant. It's the least I can do."

Gibbons leaned back against the pillows as he watched the inspector leave. He was curiously tired, as if focusing on their conversation had tried his strength.

But it had also given him new food for thought. In all the confusion of waking in an unknown hospital with a painful wound in his abdomen, he had nearly forgotten about the case he had been working on less than a day ago. He turned his still-fuzzy mind to it now, but dozed off again before he had got very far.

Inspector Davies hesitated as he left the hospital. He did not like to interfere in any way with Chief Inspector Carmichael's investigation into the events of Tuesday night—shootings were, after all, much more in the chief inspector's line of country than in his own—but having spoken to Gibbons, a certain step seemed essential. He supposed it would not do any harm to wait until Carmichael was back on duty and could think of it himself, but concern over the chief inspector's temper seemed a poor reason to delay such an obvious precaution.

After debating with himself for a few minutes, Davies pulled out his mobile with a sigh and rang the number for the Scotland Yard forensics laboratory. He was surprised to have his call answered by Ian Hodges himself, since the scientist was notorious for never even checking his messages, much less actually answering the phone.

"Mr. Hodges," he said politely, "Detective Inspector Davies here. I was ringing about Sergeant Gibbons's case."

"Well, I'm working on it, aren't I?" demanded Hodges. "You detectives all seem to think forensics is some kind of magic, accomplished with a snap of the fingers."

"I'm sure you're doing an excellent job, Mr. Hodges, just as you always do," said Davies soothingly. "I wasn't calling for results. I've just spoken to Sergeant Gibbons, you see, and he doesn't remember much of yesterday. I thought perhaps you might send someone along to have a look at his computer at the Yard and see if we can't determine what he was working on yesterday afternoon."

"Ah, poor lad," said Hodges, immediately appeased. "How is he today?"

"He seemed very well to me," replied Davies. "I mean, considering what he's been through and all. I think he's frustrated at not being able to remember more."

"Natural enough," grunted Hodges. "Well, I'll have Michaels go collect Sergeant Gibbons's hard drive and we'll see what we'll see."

"Thank you," said Davies. "Er—I'm ordering this on my own initiative, you understand, but I think your report had better go to Chief Inspector Carmichael."

"Very well," said Hodges. "Nothing else, then? Good."

And he rang off abruptly.

Davies sighed as he closed his mobile, reflecting that he was sure to get a dressing down for this from Carmichael later in the day.

"But he probably would have been just as upset if I hadn't," he murmured to himself, and turned his attention to finding a taxi. He had heard of Carmichael, of course, as the chief inspector and his nearly miraculous clear rate was often spoken of reverently at the Yard, but last night had been Davies's first personal encounter with him. The meeting, in his opinion, had hardly been a favorable one, and he felt as though he would forever be associated in Carmichael's mind with the injury of a favorite sergeant. But there was no help for that, and he could only hope that the circumstance would not harm his career.

He met Colin James at 1 Lombard Street, an elegant establishment in the City and a favorite haunt of the investigator's, whom the atmosphere in 1 Lombard's dining room fit like a glove. James was a man who enjoyed his food. In fact, James enjoyed most things in life with gusto, and there could hardly have been a greater contrast between Davies's quiet manner and the robust enthusiasm of James.

He was a big man who worked to keep his figure and had thus far succeeded, with only the shadow of a bulge at his waistline. At forty-two, his hairline had receded sharply and in consequence he wore the fair hair that was left him clipped very short against his skull. He welcomed Davies eagerly, his gray eyes twinkling with good humor, and waved him into the chair opposite his own at the table.

Davies sat down and immediately felt the tension begin to ebb out of him. He was exceedingly glad James had offered to take him to lunch; an hour spent in James's comfortable, elegant world was just what he needed.

"Try this," James urged, pouring from the bottle of white wine that stood ready in a cooler. "It's a new discovery of mine, and really quite excellent, considering its price."

Davies raised a brow. "Not your usual extravagance, I take it?"

"Not a bit of it, my dear man," said James, setting the bottle back in the cooler and raising his own glass. "Cheap, in a word, positively cheap. Here's to confounding the criminals!"

Davies lifted his glass to the toast and tasted the wine, a light, crisp draught on his palate.

"Very good," he pronounced, though he knew James hardly needed his opinion.

"Yes, I thought you'd like it." James was eyeing him narrowly; he was a keenly observant man. "You don't look quite as alert as usual," he said. "Did you and Mrs. Davies overindulge last night? And it a school night, too." He shook his head in mock disapproval.

"Not exactly." Davies found himself curiously reluctant to broach the subject he had come about. "Something rather disturbing happened last night. Sergeant Gibbons was taken to hospital and had emergency surgery. He'd been shot, you see."

The good humor was instantly wiped from James's face and his eyes went steely cold.

"I'm very sorry to hear it," he said. "Will he recover?"

"Early days, but they believe so," answered Davies. "It was touch-and-go last night, though."

James shook his head and leaned back. "I rather wondered why I was seeing you today," he said. "I had thought perhaps you were checking up on young Gibbons's progress, and I was prepared to issue a conservatively glowing report. I never imagined anything had happened to the lad." He paused for a moment, reaching for his glass. "I expect," he added, "you want to know if I think the Haverford case could be connected with this attack?"

"Yes," answered Davies with a smile. He was used to being anticipated by James and had come to rather enjoy it. "And, more than that, I want to know if he told you where he was going when you parted yesterday."

James looked puzzled. "But I thought you said Gibbons was going to be all right?" he asked. "Surely if that's the case, he should be awake by now?"

Davies grinned at him. "It's very seldom," he said, "that I find a subject you're not well versed in. But apparently you know very little about gunshot wounds."

"I readily admit that," retorted James. "Frankly, I had never thought it would be a topic of import to me. I take it they're keeping him sedated?"

"No, that's not the problem," answered Davies. "Poor Gibbons has forgotten most of yesterday. I don't know whether any of it is likely to come back or not, but at the moment his memory stops on his way into the Yard in the morning."

"Ah," said James, considering this. "So he doesn't remember our interview with the Colemans? Or our lunch together?"

"No," said Davies, his eyes lighting up at this revelation. "You took him to lunch, did you?"

"Yes, and found him a very pleasant companion. Mind you, he's appallingly ignorant about jewels—and painting, for that matter— but he's a very intelligent sort, and picks things up quickly. I should say he's already fully grasped just how different our work is from Homicide's. And," he added, "it was rather a relief to me that he wasn't one of the country lads you sometimes send me who seem to think my slightest comment off the case is an effort to chat them up."

Davies smiled. "That was Sergeant Dent."

James simply sighed and shook his head.

"Well," he said, "let's order, shall we? And then you can tell me what happened to poor Sergeant Gibbons." He beckoned the waiter. "Shall I decide?" he asked.

It was their usual arrangement, James having a reputation as a gourmet, and Davies nodded acquiescence.

James's good humor seemed to return as he discussed the merits of various dishes and ingredients with the waiter, but with the ordering of their meal accomplished he turned serious again.

"So you think this shooting is connected with the Haverford case?" he asked.

Davies waggled a hand. "We just don't know at this point," he said simply. "Everything is being considered."

"How did it happen?"

"We don't know that, either," said Davies, frustration in his voice. "For some reason, Gibbons went to Walworth last night and was shot in the street around nine o'clock. That's the sum total of the facts at the moment."

"And your job is to either rule in or rule out the Haverford case as a connection," said James, nodding. "Well, I don't know that I can tell you much. Let's see . . ." He rested his elbows on the table and steepled his fingers in front of him while he marshaled his thoughts. "The interview with the Colemans was largely inconclusive," he said slowly. "I came away thinking it unlikely they were running a scam, though they're a difficult couple to make out. Particularly her."

Davies raised an eyebrow. "So why were you inclined to exonerate them?" he asked.

"Oh, it wasn't anything to do with our interview," said James. "It's just logic. The robbery looked quite professional, or so I gathered from your forensics lads, and I didn't see how two people only recently arrived in England would have the necessary connections. On the other hand, the fact that they may well be planning to leave the country means they could conceivably keep the insurance money and sell the jewelry elsewhere in the world. Well, I'm sure you've worked that out for yourself."

Davies nodded thoughtfully and sipped at his wine. "Yes, I explained to Sergeant Gibbons that the pieces themselves were worth more than just the value of the jewels in them, and that only someone very desperate for money would be likely to sell the jewels off individually. I take it the Colemans don't seem desperate to you?"

"Not a bit of it," answered James. "I admit that I found Mrs. Coleman very enigmatic, but there was nothing enigmatic about her clothes. Designer labels and two-hundred-pound Italian shoes—not the wardrobe of anybody desperate."

"No," agreed Davies. He shook his head. "I don't see myself that Gibbons's attack can have anything to do with the case, unless he had somehow got on to the thieves and confronted them last night."

James was shaking his head, too. "I can't see how," he said. "Unless it was all a monumental coincidence. Even if he had somehow discovered who our thieves were, your Sergeant Gibbons is no fool—he would never have confronted them without backup."

"No," said Davies with a sigh. "Did he say anything to you during lunch that might give us a clue?"

"I did most of the talking at lunch," admitted James. "We started by going over our interview, but then the conversation went from there to the arts world in general and the type of people who commit crimes involving art or jewelry. Sergeant Gibbons was pumping me for information and, well, there's no denying I have plenty to give."

"And no objections to giving it," added Davies with a smile. "What did you think of the Yard's favored son?"

"Oh, I was most favorably impressed," said James. "Although, if you want my opinion, Gibbons isn't going to stay in Arts Theft. He doesn't have that flair for the artistic that the best of us have, and although an eye for art can certainly be learned, it's just not his natural bent."

"That's more or less what I thought myself," admitted Davies. "Nevertheless, he's clever enough that I thought he would be quite useful while he was assigned to me." He looked rather glum over this lost opportunity, but then redirected his attention with an effort. "So," he continued, "there was nothing said during lunch that gave you any notion of something amiss?"

"None at all."

"And what time did you part?"

"Oh, it must have been about two or half-past. I took a taxi after we left the restaurant and Sergeant Gibbons started off for the tube. That was the last I saw of him."

"And he turned up at the Yard at about four," murmured Davies, running the timetable through his head. "So he must have stopped somewhere along the way."

"I was going to ask," said James, "what you'd found out from the other end of the case."

"Nothing." Davies scowled. "I've put feelers out, and may yet get something—it's early days, after all—but so far no one's picking up any rumor of a big theft like this. I've got one lad who's a very reliable source for this kind of thing, but he's come up empty-handed. In fact, if Gibbons hadn't been shot last night, I was planning to meet with you both today to look at the scam angle. But now you tell me there's nothing there, either."

"Well, the bloody jewelry went somewhere," said James. "And we certainly can't have Scotland Yard sergeants wandering about getting shot. I don't know that the Haverford robbery has anything to do with it, but if it does, I'll ferret it out, I promise you. I'll work double time on this case whether it's outright theft or a scam, and I won't stop until we've got it cleared up and know for sure and certain if it was the reason Gibbons was attacked."

"Thank you, Colin," said Davies. "I appreciate that, and I'm sure the sergeant will, too."

And in truth he did feel better. He was a more than competent detective, but James had what amounted to genius in cases like this.

Detective Sergeant Chris O'Leary had barely got three hours' sleep and in consequence his blue eyes were bloodshot and puffy. He was normally a rakishly handsome young man with black hair and fair skin who had much success with the ladies. He was a few years older than Gibbons and had only received his promotion to sergeant during the past summer, but despite Gibbons's much earlier promotion, the two men had been friends ever since Gibbons had joined the force.

O'Leary might be short on sleep, but his mood—at least as he presented it to Gibbons—was upbeat and full of good humor.

"We'll sort it out, never fear," he said encouragingly when he stopped by the hospital on his way into the Yard. "You just concentrate on healing up so we can have you back on the job."

Gibbons grunted. Everyone seemed very intent on reassuring him, but he did not want palliatives, or to be told that his colleagues were handling everything; he wanted to be handling it himself.

"So you didn't find out anything last night?" he asked. "No one saw anything?"

"Not that they wanted to say," answered O'Leary. "You know that neighborhood, Jack—they don't talk to the police if they can help it. But Lambeth station has everyone out this morning. I haven't been down there yet, but I rang as I was coming in, and DC Cummings tells me they're bringing in everyone who reported hearing the shots last night. They'll dig up something in the end, I'm sure."

Gibbons merely grunted again and shifted cautiously while O'Leary hid a yawn behind his hand.

"Carmichael's not turned up yet," he went on, "but Inspector Hollings is already down in Walworth, and Inspector Davies is off looking into your robbery. I don't suppose you think the shooting was connected to that, do you?"

"It doesn't seem likely, does it?" said Gibbons. "I mean, I'd barely started investigating—I don't remember most of yesterday, but I can't believe I solved the case between lunch and dinner."

O'Leary grinned. "It would be like you if you did," he said.

Gibbons waved this away. "Nonsense," he said, in no mood for flattery. "On the other hand," he added, "I can't see why anyone else would want to shoot me. I wasn't robbed, was I?"

"No," said O'Leary. "They gave me all your effects in hospital and your wallet was there and everything accounted for. You had your ID, two credit cards, an Oyster card, and twelve pounds, seventeen pence."

"That sounds about right," sighed Gibbons. "I can't remember what money I had left, but it was certainly less than twenty quid. So when did you find me?"

O'Leary obliged with a recap of the events of the previous evening, passing over his own horror at finding his colleague lying in a pool of blood on the street with a pack of frantically busy paramedics ministering to him while the rain came down.

For his part, Gibbons felt grateful for any information that helped fill the gaps in his memory. He kept thinking that with enough reminders he would remember more, but so far this hope had come to nothing.

Carmichael was thoroughly out of temper with himself. He had intended to rise early and make another visit to the hospital before getting on with the day at Scotland Yard, but instead he woke too late to do anything but shower and grab a quick cup before setting off for work. He was the more annoyed as he knew he was now at an age where he could no longer do without sleep as he had in his youth, but refused to admit it to himself.

Despite having got nearly five hours' sleep, he felt anything but alert and the messages backed up on his mobile phone testified to the fact that his underlings had got ahead of him, making him even more irritable. He left for the Yard having snapped at his wife and been tartly reproved for it, and tried to take stock of all his messages along the way. He intended to ring Gibbons when he was done, but he was still sorting it all out when he arrived at his office and in his hurry to get hold of Hollings he forgot.

When Carmichael stormed into the office, Chris O'Leary was on his sixth cup of coffee and really did not think he could stay awake much longer. The sight of his superior striding past—without so much as a glance to acknowledge the sergeant's presence—stung him to alertness, and he straightened in his chair as he watched Carmichael turn out of sight around the corner. There was a pause and then O'Leary—who was waiting for it—heard the door of Carmichael's office slam shut.

The appearance of his superior in a foul mood had given O'Leary a shot of adrenaline; he dropped the cold remains of his coffee into the bin and turned with a sigh back to the computer, whose screen was beginning to blur before his eyes. But it was only a moment before he heard Carmichael's heavy tread returning and he looked up, startled to find the chief inspector frowning down at him.

"What the devil are you doing here?" Carmichael demanded.

O'Leary swallowed. "Inspector Hollings told me to look into Gibbons's past cases," he replied, trying to keep his tone perfectly even and innocent. "To find out," he added when Carmichael continued to glower at him, "who might have been released from prison lately and be holding a grudge."

"And are there any?"

"I've only found one so far, sir," answered O'Leary. He did not mention that he had made slow going at his assigned task because he kept falling asleep and had to stop and walk around the office to wake himself up.

But Carmichael's frown disappeared. "Who is that?" he asked. "One of my cases?"

"Yes, sir," said O'Leary, turning to his notebook. "I have it here—Frank Mulligan was released a fortnight ago. He was convicted—"

He broke off as Carmichael waved an impatient hand. "Scratch that," he said. "Frank Mulligan couldn't successfully shoot anybody on the best day he ever had. Anyone else?"

O'Leary shook his head. "Not yet," he answered. "Most of the people Jack has helped to put away are still in prison."

"Well, that makes sense," said Carmichael. "Gibbons has mostly worked murder cases, and he's only been a detective for the last four years or so—murderers usually get a much longer sentence than that."

There did not seem to be much to say in reply to this obvious fact, so O'Leary contented himself with nodding agreement while Carmichael rubbed his chin and looked thoughtful.

"What's really wanted," he said, "is to nail down Gibbons's movements yesterday. Davies left me a message saying the poor lad doesn't remember Tuesday at all."

"He doesn't seem to," agreed O'Leary. "I stopped by the hospital on my way in today, and found Jack fretting over the memory loss."

Carmichael sighed. "I haven't been by the hospital yet," he said guiltily.

O'Leary wasn't sure what to say to this, either, and there was a brief silence.

"Well," said Carmichael briskly, "if Gibbons can't tell us himself, we shall just have to ferret out his movements on our own. Davies seems to have made some progress—he said in his message Gibbons had lunched with that insurance investigator. He mentioned a report, but I didn't see it anywhere on my desk."

"I think he sent it by e-mail, sir," said O'Leary. "At least, that was what he said he was going to do when he stopped by earlier. He waited a bit for you, but then went off to see if he could come up with anything on the robbery Gibbons was investigating."

Carmichael was looking cross at the thought of having to delve into his e-mail file; the chief inspector had never really taken to the new medium. In his opinion, e-mail merely gave people a chance to bother him with things they would never have thought of troubling him with back when they would have had to actually pick up the phone and speak to him. An idea occurred to him and he looked about, frowning as he failed to find the person he was looking for.

"Where's Constable Lemmy?" he demanded.

"He's here somewhere, sir," answered O'Leary. "He's been here ever since I came in."

"Probably at the bloody vending machine," muttered Carmichael. "Tell him I want him when he comes back."

"Yes, sir."

O'Leary stifled a yawn as Carmichael turned away. Blinking industriously, he tried to focus on the screen before him, then sighed and gave it up. He thought Carmichael was very likely right about where Constable Lemmy was and it reminded him that he was out of coffee.

He stretched and rose, but encountered Lemmy before he was many steps away from his desk.

"DCI wants you," he told him, jerking a thumb in the direction of Carmichael's office.

Lemmy nodded stolidly, and turned his steps in that direction. O'Leary watched him go, a little perplexed by Lemmy's lack of reaction. When he had been a newly christened detective constable, any mention of a DCI would have sent him trotting alertly off, eager to demonstrate his abilities. But since he had arrived at the Homicide Department, Lemmy had exhibited none of the bright-eyed enthusiasm, which was the normal earmark of new detectives. He was also a rather silent young man, which made him difficult for his colleagues to make out. He was amiable enough, and willing enough, but he appeared to be oddly lacking in interest in his supposed chosen profession.

When O'Leary returned with a fresh coffee, he found Carmichael waiting impatiently by his desk.

"Here I am, sir," he called, hastening his pace. "Did you want me for something?"

Carmichael muttered something O'Leary was too far away to catch, but the chief inspector's tone was not encouraging. He turned a blue-eyed glare on O'Leary.

"Did you leave here with Gibbons last night?" he demanded.

O'Leary was taken aback. Subsequent events had superseded the ordinary routine of leaving work with a friend from his mind, and the unexpected memory brought him up short. "Er, yes, sir," he said, swallowing. "We stopped by the Feathers for a pint. We often do if we're leaving at the same time."

Carmichael rolled his eyes. "And it didn't occur to you to tell me?" he said. "Even though I had just stated the importance of tracking Gibbons's movements yesterday?"

O'Leary shook his head mutely, chagrined to be so caught out.

"I'm sorry, sir," he offered. "It was such an ordinary thing, I'd actually forgotten it." He frowned. "Did Gibbons mention it in his report or something?"

"Lemmy noticed the two of you walking out together," answered Carmichael. "It's a miracle he did—it's about the first thing he's noticed since he's been here. Well, come along—out with it, lad. What time was all this? And did Gibbons give you any notion of where he was going when you parted?"

O'Leary thought furiously but had to shake his head in the end.

"No, sir," he answered. "I had a date last night, and left the pub before he did. That was about half-six."

"And nothing unusual struck you during your conversation? Gibbons didn't seem worried, or on edge, or anything?"

"No, sir," said O'Leary again, rather wishing he had something to report that was not negative. "It was quite an ordinary drink after work. He told me about these jewels that had been stolen, and I told him about the case I was working on."

"Hmm." Carmichael hitched a hip onto the edge of O'Leary's desk and folded his arms while he thought. "You're on the Pennycook murder, right? I don't remember much about the case—the victim was an old-time criminal, wasn't he?"

"Yes, sir," said O'Leary. "Alfred Pennycook was a fence down in Walworth, and had been for decades. He did a couple of stints in prison for it along the way, but he was getting old for the game. Sixty-three he was, and as far as we've been able to make out, what business he still did was mostly carried on by his nephew. The old man had emphysema and didn't get around much anymore. It's hard to make out why anybody would want to kill him—by all accounts, he hadn't much longer to go—so Inspector

Hollings and I have been looking into old grudges. There's no lack of them."

"Yes, I remember now," said Carmichael. "Old Pennycook was involved in the big McDonald jewel heist, way back in the seventies, wasn't he?"

"That's right, sir. He went to prison for that one—his first time, although from his record, he'd been in a fence for years, only nothing could be pinned on him before the McDonald robbery. He got out early for good behavior."

A smile had touched the corners of Carmichael's lips. "I remember that robbery," he said. "It made a big splash in the papers. They don't make thieves like that anymore—it's all knock 'em over the head these days, more's the pity."

"On the other hand, sir," said O'Leary, "the violent ones don't get out of prison for good behavior so easily."

"There is that, lad," agreed Carmichael. "Well, back to business. What did Gibbons say about his own case?"

O'Leary thought for a moment. "Nothing startling," he said. "Mostly he was telling me what he'd learned about jewelry, and how different Arts Theft was from Homicide."

"He didn't mention any theories he was working on?"

"No, I'd have remembered that. He was saying that Arts Theft was more interesting than he'd thought it would be, and I asked if he'd ever consider a permanent transfer there."

"And would he?" asked Carmichael, very much hoping not.

"He said not, sir," replied O'Leary. "He said he didn't think the job played to his strengths and besides, there was something visceral about a homicide investigation that he missed in Arts Theft."

Carmichael let out a little sigh of relief. "I'm glad to hear that at least," he said. "It's the first good news I've had in two days. Very well. So the two of you talked shop over a couple of pints, is that what I'm to take away from this?"

"Yes, sir," said O'Leary. "Like I said, I had a date, and after I'd finished my pint, I had to be off. Jack hadn't quite finished his bitter, but he told me to go on. So I did."

"So at half-six," mused Carmichael, "Gibbons was sitting in the

Feathers, finishing a pint. He'd want his dinner, no doubt, and so far as we know, he was done with his work for the day. He didn't say anything about needing to finish anything up, did he?"

O'Leary shook his head.

"It almost sounds as if, whatever he was up to, it didn't have to do with his case," continued Carmichael. "Still, I'll send Lemmy down to security and have them make sure Gibbons didn't reenter the building after you'd left him."

"He might have had an idea after I went and wanted to check it out," suggested O'Leary.

"Exactly," said Carmichael. "Well, I want you to think over your conversation with him, O'Leary, and let me know if anything else occurs."

"Of course, sir. I'm sorry I didn't think of it before now, but with all that's happened, it seems as though that drink we had was a decade ago."

"Natural enough, lad," said Carmichael, shifting his weight off the desk. "Let me go and read Davies's report now, and you can go back to our old cases." He paused, looking thoughtful, and then shook his head. "No," he said. "I want you to do something else for me, O'Leary. I want you to write as complete a report as you can on your conversation with Gibbons that night."

O'Leary, considerably startled, said, "Yes, sir," rather doubtfully, and Carmichael waved a hand.

"I know," he said. "It may be a waste of time. But it's the only thing we know for certain about how Gibbons spent his evening. He may have made a remark which will jog his memory, if it doesn't come back on its own. Do your best for me, O'Leary."

"I will, sir."

"And let me know if you hear from Hollings."

"Yes, sir."

O'Leary returned to his chair with a sigh, closed his case file window, opened a blank Word document, and sipped at his now-cold coffee.

4

The Haverford Case

*B*ethancourt woke last of all. The exigencies of the night before had exhausted him, and he slept like a log in consequence, not waking until a full eight hours had passed and the early-winter evening had already begun. A quick call to the hospital reassured him that Gibbons was not going to peg out just yet, so he set about his usual morning routine, walking Cerberus to the newsagent's for the paper while the coffee brewed. Back at the flat, he arranged himself comfortably at the kitchen table, black coffee and newspaper before him, lit a cigarette, took a sip of the hot brew, and opened the paper to look for any report on Gibbons's shooting.

Some two hours later, he had showered, changed, and presented himself and his dog at the door of Gibbons's hospital room, having passed Cerberus off as Gibbons's pet. The policemen guarding the door were two different men from the night before, and there was some little delay before he was admitted while they verified his identity.

Once inside, he was greeted with a scowl by his friend, who was lying in what looked like a terribly uncomfortable position.

"Oh, it's you," he said dully.

"How are you feeling?" asked Bethancourt, thinking his friend sounded hoarse and looked very weak. He settled himself in the armchair while Cerberus sniffed curiously at Gibbons's side.

"Cross," replied Gibbons, reaching out automatically to pet the dog. He eyed his friend who looked, to his mind, abominably comfortable and well rested. "My parents," he added sarcastically, "are very impressed with the accommodations Scotland Yard has provided for them. Apparently a grateful nation has stumped up for a suite at The Montague. One overlooking the garden."

"How nice," said Bethancourt, refusing to be baited. "Where are your parents, by the way? I rather thought I'd find them here."

"They've gone off to have dinner," answered Gibbons.

"Oh, yes, it is dinnertime, isn't it?" said Bethancourt, glancing at his watch. "I'm all discombobulated today. So have the doctors said anything more?"

"Not very much," said Gibbons. "They seem reasonably pleased with me and are being cautiously optimistic." He yawned.

"Are you sleepy?" asked Bethancourt. "Because if you'd rather I leave and come back later, just say so."

"No," said Gibbons. "It's just the damn painkillers. They make me drowsy—I've been napping half the day and hardly had a coherent thought."

"Better that than a lot of pain," said Bethancourt. "I don't imagine your tummy is feeling very good just now."

"Oh, there's still plenty of pain," Gibbons assured him. "But they claim it's less excruciating with the drugs than without. It's bad enough being laid up like this—it's hell not to be able to think clearly on top of it."

Bethancourt, a clear-thinking man himself, sympathized. "Er," he said guardedly, "is that really the most comfortable position for you?"

"No," said Gibbons crossly, "it is not. It is, however, the only position in which my abdomen doesn't hurt. The rest of me is cramped and uncomfortable. Eventually, the cramping will bother me enough that I'll decide the abdomen pain wasn't really so bad and I'll shift position and stay that way until the pain in my stomach gets to be too much."

Bethancourt considered this in silence for a moment. He was a person who abhorred any kind of discomfort and who had a knack of settling himself in quite cozily wherever he happened to be.

"It sounds dreadful," he offered.

Gibbons glared at him, and Bethancourt reflected that what his friend really needed was distraction.

"So what's the news?" he asked, ignoring the glare. "Have they found out who shot you yet?"

Gibbons's glare turned into a sigh of frustration. "Not that I know of," he replied. "But I haven't heard from Carmichael today."

"I'm sure he's hard at work," said Bethancourt. "I mean, think how you would feel if he was the one who was shot."

"I know, I know." Gibbons tentatively straightened one leg.

"It must be driving you crazy; not being able to help, I mean," said Bethancourt. "At least . . . well, the nurse said you didn't remember much about yesterday."

"Nor do I," said Gibbons glumly. "Everything's a blank after I left my flat to go to work."

"Well, let's come at things from a different angle," said Bethancourt, who had an inventive mind. "You rang me yesterday evening to say you had an interesting case."

Gibbons looked up. "Is that exactly what I said?" he asked.

Bethancourt shrugged. "It's easy enough to find out," he answered, reaching into his coat pocket. "I should still have the message."

He turned on his mobile and spent a moment scrolling down his messages.

"Here it is," he said, and rose to hold the phone to Gibbons's ear. "Ready?"

Gibbons grunted affirmatively. Bethancourt pressed a button and Gibbons heard his own voice, oddly unrecognizable to him.

"Got an interesting one on," said the voice. "I'd like to hear what you make of it. Ring me when you get a chance."

"That's got to be the Haverford robbery," said Gibbons as Bethancourt shut off the phone. "Even if I had stumbled onto something else, I wouldn't have used that phrase 'got an interesting one on.' That's definitely a reference to my own case."

"So what was interesting about the Haverfords?" asked Bethancourt, resettling himself in the chair.

"Nothing. There aren't any."

Bethancourt raised an eyebrow.

"Well," amended Gibbons, "it sounds as though old Miss Haverford would have been quite interesting, but she's dead."

"That's homicide, not robbery," pointed out Bethancourt.

"No, no, she died naturally. I believe she was ninety-seven."

Bethancourt let out an exaggerated sigh. "How could she be robbed if she's dead?" he asked. "Really, Jack, can't you just begin at the beginning and go on until you reach the end?"

"No, I can't," said Gibbons sharply. "At the moment, there is no beginning or ending for me—it's all jumbled together. And I don't like it any better than you do."

"Sorry, sorry," apologized Bethancourt. "I was forgetting. Truly, Jack, I don't mean to be flippant."

"I know you don't," muttered Gibbons. He took a deep breath. "Miranda Haverford," he began, "was by all accounts an eccentric old lady who knew her own mind and made sure everyone else knew it, too."

"That sounds like my grandmother," observed Bethancourt, not at all inclined to feel charitably toward this specter.

"Miss Haverford," continued Gibbons doggedly, "owned a quite fabulous collection of jewelry, inherited from her grandmother. Or perhaps it was her great-grandmother; I can't remember."

"No matter," said Bethancourt. "I am willing to take the bejeweled ancestor on faith."

"Being of sound mind, Miss Haverford made a will a few years back, leaving most of her estate to her only living relative, a second or third cousin."

"Including the jewels?"

"Well, of course including the jewels, otherwise why should I be dragging the poor git into the case at all?" demanded Gibbons.

"Right," said Bethancourt. "Just trying to keep it all clear in my head. The Haverford distant cousin now has possession of the jewels."

"No, he doesn't," contradicted Gibbons.

Bethancourt looked confused. "He doesn't?" he repeated doubtfully. "But I thought you said . . ."

"I said the jewels were left to him in the old lady's will," said Gibbons. "Her estate is still in probate at the moment."

"Ah! The light has dawned. Go on."

Gibbons rubbed his face and Bethancourt saw with a pang that he already looked tired. "Where was I?" he asked.

"The jewels were in probate."

"Oh, right. Well, they still are. Or were, until Sunday night, when they were stolen."

"Hence the phrase 'Haverford robbery,' " said Bethancourt. "Where were the jewels when they were stolen?"

"Where they always were—in a safe in the study of Miss Haverford's house. It was professionally broken into, or at least so forensics says. I wouldn't know, myself."

"Neither would I," admitted Bethancourt. "Although I've always wanted to know how to break into a safe," he mused. "I wonder how one learns something like that."

"Presumably from experienced thieves," said Gibbons. "Or perhaps from the Internet these days—most information seems to be out there somewhere."

"Yes, that's an idea," said Bethancourt. "I shall have to Google it when I get home. I wonder if it turns out to be like making a soufflé—you know, the instructions seem perfectly simple and it's only when you're in the middle of things that you realize you have no idea what you're doing."

Gibbons, who had never made a soufflé, yawned and returned to the topic at hand. "The robbery," he continued, "seemed fairly straightforward. The jewelry was famous in its way, and Miranda Haverford's obituary made all the broadsheet newspapers. Any thief worth his salt could have set his eyes on jewelry kept in an empty house."

"Very tempting," agreed Bethancourt. "So what made you think the case was interesting? It seems on the face of it to be open and shut—or at least it will be once you put a name to the thief."

"I don't know, do I?" said Gibbons grumpily. "We went over the scene-of-the-crime on Monday and met with the insurance agent, who had all the details about exactly what was stolen. Forensics hadn't finished processing everything yet, but Hodges said it looked like a professional job. We spoke briefly to the Colemans, who had reported the robbery themselves, and Davies introduced me to the insurance investigator."

"Who are the Colemans?" asked Bethancourt. "Neighbors?"

"No, no. Rob Coleman is the Haverford cousin. He and his wife visited the house on Monday morning in order to water the plants and generally keep an eye on things."

"Ah, I see." Bethancourt contemplated all this in silence for a moment while Gibbons gingerly stretched out his other leg and grimaced.

"All right?" asked Bethancourt anxiously, reflexively getting to his feet in order to help.

Gibbons glared at him. "You're worse than my parents," he said. "Do stop hovering like a mother hen."

"Sorry." Bethancourt sank back down, but behind his glasses his hazel eyes were uneasy as he watched the painful process of Gibbons resettling himself.

"That's better," said Gibbons at last, panting a little with the effort. "What was I saying?"

"The Colemans watered the plants," said Bethancourt. "I expect the insurance investigator is casting a suspicious eye on them?"

"It was mentioned," said Gibbons. "I would probably know better," he added with a frown, "if I could remember yesterday morning. Inspector Davies says I went off with Mr. James to interview the Colemans."

Again he was aware of a friendly feeling toward James, one that could not have been generated by their brief meeting on Monday.

"I think the interview must have gone smoothly," he said, breaking into Bethancourt's comments. "At least, I think James and I must have got on well together. Anyway, Davies says I wrote up a report, so we'll know about that when he comes back. Maybe it will jog my memory," he added hopefully.

"Just the thing, I should think," said Bethancourt. "And your memory may come back of itself, once you're off all the drugs."

But despite these words, he was concerned. Gibbons looked very pale and his voice was faint; Bethancourt did not think his friend was well at all.

Upon leaving the hospital Bethancourt paused, standing hesitantly on the wet pavement with the rush of traffic on Euston Road speeding past, unsure of what to do.

Having just heard the details of the case, he was keen to look into it all, but found himself at a loss without Gibbons to guide him. Normally, after having discussed a case, he would toddle off with his friend on any line of inquiry Gibbons thought might prove profitable. Bethancourt could think of several lines that might be followed up in this instance, but he had no authority with which to pursue them. One could not, he thought wryly to himself, go about questioning people if one was merely a friend of a police detective; actually being a police detective was indispensable.

Neither did he think his interference would be well received by Chief Inspector Carmichael. If he had managed to provide Carmichael with a possible motive in Gibbons's personal life, he might have wormed his way into the case by way of being a witness, but that was a closed door.

He took a deep breath of the chill, dank air, hoping to clear his mind. Cerberus, having got bored with his master's inaction, had wandered on to inspect a nearby lamppost, and Bethancourt absently followed his pet, deep in thought.

There was, he reflected, no evidence at all that Gibbons's shooting had been connected with the case he had been working on. Nevertheless, something had occurred on Tuesday which had changed Gibbons's view of the Haverford case. That, in Bethancourt's mind, was the first thing to be cleared up. And on that score there might be an avenue to follow aside from the police.

But, he reluctantly admitted to himself, not right now. It was past nine o'clock and quite dark; in front of him the rush-hour traffic along Euston Road had died down. And he had yet to return the Volvo to the rental agency.

He sighed at the thought of the number of parking tickets the

Volvo had no doubt accumulated during its stay in the neighborhood and began to walk in that direction.

"Come, Cerberus," he murmured, and the great dog fell obediently into step with him while he began to page through the telephone numbers stored on his mobile. "There we go," he said at last, and pressed the number that would dial his insurance agent. Becky Rankin would not be available now, but he could leave her a message and she would act on it as soon as she arrived at the office in the morning; Bethancourt was a very good customer.

They gathered at the end of the day, none of them at their best, all with frayed tempers from long hours of work in which very little progress had been made. Now, at nearly ten o'clock, they slouched tiredly around the conference table, its surface littered with open notebooks and paper cups of coffee.

"So," said Carmichael, his voice even raspier than usual, "have we got anywhere at all today?"

The pause before anyone ventured to answer this question spoke volumes. But as the senior man present it was Davies's duty to speak up, and he did it bravely enough, clearing his throat and saying, "We've made a little progress, I think. We've filled in some of Gibbons's day and if we haven't turned up any real leads, at least we've eliminated several possibilities."

"That's right," chimed in Hollings. He had spent all day down in Walworth, interviewing anyone and everyone who might possibly have been in the immediate area where Gibbons had been found. He and the police at the Lambeth station had done their best to find any connection, however faint, with a young detective sergeant who had been investigating a jewel theft in Southgate, but they had come up empty.

"And we've got the ballistics report back," offered O'Leary.

Carmichael snorted. "That would have been a sight more helpful if Hodges had managed to trace the gun. All we know is that it was a 9mm which had not previously been used in a crime. It might have come from anywhere."

"But, again, it rules something out," said Hollings, sticking to the optimistic point of view. "If Gibbons was shot by a career criminal in Walworth, you would expect ballistics to turn up the gun."

Carmichael nodded, if rather glumly. "At least your man Clarkson managed to find someone who saw Gibbons that night," he said. "I was beginning to believe the lad had wandered about Walworth like so much smoke."

"Well, it was a nasty night, sir," said Hollings. "Most people were keeping to their firesides. I won't deny that's complicated things."

"True, true." Carmichael sipped at his coffee and tried to take stock. Turning to Davies, he asked, "Where are you with the Haverford case? Anything there?"

Davies sighed. "I'm afraid not," he admitted. "My contacts have dried up on this one, and so far I'm not having much luck in matching the M.O. with any gangs we're currently aware of."

"That's what Sergeant Gibbons was doing," said Constable Lemmy unexpectedly.

They all turned to stare at him.

"What was Gibbons doing?" asked Carmichael, his eyebrows beetling dangerously.

"On his computer," explained Lemmy, apparently serenely unaware of the import of the chief inspector's eyebrows. "He was trying to refine the search pattern so he could get better results. Or at least Joe thinks that was what he was doing."

This was received in stunned silence.

Carmichael opened his mouth, closed it, and took a deep breath before speaking. It was clear to most of the men at the table that he was holding on to his temper with both hands.

"Joe?" he inquired.

"Joe Michaels over in forensics," supplied Lemmy. "He's the one who's been working on the sergeant's computer."

Carmichael's jaw clamped.

"Er," said Davies, trying to stem the tide, "perhaps there was some mix-up over there. I did tell them to send any reports on the computer to you."

"Oh, I don't think Joe has written up his report yet," said

Lemmy. "He just mentioned it to me while I was over there checking on the notebook."

"Perhaps," said Carmichael in a stiltedly polite tone, "the next time someone at forensics mentions something to you, you might pass it on to me. In a timely manner, I mean."

"Oh," said Lemmy, as if only just realizing the tension in the room was centered on himself. "Yes, sir. I'm sorry I didn't think to tell you earlier."

"Dear God," muttered Carmichael. He rubbed at his forehead.

"If I might, sir?" said Davies. "Constable, did Michaels say whether Gibbons had got any results?"

"I don't think so, sir," replied Lemmy. "He—Sergeant Gibbons, I mean—was working on one of those maths things."

"Dear God," said Carmichael again.

"An algorithm?" suggested Davies.

"That's it, sir," said Lemmy, with a doubtful look at the chief inspector.

"Didn't know Gibbons knew that much about computers," observed Hollings.

"Neither did I," admitted Davies. "I would have asked him to work on it if I had."

"But where does that leave us?" demanded Carmichael. There was a plaintive note in his voice.

"As far as the Haverford case is concerned," answered Davies, "it leaves all the possibilities wide open. I've looked through our database of career jewel thieves myself, but none of them match up exactly to this robbery. It could well be a simple case of a thief, knowing the house was now empty, having a go at it and getting lucky."

They all nodded; robberies at the houses of the recently deceased was a perennial problem.

"But," said Carmichael, frowning, "if the robbery was either of those possibilities, it's very difficult to see how Gibbons could have stumbled on the thief or thieves."

"I know," said Davies glumly. "The biggest connection I can think of is that half those pawnshops in Walworth are fronts for stolen goods, some of them very high end. But I can't see how Gibbons could have come at the thing from that end."

"No," agreed Carmichael, "it's not likely, is it? He'd only been with you for a couple of weeks."

"And he gave you no indication at all of how he planned to spend the evening?" Hollings asked O'Leary. "Presumably he was at least planning to have some supper."

"He may have been," answered O'Leary, "but he didn't mention it. Honestly, Inspector, if none of this had happened and you had asked me what I thought Jack did last night, I would have said he was heading home to Google Golconda diamonds, possibly picking up some takeaway en route."

Carmichael pursed his lips. "Then let's assume those were his plans," he said. "Something happened to change them after you left. That's the piece of information we really need, though I don't see quite yet how we're to get it."

Neither, it was clear, did anyone else.

"Well," said Carmichael after a moment, "let's all be off home—perhaps a good night's sleep will give us some new ideas."

They were all more than eager to comply with this sage advice. But Carmichael, rather than following it himself, picked up his overcoat from his office and went, not home, but to University College Hospital.

At 10:30 the hospital was quiet, all the bustle of the day gone from the halls, the hum and regular blips of monitors more noticeable in the hush. Gibbons's room was in shadow.

"I think he's been asleep for an hour or so," the uniformed policeman outside Gibbons's door told Carmichael in a whisper. "His parents came back from their supper after that other friend of his left, but they didn't stay long. His mum said when they went that she thought he'd sleep if he was left alone."

Carmichael nodded, his gaze still focused on the still shadow in the hospital bed.

"I thought he probably would be," he said. "But I wanted to stop in, since I missed him this morning."

"Of course, sir," said the policeman. "I'll see to it he knows you called by."

Carmichael nodded. "Thank you," he said. He stood still for another moment, knowing that his guilt sprang not only from not having visited his sergeant this day, but also from a most unreasonable feeling that if he had not let Gibbons go to Arts Theft, he would not have been shot.

Eventually, however, he turned away and started for home and his wife and the comfort of their bed.

Gibbons came awake much later, in the depths of the night, and lay blinking in the hospital bed until his gaze sharpened enough to make out the rain-flecked window. He was acutely uncomfortable, and his drugged mind flitted from thought to thought while he stared blankly at the window and tried to come to terms with what had happened to him. The idea that he had been shot still seemed an absurd one; he felt he ought to remember such a momentous event. Nor did he feel much like he had experienced a near-brush with death though that was what everybody told him. There was gravitas in such things, or at least there ought to be, but try as he might he could not come up with any emotion appropriate to the occasion. He did not feel profoundly changed, or filled with any insight into the meaning of life. He merely felt unwell. And while he pondered this, his lids grew heavy and he dropped back again into a restless sleep.

Kith and Kin

He was cold. Gibbons knew that, but he couldn't seem to figure out why. He had some notion that if only he could get up and get out of the rain, he would warm up, but he seemed unable to move. And there was something at the back of his mind that told him he wasn't wet or outside in any case. But he was still cold.

There was a rustling sound somewhere behind him. It was not at all a threatening sound, and yet it awoke terror in his heart. It was vital that he turn and see what was making it. With an enormous effort, he turned his head.

And found himself in the hospital room, blinking at Chief Inspector Carmichael, who was sitting by his bedside, reading the paper and sipping at a coffee.

"Ah, there you are, lad," said the chief inspector, laying his paper aside. "How are you doing?"

Gibbons was not at all certain of the answer to this question, although "Not well at all" sprang to his mind. It hardly seemed an appropriate response.

"All right, sir," he replied, or tried to; his newly awakened throat did not cooperate and what came out was a garbled sound. Carmichael's cheerful smile was at once replaced by a worried frown, and he leaned forward anxiously while Gibbons cleared his throat around the tube and tried again.

"I'm all right," he managed, though it did not sound very convincing even to his own ears.

"Good, good," said Carmichael, recapturing his smile, though it did not look very heartfelt. "I'm really sorry I didn't get round to see you yesterday, but I got a late start on the day and never seemed to catch up."

"Oh." Gibbons was trying to think, without much success. He knew he had wanted badly to see Carmichael, yet now he was faced with him, he could not seem to remember why. A memory stirred out of the depths of his drugged brain. "They told me you'd been here last night."

"I did just stop by," said Carmichael. "But you were already asleep." He paused. "Did you have a good night?" he asked, not knowing what else to say.

In fact, Gibbons had not, having woken or been woken at several points, either by pain or the nursing staff, but again the truth did not seem very appropriate.

"Good enough," he said.

"Getting your rest is important," Carmichael told him.

"Yes, sir."

An awkward pause ensued in which Carmichael tried to think of something cheerful to say and Gibbons yawned and rubbed his eyes.

They were saved from the lengthening silence by the arrival of Gibbons's parents, looking fresh and well rested. They, too, wore falsely bright smiles to hide the small, anxious lines between their brows, but they seemed genuinely pleased to see Carmichael again.

Gibbons closed his eyes while they greeted each other and tried to take stock of himself. What he most needed, he decided, was a bedpan and to sit up a bit. He felt stiff and achy, and very muzzy-headed indeed.

His mother seemed to divine at least one of these needs, detaching herself from the two men to come and ask if he would like the bed put up a little.

Gibbons nodded gratefully. "Yes, please," he said.

"Have you remembered anything more to help the chief inspector?" asked his mother, pressing the bedside controls.

"I've only just woken up," protested Gibbons.

A thought occurred to Carmichael. "Do you know," he said, "I've never had the chance to ask you if you could think of any reason you might have gone to Walworth. Bethancourt said he didn't know of any friends of yours who lived there, but we never asked you."

"I don't think I know anyone there," said Gibbons. "Perhaps a casual acquaintance, but no one I regularly visit."

"Well, there's Dawn," said his mother brightly. "She's in Walworth."

Carmichael stared at her. "Who's Dawn?" he asked.

"My cousin," supplied Gibbons. "Dawn Melton."

"She's my sister-in-law's daughter," explained Mrs. Gibbons. "She got divorced recently and wanted to make a new start. She found a quite good job here in London last September, and I asked Jack to keep an eye on her. It was a nice opportunity for her, but she's never lived in a big city before, and we thought it might be difficult for her just at first."

"I helped her sort out the kids' schools," said Gibbons, but with a guilty air that made Carmichael think Dawn had not been much in the forefront of his mind. "And I've taken her to lunch once or twice."

"She said you'd been a great help," said Mrs. Gibbons, smiling fondly at him.

"Well?" asked Carmichael. "What about it, lad? Could you have gone to visit her on Tuesday night?"

"I might have," said Gibbons doubtfully. "I mean, I didn't have any prior plans to, but if she rang me, I would have stopped by."

"It's easy enough to find out," said Gibbons's father. "Ring her and ask."

"I'd rather like to do that myself," said Carmichael hastily.

"Of course, of course." Mrs. Gibbons was rummaging in her capacious handbag. "I have the number and address right here somewhere . . . ah, yes, here's my address book."

She produced an old-fashioned address book with a spray of irises across its worn cover and opened it. "Here you are, Chief Inspector," she said. "And as long as I've got you here, I'll take down your address as well, if you would be so kind. I very much want to write a note to your lovely wife—she was so kind to us that first morning."

"She'd appreciate hearing from you," said Carmichael, pulling out his notebook and a pencil.

He excused himself once they had exchanged information, secretly relieved to leave Gibbons to his parents. He had never been much of a hand at visiting the sick, and he was quite anxious to talk to this Dawn Melton. If Gibbons had indeed gone to visit her on Tuesday night, then it might well have been an act of random violence that had felled his sergeant, rather than some insidious plot involving elderly pawnbrokers and/or stolen jewelry.

Or, he thought glumly to himself, the reason for the shooting could be hidden in some dark corner of Gibbons's personal life, which would make the situation even worse. As an experienced homicide detective, Carmichael knew only too well how easily lives could be destroyed by a police investigation. It would be even worse for a detective, who would have every nook and cranny of his private affairs exposed to the eyes of his colleagues. Carmichael was not sure how one could recover from that.

Detective Sergeant Chris O'Leary had started his day very early, determined to make up for yesterday's sin of omission in neglecting to mention the drink he'd had with Gibbons on the Tuesday. In truth, he had pretty well forgotten all about it until Carmichael had reminded him and he was feeling guilty over that. He was, after all, supposed to be a detective, and he ought to have realized that he had been the last known person to see Gibbons before the shooting.

So he was fully determined to discover at the very least what time Gibbons had left the pub. He had not taken much notice at the time, but his memory of the pub that night was of a quiet place, with only a few patrons scattered about. If he closed his eyes and tried to envision the scene—something he had spent a great deal of time doing since yesterday—he seemed to remember passing a group of men by the door as he left. He did not know any of them personally, but he believed at least two of them worked in the Narcotics Division. If he could track them down, they might remember seeing Gibbons leave.

But his first port of call must be to the bartender, Bob Crebbin. Crebbin was tolerably well known to all those at Scotland Yard who enjoyed the odd drink after work, O'Leary among them, but he had no notion where the man lived. He did, however, recollect that Crebbin had at one time been a detective himself, or at least a policeman, and that should make him fairly easy to find. By a quarter to eight, O'Leary had compelled the Scotland Yard computers to divulge Crebbin's current address and was on his way to Barking.

Once arrived there, however, he found an unexpected obstacle in the person of Dora Crebbin, Bob's wife. She answered the door with a cigarette in her mouth and a suspicious glint in her eye.

"Bob's not up yet," she announced flatly. "He works nights, does Bob."

O'Leary tried to summon up his most ingratiating smile, but was a little hampered by the dangling cigarette.

"But I really need to speak with him," he said. "It's a matter of a friend of mine, you see. A fellow policeman."

Dora snorted to show her opinion of the police.

"It wouldn't take long," added O'Leary, aware that a wheedling tone was entering his voice. "Bob could go right back to sleep."

Dora shook her head firmly. "He don't like to be disturbed once he's down for the night," she stated.

"I'm sure not—who among us does?—but this is really an emergency," said O'Leary. "My friend was shot, you see—he's in hospital right this minute—and he can't remember anything about Tuesday. Only Bob can tell us when my friend left the pub."

This failed to impress Dora. She seemed completely uninterested in any of the events O'Leary described, and utterly unmoved by his plight.

"He can tell you when he wakes up," she said. "Now, I got to get to my work."

And she made to close the door.

"Perhaps I could wait, then," suggested O'Leary desperately.

"Right," she said sarcastically. "And then you'd be waking him up as soon's I'd gone. I'm no fool, young man, and don't you be thinking it."

"Chris—call me Chris," said O'Leary, trying for the smile again. "And of course I don't think you're a fool—why, Bob wouldn't have married you if you had been. It's just that I'm fair desperate to speak to him. Briefly," he amended hastily, "very briefly. I'm sure he'd want to help."

"Well, I'm not," she retorted, trying again to close the door.

O'Leary was just about to give up and stage another attack after she had left the house when a shuffling footstep sounded behind her and a deep male voice said, "What's all this then?"

Dora swung round, sprinkling ash down the front of her jumper, and said resignedly, "Well, that's done it. There's a young man wants to see you—I tried to tell him you were sleeping."

"Well, couldn't you have told him in a quieter voice? Who is it anyway?"

Crebbin squinted out at O'Leary over his wife's shoulder and looked a bit surprised.

"Hullo," he said. "It's Sergeant O'Leary, isn't it? Here, let him in, Dora."

Dora acceded to this with a shrug and abandoned her post at the door. O'Leary swiftly stepped in after her lest she should change her mind, and smiled weakly at Crebbin.

"Awfully sorry to bother you," he said.

"It's all right," said Crebbin, yawning. "I can't imagine you'd be here if it weren't important. Come through to the kitchen and have a cuppa."

Inside, the furnishings were uninspired and the wallpaper in the hall was much faded, but the house was spotlessly clean and comfortably arranged. O'Leary took a seat at the Formica table and waited patiently while Crebbin poured tea from a pot already made on the counter.

"Milk?" he asked, turning.

"No, thanks," said O'Leary, and accepted the mug Crebbin set in front of him, sipping gingerly at the hot brew. It was very strong and bitter, but considering his lack of sleep, O'Leary drank it happily.

Crebbin sat opposite him and concentrated on stirring several spoonfuls of sugar into his coffee before he tasted it and let out a satisfied sigh.

"Now then," he said. "That'll do me for a bit. What have you come about, Sergeant?"

O'Leary explained his errand and the reason for it. Crebbin nodded sadly and sipped at his coffee.

"I heard about the shooting last night," he said. "But you say Sergeant Gibbons will be all right?"

"They expect him to make a full recovery," O'Leary assured him. "Mind, he's pretty under the weather just now, but they say he's healing up well."

"Good, good. That's a relief to my mind. I don't know how you young ones stand all the violence nowadays—it wasn't like that when I was on the beat."

"No, I dare say not," said O'Leary, cutting off any stream of reminiscence that might be forthcoming. "But you can see how important it is that we find out when Jack left the Feathers that night."

"Yes, of course," said Crebbin. He rubbed his chin and squinted up at the ceiling. "Let's see, that would have been the night before last, right? Yes, yes, I remember. It was a quiet night, nobody much came in. And I do remember the two of you—you sat at that little table by the end of the bar, didn't you?"

"That's right," said O'Leary encouragingly.

"And it was you who came up for the drinks," continued Crebbin.

"Yes, I owed Jack one from last week."

Crebbin was silent a moment, remembering. "I saw you leave," he said slowly. "I know that because I was thinking I had best go collect the empties, but then I saw Sergeant Gibbons was still there."

"Did you speak to him at all?" asked O'Leary.

"No." Crebbin shook his head. "And he didn't stay long after you left. Ten, maybe fifteen minutes at the most. I don't know what time it was when you took yourself off, but it was a bit before seven when I noticed the sergeant had gone. I had just glanced at the clock, you see, thinking to myself that the time was going awfully slowly, that it wasn't even seven yet, and then I turned and saw the two empty pints on the table."

"But you didn't see him go?" asked O'Leary anxiously.

"No, I'm sorry, I didn't. But like I say, it wasn't above twenty minutes after you'd gone, and I didn't notice anyone come up to talk to him in that time. I think I would have, since your table was so close to the bar."

O'Leary nodded acceptance of this. "So he just sat there and quietly finished his pint?" he asked.

"More or less. I saw him jotting something down in his notebook at one point, I think, but that was all."

O'Leary had to be content with this unhelpful information. He thanked Crebbin, apologized again for waking him, and took his leave. He was going to be late meeting Inspector Hollings for the day's work, but he didn't care. At least he had found out one thing, however small.

Hospitals, Gibbons reflected, were very busy places in the mornings. It was a pity he didn't feel up to investigating what all the fuss was about. He supposed it was good that his parents seemed to be staying on top of things, but on the other hand, it was disconcerting at his age to have his parents know more about his own body than he did.

There was no denying he was not up to much this morning. He was solidly awake, but that was about all that could be said for him. There was a sharp pain in his abdomen whenever he made the slightest movement, and the tube running up his nose and down his throat seemed even more irritating than it had yesterday. And he was still cold.

None of the people fussing over him seemed to be addressing these concerns. First had been a young man in pink scrubs who had recorded his temperature and blood pressure and heaven only knew what else. Then had come a young woman in maroon scrubs who had busied herself with changing his various IV bags while talking cheerfully to his parents and more or less ignoring him.

After that, a pretty red-haired nurse accompanied by a much less attractive assistant had come in. They had ruthlessly ignored his complaints of being cold, thrown back the blankets, removed his dressings, and pushed at his abdomen. This last had been very painful indeed, and Gibbons was grateful that they had shooed his parents out of the room beforehand.

They had replaced his dressings with fresh ones, covered him up again, and departed, promising to see to an extra blanket, which had still not materialized. What had arrived was a doctor with an inscrutable expression and a deep, velvety voice who asked him questions about how he felt and wanted him to rate his pain on a scale from one to ten. He, too, had inspected Gibbons's abdomen and had merely patted him on the shoulder when Gibbons mentioned being cold.

"You'll feel better once we've got rid of the infection," he said, and joined Gibbons's parents outside the door. The red-haired nurse returned with yet another IV bag, which she changed with one of the others on the pole, and then replaced his dressing yet again, this time without assistance.

"Do you think," asked Gibbons when she was done, "I could have that extra blanket?"

"Oh, yes, of course," she answered, pushing back the curtain. "I'll send Ronnie in with one."

His parents and the doctor had disappeared from his view, no doubt to move their discussion out of earshot of the policeman doing guard duty at the door. But they had been replaced by Inspector Davies, who was lounging against the doorjamb and chatting with the uniformed man. He looked up at the sound of the curtain being drawn back and smiled a little hesitantly.

"Is he ready for visitors?" he asked the nurse.

"Certainly," she answered. "He's all settled for the moment."

Gibbons wondered why no one asked him whether or not he was ready for visitors, but felt too listless to voice the question.

Today Davies's tie was an elaborate pattern in subtle beiges and grays. Gibbons found it fascinating.

"Were those your people I saw in the hall?" asked Davies, drawing up the armchair.

With difficulty, Gibbons dragged his gaze away from the tie and focused on his superior's face.

"That's right," he answered. "My mum and dad."

"Well, I hope to meet them later," said Davies, settling himself. "They must be very proud of you."

Gibbons did not feel at the moment like someone anyone could be proud of, but he managed a weak smile.

"And you've amassed quite a collection of flowers," said Davies, motioning to the bouquets that had been coming in all morning and now festooned nearly every flat surface in the room.

"Oh, yes," said Gibbons vaguely, who had paid these tributes scant attention and did not even know who had sent them. "They're very nice."

"So how are you today, Sergeant?" asked Davies. "You look a bit pale, but perhaps that's to be expected."

"I don't know," said Gibbons. He did not want to discuss his health; he wanted distraction. "I don't feel too well so far." His eyes fell to the manila envelope in Davies's lap. "Is that something for me?" he asked.

Davies nodded, smiling. "Yes, I've finally brought around those reports of yours—I'm sorry I didn't send them over last night, but I really hadn't a chance."

"It's very good of you to bother at all," said Gibbons automatically. "It's the report of my interview with the Colemans?"

"That's right," said Davies. "And I added the one you wrote up for the case file on our interview with Miss Haverford's solicitor. I had actually forgotten that one, until I went to look up the other."

"I've forgotten it, too," said Gibbons wryly.

Davies gave a sympathetic smile. "I rather thought you might have," he said. "Look, I'll put them in the drawer here and you can look them over whenever you like."

For the first time that morning, Gibbons felt a faint stirring of interest, a slight quickening of his brain.

"Actually," he said, "just hand them to me. I'd like to read them over as soon as things quieten down again."

Davies looked around, glancing back toward the door. "It did seem rather busy out there when I came in," he said. He raised a brow. "Not giving them any trouble, are you, Sergeant?"

"I'm just lying here," said Gibbons, a little despondently.

"I can see that," said Davies gently. "But you do look rather pale. You do your best to get well, eh, Sergeant? No fussing over these reports when you should be resting."

"No, sir," promised Gibbons.

"All right then."

Davies handed over the envelope and rose.

"I can't stay," he apologized. "I'm going to be late at the Yard as it is."

"It was very good of you to stop by yourself, sir," said Gibbons, clutching the envelope to his chest.

"I wanted to see how you were doing, Gibbons," he said. "I'll be back as time permits, and I'll keep you informed of developments."

"I appreciate that, sir."

Davies sketched a little salute and left. In a moment, Gibbons heard him speaking out in the hall; he could not quite make out the words, but by the tone of voice, Davies was introducing himself to the Gibbonses.

Gibbons was simply glad to be left alone. He pulled the printed pages out of the envelope. The words swam on the page before his eyes initially, but some industrious blinking made them settle down.

He was accustomed to reading through reports rapidly, picking out the salient details and leaving them to coalesce in the back of his mind. He was a practiced hand at it by this time, but he found now he had to concentrate quite fiercely to make sense of the thing, to understand what lay between the lines, unsaid, and yet held the key to everything.

He was so deep into the first report by the time his parents returned that he did not notice them come in.

The Jewels

*B*ethancourt was awakened that morning by the telephone. He had spent a restless night, waking up more than once with a pounding heart, thinking he must rush to Gibbons's bedside at once, before it was too late. On one occasion he had actually been halfway to the bathroom before he came to himself and realized his urgency was born of a bad dream.

Yawning prodigiously in the gray daylight, he answered the phone and was rewarded by the voice of his insurance agent, Becky Rankin.

"Phillip?" she said. "I've managed to track down Colin James for you."

"Oh, splendid," said Bethancourt, trying to read the bedside clock without his glasses; he rather thought it was just after eleven.

"I think he must be quite interested in your friend's case," she continued. "At any rate, he's agreed to meet with you at his office."

She sounded impressed, and Bethancourt propped himself up on his pillows.

"That's quite the favor, is it?" he asked.

"Well," said Becky cautiously, "Colin James is terribly well thought of. He's made a fortune out of recovering stolen jewels and art for insurance companies, and at this point he doesn't really have to bother with anything or anyone he doesn't care to."

"Then I appreciate the compliment," said Bethancourt. "When and where am I to see the great man?"

Becky read off an address in the City and added, "He told my contact he'd be there from noon till about one o'clock, and could see you anytime then. I wouldn't wait until close to one, though; James is well known for liking his lunch."

"Righto," said Bethancourt, stifling another yawn. "I'd best get dressed, then. Thanks very much, Becky—I do appreciate your taking the time."

"Anything for my favorite client," replied Becky with a laugh. "I'm glad it worked out."

Bethancourt looked sourly at his dog as he replaced the receiver in its cradle.

"No leisurely morning for us, lad," he said. "Up and at 'em." He hesitated and looked again at the clock. "Still," he added, reaching for the phone, "it won't take a moment to ring the hospital and check on Jack."

It was Mrs. Gibbons who answered the phone rather than her son, but she was able to assure Bethancourt that all was well with her presently sleeping offspring. Bethancourt experienced a wave of relief, despite knowing quite well that his worry had been occasioned by nothing more than a dream.

Carmichael tracked Dawn Melton down at the day-care center in Southwark where she worked, no doubt the "good job" Mrs. Gibbons had mentioned. He had instructed Constable Lemmy to meet him there, but when he arrived there was no sign of him, despite the fact that the constable had had an easy tube ride from Scotland Yard, while Carmichael had ridden all the way down from Euston. Fuming, Carmichael waited by the entrance, but when five minutes had passed and Lemmy had not arrived, he gave up and went inside to seek out the headmistress.

Dawn, when she came into the headmistress's office, turned out to be a pleasant, rather ordinary young woman who bore—so far as Carmichael could see—no resemblance to her cousin Jack. She was a shade overweight with a heavy fringe of dark blond hair and a fresh, rosy complexion. Beneath the fringe, her light blue eyes were large and a little wary, though her smile was sweet. Together, they gave her an air of vulnerability.

"Oh, of course," she said when Carmichael introduced himself. "Jack has mentioned you—he admires you very much, you know."

"Er, kind of you to say," replied Carmichael, a bit caught off guard by this artless remark. "Do sit down, Mrs. Melton."

She obeyed, plopping down into the chair and looking at him expectantly.

"Have you come about Jack?" she asked.

"Yes," said Carmichael. "Did you know he was in hospital?"

She looked horrified, her hands going to her mouth for a moment before she silently shook her head.

"Is he all right?" she asked faintly.

"Yes, yes," Carmichael hastened to reassure her. "The doctors say he'll be just fine."

"Thank God." She breathed, and then seemed to shake off her shock. "What happened, Chief Inspector? Oh, first, did you want his parents' number? I've got it in my bag, though I would have thought . . ."

She was already half out of her seat.

"No, his parents have been notified," said Carmichael. "In fact, they're here in London and have already been to see him."

"Oh." Dawn fell back in her chair, clearly a little at a loss to explain his presence.

"I'm sure they'll be getting in contact with you shortly," said Carmichael. "I stopped by to ask if you had seen Jack recently?"

"Well"—she ran a hand through her hair, rumpling up her bangs—"not very recently, no. He rang to ask how the girls were doing about a fortnight ago, I suppose. In fact"—she looked thoughtful—"I've been meaning to ring him and just haven't got round to it the last few days. But what has happened to Jack, Chief Inspector?"

"He was shot on Tuesday evening," replied Carmichael levelly.

Her hands sprang to her mouth again, her lips forming a silent "O," and he gave her a moment to absorb the news. "Luckily, the attack was not fatal, and the surgeons were able to stitch him up and say he'll make a full recovery. Though of course he's not feeling too well just now," he added.

Dawn nodded, her hands falling back to her lap. "I must go round to see him," she said. "And did you say my aunt and uncle were here? Are they staying at Jack's, or do you think they'd rather be with me?" A frown appeared between her brows as she struggled with the logistics of putting up unexpected guests in what was no doubt an already crowded flat.

"They're staying at a hotel nearby the hospital," Carmichael told her. "It seemed more convenient."

"Oh, yes, of course," she said with a little sigh that seemed half relief and half annoyance at herself for not having thought of this simple solution.

"I'm currently engaged," continued Carmichael, "in trying to discover whether the attack on Jack was motivated in any way by his police work."

Dawn looked puzzled at this. "But why else would anybody want to hurt Jack?" she asked.

"Well, that's what I'm trying to find out," said Carmichael. "It happened in a rather bad neighborhood, you see."

"Oh." She sighed again and shook her head. "I'd always heard how dangerous London was," she said, "but it's different, actually living here. Lots of the time it seems quite ordinary, but then something happens to remind you . . . well, I expect you know all about that."

Carmichael did, but he also knew her scant time in London could not possibly have bestowed on her the worldly wisdom she thought it had. If he was any judge, she was going to have difficulty with what he had to tell her next.

"So you didn't hear from Jack on Tuesday at all?" he asked. "You had no plans to see him that evening?"

"No." She frowned, her large eyes looking a little confused. "Did I forget a date we'd made?" she asked. "I'm usually very careful to write everything down . . ."

"I don't think so," answered Carmichael. "I only asked because the incident took place not far from your home. Down in Walworth is where Jack was found."

As he had expected, she looked quite shocked. "He was shot?" she asked. "In Walworth? And you think it might have been a random crime?"

Carmichael spread his hands. "As of yet, we just don't know," he said.

But the worried frown did not leave her face. "I know he didn't much care for the neighborhood," she said, half to herself. "But it was so convenient, and the flat was so much bigger than the others I'd seen—I thought it seemed all right."

Carmichael had every sympathy for her plight, but it was not his business to solve it, nor did he know of an answer offhand. Living in London was often a trade-off unless one was very wealthy.

"Tell me this," he asked, "is it possible Jack might have decided to drop in on you for some reason?"

She looked doubtful. "He never has before," she said. "I guess he could have, but I would have expected him to ring first before he came all that way. I mean, what if I were out?"

Carmichael nodded. "But you were at home on Tuesday?" he asked. "I mean, you would have been there if he had rung, or even dropped by?"

"Oh, yes, I was home all evening with my daughters. But we never heard from Jack."

And that, thought Carmichael, was that.

He thanked her for her help, gave her Gibbons's room number at the hospital, and escaped, feeling now as if he had wasted his time. His temper was not improved by finding Constable Lemmy waiting outside for him, his navy jumper liberally dusted with powdered sugar as if he had recently finished eating a donut.

"Why on earth didn't you come in and find me?" growled Carmichael, striding away from the day-care center with Lemmy trailing in his wake.

Lemmy looked startled. "I didn't want to interrupt anything, sir," he answered.

"If you'd come straight here from the Yard," retorted Carmichael, "you wouldn't have had to worry about interrupting—you'd have been before me. Where the devil were you, anyway?"

Lemmy seemed more perplexed by this question than concerned over his superior's annoyance. "I came straight along, sir," he said. "Just as soon as I thought you could get here from Euston."

Carmichael opened his mouth to reply, and then shut it again with a shake of his head. There was, he thought to himself, really no use in trying.

Unsure whether or not Colin James was fond of dogs, Bethancourt elected to leave Cerberus at home and duly presented himself, fortified by two cups of coffee, at James's office by 12:20. Early enough, he hoped, not to interfere with lunch.

Having never before been in a private investigator's office, Bethancourt was surprised to find it much resembled the office of a very well-to-do solicitor. The furniture was all solid oak, highly polished, and the carpet was an expensive, thick oriental. The usual shelves held books on art and jewels rather than tomes of law, and the paintings adorning the walls were more inspired than a law office's prints, but these things only gave the atmosphere a different accent rather than changing it altogether.

James's inner sanctum held his treasures. In pride of place hung a small Constable, and in one corner a small Degas sculpture stood on an eighteenth-century tea table.

James himself lounged behind an early Victorian twin pedestal desk, its mahogany surface burnished like satin. He rose to greet his guest and the two men shook hands, amiably taking each other's measure.

"Sit, sit," said James, motioning toward a leather-upholstered armchair. "Do you want a coffee or some tea or anything?"

Bethancourt, sitting as asked, declined this offer.

"So you're young Gibbons's friend," said James, resuming his own seat behind the desk. "I was terribly sorry to hear he'd been seriously injured. How is he today, do you know?"

"He was asleep when I rang," said Bethancourt, "but his mother said he was recovering well. I'll be popping by there later."

"Good, good," said James. "I don't mind telling you, I don't look any too kindly on whoever was responsible for this. If it turns out to be connected to the Haverford case, I shall be most distressed."

"It's about that that I've come," said Bethancourt. "Not being able to work on his own case is driving Jack loopy, the more so as he's forgotten nearly all of Tuesday. We spoke of it yesterday and, in comparing notes, discovered that he had apparently come across something in the course of the day which changed his view of the case."

"Did he indeed?" James was immediately alert.

"We believe so. It might not have any bearing on who shot him, but I thought it worth looking into to start with."

James took a moment to ruminate before replying, his shrewd gray eyes considering Bethancourt as he did so.

"Did Gibbons tell you about the case?" he asked.

Bethancourt spread his hands. "He outlined it for me," he answered. "A collection of valuable jewelry belonging to a recently deceased woman was stolen from her house in Southgate. Her heir and his wife discovered the theft."

"That's the bare bones of it," said James. "Did he tell you that the jewelry itself was most extraordinary?"

"He said it was antique, inherited from a grandmother or great-grandmother," replied Bethancourt.

This answer did not appear to satisfy James, who sighed.

"Did he tell you the grandmother in question was one of the most notorious actresses of belle epoche?" he asked.

"Really?" asked Bethancourt, immediately fascinated. "Who was she?"

"Evony St. Michel," said James, and when Bethancourt let out a low whistle, he added in some surprise, "You've heard of her?"

"Oh, yes," said Bethancourt. "She and Caroline Otero and Polaire and Lillie Langtry—not that I know a great deal about any of them, but my grandfather liked to tell stories of the old days, mostly culled from his father, who supposedly met Langtry. Didn't Evony St. Michel used to wear her jewels onstage, or was that Caroline Otero?"

James looked gratified. "They both did," he answered. He opened a leather-bound folder that lay on his desk and selected a photograph, which he then handed to Bethancourt. "That's Evony in costume."

Bethancourt examined the picture curiously. It portrayed a young, sloe-eyed woman who smiled flirtatiously at the camera. She was festooned in jewels and very little else, and the angles of her broad cheekbones suggested a Slavic descent.

"Exactly right," said James when Bethancourt mentioned this. "She made her reputation in Paris, and Evony St. Michel was a stage name she adopted. She was actually born and raised in Kiev." He consulted a sheet of paper from his folder. "Her real name was Ionna Hrushevsky—not really appropriate for a Parisian actress."

"Doesn't have a very romantic ring, no," agreed Bethancourt, handing back the photograph. "So she was Miranda Haverford's great-grandmother? It seems an odd relationship for a respectable English spinster. How did a Ukrainian actress in Paris end up here in England?"

"She married a respectable English button manufacturer." James smiled slyly at Bethancourt's startled expression. "Yes, it was a very peculiar way to end a most notorious career. Like to see the wedding photo?"

"I would indeed," said Bethancourt, leaning forward to take the picture James plucked from his folder.

By the style of Evony's wedding dress, the photograph had been taken around the turn of the century. She stood, stiff and proper, by her new husband's side, her cloud of dark hair liberally adorned with pearls. The groom was the possessor of a fine walrus mustache, behind which he looked quite young and rather uncomfortable.

"She was somewhere in her forties there," said James, "but she looks much younger. Charles Haverford was thirty-one when he married her, and by all accounts completely besotted. His friends and relations predicted she would ruin him, but in fact they did very well together. Apparently Evony became financially prudent in her old age, having learned from her own past mistakes, and never let Haverford spend too much money on her."

"A happy ending, then," said Bethancourt. "I take it they had a child?"

But James shook his head. "No, I imagine Evony was past that by the time of the marriage. But they did officially adopt one of her sister's children, a son by the name of Michael."

Bethancourt raised his eyebrows and James laughed heartily.

"You're a quick one, aren't you?" he said. "Yes, he is thought to be Evony's own child, whom she had foisted off on her sister after giving birth. No one knows who his father was, although he seems to have been born during the period that Evony was the mistress of the Russian Grand Duke Alexander. But of course she was notoriously unfaithful—she may not have known herself who her son's father was." James tucked the wedding photograph away and began leafing through the others in the folder. "In any case," he continued, "Grand Duke Alexander—whether he fathered Evony's son or not—is the reason we're all here now. He was an extremely generous man."

James had withdrawn another photograph from the leather folder, which he now held out for Bethancourt to take. In it was pictured an elaborate necklace, mid-Victorian in style, whose centerpiece appeared to be an emerald of nine carats or so, accompanied by smaller emeralds and diamonds forming the pattern around it. A second photograph on the bottom half of the page showed an identical necklace, only this one used rubies instead of emeralds.

Something was ringing a dim bell in Bethancourt's mind as he studied the gemstones. Glancing up, he met James's gaze, which had an expectant air. He returned his attention to the photographs, frowning as his eye picked out details.

"These aren't two different necklaces," he said slowly.

"Hah!" said James, obviously pleased. "Then what are they?"

"I would imagine," answered Bethancourt, "that this is an example of a necklace made from color-change gemstones."

James was grinning broadly. "You're as clever as Sergeant Gibbons," he said, satisfaction in his tone. "Although he was somewhat hampered in his answer by never having heard of a color-change gemstone. What you're looking at there are some of the famed Ural Mountain alexandrites."

"Yes, of course," said Bethancourt excitedly. "I remember now—the mine didn't last long, but the jewels it produced were said to be extraordinary." He glanced back at the photograph in his hands. "I'd forgotten they were red and green, though."

"The Russian imperial colors," supplied James. "In the beginning, alexandrite was only mined for royalty. It was a mark of special favor to be gifted with one; but then, Evony St. Michel was said to be the sort of woman to whom men gave special favors."

Bethancourt was still looking at the necklace. "Which is which?" he asked. "I can't tell from the picture."

"You mean natural and artificial light?" said James. "Oh, the green's the daylight, and the red electric light. This particular necklace is said to be of the very finest quality: a clear, deep green in daylight, and a rich purple-red under an electric lamp. The original appraiser's assessment goes on about it at great length. The Haverfords used to lend it out for museum exhibits—I've got some of the clippings here—but Miranda Haverford refused all requests over the last few years. Possibly it was just too much bother as she got older."

"Do you have a picture of her?" asked Bethancourt, handing back the one of the jewels.

"Of Miranda Haverford?" said James, surprised. "I think there's one in one of the newspaper clippings . . . let's see . . . yes, here it is."

It was just a small, square headshot accompanying a much larger photo of the necklace itself, both in illustration of a review of a museum exhibit in Paris. The photograph showed a woman in her sixties with widely spaced eyes and just a hint of the broad cheekbones of her forebear. It was a studio photograph with nothing of the candid about it, but Bethancourt thought he could just see in those wide-spaced eyes and the tilt of the narrow lips a hint of intelligence and humor.

"Thank you," he said, handing the clipping back.

"What did you want to see it for?" asked James, curiously. "Miranda Haverford has nothing to do with the case—there's not the slightest doubt that she died naturally, of old age."

Bethancourt smiled. "Well, they were her jewels, after all," he said. "And Jack thought she sounded interesting. I'm interested in people," he added. "It's more or less why I like to hear about Jack's cases."

"Ah, yes," said James, steepling his fingers and leaning them against his chin. "Do you mind my asking how you come to know Gibbons's boss so well?"

Bethancourt was startled. "Detective Inspector Davies?" he asked. "I don't know him—never met him."

"No, I wasn't referring to Davies," said James. "I meant Detective Chief Inspector Carmichael—who, I gather, is thirsting for my blood for having placed his favorite sergeant in peril."

"Really?" asked Bethancourt alertly. "And did you?"

"Not to my knowledge," said James ruefully. "And I like to be aware when I'm taking risks. I'm not even sure that what happened to the sergeant has anything to do with the Haverford case. Frankly, it looked very much to me as if the robbery was just another example of thieves who check the obituaries regularly. It's quite common, you know, a burglary at a house just after the occupants have died."

"No," sighed Bethancourt. "I didn't know."

"But you haven't answered my question."

"Oh, about Chief Inspector Carmichael." Bethancourt paused for a moment. In general, he liked to be as circumspect as possible about his involvement in any police matters, but he was a good judge of character and James struck him as a discreet man. And the investigator was, in any case, to a certain extent already in the police confidence. "Jack sometimes lets me tag along on some of his cases," he said. "I've naturally met Chief Inspector Carmichael during the course of those investigations."

James raised an eyebrow. "It's absolutely none of my business," he said, "but I must confess to a violent curiosity as to how you managed to pull that off."

Bethancourt smiled deprecatingly. "My father was at school with the chief commissioner," he said, inwardly sighing.

James laughed. He had a big hearty laugh, and Bethancourt found himself grinning in spite of himself.

"Not such a mystery after all then," James said, recovering. He looked to the clock over the mantelpiece and began to tuck the photos back into the leather-bound folder. "There were, of course," he said, "other jewels in the Haverford collection. In particular, a beautiful pair of ruby earrings, a Golconda diamond brooch, and a Colombian emerald ring and bracelet. Not to mention the pearls. I have the complete list, of course. Plus a little tract Miranda apparently wrote herself, trying to trace the various jewels to the men who had given them to Evony."

"I'd like very much to see that, if it's possible," said Bethancourt, whose interest had been piqued by the story of the jewels.

James gave him a sharp glance. "It's perfectly possible," he answered. "Miss Haverford had several copies of it printed up. It will hardly have any bearing on what happened to Sergeant Gibbons, however—I don't believe he'd even read it."

"I know," said Bethancourt, feeling faintly guilty for having let himself become distracted from the reason for his visit. "It just sounds interesting, that's all."

"I found it so," admitted James. He set aside the folder and regarded his guest thoughtfully. "I'm trying a new restaurant for lunch," he said. "I wonder if you would care to accompany me, and we could discuss the case further there."

To this Bethancourt happily agreed and after James had instructed his secretary to add one to his reservation, James ushered him out.

7

The Pennycook Case

Upon returning to Scotland Yard, Carmichael cast about for an errand to send Constable Lemmy on in order to get the young man out of his hair, and belatedly remembered he had wanted to have the Scotland Yard security footage from Tuesday night examined for any sign that Gibbons had returned to the Yard after his pint with O'Leary. Lemmy accepted this task amicably, without the resentment that most aspiring detectives would have shown. Carmichael barely noticed. With the constable out of the way, he went off in search of O'Leary, only to find that Inspector Hollings had apparently laid claim to his own subordinate today, and had sent O'Leary off to investigate the Pennycook murder down in Walworth.

"And Hollings may be right at that," said Carmichael to himself.

He paused thoughtfully, frowning. He had, during the course of yesterday, glanced over both the Pennycook case file and the report O'Leary had prepared on his conversation at the pub with Gibbons. But he found that he remembered little about either today. He was quite put out with himself.

"Old man," he muttered. "Can't do without sleep anymore. Useless, that's what you are. Bloody useless."

He tramped into his office and found both files shoved to one side of his desk, where he vaguely remembered placing them when he had begun to feel another moment reading in his chair would put him to sleep. Had he ever gone back to them? He wasn't entirely sure, but he was beginning to suspect not.

Heaving a great sigh, he pulled out his desk chair and settled himself in it, drawing O'Leary's report toward him. It would be by far the shorter of the two and with any luck he could be done with it quickly.

"On Tuesday, at approximately five thirty P.M.," O'Leary had written, "Detective Sergeant Jack Gibbons rang my office phone to ask if I would be free to have a pint with him after work. This was not an unusual occurrence, although I had not seen him since he began working with the Arts Theft Division some two or three weeks ago. In reply to his invitation, I said I was planning to leave the office at about six and would like to join him for a drink, but that I could not stay long as I had a date at seven thirty. Accordingly, I rang him when I was done for the day and we met in the lobby, proceeding across the street to the Feathers Pub . . ."

"Bloody long-winded," muttered Carmichael under his breath, and quite unfairly. Reports were supposed to be crammed with as much detail as the detective could remember in case an apparently irrelevant point later proved significant, and all detective candidates were trained in this style of writing. Carmichael sighed and slogged through a thorough description of the Feathers, of O'Leary's impressions of the patrons that night, of what he and Gibbons had ordered, and of their brief conversation with the bartender while their orders were being filled.

Having got them seated at a table near the bar, the cleanliness of which was meticulously described, O'Leary at last passed on to his estimation of Gibbons's mood: perfectly normal. Here Carmichael removed his reading glasses and rubbed the bridge of his nose for a moment.

"I then asked him," continued O'Leary, "how he liked Arts Theft after working Homicide for so long. He replied that he found it very interesting, but very different. He went on to explain that it was not just the work that was different—he had expected that—but the atmosphere of the office and the attitudes of the detectives were also quite different to that of Homicide. He said the air at Arts Theft was at once lighter, but also more rarified, that it was altogether a more cerebral atmosphere than Homicide. We continued discussing these differences for a little time, though I do not remember exactly what was said. I received the impression from DS Gibbons that although he was enjoying learning something new at Arts Theft, he also missed investigating murders and did not think Arts Theft was the niche for him."

"Thank God," muttered Carmichael, and turned the page.

"In the course of this discussion," O'Leary went on, "DS Gibbons, prompted by questions from me, told me something about the case he was working on, a large jewelry theft from a private home in Southgate. What struck me at the time was the amount of knowledge DS Gibbons was supposed to acquire about the jewels themselves."

Here O'Leary dutifully recorded all he remembered Gibbons telling him about gemstones in general and the Haverford jewelry in particular, which to O'Leary's credit was enough to fill a page and a half. Grumbling, Carmichael worked his way through the rudiments of gemology, a subject that interested him not at all.

Having dealt with the odd discrepancies between investigating murders and jewel heists, O'Leary moved on to what he had told Gibbons about his own case.

Carmichael had not paid much attention to the Pennycook murder, principally because it struck him as so very out of character for Gibbons to meddle on another man's patch. If he had had a thought about the case, he would have rung O'Leary with it, not gone haring off to investigate on his own.

But now it occurred to him that anything might contribute a piece to the puzzle that was a criminal investigation; it was perfectly possible that some facet of the Pennycook murder had given Gibbons a new angle on his own case.

So he read on with interest, although here O'Leary was less precise than he had been earlier, owing to being unsure what points he might have skipped over in the course of conversation.

Albert Pennycook had been found dead in his pawnshop in East

Street a week ago last Wednesday. The chief suspect was Frank Pennycook, the murdered man's nephew and heir, who seemed to be the sole person who gained from his uncle's death. But Pennycook had been found with a bashed-in skull, and Frank had never in his forty years shown any sign of violent tendencies; to the contrary, he was known to be a physically timid man. That left, as O'Leary had mentioned yesterday, old grudges, which he and Hollings were ferreting out and investigating.

It seemed to Carmichael a very ordinary kind of murder, Albert Pennycook being a person leading a reprehensible life that had finally caught up with him. He could not see, on the face of it, anything that might have inspired Gibbons to solve a jewel robbery.

"I remarked on the coincidence," continued O'Leary, "of my investigating the murder of a well-known fence while DS Gibbons was investigating the theft of a valuable jewel collection. DS Gibbons laughed in reply to this and asked me if I had happened on any nineteenth-century alexandrite necklaces in the pawnshop."

"The devil," swore Carmichael, suddenly sitting up and paying attention. "How could I have missed that?" he muttered, turning back a page. "Where the hell is that shop—there it is. Bloody hell."

He stared at the words "pawnshop in East Street" in disbelief at his own dull-wittedness. East Street, in the heart of Walworth. East Street, just round the corner from where Gibbons had been shot.

But what was the connection between the two cases, other than that they both had been discussed in a pub by two detective sergeants? Alfred Pennycook could not have had anything to do with the Haverford robbery; he had been dead for more than a week when the jewelry had been stolen.

Carmichael leaned back in his chair, his eyes fixed on the middle distance, and reached into his desk drawer for a cigar, which he proceeded to roll back and forth between his fingers. If Pennycook could not have been involved in the actual robbery, might he still have had something to do with the planning of it before his death? Could he have been killed for backing out of the plan to steal it?

Carmichael stuck the unlit cigar in his mouth and seized the phone, speed-dialing Inspector Hollings's mobile.

But Hollings, when he answered, seemed largely puzzled by Carmichael's sudden interest in the Pennycook case.

"But we looked into that yesterday," he protested. "As soon as I heard O'Leary had been telling Gibbons about the case, I looked for a connection. I sent you an e-mail about it."

Carmichael scowled, but since Hollings could not see it, he was not intimidated.

"I must have missed it," lied Carmichael.

"Well, it was mostly negative," Hollings told him. "It's true Pennycook was a big player in things like the Haverford robbery at one time—between his bouts in prison, that is. But he'd been out of that high-end sort of business for years, ever since his health started to fail. The shop in Walworth was nothing like any of his old storefronts—it's just a pawnshop. Mind you, I'm not saying that no stolen goods ever pass through there, just that they don't include million-pound jewelry collections. The odd gold wedding ring is more like it."

"And this nephew of Pennycook's?" asked Carmichael.

Hollings snorted. "Frank Pennycook hasn't got the gumption to involve himself in anything like that. There's some evidence he tried to go into the family business in his youth, but he was convicted of grand larceny some fifteen years ago, and ever since he got out of prison he's stayed on the straight and narrow. He hasn't collected so much as a speeding ticket in the last ten years."

It seemed Pennycook was a dead end, and yet Carmichael still disliked the coincidence. He rang off, leaving Hollings to get on with his own investigation, and thoughtfully lit his cigar. He opened the Pennycook case file, laying it beside O'Leary's report, and leafed through it, picking out the salient points. Pennycook had been at his shop with his nephew on the day of his death, and they had closed the place together as usual at six. Pennycook had gone home to his supper, but afterward informed his wife that he had to return to the shop that evening for an appointment. She had not bothered to ask with whom, knowing from long experience that no answer would be forthcoming. According to her testimony, he had set out at about 8:30 and had rung her when he had reached the shop to reassure her that he had arrived safely.

She had expected him back around ten, but had not begun to worry unduly until 10:30 or so, at which point she had rung the shop, but received no answer. She had waited another twenty minutes for him to return, and then had called on her nephew to go and look for his uncle.

Frank Pennycook affirmed that he had received such a call at about 10:50 and had proceeded back to the shop, looking for his uncle along the way. He reached the place without sighting him, however, and let himself in by the back door. The lights inside were on, and he found his uncle lying on the floor of the little office in the proverbial pool of blood. He had felt quite faint and had had to go sit down and recover himself before ringing the paramedics. ("Very likely he was clearing out anything he didn't want the police to see," Hollings had noted.)

The working theory was that whoever Pennycook had gone to meet had killed him, but no one seemed to know who that might have been. An alternative theory had either Frank or Pennycook's wife committing the murder, as they both had keys to the shop's back door.

Carmichael pushed the file aside and smoked meditatively for several minutes. As experienced a detective as he was, he found it impossible to create any kind of reasonable scenario in which the Pennycook and Haverford cases were related, particularly if he accepted as given that Gibbons would not have interfered in someone else's case.

Carmichael examined that assumption carefully. It was just possible, he admitted to himself, that Gibbons might have had an idea so out of the ordinary that he had been reluctant to pass it on without first checking it out. That would not be at all out of character; Carmichael had known his sergeant to produce quite unique views many times before. And if he had shared such an idea with anyone, Carmichael strongly suspected it would have been with Bethancourt, whom Gibbons had rung and left a message for.

Which reminded him that he had never finished O'Leary's report.

"We joked about our cases being related for a bit," continued O'Leary, "and then DS Gibbons asked where in Walworth Pennycook's pawnshop was. When I told him it was on East Street off Walworth

Road, he looked concerned and mentioned that his cousin lived very near there. I was surprised to hear it, since that part of Walworth is a notoriously bad neighborhood, and I asked DS Gibbons how he had come to let her move in there. He replied that it was all done before he heard about it, and he had not had much luck in persuading her to move. He seemed to feel a little guilty about this, and I gathered that he had been asked by his mother to see this cousin settled, but it had occurred last fall while he was in the Cotswolds, and he had rather shirked his family duty in preference to his official ones. We then discussed how awkward balancing personal and professional lives could be, at which point I remembered my personal life was waiting, and told him I had to go. DS Gibbons said I should go ahead, that he would just finish his pint while he decided what to pick up for dinner. We said good-bye quite cheerfully, and he seemed to me to be in much the same mood as when we had sat down. Nor did I at any time during the conversation feel he was particularly struck by anything I or he said."

Carmichael was willing to bet those last pronouns had been struggled over, and probably changed more than once, and he wished (not for the first time) that he had had recourse to a computer and word processor back when he had first been a detective sergeant and laboriously writing out reports.

He leaned back in his chair, sipping at coffee gone cold, and tried to put himself in Gibbons's place. There he was, a smart, ambitious young officer, his head full of a lot of new information about jewelry and jewel thieves, having a pleasant pint after work and chatting about somebody else's murder case. What might have struck him? And had Gibbons really been giving much thought to the Pennycook case, or did his mind revert back to his own case as soon as it had the chance, just like Carmichael's always did? Could something O'Leary had told him about the Pennycook murder have illuminated some aspect of the Haverford case for him? But then why would he have gone to Walworth?

Carmichael sighed and shook his head. The best thing, really, would be to have Gibbons read O'Leary's version of events and see if whatever he had thought of that night would recur to his mind. But

Carmichael, remembering his sergeant's pale face and dazed expression that morning, was not sanguine about the outcome of such an experiment. Still, he decided, it would do no harm to drop a copy off at the hospital on his way home that night, and Gibbons could look at it whenever he was feeling better.

And that reminded him of another unpleasant chore he had been avoiding. Sighing mightily, he shrugged back into his coat and left the office.

After his lunch with Colin James, Bethancourt felt he would be a much better informed and more knowledgeable shopper the next time he went to buy jewelry for Marla. He was also feeling considerably more cynical toward the human race than he normally did, owing to various stories James had told over the meal; apparently in the investigator's experience there was absolutely nothing people would not do where fine jewels or high-end art were concerned.

The lunch had been otherwise excellent. Morgan M was a restaurant in Camden Town whose cuisine had a well-deserved reputation, and Bethancourt enjoyed himself heartlessly, with hardly a thought for poor Gibbons on a restricted diet in his hospital bed.

As they made their way out, ushered on their way by beaming smiles from the wait staff, Bethancourt reached for his cigarette case and asked, "Do you mind my asking if there's any particular reason you chose north London for lunch today?"

James smiled lazily. "Possibly it was because this place is not far from the Colemans' flat," he answered. "Although I was no doubt influenced by the very high recommendation a friend of mine gave the restaurant."

"No doubt," said Bethancourt, amused. He paused as they emerged onto the street to light his cigarette and then said, "I would be very interested to meet the Colemans."

"Do you know, I'm not at all surprised to hear that," said James. He glanced sideways at his companion. "Planning to act as Sergeant Gibbons's eyes and ears while he's sidelined?" he asked.

"As best I can," replied Bethancourt.

"Then let us take a little postprandial stroll in that direction," said James, indicating the way with a wave of his hand.

Bethancourt went willingly, pleased that James had evidently decided to help him. He put that down to a mutual interest in jewels and food, and the positive impression Gibbons himself had apparently made on the man. In addition, Bethancourt sensed James rather enjoyed demonstrating his expertise and, robbed of one apprentice, was not displeased to have found another.

They walked toward the canal until they came to a row of Victorian warehouses, long since converted into flats.

"Here we are," said James. He shot back his cuff to check his watch. "Right on time," he added, reaching out to ring the bell. "The Colemans are on the second floor—it's a furnished flat. They initially stayed at the Dorchester when they first arrived, but found this place after a fortnight or so. Landlord has no complaints of them thus far."

"How long have they been here?" asked Bethancourt, following James into the building.

"Four months. The lift's over here."

The lift was still of a size to transport large loads, but the once-utilitarian interior had been completely refurbished to reflect the building's rise in fortunes with glossy paneling and thick carpet. The usual wooden guard gate had been replaced by an ornate grille, which slid silently closed when James punched the second-floor button and opened again on a mahogany door. There was the sound of a soft chime and in another moment the door slid back.

Standing just beyond it was a young man with curly dark hair and bright brown eyes. He was smiling in welcome and, indeed, looked uncommonly pleased to see them.

"Mr. James!" he exclaimed, reaching to shake the investigator's hand. "Do come in. And who's this you've brought to see us?"

He had the too-perfect British accent of someone not native to the UK, but Bethancourt could not place the original, underlying accent. In any case, Coleman sounded absolutely delighted to find he had an extra guest, and held out his hand almost eagerly to Bethancourt while James performed introductions.

"My colleague, Phillip Bethancourt," he said. "This is Rob Coleman, Miss Haverford's great-nephew."

"How do you do," said Bethancourt, rather lamely in the face of Coleman's enthusiasm.

"Brilliant, thanks," said Coleman, closing the door behind them. "This way, please. Can I offer you a coffee? My wife's just brewing a fresh pot."

The loft was furnished in the very latest in modern design, everything sleek and clean-lined. In one angle of the huge space was a sitting-room arrangement where a slender young woman was just setting down a tray on the glass-topped coffee table. Bethancourt, who was uncommonly fond of coffee tables, eyed it covetously, but then had his attention redirected to their hostess.

"My wife, Lia," Coleman was saying. "This is a colleague of Mr. James's, dear—Phillip Bethancourt."

Bethancourt reached to shake her hand while she smiled and welcomed him. Lia Coleman's smile was more reserved than her husband's, though Bethancourt did not count that against her as he had never encountered a more beaming expression than that of Rob Coleman. For the rest, she was a very attractive brunette with straight, shining hair cut at the level of her shoulder blades and, in contrast, a very pale complexion. She was a little above average height, all her curves gone to slimness, and showed a natural grace as she sat and began to pour out.

"So have you any news for us, Mr. James?" asked Coleman, seating himself beside his wife and leaning forward eagerly, elbows on knees.

James shook his head dolefully. "Nothing good, I'm afraid," he replied. "But you mustn't be discouraged by that, Mr. Coleman. These things can often take some time, and we usually get there in the end. After all, the jewels have to be somewhere!" James gave a bark of laughter at his own joke and everyone else grinned in response. Coleman in particular seemed pleased to have a bit of good humor injected into so serious a subject.

"Unfortunately," James was continuing, "we seem to have had a bit of a setback, though I can't say it's directly connected to your case."

"Oh, yes?" said Coleman, looking slightly confused.

"It's Sergeant Gibbons," said James. "He was badly injured on Tuesday night, and in consequence has forgotten some of what he learned about your case that day."

Both Colemans looked startled by this news, though the slight change in Lia's expression was once again in contrast to her husband's more exaggerated reaction. His surprise, however, went swiftly from surprise to deep concern.

"Is the sergeant all right?" he asked.

"He's doing as well as can be expected," replied James. "I'm told he should make a full recovery in time. But it's most inconvenient as far as your case goes, as he was following up some quite promising leads. He hasn't been in touch with you since our chat on Tuesday, has he?"

Coleman shook his head. "No," he answered. "Your call this morning was the first we've heard from anybody, police or insurance. But what happened to Sergeant Gibbons?"

"There was an incident in Walworth," said James. "The sergeant was attacked, but as I said, he's expected to be just fine."

"How terrible," murmured Lia, while her husband shook his head and said, "I've heard Walworth can be a rough area, but I never . . . well, never mind." A thought occurred to him, and he looked suddenly concerned. "It wasn't anything to do with our case, was it? I should feel awful if—"

"No, no," said James hastily, stemming this no doubt heartfelt outburst of feeling. "We haven't really any notion why he was there. And even if it had been your case, well, that's a policeman's lot, as it were. In the meantime, I have one or two little questions I'd like you to clear up for me."

"Yes, of course. We'll be happy to tell you anything you like."

"You said on Tuesday you didn't know the combination to Miss Haverford's safe."

"That's right," said Coleman, with a little shrug. "We'd never actually thought about it."

"But if you had wanted to open it," continued James, "where would you have looked for the combination?"

Coleman exchanged a glance with his wife, who said, "If we'd wanted to open the safe without Miranda, I expect we'd have got Rose to do it. I'm sure she knew the combination."

"Rose," repeated James, as if trying to come up with a connection.

"Rose Gowling," said Coleman. "Aunt Miranda's housekeeper. Didn't we mention her to you the other day?"

"I don't believe so," said James, his tone indicating a deep disapproval of this omission.

"I thought we had," said Coleman, frowning and looking at Lia again. "When we were talking about the keys to the house. But perhaps that was on Monday, when the police were there."

"I really should have interviewed the housekeeper before this," said James reproachfully.

"Oh, you can't," Coleman told him. "I'm sorry, I didn't mean to give you a wrong impression. Rose is dead."

James rolled his eyes. "Then how could she possibly have been of help with the safe combination?"

"Well, she couldn't, not now," replied Coleman practically. "But she hasn't been dead long, and what Lia meant was, if we had wanted anything to do with the house while Aunt Miranda was unavailable, we would have asked Rose before anyone else. She'd been with my aunt for years and years."

Lia nodded agreement. "You see, Rose hasn't been gone long enough for us to consider other ways of dealing with things."

"Well, she's not here now," pointed out James practically. "Suppose the safe hadn't been broken into and you couldn't wait to have a look at your inheritance. Where might you have searched for the combination?"

The Colemans smiled at each other.

"It did occur to us," admitted Coleman. "I mean, we'd seen the pictures and all, and we were curious to see the real thing. If we'd known the combination, I can't say we'd have been able to resist having a peek."

"As it was," said Lia, "we didn't go beyond wishing. But if we had . . ."

She put a finger to her lips while she thought.

"I expect I'd have looked in the desk in the study," put in Coleman.

"You don't think that's rather obvious?" asked Lia.

"Well, yes. It's why I thought of it. Do you think Aunt Miranda would have been more devious?"

Lia paused in thought before she answered. "Perhaps not," she said at last. "She didn't seem to take the idea of security very seriously."

"The desk for me, then," said Coleman, turning back to James.

"Or the filing cabinet," added Lia. "Miranda did once mention that she kept all her instructions and manuals in there. If she wasn't trying to be particularly secretive, I don't see why she wouldn't have just written the number down on the manual."

James nodded. "I'll check on both of those places," he said.

"You think the thief found the combination then?" asked Coleman, sounding a little disappointed. "Don't they have safecrackers anymore?"

"Certainly," said James. "But it's not a method used much by criminals. For one thing, it takes considerably longer than they lead you to believe in films. No thief wants to stay in a house he's broken into for longer than necessary."

"Ah," said Coleman thoughtfully.

"Do you mind my asking," said Bethancourt diffidently, "if Rose lived in? I'm just trying to get an idea of how the house was run."

Coleman chuckled and his wife smiled. "Oh, yes, Rose lived in," he answered. "She was a martinet, was our Rose. I don't think she took to us very well, do you, Lia?"

Lia shook her head in agreement. "I would describe her attitude toward us as one of deep resentment."

"And suspicion," chimed in Coleman. "As far as Rose was concerned, we were there to steal the silver. Really, one could hardly blame her. She was like family herself."

"Yes, I know the type," said Bethancourt. "Was her illness prolonged?"

"Oh, no," said Coleman. "No, not at all. Rose was elderly, but quite hale and hearty right up until the end. She was a good bit younger than my aunt—" He broke off and looked a question at his wife.

"About twenty years younger, I believe," she responded.

"Mind you, that didn't make her a spring chicken," said Coleman. "She was well into her seventies, and a bit past the heavy cleaning. We suggested to Aunt Miranda that she have a charwoman in once a week or so, but she refused. Said she didn't want to upset Rose." His face fell. "But that was probably because she couldn't afford it. We didn't know," he added in a tone of wounded innocence, "that she was hard up."

Bethancourt frowned, but let this pass without comment.

"Well in any case," Coleman was saying, "after Rose died—which was quite sudden and unexpected, mind you—we were in a pretty fix. I said to Lia, 'Do you know, if we had never come, we shouldn't be responsible and we wouldn't care in the least.' To which, of course, she pointed out that as we had come, it was all a moot point."

James had leaned back and was drinking his coffee while looking a touch bemused. Letting witnesses reminisce randomly was clearly not his usual interview technique, but having allowed Bethancourt to introduce it, he was apparently content to let it continue and see what came of it.

"A moot point indeed," he murmured, half to himself, and then, "What, exactly, was moot?"

"Well, how we would have felt if we hadn't come," explained Coleman.

"Ah."

"Why did you, by the way?" asked Bethancourt.

Coleman looked a little surprised. "Why, Aunt Miranda asked us to. She sent a letter. I hadn't any idea I was her heir before that—I mean, it's really quite a distant relationship, for all I call her my aunt."

"But you knew, of course, about the jewelry collection?" asked James.

"Oh, yes." Coleman grinned. "It's quite legendary in my family. My grandmother only ever referred to it as 'the wages of sin.'"

"Then presumably she wouldn't have wished to inherit it," said James dryly.

"Heavens, no. But I'm not so pure-minded as my grandmother." Coleman grinned again.

"Mr. Bethancourt was asking about Rose's death, Rob," prompted his wife softly.

"Right. Well, the poor old girl just keeled over one day, carrying a tray up the stairs. Aunt Miranda's early tea, it was. It made a frightful clatter that even Aunt Miranda could hear, and she rang for an ambulance, but it was too late. The doctor said Rose was probably dead before she hit the bottom of the stairs. A massive coronary, you see."

"I think her death rather shook Miranda," said Lia in her quiet way. "I don't think she had ever imagined she would outlast Rose. She seemed—much less herself, after that."

Coleman gave his wife a sympathetic look. "You always rather liked her, didn't you?"

"I did. She was interesting, I thought, for all she could be difficult."

"She was certainly difficult after Rose died," said Coleman glumly. "You have to understand," he said to his guests, "she couldn't really look after herself anymore. Rose had been doing all the cooking and housework, and making sure Aunt Miranda didn't fall down in the bath or anything. But Aunt Miranda wouldn't have anyone else in, and she wouldn't hear of moving. Lia and I were at our wits' ends. We arranged for a home health aide, but Miranda sent the first three packing in as many days. The last one seemed all right, but of course she only came in a few hours a day. Lia and I were just deciding we had better move in—even though, mind, we hadn't yet decided to settle in England—when Aunt Miranda's health took a turn for the worse and she had to go into hospital." He turned his palms up in an empty gesture. "She never came out again."

"Speaking of which," said James, "have you decided what you're going to do now?"

"Not really." Coleman shrugged and exchanged glances with his wife. "We were thinking we'd stay on here for a bit, but that was before we discovered what a mess Aunt Miranda's estate was in. On the other hand, it would be nice to find out what happened to the jewels before we leave, and you say that may take some time."

"It may," agreed James. "Although we're certainly trying to hurry it along."

"We appreciate it," said Coleman earnestly. He gave a little laugh.

"You can't know what it's like, thinking that quite soon you'll be the owners of a fabulous collection of jewels, only to find out the next day that you'll never even get to see them."

James smiled sympathetically. "Very frustrating, I'm sure," he said, rather perfunctorily. "Well, thank you very much for your time, Mr. Coleman, Mrs. Coleman. We must be getting on—lots to do, you know. Do ring me if you have any further thoughts on the matter. I'll be in touch."

And with this little speech, James maneuvered them out of the sitting-room area and over to the door. He shook hands cordially with Coleman, complimented Lia on the coffee, and then whisked Bethancourt into the lift.

His genial smile faded as soon as the lift doors closed and his gray eyes turned coldly shrewd.

"And so what did you think of our heirs?" he asked.

Bethancourt was already considering this question. "If Rob Coleman was English," he said, "I'd say he was a dreadful bounder."

James laughed heartily. "So would I," he agreed. "But of course he's not English, or even British. He's Ukrainian, which makes him unique in my experience."

"Mine, too," admitted Bethancourt. "I've known a few Eastern Europeans, and even one or two Russians, but never a Ukrainian."

"Which means he may not be a bounder at all," said James with a sigh.

"Even if he is," pointed out Bethancourt as the doors slid open and they emerged into the lobby, "it doesn't mean he's a jewel thief or a murderer."

"Alas, no. If it did, my job would be much easier and I would be a richer man than I am. Oh, dear, it's raining again."

James paused for a moment to regard the cold drizzle outside sourly.

"Well," he said, recovering his aplomb and pulling out his mobile, "we needed a taxi in any case. I'm going to have another look at the Haverford place," he added to Bethancourt as he scrolled through his contacts. "You're welcome to come if you think the scene of the crime would interest you."

"I'd like to see it," said Bethancourt. "It's very good of you to offer."

James waved this away as he dialed and lifted the phone to his ear.

Carmichael surveyed the door of Gibbons's flat carefully before he stepped forward to insert the key in the lock. So far as he could see, it showed no signs of having been forced or otherwise tampered with.

The key turned smoothly, and let him into a pleasant sitting room with double windows that let in the afternoon light. It was not a large room, but it was arranged comfortably enough, with a pair of overstuffed chairs, which needed new upholstery, a stout oaken coffee table, and a brightly colored rug. There was a drop-leaf table against the wall by the windows, with two straight-backed chairs set by it. Everything was quite neat and clean, with the exception of a coffee mug on the coffee table, and a jumble of loose change, various receipts, and a couple of CDs without their cases that were all piled on the tiny table by the door which held the phone and answer machine.

To the right was the narrow kitchen, and beyond that the doors to the bedroom and bath, both of which were ajar.

Carmichael stood just within the front door, contemplating the room before him. Gibbons had not been gone long enough for the flat to have a disused air, and the only sign that all was not business as usual was the coffee mug, in which the dregs of Tuesday morning's coffee had dehydrated into a thick black coating at the bottom of the mug.

Carmichael had never been here before; sergeants did not commonly invite detective chief inspectors to their homes, especially not when the home in question was a bachelor flat with little in the way of amenities. But the place spoke to him of Gibbons, and he felt an intruder into his subordinate's private life. He did not like to venture farther in without invitation.

But he knew his job. He drew a pair of latex gloves from his pocket, pulled them on, and moved to the drop-leaf table where Gibbons's laptop lay. This would be the sergeant's personal machine, and it was with great reluctance that Carmichael started it up. He stood while it booted up, dreading what he might find once it was running.

It was not that he suspected Gibbons of any criminal activity; it was only that he hated probing into what was none of his business. He did not want to know what, if any, political sites his sergeant had been visiting on the Internet. He did not want to read Gibbons's private e-mails. He liked their relationship very well the way it was, and he would greatly prefer not to know things Gibbons had chosen not to share with him.

On the other hand, better he than anyone else. He at least had Gibbons's best interests at heart, and if he found things today that troubled him, he would take care to bury them deep, as deeply as he could, even if he could not rid himself entirely of their memory.

The computer was on. With a sigh, Carmichael brought up the browser and checked the history. The most recently visited site was the *Guardian*'s on Tuesday, probably a morning ritual as Carmichael saw no sign of a physical newspaper. The next lot of sites were gathered under Monday's date, and there were a great many of them. Running his eye down the list, Carmichael smiled. They were all, every last one, sites dealing with gemstones and heritage jewelry. Gibbons had simply been doing his homework.

Further back, there were other sites visited, but Carmichael was relieved not to find anything to be embarrassed about. Probably buried somewhere in the computer's bowels was something he did not want to know, but it looked very much as if he would not have to dig it out, and that was a great relief.

Gibbons's e-mail was password protected, which made it quite beyond Carmichael's ability to open. He bit his lip at that, but there was no help for it: some anonymous scientist in forensics would see the correspondence before Carmichael could vet it. He could only hope Gibbons's e-mail was as innocuous as his Internet habits.

He wasn't much looking forward to inspecting the bedroom, either, but here again he found nothing to distress him. Gibbons apparently had not had time to make his bed on Tuesday morning, and he had read himself to sleep on Monday night with Ian McEwan's latest novel. His clothes hamper was nearly full, and he did keep a supply of condoms in his bedside table drawer, but that was only to be expected in a young, single man. A chair held some discarded clothing, and on the top of the bureau was a collection of things from Gibbons's pockets. Carmichael went through the drawers perfunctorily, finding only what one might expect.

In the closet he did find a collection of used notebooks, but they all referenced past cases.

And that was really the only thing in the flat that had anything to do with Gibbons's work. Carmichael had rather expected it to be so; he knew from his own experience that detectives spent so much time at work that many of their personal effects ended up at the Yard, rather than Yard business at the home. Still, he had had to make sure.

There was in the end only the computer to be taken back to forensics. With a better heart, Carmichael took extra care to make sure he had left as little trace of his presence as possible before wrapping the computer in a polythene bag and tucking it under his arm. He locked the door behind him and sought out the stairs, thinking to himself that he should have known Gibbons would not let him down, not even in this.

The House in Southgate

This is it," said James.

The taxi made the turn down what in summer would be a green, leafy street but which in November was merely a wilderness of stark, bare limbs. On James's instructions the taxi rolled to a stop in front of a pleasant house, set back from the street and partially obscured by a large plane tree in the front garden. It was a big building, but very well proportioned, and unaltered from early Victorian times.

James asked the taxi to wait and then led the way through the rain into the porch and the front door.

"Most of the land is at the back, of course," he said, patting his pockets in search of the key. "These places are all like that. A nice bit of property, though, if you ask me."

Bethancourt merely nodded agreement; he had taken his glasses off and was drying the lenses with his handkerchief while he squinted about him. A slight frown appeared between his brows and once he had returned the horn-rims to his nose, he observed, "It's not very well kept up, though, is it?"

"No, the old lady had let things go of late years," agreed James, at last uncovering the key in his pocketbook and inserting it into the lock. "Everyone thought, of course, that it had merely become too much for her in her old age, but in fact she had pretty much run out of money. The property is heavily mortgaged."

Bethancourt looked startled at this bit of information. "She can't have been that hard up," he said. "She had a jewelry collection worth a million pounds."

"Well, yes, but that doesn't actually produce income, does it?" said James.

"Perhaps not," admitted Bethancourt. "But if she was in difficulties over money, a single auction would have netted her a small fortune. Or she might have sold off just a few pieces and invested the proceeds."

"But if she didn't choose to sell it," said James, holding open the door and ushering Bethancourt in, "the jewelry actually cost her money rather than making it. I mean, there were the insurance fees and things."

Bethancourt looked blank. "But why wouldn't she have sold it?" he asked. "It's not as if she ever wore it, or was holding it in trust for a beloved daughter or something. In fact, she barely knew her heir."

James paused, his hand on the doorknob, and looked upward at the cracked lintel. "I think it was pride," he said, "though of course I don't really know. Why did she keep this house? She couldn't afford it and she didn't need anything nearly this big, but she refused to sell. I think it was because it was her family home, her birthright, and she wasn't going to admit that she couldn't afford it any more than she would admit that, unlike her forebears, she had to sell her gems."

This was a new take on the woman whose jewelry had brought them here, and Bethancourt was thoughtful as he looked about the foyer, which badly needed new wallpaper.

James punched in a code on the alarm and closed the door before joining him. "Faugh," he said with an energetic snort. "It's amazing how quickly a closed-up house becomes fusty, isn't it? The study's at the back—down the hall this way."

Bethancourt obediently fell into step beside him.

"The alarm wasn't triggered on the night of the robbery?" he asked.

"Not a bit of it—these chaps knew their business," replied James. "They also knew their parsimonious old ladies—the windows above the ground floor aren't wired. How she got that by the insurance company I can't imagine, especially in this house with convenient porch roofs jutting out all over the place. It was child's play for the thieves to climb up, break a window, and let themselves in. Here's the study—we shall ignore the police tape if you don't mind."

Bethancourt obligingly ducked beneath the tape to enter the study. James followed him and then produced latex gloves from his coat pocket.

"Here," he said, offering a pair to Bethancourt. "We don't want to leave any fingerprints for the police forensics department. A long and varied life has taught me that they are picky about such things—though in this case, I very much doubt whether they'll be back."

"Still, you never can tell," said Bethancourt, putting on the gloves.

"Exactly." James paused to look around and take stock. "I was only here the once," he said. "On the Monday, when I met your Sergeant Gibbons. The place was crawling with forensics and policemen of every possible stripe then. There was so much bustle it was impossible to think, much less investigate."

Taking this as a cue to keep quiet and out of the way, Bethancourt only nodded and turned his attention to the room, more in search of hints to Miranda Haverford's personality than in the hope of finding any actual clues. He knew his limitations and much preferred to leave clues to the professionals.

The study was a large room with windows looking out over the back garden, a somewhat overgrown expanse of lawn and large trees with bare patches that in summer would no doubt hold flowers.

It was a lived-in room, with a leather sofa and armchair arranged to look out at the garden and two oak filing cabinets standing in for end tables. The safe stood in the darkest corner of the room, a squat, weighty thing with its door hanging open to reveal an empty interior.

Set against the opposite wall was a large cabinet desk. It was ornate and heavy, a late Victorian creation with its finish much worn beneath a liberal smearing of black fingerprint powder, and its pigeon holes crammed with bits of paper. It bore very little resemblance to its elegant cousin in James's office. James stood in front of it with fierce concentration, hands on hips, as though he might be communing with the desk, drawing its secrets out of it psychically.

Along the back wall of the room were bookshelves, and after a moment Bethancourt strolled over to inspect them, drawn by several rows of ledgerlike volumes. They were ranged along the bottom shelves, below a leather-bound collection of the novels of James Fenimore Cooper. The Cooper books were not in the best condition, and were not first editions, but they were a nice set from the turn of the century, and Bethancourt thought they should be worth a bit. Which led him to wonder whether they, too, were a treasured family inheritance, or whether Miranda Haverford had simply not realized their value. They had certainly not been kept for their own sakes; the one volume he selected at random had several uncut pages.

The ledgers were a different matter. They were as old as they had looked from across the room, their tops liberally bestowed with dust, and were apparently the household accounts from the period when Evony St. Michel and her button manufacturer had lived here. Bethancourt, who liked that sort of thing, settled himself on the ottoman, opening one of the volumes on his lap, and began to pore over the references, in faded ink, to "three cords of firewood—1 pound, 4 shillings, & sixpence" sitting just above the entry "silk shawl embroidered with roses, from Paris—25 guineas."

James meanwhile had seated himself at the desk and, with a delicacy of touch unexpected in a big man, begun to carefully go through each pigeonhole's contents.

The silence, broken only by the rustling of paper and the steady drone of the rain outside, continued for some time. James, having dealt with the pigeonholes, moved on to the desk drawers, while Bethancourt slowly began to build a picture of a marriage. Haverford had apparently realized that even jewelry from the best shops in London could not compete with the jewels previously bestowed on his wife by dukes and kings; there were virtually no entries in the ledger for payments to jewelers. A few years into the marriage there was one large expenditure for copies to be made of some of Evony's jewelry, and there was another on the couple's tenth anniversary for a ruby ring, but apart from that the only jewelry purchases were of inexpensive items, like an enameled brooch.

Evony's dressmaker's bills, on the other hand, were large and frequent, dwarfing the salary of her lady's maid. In fact, Bethancourt noted, none of the servants' wages came anything close to the amount he was accustomed to pay his charwoman. All in all, the household expenses, though certainly well above the norm, were quite reasonable for a wealthy Victorian household.

The ledgers were all meticulously kept in a neat hand, and Bethancourt wondered if they had been penned by Haverford himself. There was no record of a bookkeeper being paid, but Haverford might have had someone in from his office to do the household accounts.

"What the devil are you reading there?" demanded James, interrupting this reverie. "It's not the damned Fenimore Cooper, is it?"

"No," answered Bethancourt with a grin. "It's the household ledgers—from Evony's time. Rather interesting, really."

James raised an eyebrow. "Read history at University, did you?"

"Close," answered Bethancourt. "I took a degree in classics."

"Did you, indeed?" James was slightly surprised. He absorbed this information for a moment, eyeing Bethancourt the while, and then a slow smile spread over his face. "And got a first, I'm betting."

Bethancourt inclined his head modestly.

James gave a bark of laughter. "There's more to you than meets the eye," he declared. "I had quite put you down as a dilettante. But I should have known—I knew Sergeant Gibbons had a first from Oxford. Is that where you met, by the way?"

"Initially," said Bethancourt. "We were in different colleges, and didn't really become friends until after we had come down." He grinned. "We ran across each other in a pub in Bayswater one night and the rest is history."

"Drowning your woes together, eh?" said James, amused. "Well, great friendships have been founded on less. Anyway, I've found our combination—look here."

He exhibited his find, a small black leather-bound notebook, holding it carefully by the edges with his gloved fingertips.

"It's one of those little address books they used back in the forties and fifties," he said. "The kind of thing a woman would slip into her purse or a man into his breast pocket, before we all had mobile phones and BlackBerrys and PDAs. It doesn't seem to have been used much—there's only a few addresses in it—but here in the back where one's supposed to write down birthdays or what have you, there's a list of names and dates. And then, at the bottom, there's a series of numbers written in fresh ink."

He held the page open for Bethancourt's examination.

"How odd," said Bethancourt, adjusting his glasses and peering down at it. "The numbers she used for the combination are the same as this chap's birthday."

"Which chap?" asked James, turning the little book back so he could read it. "Ah, this one at the top—Andrew Kerrigan. I didn't notice that. I wonder who he was."

"A lost love perhaps?" suggested Bethancourt.

James snorted. "You young people are all obsessed with romance," he said. "He was probably her milkman. Well, I think we'll pass this along to Scotland Yard forensics, for all the good it will do."

"You don't think the thief left his fingerprints?"

"Do you?" retorted James. "No, I expect them to find this little gem wiped clean. However, if it's not . . ." He tapped his chin thoughtfully with one finger.

"Then it will mean the thief already knew the combination," supplied Bethancourt.

"Yes," affirmed James. "And that would be a pretty little twist, but it's very unlikely." He stood silent for a moment, his eyes passing over the room and its contents. "The thief knew the safe was here," he said musingly. "Nothing else in any of the other rooms was touched. Not, mind you, that there was much worth stealing in any of them apart from a bit of sterling in the dining room."

"And the Fenimore Cooper," added Bethancourt with a jerk of his head.

"Good grief, what thief in his right mind would steal those?" said James. "No, he knew about the safe, right enough. The question is: did he know what was in it?"

"In other words," said Bethancourt, following this logic, "was it a crime of opportunity, or was he specifically after the jewels?"

"Exactly," said James. "The jewelry was mentioned in the obituary naturally enough, but one wouldn't necessarily expect to find it on the premises. Most people," he added with a scowl, "keep their valuables in a safe deposit box."

"But anybody who owned a fortune in antique jewels might be presumed to have other things worth stealing," said Bethancourt.

"So one would have thought," agreed James dryly. "I certainly did."

"So did I," agreed Bethancourt. He looked about him at the worn spots on the leather sofa, and the spoilt finish of the tops of the oak filing cabinets, at the damp spot on the wall in one corner, and said, "I hope to God that I'll have the sense to sell my grandmother's jewelry if I end up penniless at the end of my life."

James looked interested. "Does your grandmother have particularly nice jewelry?" he asked, and Bethancourt laughed.

"It's all earmarked for my sister in any case," he said. "Everything but the engagement ring and wedding pearls."

"Then you'll have to steal it first," said James. "I do hope they're not insured through one of my companies."

Both men grinned at this jest as they left the study, ducking under the police tape again and carefully closing the door behind them.

"Do you have any interest in seeing the rest of the house?" asked James, leading the way back to the foyer.

Bethancourt admitted that he did and James, who clearly did not, took him on a whirlwind tour of a once-graceful home that now showed signs everywhere of neglect. Some of the furnishings had been preserved from Evony's time, but they were universally so worn and with so many defects that even the nicest of them was no longer fit for anything but the secondhand shops.

Back at the front door, James glanced at his watch and said with satisfaction, "Just in time for me to get home and walk the dog."

"Me, too," said Bethancourt, consulting his own watch. "What kind of dog do you have?"

"English bulldog," said James proudly, and then he added, with a rather abashed look, "His name's Churchill, but I didn't name him. What kind is yours?"

"Borzoi," answered Bethancourt. "He was an unexpected gift from my sister, but it's turned out rather well in the end. His name's Cerberus, for which I am responsible."

James gave a bark of laughter. "Ah, yes, that degree in classics," he said as he locked the front door, struggling a bit with the key. "Well, can I drop you anywhere? I'm headed to Hampstead. Or you can take the taxi on from there if you like."

Bethancourt agreed to this latter plan, and arrived back in St. Loo Avenue just in time to catch the porter leaving the building with Cerberus. Mr. Kenilworth owned three dogs of varying sizes and pedigrees and had cheerfully agreed to take Cerberus along on their walks whenever Bethancourt was not at home.

Cerberus, whose tail wagged with violent enthusiasm upon sighting his master, was far less pleased when Bethancourt guided him away from a delightful run in the park with his friends, and instead ushered him into the Jaguar.

"We'll have a good run later, lad," apologized Bethancourt. "Right now it's time to go visit Uncle Jack and cheer his no doubt flagging spirits."

Cerberus wagged his tail resignedly.

Gibbons wondered vaguely if he was becoming a morphine addict. He had certainly dosed himself into a stupor on account of the hideous pain resulting from the nurse's insistence that he get up and sit in a chair. He rather thought that being a drug addict would interfere with his career as a police detective, but that didn't seem to matter as much as it had a little while ago.

"Here we go," said the nurse, bustling back in with a footstool.

Gibbons glared at her, his normally fierce eyes mere glints of blue between puffy, sleep-swollen lids. It was grossly unfair, he thought, that a woman as pretty as the nurse should turn out to harbor sadistic tendencies. There was really no other explanation for anyone referring to his present agony as "discomfort."

"I can't imagine where the one from this room went," the nurse continued, kneeling to place the stool by Gibbons's feet. "I think you'll be more comfortable with your knees up a bit. I'll help you get your feet up. Ready?"

Gibbons was not ready, but before he could say so, the nurse—who also seemed to be much stronger than her diminutive size suggested—had lifted his feet in one smooth motion and rested them on the footstool. He let out an inarticulate moan of pain.

"I know," she said soothingly, rearranging the small blanket she had placed over his knees. "I know it's difficult, but you'll feel better for it in the end."

Gibbons, whose eyes had closed reflexively with the pain, opened them again to glare at her, but instead encountered a shocked-looking Bethancourt standing in the doorway.

"Er," said Bethancourt. "Should he really be out of bed?"

The nurse swiveled on her heels and smiled brightly at this newcomer before noticing the large hound accompanying him.

"It's all right," added Bethancourt hastily. "This is Sergeant Gibbons's dog—I've cleared the visit with the matron."

He smiled down at her.

"Well, if Matron okayed it," she replied doubtfully.

"Oh, she has. Cheerful patients do better and all that." Bethancourt's worried eyes belied his smile as his gaze strayed back to Gibbons. "I hadn't thought," he said, "that Jack would be out of bed for a while yet."

"Oh, no," the nurse assured him. "We like to get them up and moving as soon as possible. After all, it's bad enough to be shot in the abdomen—we don't want him developing any other problems."

"Er, no, of course not," said Bethancourt doubtfully.

"Do I get a vote?" asked Gibbons hoarsely.

The nurse shook her head at him as she rose. "I'm afraid not," she said, not unsympathetically. "I know this probably doesn't feel right to you, but you'll have to trust me that it's for the best."

"I'd rather trust a—a—" began Gibbons grumpily, and then foundered as he failed to come up with an example of untrustworthiness.

"A traitor?" suggested Bethancourt brightly.

The nurse chuckled. "I'm sure a lot of my patients feel that way," she said, shaking her head. "But there's no help for it—I have to look after their welfare before I worry about whether or not they like me."

"And I'm sure they're grateful in the end," said Bethancourt with a gallant smile.

"No, they're not," muttered Gibbons, but no one took any notice of him.

"So long as they leave healthy," said the nurse.

Bethancourt was still smiling down at her. "I'm Phillip Bethancourt," he said, holding out his hand. "Friend of the injured."

She smiled as she shook his hand. "Alice Pipp," she said. "Pleased to meet you."

"I'm sure we'll be seeing a lot of one another," said Bethancourt, beaming at her as if this would be the highlight of his day. "At least, I take it Jack here will be under your care for a few days."

"Oh, yes," she said, glancing at her patient. The shadow that passed over her features as she did so was faint, but Bethancourt noticed it. "A few days at least," she echoed. "Well, I must be about my rounds. You ring for me, Mr. Gibbons, if you want anything. It was nice meeting you, Mr. Bethancourt."

"A delight," said Bethancourt, looking after her as she left the room, closing the door softly behind her.

"If you've quite finished chatting up my nurse," said Gibbons coldly.

"Oh, don't be silly, Jack," said Bethancourt, turning to his friend. "How on earth do you expect me to get Cerberus in here if I'm not nice to the staff?"

"She's a redhead and she has big breasts," insisted Gibbons.

"Her hair color comes out of a bottle," retorted Bethancourt. "And nobody who dates a fashion model can be said to be fixated on breast size. Besides, I don't have a particular thing for redheads—just for Marla."

"Marla?" asked Gibbons, who had already lost track of what they were talking about. "Is she here?"

"No—she doesn't get in until tonight." Bethancourt considered his seating options, which, with Gibbons occupying the chair, came down to a padded stool on castors. He looked at it disdainfully and sat down on the bed. "So," he said, "why is your nurse worried about you?"

"Probably because she's nearly killed me, getting me out of the bed," said Gibbons. He squinted at Bethancourt. "There's an idea," he added. "You can lift me back in."

"No, I couldn't," retorted Bethancourt, although privately he wished he might. Gibbons looked pale and unwell to his eye, and not fit to be anywhere but in bed. "Is that a different IV drip they've given you?"

"God knows," said Gibbons fretfully. "They've got so many things running into me and out of me, I hardly know if I'm coming or going. All I know is that this one's the morphine." That reminded him of his earlier concern, and he asked, "Phillip, do you think I'm becoming a morphine addict?"

"What?" said Bethancourt, startled. "No, of course not."

"I've given myself quite a lot," confessed Gibbons.

"I think you're supposed to," said Bethancourt. "And you can't overdose on those machines—they're programmed not to let you."

Overdosing had not occurred to Gibbons and he frowned. "I certainly didn't mean to do that," he said. "I don't want to die. Not now, at least. I'd like to kill that nurse."

"Nurse Pipp," supplied Bethancourt absently. He was eyeing his friend with concern; Gibbons's speech was a little slurred and he seemed to be having difficulty keeping his eyes open and his thoughts straight. Bethancourt felt quite helpless, and he was not accustomed to that.

"So have you found out anything?" asked Gibbons.

"About the case, you mean?"

"What the devil else would you think I meant?" snapped Gibbons.

"Sorry, sorry, old man," said Bethancourt, leaning comfortably back on one elbow. "My thoughts were elsewhere. Let's see. I've met your Colin James, and he very kindly took me round to meet the Colemans."

He paused, as Gibbons seemed to be having difficulty assimilating this information.

"The Colemans," Gibbons said slowly, rolling the name on his tongue. Just as James's name seemed to come attached to friendly feelings for which he had no reference, so the Colemans dredged up feelings that could not be explained by the brief encounter he remembered having with them. These feelings, however, were far more ambiguous and in his present fuzzy-minded state, he did not feel up to sorting them out.

"Davies sent round my report on the interview I had with them," he offered at last. "It's in the drawer there if you want to look at it."

"That was good of him," said Bethancourt, moving leisurely off the bed to fetch the report. "Did it ring any bells?"

"No." Gibbons shook his head. "It was very odd, reading it. I could recognize it as one of my reports, but I have no memory of writing it. Or of the events I wrote about. It gives one a rather queasy feeling."

"I can imagine." Report in hand, Bethancourt settled himself back on the bed and gave his attention to it while Gibbons tried and failed to find a comfortable position in his chair. Cerberus, who seemed to sense something was wrong with his master's friend, padded over to lay his head gently on Gibbons's knee. Gibbons patted him feebly.

"This," said Bethancourt, rapidly scanning, "seems to be a record of your interview with Miss Haverford's solicitor."

"Oh, right," said Gibbons. "Davies sent that one along, too. It's not very interesting—just a report for the record."

"Well," said Bethancourt, "if I'd read it earlier, I shouldn't have been so surprised to find out Miss Haverford was broke."

"It seems very odd," agreed Gibbons. "Though I do remember thinking the house wasn't very well kept up."

Bethancourt looked up from the report at once. "You're remembering things?" he asked.

Gibbons grimaced. "No, I'm not," he said, a little shortly. "I was at the house on Monday. It's Tuesday I can't remember."

"Oh. Yes, of course." Bethancourt hesitated, decided words of sympathy would not be welcome, and returned to the report. "So," he said in another moment, "she hadn't changed her will since the death of her maid."

Gibbons moved restlessly. "No, I expect not. But I only vaguely remember the Colemans mentioning the maid on Monday night. That," he added petulantly, "is why detectives keep notebooks—so that they can refresh their memory of incidental remarks."

For an instant Bethancourt did not understand the significance of this remark, but then the light dawned.

"I'm sure Carmichael will let you have a copy of yours once forensics is done with it," he offered.

"Yes, but it's mine," burst out Gibbons. "Damn it all, Phillip, I'm not dead. I want my things."

"Well, of course you do," said Bethancourt. "Anybody would. But it's quite hopeless—you know better than anyone that once forensics has got its hands on something, they never let it go."

Gibbons merely grunted in a thoroughly dissatisfied way.

Bethancourt turned back to the report, and then looked up again as a thought occurred to him.

"Do you want another notebook?" he asked. "I mean, I know you couldn't look things up in it, but would you like to make notes as you go now? Just to keep track of your thoughts, you know."

Gibbons did not answer at once; he seemed to be turning the idea over in his mind.

"I don't know," he said at last with a sigh. "My mind's so fuzzy and I feel so rotten. But maybe having a notebook like I usually do would help."

Bethancourt nodded. "I'll bring one round tomorrow," he said, returning to the report.

"You don't have to," said Gibbons, but not as if he meant it.

"I know that," replied Bethancourt, laying aside the first report. "Well, the will seems fairly straightforward, particularly as there turned out to be so few assets. Just bequests of particular items to the maid and the neighbors, and this friend—what's-his-name—Ned Winterbottom, and the residue of the estate goes to the Colemans. Not," he added, turning to the next report, "that there is any residue."

"There was the jewelry," pointed out Gibbons.

"Mmm," said Bethancourt, his attention on the papers in front of him.

There was silence for a few minutes, while Bethancourt scanned the report and Gibbons closed his eyes and rested his head against the back of the chair.

"So," said Bethancourt, "you thought Rob Coleman was 'personable' and his wife 'attractive.'"

"Which means I couldn't make her out at all," translated Gibbons, opening his eyes. He frowned. "I remember what she looked like, from Monday night," he said, "but I don't recollect that she said very much, and all I was left with was an impression of her looks. It's odd, though, that I didn't do any better the next day, in a longer interview."

Bethancourt drew his knees up onto the bed thoughtfully. "She doesn't give much away, our Mrs. Coleman," he said. "She just—is. I mean," he added as Gibbons raised an eyebrow at him, "she doesn't react very much, and she says even less. 'Attractive' describes her very well."

"And yet not well enough," muttered Gibbons, closing his eyes again.

"Well, no, possibly not," admitted Bethancourt. "Still, need we describe her very well? Colin James seemed to think it unlikely the Colemans had a hand in the robbery."

"It is unlikely," agreed Gibbons, but he did not open his eyes.

Bethancourt regarded him from the bed with concern. Gibbons, shifting gingerly in the chair, did not appear to notice his friend's sudden silence. Bethancourt sat up, swinging his legs off the bed.

"If you don't mind," he said, "I think I'll just nip out and get a coffee—I think I need a little pick-me-up."

"Sure," said Gibbons, cracking his eyes open. "Are you coming back?"

"Right back," Bethancourt assured him. "Cerberus will stay with you."

He motioned to the dog, who settled back at Gibbons's feet, and then he slipped out in search of the red-haired nurse.

In the corridor, it was apparent that it was meal time for those patients who unlike Gibbons were taking solid food. An unappetizing smell wafted from the cart of covered trays parked outside one doorway, and Bethancourt immediately wished for a cigarette. Instead he turned to the bored-looking uniformed policeman sitting outside Gibbons's door and said, "Jack doesn't seem very well today."

The policeman glanced back into the room. "No," he agreed with a sigh. "It's a pity about the peritonitis, though according to the nurse it's not unexpected."

"Ah," said Bethancourt. "And what's peritonitis when it's at home?"

"Infection," said the policeman succinctly. "It can happen when the peritoneum gets contaminated."

"Oh." Bethancourt thought a moment. "I assume 'peritoneum' refers to the bowels?"

"As near as I can make out," agreed the policeman. "The way the nurse explained it was that when your intestines are perforated, what's inside them can leak out. And since that's not supposed to be outside, it can cause an infection."

Bethancourt nodded understanding. "It doesn't sound good," he said. "I thought they expected him to make a full recovery."

"Oh, they still do," the policeman hastened to reassure him. "This is just—what did they call it?—a complication. He may be in hospital a bit longer, but it'll be all right in the end. They expect the antibiotics they're giving him now to make short work of this peritonitis, and the nurse says it's not a bad case so far."

"That sounds a bit better," said Bethancourt, much relieved. He glanced back at his friend, who was still lying in the chair with his eyes closed. "I expect," he added, "Jack's got a fever now, and that's why he's so poorly."

The policeman nodded. "His temperature went way up this afternoon," he said, "but I think it's come down a little now—leastways, Nurse Pipp said it was good enough that the sergeant could get out of bed for a bit."

"I see," said Bethancourt, who still harbored doubts about the wisdom of this. "Well, thanks for filling me in—I was worried. Here, get yourself a pint when you get off duty."

"Why, thank you, sir," said the policeman, pocketing the note Bethancourt slipped him. "I'll do that."

Bethancourt nodded and wandered back into the room. At the sound of his step, Gibbons opened his eyes and smiled weakly. "Where's the coffee?" he asked.

"Finished it outside," said Bethancourt. "I was having your guard tell me how you were today."

"Oh?" said Gibbons. "And how am I?"

"You've got peritonitis," Bethancourt told him.

"Right," agreed Gibbons, but not as if it mattered much. "I'd forgotten what they called it this morning, but that was the name. It makes one feel awfully rotten."

"I imagine it does," said Bethancourt, smiling a little at this confidence.

"Although the pain's worse," Gibbons added, frowning as he shifted a little. "I never imagined just sitting up could hurt so badly."

Bethancourt gave a sympathetic wince. "You're young," he said, trying to sound encouraging. "They say you'll heal fast—it's having your stomach muscles torn up that hurts so much."

"Thanks for the diagnosis," said Gibbons dryly.

"Sorry," said Bethancourt.

The door opened behind him and he pivoted to see Gibbons's parents. His mother, in the lead, looked pleased at first to see her son sitting up, but her expression changed swiftly as she took stock of the pain reflected in Gibbons's face and the awkward way in which he held himself. Beside her, Mr. Gibbons's mouth tightened and he laid a hand on his wife's shoulder.

Another young woman had accompanied the Gibbonses; Bethancourt did not recognize her, or the two little girls she held by the hand, but assuming them to be family, he politely made his excuses and left them alone.

Cerberus, released from attendance on the wounded, was extremely eager for his walk. Upon emerging from the hospital, he turned west toward Regent's Park in a determined and no-nonsense sort of way, and Bethancourt followed behind resignedly, letting the great dog have his way for a moment before calling him back to heel. Hierarchy between master and dog reestablished, Bethancourt paused to light a cigarette, hunching away from the brisk west wind before continuing on their way.

It had rained while they had been in the hospital, leaving puddles on the pavement and making the turf in the park soggy underfoot. Bethancourt sniffed the wind and decided it would shortly be raining again. He let Cerberus loose and pulled out his mobile to check his messages while the great dog inspected an interesting scent amid the hedges. Both Marla and Spencer Kendrick had rung, leaving almost identical messages in which they announced their landing at Heathrow, asked after Gibbons, and wanted to know where Bethancourt was.

He rang Marla back first with the idea of meeting her somewhere for dinner, but she declined the invitation.

"I'm knackered," she said. "And it's a beastly night out in any case. My plans for the evening are to order in some Indian takeaway, and then get into bed early and watch the telly."

Bethancourt had to agree the weather was unpleasant, and as the rain started up again, he was beginning to wish for his own warm, comfy flat. He tucked his mobile safely away and stood a moment in the driving rain. He had learned a great deal more about the Haverford case, and admitted to himself he had become rather intrigued by it. But he had not, in all his researching during the day, found anything that might have made Gibbons ring him on Tuesday evening and declare he had "an interesting one on."

"But it's early days yet," he said to himself, trying to assuage his vague feeling of guilt that he had not come up with the answer. "I did have to catch up to where Jack was with the case before I could expect to see developments from his point of view. Perhaps tomorrow . . ."

But there his thoughts trailed off, as he had not the least notion of what he should do tomorrow. He sighed and whistled for his dog.

"Let's get home, lad," he said as Cerberus bounded up and then paused to shake himself vigorously, flinging water over his already drenched master. Bethancourt, accustomed to this performance, was unfazed. "I reckon you want your dinner," he continued, leading the way back toward the street. "I'm still feeling rather full of lunch, myself. I think an omelette and a salad will suffice for me tonight."

When at last they had negotiated their way from north London down to Chelsea, Bethancourt found a package waiting for him, delivered by messenger that evening from Hampstead. Curious, he tore open the envelope and removed a small tract of about fifty pages, complete with colored photographs. It was entitled "A Short History of the St. Michel Jewels," while the note tucked into the front cover read, "Hope you enjoy. I found it quite fascinating.—CJ."

"Excellent," said Bethancourt, smiling as he flipped through the pages. "Just the thing for a rainy November night. Whoa, Cerberus—not that way. It's the bathroom for you until I've got you dried off."

He herded his dog into the bathroom, stripping off his own wet things as he went, and spent some fifteen minutes rubbing the borzoi's long coat dry. He repeated the procedure on himself with a fresh towel and then headed to the kitchen to take care of man and dog's bodily needs.

It was not until after he had eaten his omelette and salad that he settled himself in one corner of the sofa, a glass of cognac on the table and his dog curled at his feet, and at last opened the tract in which Miranda had traced her great-grandmother's affairs and the jewels that had resulted from them.

9

A Pint After Work

*B*ethancourt was awakened the next morning, as he had been the morning before, by the persistent ringing of the telephone. In the normal way of things, he ignored such importunate intrusions, but with his sleep haunted by visions of a dying Gibbons, he found himself reaching to answer the phone before he was even truly aware.

His groping hand found the telephone receiver, and he cleared his throat loudly before saying, "Hullo?" in a groggy tone of voice.

"Bethancourt?"

He knew the voice, but in its present context he was unable to identify it.

"Yes?" he mumbled.

"It's DCI Carmichael here."

"Oh!" Bethancourt's eyes sprang open and he struggled into a sitting position. "Good to hear from you, sir," he said, recovering. "Is Jack all right?"

"He's no worse," Carmichael reassured him. "Still running a fever, but I gather they had expected that. No, I had another reason for ringing you. I was wondering if you might stop by the Yard this morning. There's a report I'd like your opinion on."

Bethancourt could not have been more surprised, but he jumped at the opportunity to have any kind of involvement in the police investigation.

"I'd be delighted to, sir," he said. "I could be there in an hour or so, if that would be convenient."

"Brilliant," said Carmichael. "I'll see you shortly, then."

Bethancourt rang off and lay blinking in the bed for a moment, trying to assimilate this sudden occurrence. He reached for his glasses and squinted at the bedside clock, letting out a long groan when he saw the time. It was 8:15.

Cerberus, standing at the edge of the bed, wagged his tail and Bethancourt regarded him severely.

"It is far too early," he announced. "Particularly for someone who sat up till two reading a tract on antique jewelry. Oh, dear," he added, yawning as he swung his legs out of the bed and reached for his dressing gown.

The day outside was not very inspiring to one who had not got his usual quota of sleep. The view from the windows of the Chelsea flat, when its owner eventually looked out, was gray and bleak, with light splatterings of rain blown against the panes by intermittent gusts of wind. It was against this background that Bethancourt hastily showered, shaved, and dressed, gulping down strong black coffee the while. Despite all the caffeine, he was still not feeling particularly alert when he arrived at Scotland Yard, a fact he tried very hard to hide as he and Cerberus emerged from the lift and made their way to Carmichael's office.

The chief inspector was at his desk with a pair of reading glasses perched on his nose and a paper cup of coffee by his hand. He looked up as Bethancourt appeared in the doorway and motioned the young man in.

"Good morning," said Bethancourt, as cheerfully as he could manage. He moved to take one of the chairs positioned opposite Carmichael's desk, and Cerberus, after a friendly tail wag in the chief inspector's direction, laid down at his master's feet.

"Good morning," replied Carmichael, laying aside the paper he had been reading. "I'm hoping you can help me with something."

"Anything you like," responded Bethancourt. "I'd be grateful for the chance to do something to help with Jack's case."

Carmichael nodded understanding of this sentiment. "It's been a shock to us all," he said. "The more so as he'd just begun his stint in Arts Theft—traditionally one of the less violent divisions at Scotland Yard."

"It had never occurred to me that Jack might be hurt in the performance of his duties," admitted Bethancourt. "I knew, of course, that you often dealt with violent people, but the corollary never came to mind."

Carmichael nodded again, thinking to himself that he, too, had once been that young, that inexperienced, and had the same belief in his own omnipotence.

"It's not something one does think about," he agreed. "But it does sometimes happen, and it's up to me to sort it out when it does."

Bethancourt looked sympathetic, while Carmichael leaned forward to sift through the various papers and folders spread out across his desk.

"I wanted your input on this report of O'Leary's," he said, frowning a little as the said report did not immediately come to light. "He had a drink with Gibbons after work that evening, you know."

"No, sir, I didn't," said Bethancourt. "I don't think," he added, a little hesitantly, "that was anything out of the ordinary, though—Jack has often mentioned having a pint with Chris O'Leary."

"Yes, yes," said Carmichael absently, his attention taken up with burrowing to a deeper level in the piles on his desk. "Ah, there it is! I was beginning to think I'd lost it."

Bethancourt, viewing the chaos on the desk, privately agreed that this was a possibility, but kept the thought to himself.

"The thing is," continued Carmichael, turning back to his guest, "O'Leary is currently working a murder in Walworth. It's just possible that something he said about the case might have been the reason Gibbons went down to Walworth on Tuesday night in the first place."

"But surely," objected Bethancourt, "if Jack had an idea about the Walworth murder, he would have told O'Leary?"

Carmichael nodded, pleased to have his own estimation of his sergeant's character confirmed. "So I would have thought," he agreed. "But I suppose it's just possible his idea was so extraordinary he felt the need to check it out a bit before mentioning it. Gibbons does sometimes come up with quite, er, unique views of a case. I was thinking that perhaps he had rung you up to see what you thought of it. His call to you was placed not long after he left the pub where he and O'Leary had been drinking."

"I see," said Bethancourt. "Yes, I expect that might have been what he wanted." In truth, he was thinking that most of the ideas Carmichael found so unique were probably his own. It was Bethancourt, not Gibbons, who was prone to flights of fancy, and every once in a while one of those flights would lead somewhere. But he could hardly tell Carmichael that.

"In any case," said Carmichael, "I dropped off a copy of O'Leary's report on their conversation for Gibbons to look at, but he was so under the weather last night, I doubt he's even seen it yet."

"You thought if he read a transcript of the conversation, the same notion—whatever it was—might occur to him," said Bethancourt.

"Just so," answered Carmichael. "Always assuming that was indeed what took him to Walworth Tuesday night. But as I say, Gibbons isn't up to much at the moment, and then I thought of you. You know him better, I think, than anyone else. I imagine he's more open with you about his thought processes than he is with me or with another colleague."

Carmichael looked at Bethancourt hopefully.

"We do sometimes brainstorm together," admitted Bethancourt. "I don't know that reading over a conversation of his would give me the same ideas as he had, though. I could try, I suppose."

"That's all anyone could ask," said Carmichael. He proffered the manila envelope he had dug out of the pile on his desk. "Let me know what you think," he said. "I'm afraid I must ask you for the report back once you've finished with it. And, mind you, no one else is to see it."

It was clear Carmichael had some qualms about bringing a civilian in on the police side of an investigation, and Bethancourt did his best to reassure him.

"I understand completely, sir," he said, taking the envelope. "I'll have it back to you as soon as I've digested the information. To tell the truth, this is the first I'd heard of any other case being involved in the attack on Jack."

Carmichael sighed and leaned back in his chair, polishing his glasses absently on his shirtfront. "It's probably not," he said. "Still, the fact remains that Gibbons had a conversation about a crime in Walworth and then popped up there some three hours later. And there doesn't seem to be another reason for him to have been in that neighborhood."

Bethancourt nodded.

"By the way," said Carmichael, "were you aware that a distant relation of Gibbons had recently moved into the Walworth area? A woman," he added as Bethancourt frowned, "named Dawn Melton."

"Oh, yes." The frown cleared from Bethancourt's brow. "I'd forgotten. Jack has mentioned her occasionally. I believe she's a first cousin of his, though I don't recollect which side of the family she's from. He wasn't best pleased that she ignored his advice and moved into Walworth. But I don't think he sees much of her—I take it she wasn't the reason Jack went down there that night?"

"Apparently not," answered Carmichael, in the manner of a policeman who never rules anything out until the whole solution is bare before him. "I just wondered if you knew her."

"No, we've never met," said Bethancourt. "I only know about her because of remarks Jack's made. I gather he didn't think much of being given the job of looking after the lamb in London, but couldn't tell his mother so."

This coincided exactly with the impression Carmichael had formed, but he was happy to have the confirmation from Gibbons's best friend.

Bethancourt was hesitating. "I did wonder, sir," he said, "if you'd discovered anything about Jack's movements that night."

"Not very much." Carmichael sighed. "It's rather unusual, having this blank slate to fill. Normally, we're checking a statement given to us and when we find a deviation, we look into it and one thing leads to another, so to speak. With this, we have no idea what direction to take. The only thing we know for certain is that Gibbons didn't go straight home. Was he thinking about the Haverford case? About the Pennycook murder? About something else altogether? Did his conversation with O'Leary remind him of his familial responsibilities and send him off to check on his cousin?" Carmichael threw up his hands.

"I see," murmured Bethancourt pensively. "I hadn't thought of it in that way before. Jack thinks," he added, a little tenuously, "that his call to me referred to the Haverford case."

Carmichael nodded. "I wouldn't be surprised if that were true," he said. "I know myself, when I'm on a case, it's always there in the back of my mind, waiting to come out the moment I'm not occupied with something else."

That was an interesting take on the mindset of a professional detective, something Bethancourt tucked away to mull over later. It was certainly quite different from the way he personally approached things and he couldn't help but wonder if that reflected his lack of professionalism, or merely a characteristic eccentricity.

They were interrupted by the telephone, which Carmichael reached to answer, holding up a finger to tell Bethancourt to wait. He listened for a moment, frowned, and then asked the caller to excuse him for a second.

"I've got to take this," he said, returning his attention to Bethancourt. "You'll look at the report and let me know?"

"I will, sir," said Bethancourt, tucking the envelope under his arm as he rose. "You'll hear from me by tonight."

He clucked at Cerberus to bring the dog to heel and retreated from the office. He was greatly tempted to linger within earshot of the chief inspector's conversation, but the penalties for being caught outweighed the possible benefits.

So he went back out into the cold drizzle. There was a café just down the street and he turned into it gratefully, ordering a large latte and settling into a corner at the back where there was room for Cerberus to lie down. Thus fortified, he lit a cigarette and opened the manila envelope.

Unlike Carmichael, Bethancourt was unaccustomed to reading police reports and found the style stolid. He skimmed quickly over it, only slowing when he came to the depiction of the conversation. He read that section over twice, and then leant back to let his thoughts roam.

He was rather glad no one had mentioned the Pennycook case to him before this, since clearly Gibbons had heard of it for the first time that night.

"So," he said to himself, "here I am, sitting in a public place, having a drink of something, knowing quite a lot about the Haverford robbery and having just heard about the murder of an old-time fence. Just like Jack that night. Only the wretched Pennycook case seems to have shifted his train of thought about his own case onto a different track, and it's not doing a single thing for me. Damn."

This last was said aloud and Cerberus raised his head, looking a question at his master.

"Well, is it doing anything for you?" demanded Bethancourt of his dog. "No, I thought not. Still," he added thoughtfully, "stolen jewels must be fenced—could Jack have gone down to Walworth to look at a pawnshop? Well, let's go and ask him, shall we, lad?"

Cerberus, who had rather been hoping for a piece of any of the foodstuffs he could so clearly smell, abandoned hope and resignedly got to his feet as Bethancourt pulled on his gloves.

Remembering his promise of yesterday, Bethancourt stopped at a stationery shop to buy one of the notebooks Gibbons favored, as well as a couple of the inexpensive mechanical pencils he knew his friend habitually used. But as he was paying for his purchases, another thought came to him.

He had, on the occasion of Gibbons's promotion to detective sergeant a few years ago, presented his friend with a monogrammed leather cover for his notebooks. It was no doubt now in the possession of the forensics laboratory, but the thought that gave Bethancourt pause was whether the cover would ever be fit to be used again. He had a very vivid picture in his mind of Gibbons lying bleeding in a Walworth street, and he knew from Carmichael that he had been found facedown in the rain. Now that he thought of it, it seemed very unlikely that the leather would have survived the experience, at least not in any shape to resume its former duties.

Outside, both the rain and the wind had picked up. It was as nasty a November morning as Bethancourt could remember, and he promptly abandoned the idea of walking Cerberus across St. James Park and instead sought out a taxi to take him to New Bond Street and Smythson's, where he could order a new leather cover.

Gibbons cracked open one eye to confirm that it was indeed sunlight coming through the window, and then closed his lid again immediately. He felt some relief that apparently the long night was over, but he wasn't much looking forward to another day.

He was unspeakably tired, but rest seemed out of the question. The constant pain made it difficult to sleep, and when he did manage to drop off, he was invariably awakened by someone checking his blood pressure, or temperature, or whatever other bits of him they were monitoring. He was beginning to feel that if only he could get a solid night's sleep, he would really be quite all right.

There was someone in the room with him now, moving about very quietly, from which he deduced that it was probably his mother, settling herself in to wait till he woke up. He decided nothing much would be gained for either of them by his advancing this moment; there was not much to talk about between parent and child when the child in question had been shot, felt quite horrible, and was in hospital running a fever, and the long silences were beginning to get on Gibbons's nerves. At the same time, he took comfort from his parents' presence and had not been able to summon the fortitude to tell them that he would be all right and they should go home. Quite irrationally, he wanted them here, even if their hovering got on his nerves, and that made him feel guilty.

So he lay quietly, trying to rest despite the pain, listening to the sound of his mother turning the pages of a magazine. She was not much of a reader—his father was the one for that—but she liked to look through a magazine occasionally. Since her arrival, he thought glumly, she had probably been through every magazine ever published twice over. This, too, made him feel guilty, and he sighed.

Some time had passed when he was roused by the unexpected sound of a dog's nails clicking on the linoleum floor. That this heralded Bethancourt's arrival was obvious, but Gibbons felt immediately disoriented, believing the day must be much further advanced than he had thought, as his friend was seldom out and about before late morning. Yet, when he opened his eyes, the clock on the wall proclaimed it to be only 9:15.

"There, you're awake," said his mother, closing the magazine in her lap at once.

"Oh, dear," said Bethancourt, halting just inside the doorway. "Did I wake him? Sorry, old man. I thought they'd have you up at dawn in this place."

"They did," grunted Gibbons, cautiously moving. "They're always waking me up."

"Here," said his mother, "let me put the bed up for you."

Behind his glasses, Bethancourt's hazel eyes were full of concern as he watched the agonizing process of Gibbons shifting to a sitting position in the bed.

"It's not as bad as it looks," gasped Gibbons as he made a last adjustment.

"I'm sure it's bad enough," replied Bethancourt. "I'm awfully sorry you've come in for this, Jack."

"So am I," retorted Gibbons.

He laid his head back on the pillow and closed his eyes for a moment, needing to recover from his efforts. Bethancourt had brought a coffee in with him, and the smell was driving Gibbons wild, both attracting and repelling him at the same time. He swallowed uneasily past the tube in his throat.

"So what brings you out so early?" he asked at last, opening his eyes again.

"Your guv'nor," answered Bethancourt, who had settled himself in a second chair. "He rang me at dawn, apparently thinking I would be up and ready for anything by that time."

Gibbons smiled, though his mother—to whom the idea of sleeping past seven was entirely alien—looked a little puzzled. It suddenly occurred to him to wonder what his parents were making of Bethancourt. They had met before, of course, but they had never spent much time alone together before this.

"What did the chief inspector want then?" he asked.

Bethancourt looked rather pleased. "He wanted me to read a report of a conversation you had with Chris O'Leary on the night you were shot. He has an idea that I might be better at reconstructing your thought process than he is himself."

"Does he now?" Gibbons's eyebrows shot up. "Is there some reason he doesn't think I would be equally good at it? It's my bloody thought process after all."

"I don't know," answered Bethancourt cheerfully. "I wondered the same thing."

"He's probably trying to spare you any stress," put in his mother practically. "He's really very concerned about you, you know."

Her expression, if not her tone, showed clearly that Carmichael was not alone in this. Gibbons narrowed his eyes at her.

"There's nothing you're not telling me, is there?" he demanded.

She just sighed and shook her head, so he transferred the glare to Bethancourt.

"Don't look at me," said his friend. "I told you what I found out—you have peritonitis and will be feeling poorly until the antibiotics manage to knock it out of you."

"I was feeling plenty poorly before," muttered Gibbons.

"This is a different sort of poorly," explained Bethancourt.

"You are very ill indeed," interrupted his mother. "They still expect you to make a full recovery, but it will take some time."

Gibbons didn't want it to take time, he wanted to feel better at once. Most of all, he wanted the pain to go away. It startled him to realize that he could no longer remember a painless existence. He knew quite well the pain had not always been there, and could remember going about his business without such an encumbrance, but the actual sensation of being without pain no longer seemed to be stored in his brain.

The door opened and Nurse Pipp appeared, smiling brightly. "Good morning, everyone," she said.

Bethancourt and his mother returned murmured salutations while the nurse moved briskly into the room, her eyes immediately seeking out the monitors.

"Well, you're not doing too badly, all things considered," she said, smiling down at Gibbons and gently taking hold of his wrist to check the pulse. "How do you feel?"

Gibbons had given up trying to pretend he was all right. "Pretty rotten," he answered. "I feel awfully weak."

"That's only to be expected," she answered, folding back the covers and bending to listen to his abdomen with a stethoscope. "That infection will have you feeling as weak as a baby for a bit yet." She frowned, concentrating and shifting the stethoscope a bit. "I think I'm beginning to hear some bowel sounds," she said with satisfaction, straightening. "That's very good, very good indeed."

Gibbons felt a warm glow, as if he had accomplished something, though in fact he had no control over the functioning of his bowels. He grinned up at Nurse Pipp like a schoolboy at a teacher who has given him a gold star.

She continued checking him over while his mother listened anxiously and Bethancourt excused himself lest his presence prove an embarrassment. Gibbons submitted to her ministrations more or less gracefully, largely because his mother was present.

"Oh," said Nurse Pipp as she was tucking the blanket in around him, "I almost forgot—there's something for you out at the nurses' station. I meant to bring it in with me."

"What is it?" asked Gibbons.

"Well, I don't know, do I?" replied Nurse Pipp. "That nice chief inspector of yours came by and handed it to the night nurse last night while you were asleep."

"Carmichael?" said Gibbons, surprised. "He was here?"

"So Julie said." Nurse Pipp stepped back and cast an expert eye over him. "I'm going to have to get you up later, you know," she warned.

Gibbons could not suppress a grimace. "I can't see," he said, "what difference it makes if I'm sitting up in bed or sitting in a chair."

"It makes a world of difference to your circulation," she told him. "Don't forget, you've had a serious operation."

"I'm hardly likely to forget," snapped Gibbons miserably. "It hurts like bloody hell."

"Jack," chided his mother. "You shouldn't use such language to Nurse Pipp. She's only got your best interests in mind."

Gibbons gritted his teeth. "Sorry," he managed.

"It's all right," said Nurse Pipp, smiling to show that it really was. "I've heard worse in my time—and you can hardly expect people to be on their best behavior when they're in hospital. Now, you ring if you want anything, and I'll send an orderly in with that envelope."

Gibbons, who knew from recent experience that the orderly might show up in the next five minutes or the next five hours, cast a desperate glance at his mother. But she was smiling up at Nurse Pipp and did not see him.

Happily Bethancourt must have been waiting just outside, because he poked his head back in almost as soon as Nurse Pipp was gone, smiling tentatively and saying, "All settled again?"

"Yes, yes," answered Gibbons impatiently. "Carmichael left an envelope for me last night—can you run after her and find it?"

"Righto," said Bethancourt, and disappeared again.

Gibbons leaned back against his pillows, enervated by this little effort. His mother frowned at him.

"You should rest," she said gently. "I don't see why you can't leave other people to do their jobs. You're just like your father."

Gibbons ignored this. "Where is Dad?" he asked.

"He didn't have a good night, so I let him sleep in," his mother replied.

A smile touched Gibbons's lips because that was so like his mother, always taking care of everyone, making sure they all were fed and rested and set up as best she could see to it. Sadly, he reflected, none of that seemed to be doing him much good in the present case. His father, he was sure, was suffering from being the only one available for his mother to take care of.

He sighed, turned his head more comfortably on the pillow, and dropped into a doze.

He woke again, as he nearly always did now, because of the pain. Once on the threshold of consciousness, the combination of the sharp ache in his belly and a general malaise prevented him from drifting back off and so, like a hippopotamus heaving itself out of the muddy shallows, his mind struggled back to reality and his hospital room.

His mother had resumed her perusal of her magazine, although he could tell she was not really taking any of it in, and Bethancourt had returned and was comfortably ensconced in the second chair, long legs negligently crossed while he paged through some papers, a thoughtful expression on his face. Cerberus alone seemed to realize Gibbons was awake again, lifting his head to look at the patient in an inquiring manner.

The movement caught Bethancourt's attention and he, too, looked up, smiling when he saw Gibbons's eyes were open.

"Back among us, are you?" he said.

His mother also smiled. "Did you have a nice sleep, dear?" she asked.

Gibbons merely grunted in reply, but Bethancourt, with customary aplomb, smoothed over the moment by saying, "I winkled your envelope out of Nurse Pipp—here it is."

He rose to hand Gibbons a manila envelope, sealed and stamped with the Scotland Yard crest. Gibbons eyed it hungrily.

"Open it for me, will you?" he asked, knowing his fingers would fumble it.

Bethancourt efficiently ripped the envelope open and handed it to his friend, relaxing back into his chair while he watched Gibbons pull out the papers within and then blink rapidly to focus on them.

"It seems to be O'Leary's report," he said in a moment.

"Ah," said Bethancourt. "Then Carmichael was only hedging his bets when he gave a copy to me. You have a go at it now, and then we can brainstorm."

Gibbons was not sure his brain was currently capable of brainstorming, but nothing could have stopped him from reading the report. His mother, he noted, had her lips firmly pressed together and a doubtful look in her eye, an expression he translated as meaning that she was unsure as to whether this exercise would be good or bad for her newly wounded son. Before she could make up her mind, he began to read, thereby settling the question, or so he hoped.

His hopes were justified when he heard her sigh and say, "I'll leave you two to work it out, then."

"There's no need for you to go," said Bethancourt quickly. "If any of this was classified police business, Carmichael would never have let me see it. You might have some thoughts of your own."

She laughed heartily at this idea, and shook her head. "You're a kind lad, but I'd never keep it all straight. I'll go find myself a cuppa and have a chat with the nurses."

"Thanks, Mum," said Gibbons, smiling at her to show he appreciated her tact.

"Don't you tire yourself out," she replied. "You see to it he doesn't, Phillip."

"Yes, ma'am," said Bethancourt meekly.

Grinning faintly, Gibbons returned his attention to the report. His vision seemed oddly fuzzy, and he had to blink rapidly several times to make the print come into focus.

It was very strange indeed to be reading about his own actions—and to recognize himself in some of the dialogue quoted—and yet to have no recollection at all of the events described. He read doggedly, rather admiring the amount of detail O'Leary managed to cram in, although privately he thought his own writing style was superior. He tried to drink in all the detail, but found himself reading many parts twice in an effort to keep it all in his head, something he would never have had to do in the normal way of things.

All in all, it was quite some time before he reached the part where O'Leary mentioned the Pennycook murder.

"Pennycook?" he said, feeling confused. "In Walworth? Is that why I was there?"

He looked up to find Bethancourt stifling an enormous yawn.

"What?" said Bethancourt, reaching up to resettle his glasses on his nose and push his hair out of his eyes. "Oh, right, the murder. Well, no one knows why you went haring off to Walworth. Do you think you would have, if you had a good idea about the case after O'Leary left?"

Gibbons frowned and looked doubtful. "It doesn't seem very likely, does it?" he asked. "I mean, why wouldn't I simply have rung

O'Leary? Why should I take myself all the way down to Walworth when it's not even my case? And," he added, more practically, "it wouldn't have taken me till nine to get from St. James to Walworth in any case."

"No," agreed Bethancourt. "But we don't know what time you did get there. You might have been investigating for hours."

Gibbons was unconvinced. "No." He shook his head. "If I'd had an idea about O'Leary's case, I might just have checked it out a bit before telling him, but I would never have spent hours investigating it without him."

"True," said Bethancourt, stroking his chin and looking thoughtful. "I hadn't thought of it that way. So you must have been fairly recently arrived when you were shot."

"Only if I was there looking into the Pennycook thing," said Gibbons. "If I was there for some other reason, well, there's no telling really."

"Might you have gone to look at a pawnshop?" suggested Bethancourt.

"What?" demanded Gibbons, looking totally lost. "Why on earth should I have done that?"

"Well, you were investigating a jewel robbery," explained Bethancourt. "Stolen jewelry has to be fenced, doesn't it?"

"It doesn't have to be fenced in Walworth," retorted Gibbons.

"But I was thinking that O'Leary's talk of pawnshops and jewelry might have made a connection in your head."

Gibbons closed his eyes. "If it did," he said in a moment, eyes still shut, "it's not there now. And I still don't see why I would have gone to Walworth, particularly not after all the shops were shut."

"Oh," said Bethancourt, crestfallen. "Yes. They would have been shut by then, wouldn't they?"

"Good Lord," muttered Gibbons wearily. "Things have come to a fine pass when your thinking isn't any clearer than someone whose head is stuffed with morphine." In fact, he rather resented Bethancourt's muddied thinking. It seemed to him that if anyone was justified in having impaired reasoning, it was himself, not his friend.

Bethancourt grinned sheepishly.

"I had this whole Pennycook connection thrown at me too early this morning," he complained. "There I was, all absorbed in elite jewel thefts, and then Carmichael wakes me up at an ungodly hour and tosses this grotty little murder at me. What do you expect?"

Gibbons started to laugh, which shifted the tube in his throat and made him cough instead. Which in turn made him cringe with the pain and curl onto his side, shivering.

"God, I'm sorry, Jack," said Bethancourt, truly penitent. "I never thought—I'm sorry. Do you want me to do anything? Should I ring—"

Gibbons waved a hand at him to quiet him, and Bethancourt obediently fell silent. But Gibbons, even with his eyes closed, could feel his friend hovering, tensed and ready to leap into whatever action might be called for.

Slowly the worst of the pain receded and he was able to catch his breath and ease himself back up on the pillows. Bethancourt was sitting bolt upright in his chair and Cerberus was on his feet, watching him as if deciding whether or not he needed rescuing. Gibbons managed a wan smile to reassure them, but in truth he was done in for the moment.

"I think we'd better finish this later," he said hoarsely.

"Right," said Bethancourt, popping to his feet. "I really am dreadfully sorry, Jack."

"You don't have to be sorry," said Gibbons, a little irritated by this third apology. "Just come back later, all right?"

"Certainly," said Bethancourt, gathering up his coat. "Count on it. Cerberus, come."

Gibbons, left alone, swallowed carefully, shifted his position slightly, and then lay very still until he fell into a fitful doze.

10

Dead Ends

*T*wo days' worth of work had produced a wealth of negatives, thought Carmichael sourly as he gazed down in frustration at the list he was endeavoring to make of Gibbons's movements on Tuesday evening.

He was compiling the schedule from a wealth of brief reports that had been filed, it seemed to him, by half the London constabulary, and which outlined some of the many things Gibbons had not done on Tuesday night. He had not returned to the Yard, or been seen at his flat in Hammersmith or at any of the nearby establishments that he was known to patronize there. Here his landlady, who lived upstairs, had been very helpful, pointing out the various pubs, restaurants, and shops Gibbons often went to.

Gibbons had not entered the underground station at St. James, and interviews with various bus drivers were still ongoing. He had not eaten at any of the usual haunts of young detectives in the area.

But in all the piles of paper before Carmichael, there was not a hint as to where Gibbons had gone or what he had done when he got there.

"Why the devil," muttered Carmichael to himself, "couldn't it have been a balmy summer night with half the population out on the street? That would have been some help."

But, of course, it hadn't been. It had been a nasty, blustery, cold November night, the kind of night on which everyone hurried home as quickly as possible, their attentions firmly fixed on their own warm firesides.

The phone rang and Carmichael picked it up with a growl. Ian Hodges, however, had never been known to be impressed by anybody's temper but his own.

"The mobile's done," he announced without preamble. "I'm faxing the list of numbers over to you now."

"Gibbons's mobile?" said Carmichael, rather surprised.

Hodges snorted. "Of course Gibbons's," he answered scornfully. "Would I be ringing about anyone else? And don't bother me about the notebook," he added in a warning tone. "It's in awful shape and we're working as fast as we dare. If you want it unreadable, you can have it now."

"It won't do me any good if I can't read what's in it," retorted Carmichael. A sudden awful thought occurred to him. "You are going to be able to salvage it, aren't you, Hodges?"

"Remains to be seen," replied Hodges shortly. "There. Jennings says your phone list has gone."

And he rang off.

Carmichael picked up the fax himself, but then sent Constable Lemmy to make copies of it and to do the tedious work of matching the unidentified numbers with their owners. In his present mood, he hadn't really much hope the numbers on Gibbons's mobile would lead anywhere, but at least it was something new to work on.

The rain had stopped when Bethancourt emerged from University College Hospital, so he turned without much thought in the direction of Regent's Park. He liked to walk when his mind was occupied; strolling along with his dog at his side and perhaps smoking a cigarette was his preferred method of letting his thoughts wander and seeing what came of it. And Cerberus was more than happy to let his master indulge himself in this.

So they turned into the gray world of the park in winter, walking briskly to keep warm and trying to avoid the puddles—as well as the raindrops, which periodically blew off the tree branches—while Bethancourt tried to avoid thoughts of Gibbons wrung out with pain in his hospital bed. There was no doubt the incident had unnerved him.

"Life's a funny old thing," he observed to his dog while he strolled along and tried to recover his composure. "One thinks one's prepared for it, but there's always something around the corner one's never thought of."

Cerberus wagged his tail, keeping most of his attention on a squirrel running across the lawn some distance away.

"Right," said Bethancourt. "Back to business. Only I don't seem to be getting very far with this business. It could be," he added, somewhat despondently, "that I'm not much of a detective without Jack."

Cerberus's silence was disdainful, or so it seemed to his master.

Bethancourt sighed, and tried to think positively. Surely there was some line he could pursue on his own. He could hardly hope to find the jewelry himself, not with both Colin James and Scotland Yard hot on the trail, but perhaps he might contribute some color to the picture they were painting.

"What about the other people mentioned in Miss Haverford's will?" he asked aloud.

After all, so far as he could make out, the Colemans had not, until recently, played much of a role in Miranda Haverford's life. It could be possible that either her maid or this Ned Winterbottom had believed they would inherit the jewelry, and upon discovering that they did not, had taken steps to insure that they would receive it anyhow. If Gibbons had suspected that, it would provide either of them with motive to shoot him. Well, Bethancourt corrected himself, not the maid, since she was dead, but her heirs.

He rather suspected that this was exactly the kind of flight of fancy that Carmichael had been referring to earlier, but it was all he could think of.

"I'll need to talk to the solicitor," he muttered to himself. "Which means I'll need an introduction. Someone must know the blighter."

Cerberus had paused to inspect the base of a tree, so Bethancourt took the opportunity to take out his mobile and ring his own solicitor. Ronald Fairclough, Esq., was meeting with another client, but his secretary assured Bethancourt he would ring back at the earliest opportunity.

"It's nothing important," said Bethancourt. "I only want a favor. Tell him to take his time."

That accomplished, and the tree duly marked by Cerberus, the two moved on. And Bethancourt, looking down at his pet, had another idea.

"I can't very well demand Chief Inspector Carmichael or Colin James keep me abreast of their investigations," he said. "But James does appear to enjoy walking his dog of an evening. And you've not been for a nice ramble on Hampstead Heath for a long while, have you, Cerberus? A casual meeting on the Heath isn't at all the same thing as importuning a mere acquaintance."

Cerberus seemed to agree; at least he wagged his feathered tail in what seemed to Bethancourt to be approval.

"We'll go this evening, then," he said, well satisfied with this plan.

That left what he should do at the moment. It was beginning to rain again, so he whistled to Cerberus and turned back, still puzzling over this question. He had just decided that he had better find some other distraction while he waited for word from his solicitor when his mobile rang. But it was not Fairclough.

"It's a perfectly awful day out," said Marla. "I just nipped out to pick up some salad doings, and I got chilled to the bone. So I bought some champagne and orange juice."

A smile was playing about Bethancourt's lips. "You're a woman of infinite resources," he said. "Are you warm again now?"

"I could use a bit of help there," Marla admitted. "Also, I think I could use some help with this champagne. Now I've got it home, it looks an awfully big bottle."

"I am at your command," said Bethancourt. "I shall be round at once."

"Good," she purred. "I'll get out of my boots and coat and see you soon, then."

Inspector Grant Davies smoothed his tie and regarded Martin Bloore thoughtfully.

They were sitting in a pleasant pub just off New Bond Street. The establishment had been refurbished for the tourist trade with pale woods, cozy upholstery, and wide windows that let in the thin afternoon light.

Across the table from Davies, Bloore sat at his ease, an overweight man with a cherubic face and round blue eyes, dressed in bespoke tailoring. He habitually wore a slight smile, indicative of arrogance, but it was absent at the present moment in the interests of sincerity. The problem was, Davies believed him.

"Truly, Inspector," Bloore said. "I haven't got your jewels."

Davies smiled. "But, Martin," he said, "that's what you'd tell me if you had got them."

"Nonsense," replied Bloore automatically. "If I had found them, I would naturally alert the police at once like any good citizen."

Davies let this pass at face value. "Of course you would," he answered. "I never implied otherwise, did I? I merely asked if, in the course of your business transactions, you had possibly heard of some less principled citizen who might have an eye for heritage jewelry."

But Bloore shook his head. "Odd things do sometimes come to my ears," he admitted. "Only rumors, of course, but they stick in the mind nonetheless. But not in this case, Inspector. If you ask me, somewhere out there is a group of smash-and-grabbers, scared out of their wits. They're probably sitting on the jewelry with their knickers in a twist even as we speak."

"But in that case," objected Davies, "you'd have thought they would have tried to unload their bounty before they realized what they'd got. I understand, of course, that sort of thing would be beneath your radar, but I'd have expected my own sources to get wind of it."

"True, true," said Bloore, shaking his head with an exaggerated sigh. "It's a mystery."

And Davies, however unfortunately, believed it was as much of a mystery to Bloore as it was to himself. But Bloore would be looking now and some judicious surveillance should alert him if the old criminal found anything.

"Well, thanks for meeting me, Martin," he said, swallowing the last of his beer.

"Always a pleasure to be of help, Inspector," replied Bloore, the slightly condescending smile returning to his round face.

But it was very odd, thought Davies, as he buttoned up his overcoat and adjusted his scarf before leaving the pub. He had contacted Bloore because if a big heist like the theft of the Haverford jewels had been in the planning, he would have expected Bloore to get wind of it. Not necessarily that Bloore would have known exactly what was afoot, but he would have been aware that certain people had disappeared from the scene, and he might have been willing to mention a name or two to Davies. Particularly if Bloore had no reason to believe he himself could lay hands on the jewels. Bloore knew well enough that if Davies could take him down, he would, but thus far Bloore had avoided that fate, and by occasionally making himself useful, he ensured that he did not become Davies's top priority.

But if Davies was any judge, Bloore had heard and noticed nothing. And considering how easy the theft had been to carry out, that might mean that it was an amateur job, which would leave the field wide open.

When Gibbons next came to, his father had arrived and it was apparently lunchtime on the ward from the sounds of carts and trays coming in from the hallway. His father was hunched over a battered paperback edition of *Far from the Madding Crowd*, his thick fingers keeping the pages spread apart on his lap. He looked up when he heard his son stir.

"Hullo, lad," he said, smiling a little, but not as falsely or brightly as his wife. "How are you doing, then?"

Gibbons blinked and remembered to swallow cautiously around the tube in his throat before answering, "Well enough, I suppose."

"You're a bit pale," said his father, eyeing him judiciously, as if evaluating the quality of a cut of meat. "It's a pity about this infection thing."

"It's more the damn tube than anything else," said Gibbons. "Have they given you any idea when I can have it out?"

"Not much longer, I don't think," his father answered. "They said they only leave it in for a few days after surgery. And of course they wanted to make sure no further surgery was needed. But they seem to have decided you're holding together all right."

He grinned at his youngest son, and Gibbons managed a wan grin back.

"I'm glad of that, at least," he said.

"There was a young man here," continued his father. "Said he'd come back when you were awake."

"What did he want?" asked Gibbons suspiciously.

"He didn't say. He only had a clipboard, though. Maybe it's something about the national health."

"Brilliant," muttered Gibbons. The very last thing he needed was to have a bureaucrat added to his endless list of medical visitors. It felt as if they could not leave him alone for five minutes.

"Ah," said his father. "Here's the lad come back again."

"Hello, Mr. Gibbons," said the new arrival. "I'm Ernest Fursdon, your physiotherapist."

Gibbons regarded him sourly. Fursdon was a trim, painfully fit young man about Gibbons's own age, and looking at him reminded Gibbons that before he had been shot, he had been meaning to make a few sit-ups part of his morning routine. Fursdon's regular features were attractive without being handsome and somehow made his face very forgettable, at least in Gibbons's opinion.

"I'm here to get you moving again," continued Fursdon. To his credit, he said it quite seriously, without the trace of a cheerful smile.

"So soon?" asked Gibbons's father doubtfully, while Gibbons continued to regard this apparition from his bed with a baleful gaze that suggested he was sizing up his chances of successfully strangling the man, or at least turning him out.

Fursdon turned to the elder Gibbons readily. "I know it seems awfully soon," he said. "But you have to remember how young your son is and how well he's healing already. The danger now is not that he'll do further damage to his wound, but that he'll have complications from lying about too much. If we can get him moving early, his body will be free to concentrate on healing the original injury, instead of getting sidetracked by other problems."

Gibbons wanted to ask exactly what other problems they were worried he would develop, but the truth was that he could already feel, beneath the pain of his wound and the ache from his fever, odd kinks in his back and legs. There was no denying his body was accustomed to spending a good part of every day moving fairly energetically about, and was beginning to feel the change.

"Oh, very well, if you insist," he said, giving way ungracefully.

"I'm afraid it really is for the best," said Fursdon apologetically, laying his clipboard aside. "I've brought you some slippers to wear—the floors are chilly this time of year."

"Is this really going to help?" gasped Gibbons as he tried to sit up and was assailed by a fire blooming in his belly.

"Oh, yes, certainly," replied Fursdon, catching his arm in a practiced move and easing him into a sitting position. "You'll definitely be back to your old self much sooner if you can manage to move about a bit."

And that gave Gibbons the strength of mind to endure the sheer torture that was his lot for the next five minutes. With Fursdon's guidance, he shuffled painfully over a distance that he would once have encompassed in a couple of steps. He was quite pale and sweating with the effort when Fursdon at last returned him to his bed.

"I know that was rough," he said, lifting Gibbons's legs back into the bed, "but you did remarkably well. You're making a quite miraculous recovery."

Gibbons was too exhausted to reply. The physical activity—if it could really be classified as such—had put his temperature back up and he was almost shaking with the ache that seemed to seep out of his very bones. The fire that had begun in his abdomen with the first movement had coalesced into a fierce blaze that would not abate.

He was barely aware as Fursdon drew the blankets back over him and rearranged the IV tubes. Before the therapist had left the room, he had already dropped into the gray world of half-consciousness.

Colin James frowned as he replaced the telephone receiver, severing the connection with his contact in Amsterdam. Jan Stoeltie was a renowned diamond expert, one who kept a sharp ear to the ground for any deals concerning the brilliant gems. But he had heard nothing at all about an antique Golconda diamond like the one from the Haverford collection.

"Though it does rather remind me of one that was on the market a number of years ago," he had told James. "Sold on the quiet, as I recall, but a most remarkable jewel. Twelve carats, like the one you're describing. It would have fetched a fortune at auction."

"How long ago was this?" asked James, his interest piqued.

"Oh, quite some time ago," Stoeltie answered, searching his memory. "Fifteen years? Something like that at any rate."

James's interest evaporated. "No good to me, then," he said, a little reproachfully, but Stoeltie did not seem to notice the tone.

"No," he agreed cheerfully. "Still, diamonds like that tend to stick in the mind. I'll put some feelers out for you, Colin. But to be honest, I can't really imagine there's a stone like that out on the market that I haven't heard of."

And this, James admitted to himself, was probably true.

His eyes narrowed as he swiveled in his chair to gaze out the windows of his City office. The cold gray of the sky reflected the equally cold gray of his eyes as he ruminated on what he had learned—or, more accurately, had not learned.

The alexandrite necklace was by far the most recognizable piece in the Haverford collection, but there were other notable elements. The Golconda diamond brooch, for example, or the Colombian emerald ring. Or even the pearls. When he had not been able to find any trace of the alexandrite necklace, he had begun to search for word of the other pieces, thinking that any intelligent thief might reason that the famed necklace was better sat on until after the uproar had died down. But there was, so far as he could determine, no hint of any of the jewels on the market at all. And that was peculiar.

His fingers tapped an impatient staccato on the arm of his chair, while he shuffled through possibilities in his mind. None of them were promising, and some were too extreme to undertake until all other lines had been followed. As determined as he was about solving this case, James was not yet ready to go to extremes.

There was a discreet knock on his door and his secretary Vivian appeared, cool and stylish as usual, with her shining dark hair done up in a French twist. Oddly contrasting with this sartorial elegance were the pair of baggy latex gloves, which covered her slender hands.

"Mr. Loggins is on line one about the Barshot case," she murmured.

"To hell with the Barshot case," retorted James. "I don't give a fig for it."

Vivian's habitual calm was broken by the slightest of smiles. "But Mr. Loggins does," she reminded him.

"He would," snorted James, swinging round to his desk and noticing the gloves for the first time. "Oh, damn it, Viv, are you still on about that?"

"I know police procedures just as well as you do," she assured him.

"We don't need to follow police procedures because the police aren't going to be called in," said James. "If I've said it once, I've said it a thousand times: they're just crank letters."

"Of course they are," Vivian answered with false sincerity. "And when their writer has murdered you, I shall have all the letters with their envelopes for the police, uncontaminated by fingerprints."

"Great heavens, woman, you're enough to try the patience of a saint!" thundered James. "Out with you! Out!"

Smiling more broadly now, Vivian withdrew while James swore at her and reached for the phone to placate Mr. Loggins.

11

The Witness

Carmichael was ordered to report to Detective Superintendent Walter Lumsden, a necessity that made him scowl. He hated to be interrupted by his superiors in the course of an investigation, although—he admitted to himself—he ought to be used to it by now. Still, he wished he had put on his gray suit this morning instead of just a sports jacket, and he spent some time assuring himself that his tie and shirtfront were free of coffee stains.

Lumsden, of course, merely wished for an update both on the case and on Gibbons's condition, as well as to convey his sympathies. He offered coffee to convey the personal nature of his inquiries, and Carmichael perforce had to sit for ten minutes and converse politely in order to satisfy his superior's need to feel in charge. Ten minutes was not long in the scheme of things, but Carmichael found it irritating nonetheless, and was in no very good mood when he returned. Nor was his temper much improved when he found Hollings had rung while he was out.

"I've just turned up a little thing," said Hollings when Carmichael rang him back. He sounded cheerful, which Carmichael took as a good sign despite his cautious words. "Probably not much help in the grand scheme of things, but I thought you'd want to know."

"I do want to know," said Carmichael firmly. "What have you got?"

"Well, I've found someone else who saw Gibbons that night," said Hollings, unable to keep the pride from his voice. "At least, he's reasonably sure it was Gibbons, and if he's right, then he puts Gibbons's arrival in Walworth at about half eight that night."

"That's good work, Hollings," said Carmichael. "I didn't think we'd get any more there. I'll want to talk to this fellow."

"Thought you would," said Hollings. "He says he'll be at his flat all afternoon today. Shall I give you the address?"

"Yes, go ahead."

Hollings read off a name and address, which Carmichael scribbled on the back of a sheet from one of the many reports on his desk.

"Got it," he said. "I'll run down there now. Thanks, Hollings—you're a wonder."

Carmichael rang off, crammed the paper with the address into his pocket, and rose, snagging his jacket off the back of his chair as he headed for the door. There he nearly ran headlong into Constable Lemmy, who loomed up in the door frame at the last possible moment, causing Carmichael to draw up sharply. The encounter was so unexpected that Carmichael scowled at his subordinate without meaning to.

"Sorry, sir," said Lemmy, stepping back.

Carmichael remembered that he was not supposed to resent his assistants and resettled his features into a neutral expression.

"You'll have to walk with me, Constable," he said. "I'm on my way out. What have you got?"

He started down the hallway and Lemmy scurried to keep up with him.

"Got, sir?" he inquired doubtfully.

"Yes." Carmichael wondered if he would ever have a conversation with Lemmy in which he would not have to manfully restrain his temper after the first two sentences. "I assume there was a reason you came to see me?"

"Oh. Yes, sir. I was just wondering, sir, if you remembered the name of Sergeant Gibbons's cousin?"

Carmichael quickened his pace as he rounded the corner and saw the lift doors just opening up ahead.

"Gibbons's cousin?" he repeated. "You mean the day-care woman?" He was, he realized, unreasonably annoyed that Lemmy did not remember himself, although the constable had not been present for the interview. "Dawn Melton," he answered.

"Yes, I thought that was it." Lemmy nodded.

"Hi, there!" called out Carmichael as the lift doors began to close again. "Hold the door, please!"

The doors reversed their motion and a head peered out.

"Did you need anything else?" asked Carmichael as he reached the lift and nodded to the man holding the door open.

"Oh. No, sir. That's what I wanted."

"Good, good," said Carmichael, stepping in. "I'll be back soon, Constable. See how many of those phone numbers you can get through while I'm gone, eh?"

And with that he stepped into the lift and felt his shoulders relax as the door closed. He was quite certain that never in the long course of his career had he had a subordinate so aggravating.

When Carmichael knocked on the door of Tom Gerrard's flat in Walworth, it was opened by a young giant of a man, well over six feet tall and very fit-looking, dressed in an ancient football jersey and a pair of faded jeans. He was also, however, very soft-spoken, and asked the detective in politely, though something in his eyes told Carmichael Gerrard was not altogether comfortable talking to the police. Since his accent placed him as a native of the Walworth area, Carmichael deduced that this reluctance was more an ingrained result of growing up in a poor London neighborhood than anything specific to Gibbons's case. He was rather surprised the young man had come forward at all.

Gerrard motioned Carmichael to a chair and took the sofa himself, sitting uneasily on its edge with his hands clasped between his knees.

"I work for Ryman, the stationery shop," he told Carmichael. "I'm a supervisor at the Lower Marsh shop, and I was to go down to the Brighton shop for a couple of days' training. They wanted me there early Wednesday, so I left on Tuesday night."

Carmichael nodded; this fit in with his first assessment of Gerrard: a young man from a poor background who was working his way up.

"You took the bus to the train station?" he asked.

"That's right," said Gerrard. "My train went from London Bridge, so I caught the number forty bus out on Walworth Road. It goes right by the station."

"But no doubt you had to wait for it?" asked Carmichael encouragingly.

"Only because I missed the first bus," replied Gerrard gloomily. "I was coming along East Street, nearly to Walworth, when I saw the bus on the other side of the street. I tried to hurry, but there was no way I was going to make it across in time. In fact, I had to stop and wait for the light at the corner."

"Aggravating," said Carmichael sympathetically. "Was that when you saw my man?"

"Well, no, I saw the other one first," said Gerrard.

Carmichael's brows shot up; Hollings had not mentioned this. "There was another man?" he asked.

"That's right." Gerrard nodded. "I was waiting to cross the street, see, and wondering if I would still make my train. I checked my watch and it was half eight, which meant I still had time. And it was then the taxi pulled up to let his fare out, and I did just think of taking the taxi myself for a moment. It was a nasty night out, and I had the money on me. But I didn't know how much I'd need to spend in Brighton, and after a second, I decided to stick to the bus."

Carmichael nodded understanding; he was quite familiar with the momentary temptation to spend more than one should on some little luxury. Like Gerrard, he seldom gave in to it.

"It was a young man got out," continued Gerrard. "He headed toward East Street, I think. I didn't notice all that particularly, it's just that down here you tend to take note of people around you, especially at night."

"Of course," said Carmichael, a little at a loss to see what this had to do with Gibbons.

"It was then I saw your man," said Gerrard. "At least, I saw another taxi had stopped up the street and that fare was just getting out. He came down the street toward me, and I think it must have been your man. Bloke about my age, average height, stocky build."

"That would be right," said Carmichael, nodding. "Tell me, isn't it a bit unusual to see so many taxis in this area on a Tuesday night?"

For the first time, Gerrard relaxed enough to grin at him.

"You've got that right, guv," he said. "I thought it was downright unfair at the time, tempting me with all those taxis when I couldn't afford them. But that's what made it all stick in my mind, see, and when I got back today and heard you were looking for information about one of your own on that night, I thought to myself, well that's why there were two taxis: this police bloke was following someone."

Carmichael tried to contain his excitement at this information. It was better than merely putting a time on Gibbons's arrival in Walworth; it also gave the first clue as to why he had been here in the first place.

"That's very good indeed," he said. "Did you see where my man went?"

Gerrard shook his head regretfully. "No, sir," he said. "It was then the light changed and I was off across the street to wait for my bus."

"You've still been a very great help," Carmichael told him. "Most people never notice anything, you know. And it's very lucky for me you had a train to catch—we'd no notion of when my man had arrived here until you came forward. Thanks very much for letting us know—we do appreciate it."

Gerrard accepted this praise modestly, but Carmichael sensed he was both pleased and relieved.

"Glad I could help," he said.

Carmichael left Gerrard's elated. Observant witnesses were a rarity, and Tom Gerrard was a perfect gem. For the first time Carmichael felt that some of the pieces of this puzzle were falling into place. It was true that they still had two hours to account for, but if they could find the taxi and discover where he had picked Gibbons up, they might be well on the way to figuring out how he had spent his evening before being shot.

Inspector Hollings was still working at Lambeth station, so Carmichael headed there, eager to see how the search for the taxi was progressing.

"There's no news yet," Hollings told him. "I've put out the word to all the taxi companies, and arranged for advertisements in all the major papers tomorrow, but you know the drill, sir. There's not a lot to be done besides sitting back and waiting."

Carmichael did know the drill, but that did not keep him from wishing it were otherwise.

"How about the news tonight?" he asked.

"I've put public relations on that," replied Hollings. "They're going to have a spokesman do an announcement on the telly tonight, and they're preparing another one for the radio, but I don't think they've got it on yet."

Hollings looked up at his superior, who was chewing his lip, and added sympathetically, "I'm sure we'll hear something soon, sir. If not tonight, then by morning. We've just got to give it a bit of time, let the word get out, and the cabbies will turn up. They most always do."

Carmichael sighed. "I know," he said. "And my fussing at you won't make it happen any sooner."

"No, sir," said Hollings with a smile. "How are things coming from your end?"

"More waiting," growled Carmichael. "Only I'm waiting for forensics instead of taxi drivers. Although," he added, "they did come up with the list of phone numbers off Gibbons's mobile today. I've got Lemmy going through—oh, bloody hell!"

This exclamation came from out of nowhere, and Hollings was immediately alert.

"What is it, sir?" he asked.

"Lemmy." Carmichael spoke the name like a swear word, while he dug in his pocket for his mobile. "He was asking me as I was leaving about Gibbons's cousin, the one who lives down here. I've only just remembered."

"Do you think he's found something, then?" asked Hollings.

"I'll damn well bet he has," said Carmichael, clicking on his phone. "I'd set him to go over the phone numbers. I should have realized earlier that his asking about the bloody woman meant he'd found her number on the list."

Hollings looked startled. "But surely he'd have said so, wouldn't he?"

Carmichael glared at him in response while he held his phone to his ear. "It's Constable Lemmy we're talking about, Hollings. What do you think?"

Hollings, who had not had much to do with the constable, did not think it possible that anyone who had made detective could be that obtuse. He opened his mouth to say so, but Carmichael waved him to silence while he barked into the phone, "Constable? Yes, it's Carmichael. Did you find Dawn Melton's phone number on that list?"

Hollings, watching, was alarmed to see Carmichael's complexion redden with fury.

"And when did Sergeant Gibbons ring that number?" he demanded. He listened for a moment, and then said, in a voice dripping with sarcasm, "Thank you so much for letting me know, Constable," before ringing off without waiting for Lemmy's reply.

Hollings raised an eyebrow, but refrained from comment until his superior had finished venting his temper by swearing a blue streak.

"I take it," he asked mildly once Carmichael's invective seemed to have run down, "that Gibbons rang his cousin that night?"

"Too bloody right he did," snarled Carmichael. "She was the last call he made before he rang and left that message for me. And she swore she hadn't heard from him in weeks. Oh, damn and blast, why couldn't the idiot have told me earlier?!"

To this Hollings wisely made no reply.

"I want her brought in for questioning," Carmichael told him, and Hollings did not envy Dawn this summons. "Have her brought to the Yard," continued Carmichael. "I want to put the fear of God into the little chit."

"Do you think," ventured Hollings, "that she really might have shot Gibbons?"

"I don't know." Carmichael seemed to deflate suddenly and his eyes looked bleak. "I hope not. I've hoped all along that this mess has nothing to do with Gibbons's personal life. An investigation is such an awful intrusion. But I can't think why the woman would have lied about a phone call from her own cousin."

The two men exchanged grim looks, neither of them having to voice what they knew of the horrors that could be uncovered in family life.

"I'll send some uniforms to pick her up," said Hollings. "What's the address of that day-care center?"

Carmichael gave it to him from memory.

Gibbons was blessedly alone when he woke again. He could not remember the last time that had happened and lay quietly, reveling in the peace. His abdomen still throbbed, but he thought he felt a little less nauseous than he had been.

He could not tell how long he stayed like that before he began to idly pick out the details of the room. Someone had shifted the chairs about while he had been sleeping; they were pushed back against the wall by the bureau instead of drawn up to the bedside as he last remembered them. The small detritus that had been left on his bed-tray table was gone and in its place the police envelope containing O'Leary's report sat with its corners neatly aligned with that of the table. Beside it lay a small shopping bag that he did not recognize.

Gibbons frowned at it. He was quite certain no one had brought in anything for him in the course of the day, nor did he remember any of his many visitors coming in with it. And yet, one of them must have. He hated that even such a small thing had escaped his notice, and he glared at the bag as if affronted by it.

But gradually indignity began to give way to curiosity. Part of what made Gibbons such a good detective was his perennial curiosity—he simply was incapable of leaving a question unanswered. Right now, nothing hurt very much and he did not want to move and disturb that status quo. But he had to know what was in the bag.

Gingerly, he shifted himself up on one elbow, bracing himself against the expected sharp spasm of pain, and reached out to grab the bag off the table and drag it onto his lap. Panting a little with the effort, he peered down into the open top.

The contents were not very exciting, only a couple of notebooks with cardboard covers and four plastic mechanical pencils. But it made Gibbons smile.

There was a telephone on the bedside cabinet, which was positioned somewhere behind him. He had seen it as he had tottered back into bed that morning, and it had particularly struck him as he had not suspected its existence before.

He tilted his head on the pillow, craning his neck to peer up behind him. Beyond the bed railing he could just see the square little chest with the old-fashioned white telephone perched on it. It was quite definitely out of reach.

Gibbons sighed and considered his choices. He could ring for help and some helpful person in scrubs would no doubt come and give him the phone. Or he could wait, enjoy his peace and quiet until the inevitable interruption, and ask for the phone then. If, he added to himself sourly, he was still awake. Lastly, he could screw his courage to the sticking point, endure the pain, and fetch the phone himself.

He contemplated these unenviable choices and began to wish he had never thought of ringing Bethancourt. But he knew, really, which choice he would make in the end.

"They keep telling me moving is good for me," he muttered, and he pushed himself into a sitting position. The pain was as intense as he had expected and he paused for a moment, absorbing it, before moving his legs out of bed. That, of course, engendered a new wave of pain, but what he had not anticipated was the shakiness that being upright caused. He felt quite dizzy and weak and had to sit on the edge of the bed for several minutes before he could once again focus on his goal. He glared at the telephone, which was now within easy reach of anyone who had not recently been shot. Hanging on to the bed rail, he pushed himself to his feet, shuffled forward a step or two, and seized the telephone. Clutching this prize to his chest with one hand, he staggered back to the bed and eased himself back down with a grateful sigh. Lifting his feet back in cost him an effort, and he had to rest and recover from the exertion, but he had possession of the phone and in a little while, curled on one side against the pain, he picked up the receiver and dialed with a sense of satisfaction.

"Wake up, Phillip."

Bethancourt had not meant to fall asleep, but he came out of a deep slumber at the sound of Marla's voice. She was wrapped in a satin quilted dressing gown, her hair still tousled from the pillows, and was kneeling on the bed and holding out his mobile.

"It's University College Hospital ringing," she said, pushing the phone at him.

"Ta," said Bethancourt, his heart suddenly in his throat. He flipped the phone open. "Hullo?"

"Phillip?" said Gibbons. "It's Jack."

He sounded weak to Bethancourt's ears, but his tone was determined. And he was clearly no worse off than he had been that morning. Bethancourt relaxed.

"How are you, old man?" he asked, pulling the pillows up behind him.

"I'm making a miraculous recovery," said Gibbons sarcastically.

"Good to hear," said Bethancourt. "Better than the long, slow kind I would imagine."

"I don't know about that," replied Gibbons. "I'm beginning to wonder, actually."

"Let's hope you don't get the chance to find out," said Bethancourt. "Nurse Pipp told me you'd had the physio in today."

"It turns out," said Gibbons, "that 'physiotherapist' is just another term for 'sadistic bastard.'"

"I'm sorry to hear it," said Bethancourt. "I'd gathered some recovery time was necessary."

"It wouldn't have been if I'd not been tortured in the first place," grumbled Gibbons. "Oh, never mind. I rang you to talk about the case, not the damned hospital."

"Ah?" said Bethancourt. "Have you had any new thoughts?"

"None to speak of." Gibbons sighed. "If talking to O'Leary that night sent me off on a new track, I don't know what it could have been."

"Tell me this, then," said Bethancourt, settling comfortably back in the pillows and arranging the duvet over himself. "When you've got a case, does your mind automatically revert back to it the moment you're left to your own thoughts?"

"I don't know," answered Gibbons, sounding slightly exasperated. "I never thought about it. I suppose it might—I tend to be a bit obsessive at times."

Bethancourt smiled at this self-description, having had personal experience of the phenomenon on many occasions. "So let's think it out," he urged. "There you are, having had a nice after-work pint and heard about the latest murder down in Walworth, not to mention Chris O'Leary's new flame, but now you're alone. Your mind goes back to the Haverford case."

Gibbons was silent for several moments. "Probably," he admitted in a low tone, "I would have wasted a few minutes being jealous."

"Very natural," said Bethancourt, though he was startled by the admission. It was not the kind of thing Gibbons would normally divulge.

"And," added Gibbons more practically, "I would likely have thought about what I was going to do—what I might pick up to eat, what tube station would be nearby, that kind of thing."

"Yes, you would want your dinner, wouldn't you?" agreed Bethancourt.

"Of course, Chris doesn't know how long I stayed after he'd gone," continued Gibbons. "If I had just a drop or two left, I would likely have sat on for a couple of minutes deciding where I wanted to eat and then been on my way."

"And if you had more than a mouthful or two in your glass?" asked Bethancourt.

"Then I probably would have begun mulling over the Haverford case again," said Gibbons. "But it's no good, Phillip. Look here, haven't you ever wrestled with a problem and then had to put it aside in order to keep a date, or answer a phone call, or something? And then when you come back to it, suddenly you see a solution?"

"Certainly," answered Bethancourt. "I should think everyone's had that experience at one time or another."

"That's why this is so futile," said Gibbons. "I don't know what I was thinking about the case before I went to have a pint, so there's really hardly any chance I'm going to guess what my subconscious came up with while I was chatting with Chris."

"Well, when you put it that way," said Bethancourt. "Still, you did ring me afterward to say you had an interesting one on."

"But that wasn't necessarily a result of something Chris told me," pointed out Gibbons. "I might have had that thought earlier, and just not have had time to ring you."

"You mean you'd forgotten about me," said Bethancourt accusingly.

"Well, you were out of town," protested Gibbons. "And you're only interested in murder cases in any case."

"I wouldn't say that," answered Bethancourt. "It's just that all your more interesting cases have happened to be homicides."

Gibbons considered this. "They have, haven't they?" he said. "One loses track over the years, and—oh, bloody hell."

"What?" asked Bethancourt, arrested in the motion of reaching for his glasses on the nightstand.

"It's my gorgon of a nurse," said Gibbons glumly. "She's going to poke at my stomach again."

In the background Bethancourt heard a female voice but could not make out what it said.

"She is no respecter of persons," grumbled Gibbons. "She says I have to go."

"Then you had better," said Bethancourt. "I'll speak to you later."

Gibbons rang off and Bethancourt closed his mobile, half smiling.

"I take it the news is good?" asked Marla from the doorway.

"It's good," replied Bethancourt. "He's recovering nicely, and wanted to talk about the case."

"That's a relief," said Marla. "Do they know who shot him yet?"

"Not yet," said Bethancourt, careful to give no indication that he himself was engaged in the investigation. Marla normally detested his involvement in police work; he reckoned he had some leeway in this particular instance, but he was not eager to use it up too quickly.

"Well, I'm glad he's going to be all right," she said, and turned away.

Bethancourt reached to set the phone down on the nightstand and picked up his glasses. He polished them absently on the sheets before settling them on his nose and glancing at the clock.

"Good Lord, is that the time?" he exclaimed, and was out of bed in an instant, muttering to himself while he hunted for his underwear amidst the bedclothes.

"Have you got somewhere to go?" asked Marla, wandering back in from the bathroom.

Bethancourt grinned up at her. "Got to see a man about a dog," he said.

"Oh, really," she said, and turned away again.

12

A Relative Complication

There was only a glimmer of light left in the western sky when Bethancourt reached Hampstead Heath. Nonetheless, there was no lack of dog owners, home from the day's work and out to exercise their pets, though hardly anybody else had ventured out. Bethancourt, with Cerberus loping at his side, walked briskly, his eyes searching for a tall man with a bulldog. It was perfectly possible, of course, that Colin James exercised his dog on some other portion of the Heath, but Bethancourt was betting that on a chilly November night, he would keep to the area nearest his house.

Though he kept his mind on his mission, Bethancourt was enjoying himself. He liked dogs and he loved to people-watch, and there was more opportunity for both on this rather dreary winter evening than he would have thought. He was stopped more than once by people admiring Cerberus, which the great dog took as his due, and had a very pleasant conversation with a young man who owned—of all things—a papillon and a Great Dane.

He had been on the Heath for nearly forty-five minutes before he sighted James striding into the park with Churchill on a lead. Bethancourt smiled and angled his path to intersect theirs, whistling to summon Cerberus. His quarry in sight, he avoided meeting the eyes of the other dog-walkers as he passed, though he could not help but notice one woman with an Afghan hound whose long, straight hair exactly mimicked that of her pet.

"Good Lord," came James's voice at that moment. "Is that you, Phillip?"

Bethancourt turned to find Churchill, now off his lead, making a beeline for Cerberus, while his master strolled along behind, hands thrust deep into the pockets of a camel hair's overcoat.

Bethancourt grinned. "There you are," he said. "I did just think I might meet you here."

James's gray eyes twinkled. "And here I thought you were going to claim it was all coincidence," he said.

"I might have," said Bethancourt, "if I had thought you would believe it."

James laughed. "Very flattering to my perspicacity," he said. "In fact," he added, running his eye down Bethancourt's figure, "very flattering for me altogether."

Bethancourt, untroubled by this admiration, merely laughed at him, and James shook his head dolefully.

"But I doubt," he said, "that it's my personal charms have brought you out this evening. Here, we'd best move on—the dogs are getting away from us."

Indeed, Cerberus and Churchill, having inspected each other thoroughly and decided on amiability rather than belligerence, were now chasing each other about the lawn, dodging in and out amongst the trees. Bethancourt and James turned in that direction, quickening their pace in order to catch up to the dogs.

"Who was that?" asked James, and Bethancourt, turning, just caught sight of a figure without a dog hurrying away.

"I don't know," he answered. "I didn't notice him. Why?"

James shrugged. "I thought I knew him for a moment there," he said. "It's the dim light, no doubt. I often thank God at this time of year that Churchill has that nice, big white patch. I'd have lost him twenty times over otherwise."

"Yes, I've often thought the same about Cerberus," agreed

Bethancourt. "Churchill's quite a lovely bulldog, by the way. Very good form."

"His previous owner was a breeder," said James, a bit of pride in his voice. "One of his dogs won the breed at Crufts one year."

"But Churchill wasn't shown?" asked Bethancourt.

"No—hadn't the temperament, or so I understand," replied James. "I don't know a great deal about dog shows, myself."

"Nor do I," said Bethancourt. "I like to watch, though."

"Me, too."

They walked on amiably together.

"How's Sergeant Gibbons getting on?" asked James.

"Slow but steady progress," answered Bethancourt. "He still feels quite dreadful at the moment, but they say he's making a good recovery."

"I'm glad to hear it." James frowned a little. "This is a funny business sometimes," he said reflectively. "I'm not saying I've never encountered any violence in it, mind you. But seldom so unexpectedly. I really didn't think the Haverford robbery would be much to trouble over, frankly."

"But Jack's getting shot may have nothing to do with that," Bethancourt reminded him.

"True, true—oh, dear, they've really taken off this time, haven't they? And I so didn't want to have to chase after Churchill tonight."

"Let's see if he'll come back with Cerberus," suggested Bethancourt, halting James's sprint forward.

He put two fingers to his lips and gave a piercing whistle that immediately brought the borzoi bounding back in his direction. Churchill, finding he had lost his playmate, hesitated for a long, confused moment and then began to gallop after Cerberus.

"Well, look at that," said James. "You've got him trained a treat, haven't you?"

"It's not much use running after a dog that size," said Bethancourt.

"No, I suppose it wouldn't be," agreed James. "Here, Churchill! Here, boy!"

Having gathered their pets, they turned back by mutual consent.

"Thanks for sending round the pamphlet on the Haverford jewelry," said Bethancourt. "I quite enjoyed it—fascinating stuff, really."

"I thought so myself," said James. "But then, I'm interested in that sort of thing, obviously."

"I haven't made a study of it," admitted Bethancourt. "In fact, I didn't realize the history of particular jewels could be so engrossing."

"It has always amazed me," said James, "the things men will do for gems. And it's not just their monetary value—it's their beauty as well. I would have liked," he added, a little wistfully, "to have seen the Haverford necklace before someone made off with it."

"I take it you don't see much chance of viewing it in the future, then?" asked Bethancourt.

"Not a great fat lot, no," replied James with a shrug. "I haven't got so much as a whiff of the jewels, and neither has Davies. Whoever's got them is sitting on them like a mother hen on an egg."

"Is that unusual?" asked Bethancourt. "It would seem to me that with such a well-known collection, a cooling-off period would be a logical precaution."

James grinned. "You'd think it was obvious, wouldn't you?" he said. "But most thieves don't plan that far ahead, not even the smart ones. They like to get the goods off their hands."

"I suppose," mused Bethancourt, "it would be rather nerve-wracking having a million pounds' worth of jewels in the hall closet."

James laughed. "I think I could come up with a hiding place a little better than that, myself," he said. "The thing is," he added in a more serious tone, "you have to remember that the criminal element is talking about the robbery, just like we are. They're all wondering who did it, where the jewels are now, where they're likely to end up, and whether or not they can get in on the action. It's the kind of atmosphere where rumors flourish, some more solidly based than others."

"Just like all rumors," murmured Bethancourt.

"Just so." James smiled.

"And if one knows the right people," continued Bethancourt, "I should imagine one could hear these rumors and judge their veracity for oneself."

"Exactly. But in this case, there are no rumors—only speculation."

Bethancourt raised an eyebrow. "And in your experience, that means what?" he asked.

"It's hard to know." James's sharp gray eyes lost their focus as he considered the problem. "When I first heard about the robbery," he said slowly, "my immediate thought was that this was a case of some petty thieves getting lucky. Easy enough to track down some panicky thieves. Mind you, that's not my bailiwick, but I have great faith in the metropolitan police."

"So do I," said Bethancourt. "But they don't seem to be having an easy time of it."

"Which would seem to indicate that my first instincts were wrong," said James. "But none of the other avenues seem to be panning out either. And that makes no sense."

They turned out of the Heath and paused on the sidewalk, turning their backs to a sudden gust of wind.

"So," said Bethancourt, "the fate of the Haverford jewels remains a mystery."

James gave a short bark of laughter. "You've got a dramatic turn of phrase, haven't you? It's a mystery for the moment, my lad, but I've never yet failed to nail down the merchandise. Of course," he added, "it's sometimes taken quite a while. Several years on occasion."

Bethancourt sighed.

"I know," said James sympathetically, "none of it does us any good as far as poor Gibbons is concerned. And in the end, the Haverford investigation may have nothing to do with what happened to him. But it has to be cleared up before we can know that for sure."

"There seems to be quite a lot that needs clearing up," complained Bethancourt. "Every time I turn around, there's another angle to be looked into."

James cocked his head in question. "Such as?"

"This murder down in Walworth," said Bethancourt. "I only found out about it this morning, but apparently a colleague had been talking to Jack about it earlier on Tuesday evening. Carmichael's looking into the possibility that it was that conversation that prompted Jack to go down there that night."

"Who got murdered?" asked James.

"A man named Alfred Pennycook," answered Bethancourt. "He was an old-time fence, I understand."

"Good Lord," said James. "Old Pennycook is dead? Well, well. I hadn't heard."

"You knew him, then?" asked Bethancourt.

"Knew of him," corrected James. "His active days were a bit before my time. He's been out of the picture for donkey's years now, but it's still a name known in certain circles. What happened to him?"

"Well," began Bethancourt, just as another gust of wind assaulted their backs. "Look here," he said, "isn't there a pub or something we could step into?"

"Yes, of course," said James. "I was just thinking the same thing myself. This way."

James led the way down East Heath Road, turning off at Well Walk and ending at a large pub, while Bethancourt gave him the details of the Pennycook murder as far as he knew them. He broke off while they settled themselves and their dogs in the cozy warmth of a corner table and fetched their drinks from the bar.

James took a mouthful of his cognac, sighed in pleasure, and then asked, "Well, where were we? Poor old Pennycook was having his skull bashed in for him, I believe."

"So he was," said Bethancourt. "There's not a lot more to tell, really. Nothing from the shop was stolen—not that there was anything there worth very much—and the police are trying to discover who it was he had the appointment with that night."

"It just goes to show," said James with a doleful shake of the head, "that one's sins catch up with one in the end. But I can't see how it ties in with our business. Pennycook had been out of circulation for some years and even if he hadn't, he was already dead when the Haverford jewels were stolen."

"No," Bethancourt admitted ruefully, "I couldn't see much connection either. I suppose it's possible Jack had an idea about the case and went running down there to look into it, but it's difficult to see how he could have got himself into trouble, even if that were true."

"More likely a random act of violence," agreed James. "It's not unknown in that neighborhood. Still, all coincidences are suspect in my philosophy, and old Pennycook did at one time involve himself in some very high-end jewel thefts. It bears keeping in mind."

"I was thinking," said Bethancourt, "of looking into the other beneficiaries of Miranda Haverford's will."

"What other beneficiaries?" demanded James. "You surely can't mean that ancient relic and the dead housekeeper."

Bethancourt smiled. "I did, in fact—if by 'ancient relic' you mean Ned Winterbottom."

James waved a hand. "I believe that was the name," he said. "But why on earth should you want to talk to him?"

"Well, there are only limited avenues for me to explore," explained Bethancourt. "I thought if Ned Winterbottom—or someone else like him—had thought they would inherit the jewelry, they might have taken steps to see that they received it in the end."

"It's not a bad theory," said James thoughtfully. "Only I can't see why they would have thought such a thing. By all accounts, Miranda Haverford spoke her mind and was a shrewd old biddy into the bargain. But have at it by all means."

"I might as well," said Bethancourt modestly. "I'm trying to get in touch with the solicitor now."

"Good Lord, why didn't you say so?" demanded James. "I can get you in to see old Grendel what's-his-name. I'll tell him you're my colleague with whom I am consulting. Vivian will set it up for you tomorrow."

"That's awfully good of you," said Bethancourt, truly grateful. "I do appreciate it."

"It's nothing," said James, dismissing the thanks with a gesture. "The very least I can do, seeing as how I've failed to come up with any answer to the Haverford case. But ever onward." He raised his glass and drank off the last of his cognac. "There," he said, setting the glass down and shooting back his cuff to check his watch. "I'm afraid I must be off. I'll be late for dinner if I don't get home and into the bath at once."

Bethancourt finished his own drink with alacrity. "Thanks for taking the time to speak with me," he said. "I'm afraid I'm becoming something of a nuisance."

"Not at all, not at all," said James, pulling on his gloves and rousing his dog, who appeared to have fallen asleep in the warmth of the pub. "We must keep each other up-to-date on this thing. Have I got your card? Splendid. I'll have Vivian ring you tomorrow."

And he was gone, sweeping out ahead of Bethancourt and Cerberus, who made their way more slowly toward the door.

"James is a very good contact to have made," Bethancourt told his dog. "I must remember to thank Becky specially for arranging the introduction. Flowers or something, I think."

When Carmichael arrived back at Scotland Yard, he had his temper under control although he made no secret of the fact that he was mightily displeased. Constable Lemmy apologized, but Carmichael had the distinct impression that the young man felt his superior was being unfair. That, of course, only infuriated Carmichael further, but he put that aside when he learned that not only had Gibbons rung Dawn Melton's number that night, but that she had apparently rung him during the day but had not left a message.

"Her number's on the missed calls log, sir," said Lemmy. "See, right here, at one sixteen P.M. But there's no corresponding message on the voice mail."

Carmichael's eyebrows began to bristle just a little less as he considered this. "Gibbons would have been at lunch with James at one fifteen," he said. "No doubt he still had his mobile switched off. And when he turned it back on, he probably only checked his messages rather than the missed calls. The question is: did he happen to look at the missed call log later, when he rang the Melton woman back? Or did he think of her because he happened to be in Walworth?"

"He probably checked his missed calls," said Lemmy practically.

Carmichael, who had been talking to himself, frowned at this interruption of his thought process. But another, less acceptable idea had occurred to him.

"I wonder," he said, "if Gibbons actually spoke to Dawn or not? And if not, whether or not he left a message."

Lemmy was thankfully silent.

"I had better get a warrant for both her home phone and her mobile," decided Carmichael. "Put her in an interview room when she arrives, Constable. It won't do any harm for her to wait about a bit."

Carmichael leaned back a little in his chair and regarded Dawn Melton with distaste. He had never liked blubbery women and while many women who had sat in this room opposite him had cried over the years, they had not done so after merely being confronted with an inconsistency in their stories. In fact, Carmichael had usually found that women, far more than men, tended to declare that there was no inconsistency at all and feel that the matter was thus settled.

He threw a wry glance at Woman Police Constable Willis, who stood impassively to one side. She merely arched an eyebrow at him in reply as if to say, "It's your problem, you're the one who made her cry."

This was no doubt true, but also unhelpful. And in any case, Carmichael hadn't meant to make his suspect cry; he had merely pointed out to her that she had lied when she said she had not contacted her cousin in some time. He was willing to admit that his expression had probably been severe as he spoke, but that should hardly have been enough to provoke the waterfall currently before him.

"Mrs. Melton?" he said, trying to sound gentler but only partially succeeding. "Is there a problem?"

This merely produced fresh wails and an incomprehensible babble between sobs.

"Are you sure, sir," asked Willis in an undertone, "that she's really related to DS Gibbons?"

"Doesn't seem very likely, does it?" snorted Carmichael.

He waited a few moments, but Dawn showed no sign of pulling herself together. She had worked herself into hysterics and apparently meant to let it run its course.

"Mrs. Melton," he said again. "Have you got your mobile with you?"

She nodded, watery blue eyes looking fearfully at him over her rumpled handkerchief.

"May I see it, please?"

Carmichael had decided against informing her of the warrant in his pocket unless he had to; he rather thought a warrant would merely be cause for more weeping. The second warrant for her home telephone had turned out to be unnecessary—she relied entirely on her mobile and did not have a phone at home.

She fumbled in a capacious leather handbag, sniffling and dabbing at her eyes the while, and eventually produced a mobile phone which she handed across the table to him. He took it with a nod, surreptitiously wiping his fingers dry on his pants leg, and began to scroll through the numbers dialed.

"Ah, there we are," he said, and turned the phone so she might see the screen. "That, Mrs. Melton, is Sergeant Gibbons's phone number. Yet you claim not to have spoken to him in weeks."

"I didn't," she sobbed. "He didn't answer."

This answer was much obscured by both her weeping and the handkerchief, and it took Carmichael a moment to work it out. When he had, he sighed.

"Mrs. Melton," he tried again, "do you mean to tell me that when we spoke yesterday, you did not intend to give me the impression that you had not attempted to contact your cousin in some weeks, and that he had not attempted to get hold of you either?"

"We didn't," she wailed, but what precisely she meant by it was, in Carmichael's mind, open to question.

He returned his attention to the phone, moving on to the Caller ID list, on which he easily found Gibbons's number listed. This, too, he showed to Dawn.

"And here is evidence that he rang you," he said.

She actually paused for a moment, blinking furiously in an effort to clear her eyes enough to see the small screen.

"He did?" she hiccuped.

"Apparently so," said Carmichael.

"Well, I never knew it," she declared. "I thought he'd be such a help when I first moved here, but he's always busy and out of town half the time, and I don't know anything about the city or living here . . ."

Carmichael lost the rest of this in the fit of weeping that overcame her, but he didn't think it sounded interesting in any case.

"Excuse me a moment," he murmured, pushing his chair back. "I'm just going to step out and hand this over to forensics," he added to Willis, who nodded. He paused, looking back at his tearful witness, and said, "If you think you can get anything out of her, by all means give it a go."

Outside, one of Ian Hodges's minions was waiting impatiently for the phone.

"The numbers are on it," Carmichael told him, handing the mobile over. "I'm most interested in those, but you might as well run everything."

The forensics man looked disdainful. "Of course, sir," he said. "We always run everything."

Carmichael decided that this simply was not going to be his day.

"As you say," he replied, waving a dismissal as he turned away.

Then he paused, considering. In his opinion, there was absolutely no point in his returning to the interview room; he was convinced his presence was merely exacerbating the situation. So he strolled back to his office. He would have a cigar, he thought, and relax for a few moments. Perhaps by the time he was done, Dawn Melton would have stopped crying.

He had forgotten about the Melton children, who had perforce been brought along with their mother as there was no one else to care for them, and lodged in his office with Constable Lemmy to watch them. The unmistakable squeals issuing from his office reminded him of their presence just as he was about to open the door, and he immediately turned away, cursing under his breath. He had really wanted that cigar.

But he stopped only a step or two away as the sound of the squeals penetrated his consciousness. Carmichael had raised two daughters of his own, and had recently been graced with a grandchild, and so was well acquainted with the various noises children made. This was not a sound of distress. This was the sound of little girls playing happily.

Carmichael turned back, curious, since when the children had come in they had been anything but happy. They had, as one would expect, been fearful and upset at this sudden disruption of their routine, and he had not supposed that half an hour in his office with Lemmy would cure this condition.

The scene when he opened the door was certainly unusual: his constable was down on all fours with a two-year-old perched on his back, bouncing up and down, while Lemmy pretended to menace the five-year-old, who in turn beat him back with a sheet of rolled up paper. The baby of the group was installed in one of the chairs, looking on and gurgling happily.

Lemmy looked up as the door opened, craning his neck to see who it was.

"Oh, hello, sir," he said. "Did you need me?"

"No, no, lad, you carry on," said Carmichael, thinking he had finally found a use for his constable, even if it was not one that was likely to be required often. "I just wanted to fetch something."

He stepped to his desk, smiling at the suddenly silent children, and drew a cigar out of the drawer where he kept a box handy.

"Your mother and I will be done with our chat in a little bit," he told them, and they nodded solemnly at him.

He escaped and went down to the garage to have his cigar. The sight of the children playing had put him in a better mood and he considered his interview while he smoked. Dawn Melton had lied to him, and lied deliberately; of that he was sure. Why she had lied was open to question: on the one hand it might have nothing at all to do with what had befallen Gibbons, or on the other hand he might have been following someone on her behalf that night. His first instinct said that she had not shot him herself, largely because he did not think her capable of aiming and shooting a pistol, though he was willing to admit he could be wrong about that. Whatever her reason for lying, some kind of explanation would have to come out, and if handled in the right way, she would eventually provide it. Whether it would be the truth or not was something else altogether.

But he needed to put aside his anger and his dislike of this woman in order to step up and do his job. He had thought that giving her a bit of a scare would do the trick, but it was absurd of him not to have changed tactics when the expected result did not ensue; he knew better than that. He had been doing this for decades.

He put out his cigar, carefully preserving the rest of it, and then returned to the attack in the interview room.

Dawn Melton was sniffling rather than outright sobbing when he entered, though the fearful look she gave him portended more tears. Carmichael smiled at her.

"I've just been to check on the children," he said, shutting the door behind him and coming to take his place opposite her at the table. "They've got my constable giving them piggyback rides and seem to be enjoying themselves." He smiled and shook his head. "I'd forgotten what they're like at that age," he told her, settling his bulk into the chair. "Mine are all grown now."

Dawn eyed him warily, but did venture to answer him.

"How many children do you have?" she asked, her voice a little hoarse from all the crying.

"Two," answered Carmichael. "Two girls. The eldest is a mother herself now, so you can see their days of piggybacks are long over."

Dawn actually managed a smile at this sally.

"Well," said Carmichael, "yours will be wanting their supper soon I don't doubt, so we best wrap this up. Are you feeling better now?"

She nodded very tentatively and glanced at Willis.

"The constable got me some water," she said.

"Good, good," said Carmichael. "Let's see if we can't get on a little better, then. Now, why did you say you hadn't rung Jack in a fortnight?"

"I hadn't," she said. "At least, I thought I hadn't. Honestly, Chief Inspector, I didn't remember that call. I do now," she added hastily. "But I'd forgotten I'd rung Jack that day. I'd been meaning to ring him—I told you that—but the days get so busy what with the girls and my job. I remember now, I had a few minutes free at lunch that day, and rang him from the teachers' lounge at work. But he didn't answer and I didn't have anything specific to tell him, so I didn't leave a message."

This was said with great earnestness, punctuated with sniffles, and Carmichael did not believe a word of it. He kept his face neutral with an effort, and said, "And when he rang you back that night?"

"I must have had my mobile turned off," she answered. "I often do after the girls are in bed."

"I see," said Carmichael, forcing a smile onto his face. "Now that wasn't so bad, was it? All we needed was a little clarification." He paused for a moment, reviewing his options. Any suggestion that she was lying would merely start the waterworks again, so he said carefully, "Can you tell me if you've checked your messages since Tuesday night?"

Dawn looked merely confused—which Carmichael was beginning to think was her normal state of mind—but at last managed to come up with an answer.

"I don't *think* so," she said earnestly. "You see, I don't get many calls, and I always have the phone with me, so there's no need for anyone to leave a message."

Since she had earlier claimed that she often turned the phone off in the evenings, one or the other statement was patently untrue. Carmichael hesitated, on the verge of pointing this out to her, when it suddenly occurred to him that with this particular witness he had an ace in the hole.

"I see," he said, almost genially. "Well, I'd best return you to your children, then. Willis here will show you where they are."

Willis looked considerably surprised at this instruction, but nodded and stepped forward at once.

"Pick up the kids and escort her out," he told Willis in an undertone. He was still too angry to offer Dawn a ride home, or even to call a taxi.

Carmichael sat on in the interview room once they had left, allowing them time to collect the children and vacate his office before he himself returned. He produced his cigar and relit it, using the metal wastepaper bin as an ashtray. With that inducement, he was able to contain himself and wait the necessary minutes, but then he was up and striding out, having stubbed out the cigar and left the remainder in the bin. But he was only halfway back to his office when he came upon Constable Lemmy hurrying in the opposite direction.

"There you are, sir," he said, drawing up short, and then executing a clumsy about-face when Carmichael did not stop. "I thought I'd better come and find you."

"Ah? And why was that, Constable?"

"Because of what the children told me, sir," answered Lemmy. "You did say you wanted to hear about anything I found out right away."

Carmichael's stride paused in surprise and he turned to stare at his subordinate. Lemmy, it seemed, had actually learned something.

"Yes, indeed, Constable," he said in a more encouraging tone. "What did the children tell you?"

"It was actually the oldest one, Mandy," said Lemmy. "She said her mother went out on Tuesday night, after Mandy and the other girls were in bed."

Carmichael stopped cold. "She said what?" he demanded.

Lemmy obligingly repeated himself.

"And how did Mandy come to know this?" asked Carmichael.

"Well, according to the girls," said Lemmy, "their neighbor, Mrs. Carlson, sometimes comes to sit with them if their mum has to run out for something. If Mrs. Melton goes out for the evening, there's another babysitter, but if she's just forgotten something at the store, it's Mrs. Carlson who comes round. And on Tuesday night, Mandy couldn't sleep and came out to ask for a glass of water, and found Mrs. Carlson in the sitting room watching the telly. She gave Mandy her water and let her sit up with her for a few minutes and then sent her back to bed. Mandy went to sleep then, so she doesn't know when her mother came back."

Carmichael absorbed this in silence for a moment. "And how sure do you think Mandy is about the day?" he asked.

"Oh, pretty sure," answered Lemmy. "It all came out when they were asking me what you wanted with their mum. I told them you just wanted a bit of a chat about something that had happened on Tuesday night. And Mandy said, 'Oh, the night Mummy went out.'"

"Right, then," said Carmichael. "We're off to Walworth, lad. I think we should beat the Meltons home if we drive—we've got just enough time before rush hour starts."

13

Meeting of the Minds

*G*ibbons was reading O'Leary's report over for the fifth time, desperately hoping it would jog his memory, when O'Leary himself appeared. He tapped on the doorjamb to announce himself and said, "They told me I could just come in."

"Yes, by all means," said Gibbons, beckoning. "It's good to see you, Chris. I'm just reading your report."

"Report?" echoed O'Leary, drawing one of the chairs up to the bedside and dropping into it. "Oh, about our conversation at the pub? Does it ring any bells?"

Gibbons shook his head, frustrated. "No, I wish it did," he said. "This murder you're working on—you seem to have told me about it in some detail."

"That's right," agreed O'Leary. "We spent most of the time talking about jewels and the Arts Theft Division, but you wanted to hear about the Pennycook case, and I gave you a pretty good summary of it."

"And I don't remember it at all," sighed Gibbons. "When I first saw this report, it came as a complete surprise. What do you think, Chris? Do you think I went down to Walworth on a hunch about the Pennycook murder?"

"Well, no, I don't," said O'Leary, almost apologetically. "I know what Carmichael always says about coincidences, but I just can't see it, myself. You'd put in a long day investigating a robbery and were looking forward to your dinner, and it was an uncommonly nasty night out. If Walworth had been on your way home, I would have said it was barely possible you had stopped to check something out. But as it is, no. If you'd had a thought about the case, you'd have rung me, or left a message at the Yard."

"That's the way it seems to me, too," said Gibbons, making a face at this conclusion. "Oh, never mind—I'm tired to death of trying to remember. Tell me about something else. How was your date with Brenda?"

"It would have been better if I hadn't had to leave in the middle of it," replied O'Leary. "We were just finishing our dinner when the call came in that you'd been shot."

"Oh," said Gibbons, discomfited. "Sorry."

O'Leary grinned at him. "As well you should be," he said with mock severity. "The least you could do is get shot during working hours instead of in the middle of my date."

"Very inconsiderate of me," agreed Gibbons.

"Actually, it's worked out rather well," said O'Leary. "Brenda is very anxious to soothe away the trauma I've experienced in seeing my friend lying all bloody in the street. I'm going to let her just as soon as I get a spare minute."

"Trauma? You?" snorted Gibbons. "I'm the one that's traumatized. I've forgotten an entire day, damn it all."

"Yes, but you're hardly in any kind of shape to be soothed by Brenda," pointed out O'Leary.

"All too true," agreed Gibbons sadly. He had been feeling so ill that it had not occurred to him, but it didn't take much thought to realize his sex life had just come to a standstill for weeks, possibly months, to come. "Never mind," he said, impatiently pushing this thought aside. "Tell me what's been going on."

"I don't know much," O'Leary warned him. "I've spent all day on Pennycook—as far as I can make out, Hollings is leaving me to solve the case on my own. God knows he doesn't seem interested in anything I tell him."

"Well, I'm interested," said Gibbons. "Tell me what you found out."

O'Leary smiled. "I got a break today, as a matter of fact," he said. "I've been working on tracking down some of Pennycook's old cronies, and I finally got hold of one of them today, a fellow called Reaney. He claims not to have had much to do with Pennycook in the last few years, and he didn't have much to say to me at first, either."

"But your natural charm brought him around?" inquired Gibbons sarcastically.

"That's right," said O'Leary genially. "That and the beer I bought him—I found him in a pub."

"And did he know who Pennycook was going to meet that night?"

O'Leary shook his head. "No," he said, "and I think I believe him. But he did finally say that Pennycook liked to indulge in a bit of blackmail when he got the chance. He called it his 'pension fund.' If you ask me, he had a go at blackmailing Reaney over something and that's what brought their relationship to an end. According to Reaney's daughter-in-law, he and Pennycook used to spend a fair amount of time together, though she didn't know what they got up to."

"Didn't want to know, more like," put in Gibbons.

"That's right," said O'Leary. "Willful ignorance can be a wonderful thing if applied rightly. Anyway, she claims there was some sort of dustup three or four years ago and Reaney hasn't seen Pennycook since. As she put it, they went from being 'bosom buddies' to 'hating each other's guts.' "

"Well, the blackmail gives you motive, at any rate," said Gibbons. "It didn't seem to me, reading this over"—and he tapped the report on his lap—"that someone would have murdered the old reprobate for the paltry contents of his shop."

"It would have seemed even less likely if you'd seen the place," O'Leary assured him. "I dropped in on Mrs. Pennycook after I talked to Reaney, but she's another case of willful ignorance. The police have always had it in for her Alfred—well, you know the drill."

Gibbons made a face. "All too well. What about the—nephew, is it? Frank Pennycook, I think it said."

"That's right," said O'Leary. "I had a go at him, too, but didn't get much. He admitted that his uncle had some private business from time to time, but claims he was never let in on any of it. He says he had no idea that Alfred had an appointment that night, but if he had known, he would have assumed it was for something like blackmail. I've been trying to think if there have been any jobs recently that Pennycook might have known about and tried to get in on, but so far nothing's come to me. Most of the people he knows are past active service, if you take my meaning."

"More to the point," said Gibbons, "do any of them have enough money to pay a blackmailer?"

O'Leary shrugged. "Not that I've noticed," he answered, and then looked back over his shoulder as the sound of voices attracted his attention. "Is that someone else coming in?"

Gibbons glowered. "Probably my gorgon of a nurse come to torture me again."

But it was Bethancourt, smelling of rain and tobacco, and smiling tentatively. Cerberus padded at his side; he smelled of wet dog.

"Hullo," said Bethancourt. "Is this a special police conversation or can anyone join in?"

"Come in, come in," said Gibbons. "You remember Chris O'Leary?"

"Yes, of course, good to see you again," said Bethancourt, reaching out to shake O'Leary's hand before sinking into the second chair. "Well, well, isn't this jolly?"

Gibbons glared at him.

"Well, perhaps not precisely jolly," amended Bethancourt hastily. "But a happy opportunity to compare notes and get all our minds on the same page so to speak."

"Do be quiet, Phillip," said Gibbons. "Chris here was just about to tell me how my investigation is going."

"I did warn you I'd missed most of the news today," warned O'Leary. "In fact, the only thing I heard was that Inspector Hollings had tracked down some bloke who apparently saw you getting out of a taxi at about half-eight on Tuesday night."

"In Walworth?" asked Gibbons.

"That's right. At the intersection of Walworth Road and East Street, or thereabouts."

"Eight thirty," mused Bethancourt. "That leaves an hour and a half or so unaccounted for."

O'Leary gave him an odd look, but it was Gibbons who said, "How do you make that out? Chris here left me at a pub at half-six, and I turned up in Walworth at half-eight. That's two hours difference."

"Well, yes, but you had to get from place to place, hadn't you?" pointed out Bethancourt. "I don't think it's pushing things to say you spent fifteen minutes getting from the pub to wherever you went and another fifteen getting from there to Walworth. That's pretty average for getting about in London."

"Well, when you put it like that," said Gibbons grudgingly, "it does make sense. But what on earth could I have spent an hour and a half doing?"

"You might have got a bite to eat," suggested Bethancourt.

"Not at any of the usual places, you didn't," put in O'Leary. "We've canvassed those—both the restaurants around the Yard and the ones near your flat. Your landlady told us which places you went to the most, but I don't think we missed any. We had a small army out on Wednesday hitting every possible place."

It gave Gibbons an odd and rather unpleasant feeling, hearing about the kind of search he himself had conducted on many occasions, but which on this occasion was directed toward his own movements.

"I was shot at about nine," he said, ignoring the winces this statement caused in his listeners, "so I might still have been planning to pick up something to eat on my way home—it wasn't that late."

"You could have run into someone," said O'Leary.

Gibbons shrugged. "I could have done almost anything," he said, sounding discouraged.

"What you couldn't have done," said Bethancourt, "is run straight off to Walworth after talking to Chris here—getting from the Feathers to Walworth couldn't take two hours unless you walked. I rather think this rules out the idea that you went off to check out a sudden inspiration about the Pennycook murder, don't you?"

"It does," agreed Gibbons, who was annoyed that he himself had not grasped this immediately. "Not," he added, glancing at O'Leary, "that we thought that was terribly likely."

O'Leary shook his head in agreement.

"No, I suppose not," murmured Bethancourt. "Still," he added, brightening, "it's nice to know for sure."

Gibbons eyed him. "You seem to be in a suspiciously happy mood," he said.

"I'm trying to lighten the atmosphere," replied Bethancourt.

"The atmosphere doesn't need lightening," growled Gibbons, "it needs clearing up."

"Well, we're all doing our best," said Bethancourt. "It's not easy without you, you know."

"Carmichael's going nuts without you," put in O'Leary.

Gibbons smiled at these attempts to cheer him, but it was a half-hearted expression. He didn't care if they were all finding it heavy going because he resented their having the opportunity to investigate when he did not. The fact that most of the time he felt too awful to think about anything but his personal well-being did nothing to alter this sentiment, and he was in enough of a pet that the illogic of it all left him unmoved. Then he frowned as a thought occurred to him.

"This fellow says he saw me getting out of a taxi?" he asked.

"That's right," said O'Leary. "On Walworth Road and East Street."

Gibbons's frown deepened. "I wonder why I took a taxi," he said. "I usually only do that if I'm in a hurry."

Bethancourt and O'Leary stared at him.

"That's true, isn't it?" said Bethancourt, who frequently took taxis himself.

"I don't normally take them myself," said O'Leary thoughtfully. "Although . . ."

"Although what?" asked Gibbons when this comment did not resolve itself.

"Well, I was just thinking that it was a miserable night out," said

O'Leary, almost apologetically. "It was the sort of weather that I might have taken a taxi in just to keep out of the rain."

"Did you take a taxi to meet your date?" asked Gibbons.

O'Leary shrugged. "Sure," he said. "But I was picking Brenda up, so I had to."

"But there's a financial element at work here, isn't there?" interrupted Bethancourt. "I mean, that's why the two of you don't hire taxis that often—because it's expensive, right?"

Gibbons rolled his eyes. "Of course."

"So, you normally only take taxis when you're in a hurry," said Bethancourt, "or possibly when the weather is bad enough." He paused for a moment, and then shook his head. "I can't think of a reason you'd be in a hurry to reach Walworth by half-eight, not unless you had an appointment there."

He cocked his head in question at the others.

O'Leary spread his hands. "You didn't have a date," he said. "You'd have mentioned that when we were talking. What else could you be running late for at that time of night?"

"Maybe," said Gibbons after a moment, "maybe I was just wanting my dinner and in a hurry to finish whatever it was I was doing. That and the weather might have made me decide to take a taxi."

"It'll help a lot once we find the taxi driver and find out where you were coming from," said O'Leary.

"Well, we've already got a rough idea of where he could have come from," said Bethancourt.

"We have?" demanded Gibbons.

"Perhaps I should have said we've got an outside limit," said Bethancourt. "I mean," he added as the other two men merely stared at him, "short of a dire emergency, there's a limit to how much you would spend on a taxi, particularly if you just wanted to finish an errand faster."

"That's true," said Gibbons thoughtfully.

"So how much?" asked Bethancourt. "How much would you be willing to spend for your own comfort on a cold night?"

"Less than you," muttered Gibbons, but this only produced an unrepentant grin from his friend.

"All too true," agreed Bethancourt, amiably. "I like to be comfortable. Come along, old thing, give us a number. Fifty pounds?"

"God, no," said O'Leary, startled by the idea of this sum.

"Then how much?"

"I don't know," retorted Gibbons. "It would all depend on how tired I was and how anxious I was for my dinner and how awful the weather was."

"The weather was dreadful," said O'Leary. "I know, I had to stand out in it for more than an hour."

"Well, I still wouldn't have spent fifty pounds on a taxi," insisted Gibbons. He hesitated, thinking. "I might have spent twenty quid," he said. "No more."

Bethancourt beamed at him. "There you go—that nicely limits how far you could have traveled. In fact, you couldn't actually have been too far from the Yard. If we work backward, twenty pounds would get you from Walworth back over the river, but not a lot farther."

They were all silent for a moment. Then O'Leary shook his head.

"I don't see where that really gets us any further," he said.

"Well, no," admitted Bethancourt. "It's more that it rules things out."

Gibbons sighed. "It would help if there was anything to actually investigate," he said. "Has it occurred to anyone else that Walworth has a very high crime rate? And that what happened to me might just have been an act of random violence?"

There was an uncomfortable silence.

Then O'Leary shrugged. "It's occurred to everyone, Jack," he said. "But that doesn't mean anything. If it was a random thug, we'll find him, too."

"Yes, all right," muttered Gibbons, but not as if he had great faith in the notion.

In the quiet that followed, the sound of murmured voices at the door reached them, causing Cerberus to lift his head. In another moment, Carmichael appeared and surveyed the three of them with a smile.

"Having a conference?" he said.

Gibbons, whose belly was beginning to ache quite intolerably and who had been on the verge of asking his friends to leave, immediately felt he could go on for a bit at the sight of his senior.

"Do come in, sir," he said. "You're quite right—we were just discussing the investigation."

Both Bethancourt and O'Leary had risen at his entrance and were offering him their chairs; Carmichael took O'Leary's with a nod, relegating the sergeant to the stool. He patted Cerberus absently as he sat, and then looked down at the Borzoi in surprise.

"How the devil did you get the dog in here?" he demanded.

"He chatted up my nurse," said Gibbons.

"I'm pretending Cerberus is Jack's pet," corrected Bethancourt. "Nobody seems to mind."

Carmichael shook his head in bemusement and returned his attention to Gibbons.

"So how are you doing, lad?" he asked, a little anxiously. He did not add that to him Gibbons still looked like he was at death's door, but the look in his eyes gave him away.

"They tell me I'm healing up nicely," answered Gibbons. "And my fever's down."

"He's making a miraculous recovery," said Bethancourt firmly. "His medieval torturer told him so."

"What?"

"Physiotherapist," explained Gibbons. He firmly changed the subject. "How is the investigation going, sir? Chris here told me I evidently took a taxi to Walworth that night?"

"That's right," said Carmichael. "Hollings found that out. We haven't got hold of the taxi driver yet, but at least we now have some idea of why you went there."

The three younger men all looked surprised.

"We do?" asked Gibbons.

Carmichael glanced at O'Leary. "You didn't tell them about the other taxi?" he said.

"No, sir." O'Leary shook his head. "I didn't know about it. I just heard that there was a witness who had seen Jack arriving in Walworth by taxi."

"I see," said Carmichael. "Well, there was a bit more to it than that, though most of it's conjecture. Our witness was trying to catch a bus when he saw a taxi pull up and let out a fare—another young man, he said. Then he noticed you getting out of a second taxi half a block or so behind the first. The assumption is that you were following the first fellow, though we won't know for sure until we get hold of the cabbie."

Gibbons looked a little dazed. "I wonder who it could have been," he said.

"Someone to do with the Haverford case?" suggested O'Leary.

"But who?" said Gibbons. "And what on earth could they have been doing that would have made me so suspicious that I'd follow them all the way to Walworth?"

No one appeared to have a good answer for this and there was silence in the room for a moment.

"I can't think," said Bethancourt at last. "Unless you went back to check something out at the Haverford house. If someone were there before you, that would certainly be suspicious."

"We'll just have to wait and see," said Carmichael. "The taxi driver should turn up tonight or tomorrow, and then we'll have a better idea. Meanwhile, I have something for you to investigate yourself, if you feel up to it."

Gibbons was considerably surprised. "Er," he said, "I don't know—that is, sir, I think I'm going to be in hospital for another few days."

Carmichael waved a hand. "It's not that kind of investigating," he said. "I just want you to get your bloody-minded cousin to tell you what she was up to on Tuesday night."

"Dawn?" said Gibbons, astonished. "What does she have to do with anything?"

"That's just what I should like to know," Carmichael told him.

Gibbons felt he must have missed some crucial piece of information because otherwise this made no sense.

"I don't quite see, sir—" he began, but Carmichael interrupted with, "I'm sorry, Gibbons, I shouldn't have dumped that on you all of a sudden. It's just that I've had a very frustrating day with the woman and am feeling a bit put out. Here, let me start at the beginning."

He recounted succinctly his various encounters with Dawn Melton, the evidence of both her phone and Gibbons's, and ended with what he described as "the deluge of tears" that afternoon.

"What's more," he added, "I have just come from Walworth where Mrs. Melton's neighbor, one Edith Carlson, verifies that on Tuesday evening she sat with Mrs. Melton's children while Mrs. Melton ran out to meet a friend. She was gone from about half-eight till a quarter to ten."

"Good grief," said Gibbons faintly. "She's made quite a mess of things, hasn't she? Don't worry, sir, I'll find out what it's all about. And if she won't tell me, I guarantee my mother will have it out of her in no time."

Carmichael nodded in satisfaction. "I rather thought that might be the case," he said.

"But, sir," said O'Leary, "do you really think she had anything to do with what happened to Jack?"

"I don't know, do I?" replied Carmichael. "Come, you know better than that, O'Leary. Dawn Melton has behaved suspiciously and it's got to be cleared up. The fact that I don't believe she could hit the side of a barn with a pistol has nothing to do with it."

"She wouldn't need to," put in Bethancourt. "She could merely have been the bait to lure Jack to the place where he was shot. Although," he added ruefully, "if my family is anything to go by, it's far more likely she's hiding some piece of monumental stupidity than a crime."

O'Leary grinned at him. "It couldn't be stupider than some of the things my cousins have done," he said.

"Why is it," asked Bethancourt, "that family members are so often people you would rather have nothing to do with?"

Carmichael chuckled. "So true, isn't it? I remember one time my sister attacked her own husband with a cricket bat, all because he came home a day early from a business trip to surprise her. She was red as a brick trying to explain that to the people at the hospital."

They all laughed quietly at this, and Bethancourt glanced at Gibbons, concerned that there might be a repeat of the earlier incident when he had tried to laugh. But Gibbons was no longer listening; his eyelids were drooping and he had curled up awkwardly on one side, his arms wrapped protectively about his belly.

"Well," said Bethancourt, rising at once, "I've got to be going."

"Sorry," mumbled Gibbons sleepily. "I'm all in, I think."

Carmichael and O'Leary, with a single glance at him, also rose to leave, bidding him good night while they collected their belongings and then all three men made their way quietly out.

It was dark when Gibbons woke, and from the hushed atmosphere he deduced the night was well advanced. His parents had been in to visit sometime after the others had left, and various medical people had come in and out, checking his bodily functions for all the good it did him, but he had been half asleep through most of it.

The blinds were drawn on the window, but the streetlights below crept through the slats, striping the bed. Gibbons focused on the pattern idly while he tried to remember what he had been dreaming. It had not been a comfortable dream, of that he was sure, but he could not bring it clearly into focus and so could not determine if it was a memory of his attack or merely his current discomfort that had inspired it.

And then a new idea came to him as he lay there in the dark, still curled around the pain that never seemed to quite go away, no matter how drugged his senses were. He had spent most of his waking hours striving to remember, or at least waiting to remember, what he had done on Tuesday. Now for the first time it occurred to him that his memory might never return, that in fact he was wasting time in the effort to remember. After all, he had investigated dozens of crimes, none of which he had known anything about before the case file landed on his desk. What had happened to him was just another case, whatever his personal involvement, and should be investigated as such. What did it matter that he could not remember the day? Was that truly any different, from an investigative point of view, than a witness who lied about their actions? At least there was nothing deliberately misleading about his situation. It was just a matter of paring down the possibilities, one by one, until they were left with the truth. And then he would know what he had done, and who had shot him.

It would not be the same, of course. Knowing what had happened and remembering it were two very different things. He would never, for instance, know what he had been thinking that day. He might posit the connections his mind had made that led to his actions, but he would never know for sure. But there were worse things in life. After all, he had narrowly escaped death, and that was no small thing.

It was past one o'clock in the morning and the forensics laboratory was darkened and quiet except for the area where Ian Hodges and his protégé, Guy Delford, worked. That space was brilliant with light, a white blazing pool in the midst of the black.

Neither Hodges nor Delford were looking particularly well; both men were red-eyed, their hair unkempt, their clothes and lab coats rumpled. Hodges had taken a moment that morning to shave, but Delford had not bothered and dark stubble grew in patches on his youthful face. Both of them had been at the lab continuously since Tuesday night, taking turns sleeping on the leather couch in Hodges's office.

But now, at last, they were done. Hodges lifted the photograph and displayed it for Delford's perusal.

"Oh, that's beautiful," breathed Delford. "I didn't think we'd be able to get it that clear."

Ian Hodges smiled with satisfaction. Delford might be his latest forensics genius, but he was still the master.

"Yes, I think Chief Inspector Carmichael should be pleased with this," he said, carefully laying the page of the notebook aside. "It's been quite a challenge, recovering all the pages. This one was the worst."

Delford nodded, leaning over to peer at the page, on which virtually nothing could be read. His eyes tracked to the photo, where various chemicals and lighting had combined to produce a good facsimile of the page's original, pristine state, and he sighed with pleasure.

"That's really a wonderful job," he said.

"That's forty years' experience there," said Hodges. "It bloody well ought to be wonderful. What do you say to a dram to celebrate, Guy? Just a wee one before we head for home."

"Today's great thought," agreed Delford, stripping off his lab coat as he came round the counter. Together they passed out of the door, shutting the lights behind them as they left in search of whisky.

14

Stained Evidence

here was no question but that the police would be working all weekend. Carmichael was at his desk at eight that morning, having had a decent night's sleep for the first time since Monday night. He was rather surprised to find the light on his desk phone blinking rapidly, indicating an urgent message. He could not imagine what anyone could consider urgent, yet not important enough to ring him at home for.

Frowning, he punched the button and in a moment the mystery was solved when he heard the raspy voice of Ian Hodges.

"Hodges here," he said. "I've got your lad's notebook done. You'd better send one of your myrmidons over to collect it in the morning. I'm going home to bed now, but Natalie will have it waiting for you."

"Hodges, I could kiss you," said Carmichael to the phone. "Bother the myrmidons, I'll go myself."

As usual, Gibbons was awakened early by the morning shift coming in and checking him over, presumably to ensure that the night shift had not let him die during the night. He was not certain that death would not have been preferable. He glared in a surly manner at Nurse Pipp when she came in to inspect his dressings.

"I've got some good news for you this morning," she said, checking off things on a handheld computer. "The doctor will be in soon, and if he's happy with you, he'll take that tube out of your nose."

Gibbons gazed up at her, gone from surly to worshipful in an instant.

"Really?" he asked.

She smiled. "Really," she promised.

The removal of the tube was more uncomfortable than Gibbons would have believed possible, but it was a huge relief to have it gone. He swore he felt almost himself, aside from a very sore throat. And abdomen. And some general aches and pains from his atrophying muscles, not to mention the muzzy-headedness caused by the morphine.

Still, he was much cheered by this small improvement in his situation, taking it as evidence that the rest would follow in its wake. When the orderly who regularly came to take his blood pressure appeared, he asked for the phone and had it placed conveniently on his tray table.

His mother sounded surprised to hear from him, and anxiously asked if anything was wrong.

"Just the opposite," Gibbons told her. "They took the tube out of my nose—it feels ever so much better without it."

"Oh, Jack, I'm so glad. Did you hear that, dear? Jack says they've got rid of the tube."

"And I'm to have a liquid diet," added Gibbons proudly, as if this were a personal accomplishment.

"That's wonderful, darling. Such good news."

To his ears, his mother's voice sounded suspiciously weepy.

"It *is* good news, Mum," he assured her. "I'm healing very well, they say."

"Oh, I'm so glad to hear that, dear, so very glad." His mother drew a deep breath. "We've been very worried, you know. We'll be over to see you directly after breakfast and you can give us all the details then."

"Yes, but, Mum, I rang to ask you something," said Gibbons. "I wanted to know if you were planning to see Dawn anytime today."

"Why, yes," she answered. "We were going to take her and the children to lunch and then come by the hospital. She's sorry she hasn't been able to get over more often, you know."

"That's all right," said Gibbons impatiently. "I want a word with her, Mum. When you get here, do you think you could take the kiddies and give us a moment alone?"

"Alone?" she said. "With Dawn? Whatever for, Jack?"

"Just something I want to ask her about," he said evasively. "I'd rather keep it between the two of us, if you don't mind," he added, knowing nothing less blunt would satisfy his mother.

"Very well, if you insist," she said a little doubtfully. "Oh, dear heavens, she's not involved with that man again, is she?"

"What man?" asked Gibbons.

"Oh. Oh, never mind. I expect I spoke out of turn," she said. "Dear, your father wants his breakfast, so I'll ring off now and see you soon."

Gibbons rang off wondering if his mother had just solved the mystery of what Dawn had been doing on Tuesday night.

Carmichael sat in the lab's car park, pouring over the replica of Gibbons's notebook, large glossy facsimiles of each side of every page, all of which Hodges had enlarged to make it more readily readable. The opening pages were unremarkable, merely looking a bit rumpled from having got damp, the pencil marks on them still clear to be seen. It appeared that Gibbons had started this notebook upon his transfer to the Arts Theft Division, and the first pages dealt with his orientation to the new job. Or at least Carmichael assumed they did; Gibbons, like all detectives, used his own special brand of shorthand when taking notes and there was a good deal of it of which Carmichael could make nothing. What, for example, did a triangle mean?

"Well," he muttered to himself, turning over a page, "it doesn't matter—it's far too late for me to start learning the Arts Theft business in any case."

Eager to reach the notes pertaining to the Haverford case, Carmichael shuffled through the glossy pages, periodically stopping to peer at one in more detail to see if he had got far enough yet.

There was no change in the smooth texture or the perfect clarity of the sheets, but the images on them began to be more disturbing. What had started out as photos of carelessly handled papers, the writing on them brought into sharp relief with artful lighting, began gradually to exhibit the signs of violence. The pink tinge was almost unnoticeable at first, particularly to one who was in a hurry to get on, but it gradually deepened, occluding more and more of each successive page, until the photographs were of nothing so much as a scarlet smear.

It left Carmichael shaken. He was forced to set the sheets aside and refocus his eyes on the car park around him, though he did not take in much of his surroundings. His mind's eye was turned inward as he reflected on how much had changed since the long-ago days when he had first become a detective constable. It was not that there was no violence connected with criminal investigation in those days, but the idea that you could be gunned down in the streets of London as if you were in some bad American television program was unthinkable. Back in those days, your chances of being seriously injured sprang from the danger of IRA bombs, the same as any Londoner. And even the murders he had investigated back then usually had far less to do with gunshots and a great deal more to do with poisons, beatings, or stabbings. He could not recall, in his early days, any of the detectives he worked with receiving a life-threatening injury. Though Canfield had been run over by a car that time . . .

He had not expected, back then, to ever be exposed to much blood that did not belong to a murder victim.

He shook his head to clear away the memories, and not quite ready yet to expose himself to more of Gibbons's blood, he let down the window a bit and lit up a cigar.

The tobacco had a calming effect on him and he puffed quietly for a few moments before summoning up the courage to return to the notebook facsimile.

He tried to look at it analytically, strictly as evidence. As such—and also to avoid coming unexpectedly on anything else so disturbing—he quickly riffled through the thick sheaf of photos.

He had assumed, from the bulk of the facsimiles, that Gibbons's notebook had been almost full, but in fact it had hardly been half used up. The first set of pages was a record of the notebook as forensics had received it. Hodges had not bothered reprinting the early sheets after that, as they were readable as they were without further work on his part. The last pages, however, had many incarnations, ranging from utterly obscured to almost total clarity. It was, unfortunately, these pages that referred to the Haverford case.

"I might have known," muttered Carmichael.

Still, most of it was legible and Carmichael thought that if he had written it himself, he would be able to make it all out with the possible exception of one or two jottings in the margins. Unfortunately, he hadn't written it, and he was hesitant to exhibit such evidence of the violence done to him to Gibbons's own eyes. Surely, thought Carmichael, looking at this would be overly traumatic for a man who had only been removed from the critical list three days ago.

And yet, he saw no alternative. From what he could read, there was a lot here that hadn't gone into Gibbons's official reports. That was typical of a good detective's notebook; one was not supposed to include one's hunches and guesses in official reports.

Still puffing thoughtfully on his cigar, Carmichael started up the car and eased out of the parking space. He would stop at the Yard and see what he could make out from the notebook on his own before he showed any of it to Gibbons. Constable Lemmy could help; if nothing else, he possessed a pair of younger eyes and a better acquaintance with current slang.

The phone was ringing again. Bethancourt had lost count of the number of days he had been wakened by it, but he knew he was growing very tired of the phenomenon.

"Oh, really, Phillip," said Marla.

She thrust herself up in the bed and then climbed half over him to reach the telephone on the nightstand. The ringing silenced, Bethancourt gave a little contented grunt and snuggled more deeply into the pillows.

"Here," said Marla, collapsing back beside him and clapping something hard and cold to the side of his face.

Bethancourt perforce freed a hand from the blankets and fumbled the telephone receiver over his ear.

"Mmm," he said in a vaguely interrogatory way.

There was startled silence at the other end, and then a woman's contralto voice said, "Is Mr. Phillip Bethancourt there?"

Bethancourt yawned. "Got it in one," he said. He couldn't place the voice, but at the moment he didn't care very much.

"This is Vivian Entwhistle, Colin James's secretary," said the voice. "Mr. James had asked me to arrange for you to meet with Mr. Grenshaw. As this is Saturday, Mr. Grenshaw would not normally be in his office, as you can imagine."

In his half-asleep state, Bethancourt was still groping after the elusive memory of who Mr. Grenshaw might be.

"Of course not," he replied automatically. "Why should he be?"

"I have, however, contacted him at home," continued Vivian, "and he has agreed to meet you this afternoon, if that would be convenient."

"It would be a sight more convenient than this morning," mumbled Bethancourt. "Oh, hell," he added as his brain finally jerked into wakefulness. "You're talking about the solicitor chap, aren't you?"

"Yes, Mr. Bethancourt." Vivian's voice, though still professional, took on the slight extra clarity of someone speaking to the mentally impaired. "That would be Charles Grenshaw, Esq., the late Miranda Haverford's man of business."

"I'm so sorry," said Bethancourt. "You must think I'm an idiot. I'm afraid I'm terrible in the morning until I get my first coffee. It's very good of you to spend your Saturday setting up appointments for me."

He was fumbling on the nightstand for his glasses as he spoke.

"Not at all, Mr. Bethancourt," said Vivian graciously, but with the faintest hint of reproof in her tone. She was rapidly beginning to remind Bethancourt of a particularly difficult teacher he had had in the fourth form.

"Where and when am I to meet the illustrious Mr. Grenshaw?" asked Bethancourt, having found his glasses as well as a pencil and a notepad in the bedside drawer.

"He'll be at his office at three o'clock," replied Vivian. "Do you have the address?"

"No, could you give it me?"

She read it off, pausing to give him time to jot it down.

"I think I should mention," she added, "that although Mr. Grenshaw is exceedingly eager to have Miss Haverford's affairs cleared up, and is willing to go to some lengths to see this accomplished, he nevertheless would rather have left this till Monday."

"Thank you very much for persuading him to see me today," said Bethancourt humbly.

"My point, Mr. Bethancourt, is that I would not be late for the appointment if I were you, nor would I expect Mr. Grenshaw to spend overmuch time on your interview."

"No, of course not," replied Bethancourt, feeling more like a schoolboy with every passing moment. "I wouldn't dream of it. Thanks frightfully, Miss, er—"

"Entwhistle," she replied. "Vivian Entwhistle, Colin James's secretary."

"Thank you very much, Miss Entwhistle," said Bethancourt respectfully.

"You're welcome, Mr. Bethancourt," she said, and rang off.

Bethancourt collapsed back against the pillows, still clutching the phone.

"What," demanded Marla, "was that all about?"

"Confirming an appointment with a solicitor," said Bethancourt, reaching to return the receiver to its cradle. He saw no reason that Marla need know that the solicitor in question had nothing to do with any business of Bethancourt's.

"On a Saturday?"

"Yes—that's why it needed confirming. But it's not till three this afternoon. No hurry at the moment."

"That's good," said Marla, stretching luxuriously. "Damn it, that phone call has woken me up. And I did so want another couple of hours' sleep—we were at that club rather late last night."

"So we were," agreed Bethancourt, who had turned on his side to watch her. "I thought we'd sleep in, myself. But if you're awake now . . ."

He reached for her and she came unresistingly into his arms.

Carmichael's plans to sit down with the notebook changed when he arrived back at the Yard. He found Lemmy there with a message that one of the taxi drivers had come forward.

"His name is Bradley Johnson," said Lemmy, reading it off a scrap of paper. "He's got his taxi out at the moment, but I've got his mobile number here."

"Fine, fine," said Carmichael, reaching for the phone. "Read it off, will you?"

Lemmy obeyed while Carmichael punched the numbers in and waited for an answer. It came quickly.

"Is that the chief inspector?" asked a cheery London voice.

Carmichael grinned. "It is indeed," he replied. "Wallace Carmichael here. Am I speaking to Bradley Johnson?"

"That's right. Your man says you want information about a fare I picked up on Tuesday night?"

"I do," answered Carmichael. "When can I speak to you?"

Johnson chuckled. "You live right, guv. I'm two minutes away from Scotland Yard this minute, and I've just dropped off my fare. I'll be round in two ticks of a lamb's tail."

Carmichael rang off with the faintly optimistic feeling that today might be turning out better than yesterday.

"Here," he said, thrusting the facsimile envelope at Lemmy. "See what you can make of these—it's what Hodges has resurrected from Gibbons's notebook."

Lemmy nodded and Carmichael hastened for the door, but then turned back.

"Mind," he said, "you won't be able to read all of it. Gibbons uses his own shorthand. And don't start at the beginning—skip on to the part about the Haverford robbery. Just take a sheet of paper and write out everything you can understand in longhand, all right?"

"Yes, sir," said Lemmy.

He looked as if he understood what was wanted, so Carmichael continued out, though in his mind he kept going over the instructions he had issued all the way down to the lobby, trying to work out if there was a way Lemmy could muck them up.

Bradley Johnson was as good as his word. Carmichael had not been in the lobby five minutes before a stout, fortyish man, well wrapped up against the weather, came briskly in, looking about him curiously.

He had a firm handshake and did not seem put out at all to have his workday interrupted by the police. Carmichael thanked him sincerely and led him off to an interview room.

"A couple of the other drivers," said Johnson, following along, "have tales about how Scotland Yard has needed their help. I reckon this'll bring me even with them. Can you tell me who I had in my cab? Was it a murderer?"

Carmichael was sorry to have to disillusion him. "I'm afraid not," he said, holding open the door of the interview room. "If yours is the right taxi, I'm hoping it was one of my men you dropped off that night."

"Oh." Johnson was clearly disappointed, but after a moment's thought he asked brightly, "Was he after a murderer?"

Carmichael laughed. "He might have been," he said. "We don't know yet. If not a murderer, then at least a jewel thief."

"Ah!" Johnson's eyes shone. "That'll do, guv. I don't know but what a jewel thief might be better, all things considered. It'd be different, do you see?"

"I do indeed," said Carmichael, still amused. He switched on the recording equipment and gave both his own name and Johnson's.

"Now then, Mr. Johnson," he said. "Could you tell me about the fare you drove to Walworth on Tuesday night?"

Johnson was delighted to do so.

"It was about eight fifteen," he said. "And a cold, miserable night it was, too. The streets were near empty, but every last soul on them wanted a taxi so I wasn't making out so badly. I picked up one gentleman in Brixton and took him to Waterloo Station. I sat in the queue for a minute or two, working on my logbook, with some other taxis in front of me. Then two young blokes come out, one right after the other. First one hops into the taxi in front of me, and the second man asks me if I mind following along after the first taxi."

"Does that happen often?" asked Carmichael.

"Not much," admitted Johnson. "Mostly when there's a large group, and one taxi won't do. Or at a train station, like I was that night, if someone's got a full load of luggage."

"But neither of these young men had luggage?" asked Carmichael.

"No, guv, that they did not. Not so much as an overnight case. Well," added Johnson, "at least my fare didn't. I can't say I noticed about the first man particularly."

"But your fare didn't give any explanation for this?" asked Carmichael, trying to keep the eagerness out of his voice. "He didn't announce himself as an officer?"

Johnson shook his head. "No," he answered. "I would have remembered that, see? This bloke just says as he and his friend don't want to arrive in the same taxi, and I figure it's something to do with a woman—it usually is when young men are getting up to a lot of foolishness."

"Very true," said Carmichael with a little sigh. "Please go on."

"Well, there's not much more to it," said Johnson. "I followed along behind the other taxi, straight down Waterloo, through Elephant and Castle, and on down Walworth till we got near East Street. Then my fare says, 'Here, they're pulling over. Just let me out a bit back of them.' I didn't think anything of that, not with his saying they didn't want to arrive in the same taxi. I mean, it stands to reason that if two taxis pull up right together, you may as well have just taken the one as far as camouflage goes, doesn't it?"

Carmichael nodded understanding of this salient point.

"So I pulled up half a block or so away," continued Johnson. "My man had his money ready—and a nice tip, too—and he handed it over, thanked me, and got out. Tell the truth, I never thought any more about it until today."

"I'm very grateful you remembered it today," said Carmichael. "Can you tell me what time you let your fare off?"

"Oh, it couldn't have been more than a minute or two past half eight, if that," replied Johnson. "We had a clear run from Waterloo, it being such an inclement night. We were down to East Street in no time at all."

This accorded almost exactly with what Tom Gerrard had said and Carmichael was gratified by the match.

"That's very good, Mr. Johnson," he said. "Can you describe your fare at all?"

But here Johnson fell short. "It was pretty dark," he said apologetically. "I saw him as he came toward me out of the station and passed under the light there, but I wasn't taking particular notice. Just enough to see he was young, average height. He had a cap on, so I didn't see his hair to speak of. I don't know as I could recognize him again."

"What about the chap in the first taxi?" asked Carmichael. "Do you remember anything about him?"

Johnson shook his head. "I only saw him for a moment when he and my fare came out of the station. He wasn't a lot taller or shorter than my man, and that's all I could say."

With that Carmichael had to be content, and indeed he was not displeased. He arranged for Johnson to return to sign a statement and then showed him back to the lobby with many thanks.

He himself turned back toward the elevators, ruminating on what he had just learned. Having seen the good man out, he turned back to the elevators, wondering who Gibbons had been following on Tuesday night.

It turned out that Constable Lemmy, far from mucking up, had done quite well with the notebook. Carmichael found him seated at his desk with four of the facsimile sheets spread out before him while he worked on writing their contents out in longhand as best he could. In fact, he had managed to make out a few scribbles that had eluded Carmichael.

"You're making out pretty well with it then," said Carmichael, peering over Lemmy's shoulder. He pointed. "I think that bit probably refers to the upstairs window that was broken."

Lemmy looked. "Oh, I see," he said. "Yes, that must be right, sir."

Carmichael fetched one of the other chairs and joined Lemmy at the desk, checking over the work the constable had already done.

The first page of the notebook that dealt with the Haverford case had clearly been written at the scene; indeed, it indicated as much at the top of the page, along with the date. The notes here appeared to deal mainly with the method of the burglary, expatiated with details about the house and its situation. Rob and Lia Coleman's names were written out, as was Miranda Haverford's. There were parts of it that Lemmy had not been able to translate, but to Carmichael's eye it looked like a straightforward encapsulation of the crime as later detailed in the case file.

The next page Lemmy had had a good deal of trouble with, owing to the fact that it apparently was devoted to a description of the stolen jewelry itself, with many side notations. Carmichael could not make them out any better than Lemmy could, but he judged it unimportant.

"Don't bother too much with that," he told the constable. "We'll have Inspector Davies check it out later—probably this is all stuff he was explaining to Gibbons in any case."

"I haven't been able to find anything there that didn't seem to pertain to gemstones," agreed Lemmy. "Not unless you count that at the top, but I reckoned that was just his grocery list."

It was so obviously a grocery list that Carmichael's eye had skipped right over it. "Milk" was scrawled in the top margin with "beer" and "pots" right after it, the latter of which Carmichael read as an abbreviation for "potatoes."

"Right you are," he said. "Where's the next sheet? Oh, I see. It's more of the same, looks like."

"I thought so, sir."

Slowly they went on, working out each word or symbol as best they could.

15

Quaint Traditions

*C*harles Grenshaw, Esq., had his office in Lincoln Inn. He was a neat, elderly man, nearly completely bald, with wire-rimmed spectacles. Bethancourt thought him the very picture of a conservative family solicitor.

"So very good of you to meet with me," said Bethancourt, shaking his hand. He fairly towered over Grenshaw and found himself, in an effort at amiability, hunching a bit to make the difference less obvious.

"It's a very distressing matter," replied Grenshaw. "I cannot recollect anything like it in my experience, and thank goodness for that."

"Indeed," said Bethancourt. "The situation is unfortunate."

"Although," added Grenshaw, his eyes turning inward in reminiscence, "I'm not sure but what Miss Haverford would rather have enjoyed all the upset. She had very odd tastes sometimes. Well, do come this way."

Bethancourt was intrigued by the comment, but let it go as he followed Grenshaw into his inner sanctum, where he was ushered into one of the green leather armchairs. Grenshaw moved to stand behind his desk, but then hesitated before seating himself.

"Normally," he said, "I would offer you some tea, but Miss Daniels always prepares that for me, and she is naturally enough not present today. Perhaps—it is a trifle early, but it is Saturday, after all—perhaps we might indulge instead in some sherry?"

Bethancourt was completely charmed by this speech, which reminded him of visits with his grandfather to his man of business when Bethancourt was a small boy.

"It's very good of you to offer, sir," he replied. "I should love a glass of sherry."

The sherry glasses Grenshaw removed from a cabinet were beautifully etched examples from the turn of the last century. The sherry was younger, but still aged, a very fine oloroso. Bethancourt sampled it appreciatively.

"This is excellent," he said, and Grenshaw smiled.

"I keep it for a few select clients," he said. "But I don't deny I look forward to the occasions I can bring it out. Well, now, what can I do for you in regard to Miss Haverford's affairs?"

Bethancourt reminded himself that despite his hospitality, Grenshaw was no doubt eager to return to his interrupted weekend.

"I take it from what you said earlier that Miss Haverford had a sense of humor?" he asked.

Grenshaw bobbed his head in a nod remarkably like a bird's.

"She did," he answered. "It would often come as a surprise, especially to people who were just meeting her, because she was in other ways a very autocratic old lady. Her mischievous side was not always on display, but I came to realize it was always present, though she seemed to feel it necessary to hide it."

"It sounds as if you knew her well," said Bethancourt.

"Oh, yes. Indeed, I have known her all my life, my father being her solicitor before me. When she was younger and still entertained occasionally, my wife and I were usually among her guests."

"And did you know the other people mentioned in her will?" Bethancourt asked. "It's really about them that I've come," he added. "I wanted to know a bit more about them."

"I see." Grenshaw sipped his sherry, set the glass down carefully, and then steepled his fingers under his chin. "There were not very many bequests in the end," he said thoughtfully. "Most of Miss

Haverford's friends and relatives had died long before she did. I did not know her principal beneficiaries, the Colemans, at all. But her executor, Ned Winterbottom, I've encountered several times over the years. And of course I knew Rose Gowling quite well. In late years, I saw as much of her as I did Miss Haverford."

"I expect Mrs. Gowling's bequest will go to her heirs now?" asked Bethancourt.

Grenshaw gave his bobbing nod again. "Though I don't know them personally," he said, "as they live in Lincolnshire. And of course the few pieces of jewelry and china that Miss Haverford left to her maid are not worth a great deal."

"Sentimental value, no doubt," put in Bethancourt. "Tell me, was the jewelry always destined to be left to her distant relatives?"

"Most of it was, yes," said Grenshaw. "Miranda toyed from time to time with the idea of leaving a few of the lesser pieces to the people who were close to her, and at one time—if I remember aright—a substantial part of it was to be left to her other Haverford relatives. But they all died out—many of them before their times—and so the collection reverted back to the Hrushevsky family in the Ukraine." Grenshaw paused. "I'm assuming," he added, "that Mr. James has told you of the jewels' origin?"

"Oh, yes," said Bethancourt. "I found it quite fascinating. And I've read Miss Haverford's tract about the history of the jewels themselves. Wonderful stuff."

Grenshaw smiled, pleased. "Well, then you will understand when I tell you that the Hrushevskys—Evony St. Michel's family in the Ukraine—were united in their disapproval of their black sheep. But they were fond of her son, as he had grown up among them, and there was much coming and going between the families once Evony had passed on."

"Well, then, shouldn't the son have left the Hrushevskys some of the jewels if his mother had meant them to have them?" asked Bethancourt skeptically.

"No doubt, no doubt," said Grenshaw. "But Michael didn't die until after World War II, by which time all contact with the Ukrainian branch of the family had ceased on account of the Iron Curtain.

It was only relatively recently, after the breakup of the Soviet Union, that communication was reestablished."

"Oh," said Bethancourt. "Of course—how stupid of me."

"No, no," said Grenshaw. "It's easy for people of your age to forget what a different place the world used to be."

"But wait a bit," said Bethancourt. "Where does Rob Coleman come into it then? I may have forgotten an entire era in history, but I'm relatively sure Coleman isn't a Ukrainian name."

Grenshaw received this with a small chuckle. "Your confusion is understandable," he answered. "But it's easily explained: while visiting her cousin, Evony's niece met and then married an Englishman, William Coleman. He, unfortunately, died young and his widow returned to the Ukraine with her children. Rob Coleman is her grandson."

"Ah," said Bethancourt, "I see. Family histories are always complicated, aren't they? More so than one is usually prepared for."

"I've got accustomed to it in my practice," said Grenshaw complacently. "It so often matters in estate law, you know, exactly how people are related."

"Well, yes, I imagine it would," said Bethancourt. He felt he had got rather sidetracked, and marshaled his thoughts quickly. "So Miss Haverford's plans for the jewels were well known," he said, thinking that this was more or less the death knell for his theory.

"I don't know as I'd say that," Grenshaw interrupted him. "I wonder if perhaps I have given you a wrong impression of Miranda Haverford. She had her eccentric side, but in many ways she was very traditional. I doubt anyone knew what was in her will aside from she herself; she would have considered that her business and no one else's."

"I understand," Bethancourt said with a nod, brightening again. "My own people are rather like that. Can you tell me anything about the other heirs?"

"As I said, there weren't very many in the end," answered Grenshaw. "Ned Winterbottom, the executor, is a very old friend of the family. At one time, in their youth, I believe there were some intimations of an amorous nature between him and Miss Haverford but it came to nothing in the end. He still lives here in London, although he recently had to give up his flat and move into a nursing home for health reasons. He is only a couple of years younger than Miss Haverford was, after all."

Bethancourt tried to imagine a man in his nineties with health issues climbing up onto a porch roof to break a window in order to hoist himself through it and rob a safe. It did not seem very likely, but before dismissing Winterbottom altogether he reminded himself that the elderly man need not have committed the burglary himself. Anybody could have an accomplice.

Grenshaw was going on. "Then there's Mrs. Burdall and her son. She's Miranda's neighbor on the eastern side of the property, and the Burdalls have owned that house almost as long as the Haverfords have owned theirs. Nicola Burdall is a very old friend of Miss Haverford's, and in addition her son and grandson have obliged over the years with a bit of property upkeep when it became difficult for Miss Haverford and Rose Gowling to attend to such things themselves."

Young sons were more promising as potential burglars and Bethancourt made a mental note.

"Lastly, there is May Kerrigan," said Grenshaw. "She was, I believe, Miss Haverford's best friend for many years, although the relationship lapsed somewhat since Mrs. Kerrigan moved north to live nearer her children. She, too, is now under medical care. But, as I say, none of these bequests are particularly valuable."

The name seemed to ring a faint bell in Bethancourt's mind, but he could not bring the memory into focus.

"What about the Fenimore Cooper?" he asked. "Did that go to anyone?"

Grenshaw cocked his head. "I'm afraid I don't know to what you refer," he said.

"There's a collection of James Fenimore Cooper novels in the study," explained Bethancourt. "They're old enough to be worth a couple thousand pounds or so."

Grenshaw's eyebrows rose. "I do not think," he said, "that Miss Haverford could have been aware of that. As the probate proceeds, it is becoming very clear that she had, over her last years, sold off nearly all her assets except the jewelry. That she considered more in the nature of a trust than hers to dispose of as she would, or so I gathered."

"I was only curious," said Bethancourt. "I noticed there didn't seem to be much of value left in the house, so the Cooper books rather stood out."

"Thank you for mentioning it," said Grenshaw. "The probate valuation is still under way, but I will take care that the books are appropriately accounted for."

"You're welcome," said Bethancourt.

Grenshaw shook his head. "The Haverfords have been clients of my family's for generations," he said sadly. "I knew, of course, that the tradition would come to an end with Miranda Haverford's death, and I considered that a sad thing. I never imagined it could be made worse."

"I'm very sorry you've had all this trouble," said Bethancourt, rather touched. "I do hope it can all be cleared up quickly."

"Yes," said Grenshaw, shaking off his mood. "We must try to look on the bright side. Well, I hope this has been of some help to you, Mr. Bethancourt."

"Yes," said Bethancourt slowly, thinking it over. "Yes, I do believe it has."

Bethancourt was thoughtful as he returned to his car from Grenshaw's office. Cerberus, asleep on the backseat, roused himself at his master's return and licked Bethancourt's ear as he slid into the driver's seat.

"Good lad," murmured Bethancourt, starting up the Jaguar and then sitting thoughtfully for a moment, his hands motionless on the wheel. "I think," he said slowly, "we might as well go and pay a visit to Mrs. Burdall, don't you? It's Saturday—ten to one either her son or grandson might be visiting. After all, it's just time for tea."

Cerberus did not seem to care much about this itinerary; he had rearranged himself on the backseat and as Bethancourt put the car into gear, he closed his eyes again to resume his nap.

The neighboring property was set out much like the Haverford place, and the house, though rather larger, was of the same architectural style. This house, however, was very well kept up and Bethancourt's eye picked up additional improvements as he parked the Jaguar and got out. Through the bare branches of the trees to the west he could catch glimpses of the Haverford house, but it was far enough away that the neighbors could not very well keep tabs on one another. He doubted very much that the Burdalls would have heard a pane of glass breaking, particularly not if their windows were closed as seemed likely at this time of year.

A slender girl of about fifteen answered the bell, which was not what Bethancourt had been expecting. She was dressed casually in jeans and trainers, with a Fair Isle jumper worn over a cotton turtleneck and her sleek dark hair pulled back in a ponytail. There was a mischievous look in her bright blue eyes as she looked up at him with lively curiosity.

"Hello," she said with a grin. "Can I help you? You don't look like you're selling things."

"Certainly not," said Bethancourt, grateful he had dressed to meet Mr. Grenshaw and worn a proper overcoat. "I'm Phillip Bethancourt," he said, proffering a card, which she took and read intently for a moment. "I'm a colleague of Colin James's, looking into the burglary next door. I was wondering if I might speak to Mrs. Burdall or perhaps her son, if they're about."

"Oh, they're about," she answered. "Grandma Nicky doesn't get out much anymore." She paused and leaned to peer around him out the door. "Is that your dog in the car?"

"Yes, that's Cerberus."

"You'd better have him in," she said decidedly. "Grandma Nicky likes dogs, but won't have one anymore because she says she won't outlive it."

"Very well," said Bethancourt, wondering if this was merely a ploy to take him away from the door so she could shut it. "If you think she would like that."

But rather than trying to shut him out, she accompanied him back to the car, saying, "Your card doesn't have a company name or anything. Colin James's did."

"That's because I'm a consultant," answered Bethancourt. "I'm not in Mr. James's employ."

"Well, this entire upset has certainly been an eye-opener," she said. "First we had the regular police, then we had the detective from Scotland Yard. We thought we were done then, but, no, next thing we get is Mr. James, who says he's the insurance investigator, and now we've got you. I wonder who's coming next."

"I think you may have struck bottom with me," said Bethancourt, opening the door of the Jaguar. "This is Cerberus."

"Hello, Cerberus," she said, holding out her hand to be sniffed in the time-honored manner of human greeting dog. "You're a beauty, aren't you? Yes, Grandma Nicky will like you very well indeed."

"Would you mind awfully," said Bethancourt, "telling me your name?"

"Oh!" She looked startled, but then grinned impudently up at him. "I'm Nicky Burdall. Grandma Nicky is really my great-grandmother."

"Well, it's very nice to meet you," said Bethancourt. "Cerberus, heel."

"My," said Nicky, "he's a well-behaved one, isn't he?" She turned and led the way back to the house, saying, "You'll think it odd, no doubt, all four generations of us Burdalls living here together."

"Not at all," said Bethancourt, who had been unaware until that moment that they did.

She gave him a scornful look. "You needn't pretend," she said, "everyone thinks we're quite eccentric. But it works very well, really. Dad and Granddad between them have got it all sorted, and the ruddy house is big enough, heaven knows. Here we are, then. Come this way—Grandma Nicky has her rooms at the back."

Nicky led him out of the foyer and down a carpeted hallway ending in a set of mahogany double doors. Nicky turned aside about halfway down and opened a door on the right.

"Just wait in here a minute, will you?" she said. "I've got to let Grandma Nicky know she's got a visitor—she takes a bit of preparing for anything new. I'll be back in half a tic."

When she returned, Nicky was accompanied by an older man in

his mid- to late sixties with a handsome head of gray hair and a somewhat stooped posture.

"Good afternoon," he said politely, holding out a hand. "I'm Neil Burdall, Nicola Burdall's son."

"Phillip Bethancourt," said Bethancourt, shaking hands. "I do hope I haven't come at an inopportune time—I'd be most happy to come back at some later date if it's more convenient."

"Not at all," said Neil. "My mother quite enjoys visitors as she gets out so little these days. We were just having tea—she likes the old-fashioned routines. Do come join us. Ah, is this the borzoi Nicky mentioned?"

"Yes," said Bethancourt. "She seemed to think your mother would like to see him. If he's too big—"

"Oh, no, no," said Neil. "Mother had English setters in her day—she'll like this chap. Here, this way. Nicky, you had best let your parents know where you've got to."

"I'll tell them and come right back," she answered, looking to her grandfather for permission.

"Certainly," he said, smiling. "I'll have your grandmother set out another cup. Mr. Bethancourt, if you would?"

With Cerberus at heel, Bethancourt followed him down to the double doors, which he slid open to reveal a large double reception room with arched windows and French doors leading out onto a small veranda.

At one end of the room, almost lost in the depths of a wing chair, was a frail, elderly woman with snow-white hair. A knitted afghan lay over her lap and she wore a thick cashmere cardigan over her thin shoulders. She smiled at Bethancourt as Neil led him forward, saying, "This is the gentleman, Mother. Phillip Bethancourt. He's working with Mr. James, whom you remember."

"Oh, yes. Mr. James was most amusing. How do you do, Mr. Bethancourt? And what a lovely dog!"

"This is Cerberus," said Bethancourt.

Cerberus stepped forward with great dignity, rather like one head of state greeting another, his feathered tail waving gently. He sniffed Mrs. Burdall's hands graciously and then bent his head to be petted. The old woman clearly fell in love with him on the spot.

"So nice of you to bring him in," she murmured. "I do so miss dogs. Well, I'm neglecting my duties. Please do sit down and have some tea, Mr. Bethancourt."

Bethancourt sat as she indicated, and gazed bemusedly at the formal tea service set out on an antique tea table at Mrs. Burdall's right. Today, he thought, seemed to be his day for visiting the traditions of the past.

"I'll pour out, Mother," said Neil, seating himself at the end of the sofa. "Sugar, Mr. Bethancourt?"

Bethancourt declined the sugar, but took a piece of shortbread from the offered plate and then waited politely while Neil served his mother and himself.

"You've arrived at just the right time, Mr. Bethancourt," said Mrs. Burdall. "I've always loved tea parties. My favorite kind of entertainment, really."

"Happy to be of service," said Bethancourt, smiling back at her. He sipped at his tea and was immediately transported back to his boyhood and the beverage his own grandmother had used to serve. "Delicious," he said.

Mrs. Burdall nodded complacently, as if she expected the accolade.

"Molly's learned to make it just the way I like it," she said. "I know she thought I was too picky when she first came, but she likes it herself now, doesn't she, Neil?"

"She does indeed," said Neil, sipping at his own tea. "Well, Mr. Bethancourt, how can we help you? You must already be aware that we knew nothing about the burglary until the police came round asking."

"Yes, I know," answered Bethancourt. "I shouldn't have expected you to, really. The only noise would have been the glass breaking, and the houses are too far away for you to have noticed that."

"We might have in the summer," said Mrs. Burdall, "when we have the windows open. But not now, with the central heating going and the windows shut."

"Of course," said Bethancourt.

A brief rap on the door heralded the return of Nicky, now accompanied by a boy of about ten.

"Hullo," she said. "Have you started yet? Oh, here's my brother, Dylan."

She frowned repressively at the younger child who grinned unrepentantly and marched over to have his hand shaken properly.

"Come have your tea then," said Neil. "And do be quiet, both of you. I'll warrant poor Mr. Bethancourt has already been here longer than he meant to be."

"Not at all," said Bethancourt. "You have a delightful family."

"Are you married yourself, Mr. Bethancourt?" asked Mrs. Burdall.

"No, ma'am, not yet."

"But I bet you've got a girlfriend," put in Nicky.

Bethancourt admitted that he had.

"Do let him ask about the burglary, Nicky," interrupted her brother. "He doesn't want to spend all his time telling you about his love life. So"—here he turned to Bethancourt with eager eyes—"have they caught the thieves yet?"

"No," said Bethancourt, laughing. "I should hardly be here if they had, should I? I'm afraid I don't have anything very interesting to discuss—I only wanted to know something about Miranda Haverford and those close to her."

"Well, we can certainly help with that," said Mrs. Burdall. "We've all known her all our lives, haven't we? She was a funny old thing, but I was very fond of her."

"But does this mean the police no longer believe it was a random theft?" asked Neil. "That was the theory they gave us—that it was a gang who broke into the empty houses of the recently departed."

"That may still be the case," Bethancourt told him. "But at this point the field is wide open, and I'm looking into other possibilities. To that end, I'm interested in anything you can tell me about Miss Haverford's relationships with those people she mentioned in her will."

They looked puzzled by this tactic, but complied readily enough, and it was clear it never once crossed anybody's mind that they themselves could be suspect.

In any case, thought Bethancourt, Dylan was too young, and Neil too old to have broken into the Haverford house; he rather wished he could get a look at Dylan's father. Or mother. There was no point, he reminded himself, in being sexist about the thing.

"Well, of course the Colemans inherited most of it," said Mrs. Burdall. "In fact, we gathered that was the reason they were here, though whether Miranda wanted to vet them or they wanted to be Johnny-on-the-spot when she passed on, I could never quite make out."

She looked at her son, who shook his head in agreement.

"Mind," he said, "we didn't know the Colemans before they arrived. We did wonder, when they first came, if they had come with the idea of persuading Miranda to leave them something in her will."

Nicky and Dylan both hooted at this idea.

"As if Miss Haverford would ever have the wool pulled over her eyes like that," said Nicky scornfully.

"That's true," said Mrs. Burdall, smiling at them. "Miranda was a shrewd woman."

"So you were surprised when they turned out to be her heirs?" asked Bethancourt.

"Well, no, I wouldn't say that," said Neil, looking toward his mother for confirmation.

"Not by that time," she agreed. "After all, the jewelry had to go somewhere, and Miranda hadn't anyone to leave it to. I had rather thought she would leave it to a museum, but I could understand her wanting to leave it in the family, so to speak."

"*I* was surprised," said Nicky. "I didn't think she liked the Colemans that much."

"Nicky!" protested Dylan.

"Just because you like Mrs. Coleman doesn't mean Miss Haverford did," Nicky shot back.

"Liking," said Mrs. Burdall, raising her voice to be heard, at which both children quieted, "liking does not necessarily have much to do with one's financial affairs. And I believe your grandfather asked you to be quiet while Mr. Bethancourt talked to us."

"Sorry," muttered Nicky, and nudged by his sister, Dylan chimed in, too. Bethancourt gave them a sympathetic smile.

"What about the other people Miss Haverford was close to?" he asked. "You must have known Rose Gowling, her housekeeper?"

Rose's name elicited an immediate reaction from all the Burdalls: the two elders smiled broadly while the children pouted.

"Oh, Rose was a dragon," said Mrs. Burdall. "She was fiercely protective of Miranda and took very good care of her, but she was quite a character. She never trusted anyone or anything, and was generally pessimistic."

"Her relationship with the Colemans was particularly strained," said Neil, smiling in amusement at the memory. "You would have thought from her attitude that they had come to steal the silver. No, I'm not joking, Mother," he added as Mrs. Burdall started to put in a word of protest. "I actually found Rose counting the sterling one day, and when I asked why, she told me she counted it every day after the Colemans had been to visit."

"Oh, dear," said Mrs. Burdall, but she was laughing.

Bethancourt chuckled, too. "I take it," he asked, "that your family passed muster?"

"Only because we'd known Miranda longer than Rose," said Mrs. Burdall. "Those of us who predated her were accepted as trustworthy."

"Well, I don't know about that," said Neil. "She always seemed suspicious of poor Ned Winterbottom."

"Well," said Mrs. Burdall, "she thought he was trying to marry Miranda for her money. She was quite wrong of course—Ned had been in love with Miranda from the time he was fifteen."

"Mr. Grenshaw did mention," put in Bethancourt, "that Mr. Winterbottom and Miss Haverford had once been romantically linked."

Both Nicky and Dylan were looking rather stunned; apparently it had never occurred to them that even someone as old as Miranda Haverford had once been young and very likely had fallen in love.

"That's putting it too strongly," said Mrs. Burdall. "As I said, Ned has been in love with Miranda all his life, and when he moved back to London several years ago and found her still single, I don't say that he didn't try again. And she might even have been tempted. But she never cared for him in that way, and that was that in the end."

"I believe you told me she never got over Andrew Kerrigan's death," said Neil.

This time Bethancourt recognized the name. "That's why it was so familiar," he said aloud, and all the Burdalls looked inquiringly at him.

"Sorry," he said. "It just came together in my mind. When we were looking through the house, we found an old address book with a list of names and dates at the back—birthdays, we assumed."

"And Andrew Kerrigan's name was in it?" asked Mrs. Burdall, surprised. "It must have been quite old—Andrew died in the war."

"I expect it was," replied Bethancourt. "It turned out Miss Haverford had used his birthday as the combination to her safe."

"Oh, my," said Mrs. Burdall. "I never knew that. It's rather sad, really."

Bethancourt raised a brow. "Is it?" he asked.

"They were engaged, you see," she explained. "Andrew Kerrigan was a very handsome, dashing young man back then and everyone was quite jealous of Miranda for landing him. But she worshipped the ground he walked on, as we used to say, and she was devastated when his plane went down and he was killed. I don't believe she ever looked at another man after that."

"That's tragic," said Nicky. "You never told us that."

"Well, I haven't thought about it in a long time," said Mrs. Burdall.

"But," said Bethancourt, "wasn't one of Miss Haverford's beneficiaries named Kerrigan as well? I knew the name sounded familiar when Mr. Grenshaw mentioned it, but I couldn't think where I'd heard it before."

"Oh, yes, that would be May," said Mrs. Burdall. "May and Miranda were at school together, and they were very close all their lives. Andrew was May's older brother, but the girls were friends before he and Miranda got engaged. May's up north now; her children live up in Derbyshire and as she got older they decided it would be best to have her closer to them. She's not in very good health—we all thought she would be the first of us all to go, but instead it was Rose who was a good fifteen years younger than anyone else."

"Gran," protested Nicky. "That's depressing."

Mrs. Burdall shrugged. "It's just life, Nicky."

Bethancourt was quite enjoying this stream of reminiscence—the background was giving him a far more favorable view of Miranda Haverford than he had previously had—but he didn't think the Burdalls had much more to tell him and although he had not met Nicky and Dylan's parents, he was having difficulty believing they had stolen a fortune in jewels. Still, it did no harm to ask.

"One last thing I wanted to know," he said. "Were you all aware that Miss Haverford kept the jewelry collection in her study safe?"

Neil looked toward his mother, who spread her hands.

"I never thought about it," she said. "I suppose I would have assumed it was either there or at the bank. I do know when she was much younger, it often used to be kept in the safe as she used to wear some of it occasionally. Not the more elaborate pieces, of course, but a couple of the brooches and bracelets."

"I do remember," put in Neil, "the last time she lent it out, they picked it up from the house in an armored truck." He grinned. "It's not the kind of thing you see much in this neighborhood."

"No," agreed Bethancourt, "I imagine not."

He excused himself shortly thereafter, thanking the Burdalls for their time and trouble, though in fact they seemed quite pleased with his visit, happy to add another investigator to their roster.

16

An Interview in Hospital

*I*t was somewhat unfortunate for Dawn that her visit to the hospital occurred shortly after Gibbons had finished his daily physical therapy. The therapist today had refused to return him to bed and had insisted on settling him in one of the chairs. Gibbons found it excruciating.

He tried to put the best face he could on things when his visitors arrived, but his mother sensed at once that he was both tired and cross, and it was not long before she collected the children (who were giving Gibbons a headache in any case) and her husband and left him alone with Dawn. His father, Gibbons noticed, looked utterly confused by this maneuver but acquiesced as usual to his wife's silent signals.

Dawn sensed something was in the wind, and tried to leave with them, but Gibbons's mother squelched that firmly.

"Well," said Dawn brightly when they were left alone, "I'm so glad you're making good progress, Jack."

"Thanks," said Gibbons, sizing up her demeanor. At the moment, all he wanted was to get back into his bed and see if he could find a position that would make the raging pain in his stomach abate. Since that had been ruled out by the medical staff, he supposed it was just as well that he had someone to take his temper out on. He had never been all that fond of Dawn.

"So," he said before she could trot out another inanity, "would you like to tell me what you were doing last Tuesday night?"

She managed to keep the bright smile in place. "I was home with the girls," she answered. "I nearly always am at night."

"Not according to Chief Inspector Carmichael," said Gibbons, and that name wiped the smile from her face at once. "Or according to your neighbor," he continued. "She claims you asked her to babysit while you went out for an hour or so."

"Oh, that's only Mrs. Carlson being forgetful again," said Dawn with a nervous little laugh. "She's quite elderly, you know. I did ask her to sit with the girls, but that was Monday, not Tuesday."

"Do come off it, Dawn," said Gibbons, annoyed. "You're lying and you know it. You rang me on Tuesday afternoon, and I apparently rang you back that night while you were out doing whatever it was. Just tell me what the hell's going on, can't you?"

At that point, Dawn burst into tears, protesting her innocence and accusing Gibbons of being insensitive to a struggling single mother.

"Oh, put a sock in it, Dawn," said Gibbons unsympathetically. "You may have got round Carmichael with that crap, but I'm not having any. I've been effing shot, woman. I nearly died, and if they had found me much later, I would have. At the moment I couldn't care less about your petty little problems."

This actually seemed to have some effect on her, though it did not stem her tears altogether.

"Oh!" Dawn hiccuped. "I'm so sorry, Jack. Truly I am—I wasn't thinking. I know you've had an awful time—"

"I don't need you to be sorry," interrupted Gibbons. "I just need you to tell me the truth. Let's start with why you rang me that day."

"It wasn't anything important," she assured him earnestly, dabbing at her eyes. "I was only thinking you might come out with me that night if you were free. We hadn't caught up in a while."

"In that case, why didn't you leave a message?" demanded Gibbons.

She looked hurt and bewildered. "You didn't answer," she said. "So you were busy."

Gibbons held on to his patience with both hands. "Just because I was busy at one o'clock in the afternoon doesn't mean I would inevitably be busy for the rest of the day and night," he pointed out.

"But I wasn't sure," she explained, looking on the verge of tears again. "I wasn't sure it was a good idea. So when I didn't get you, I took that as a sign."

"A sign," repeated Gibbons, quite incredulous at this piece of specious reasoning, if reasoning it could be called. "You needed a sign from above to decide whether or not you could have a drink with your own cousin."

"Oh. Oh, well . . ." Dawn made a fluttery little gesture.

"I see," said Gibbons in a moment. "You weren't sure you wanted to tell me whatever you rang about, and when I didn't answer, you decided that meant you'd made the wrong decision in trying to consult me."

Dawn did not meet his eyes, but the tears began to roll down her cheeks again, this time silently.

"And," continued Gibbons, working it out, "wherever you went that night, that was what you wanted to ask about. Perhaps you even wanted me to come with you."

She remained silent, eyes averted, but nodded her bent head.

"But what did you say when I rang you back?" asked Gibbons. "Did you just put me off?"

For a moment he thought she would not answer, and was even prepared for the sobs to start up again, but instead she said shakily, in a very low voice, "I had my mobile switched off. I didn't know you had rung. I really didn't."

Gibbons considered this. "But my phone records show I must either have spoken to you or left a message," he said, half to himself. "And if I had left a message, your mobile would have alerted you when you turned it back on. When did you?"

Dawn looked up, confused. "When did I what?" she asked.

"When did you switch your phone back on?"

She frowned, trying to remember. "I was tired," she said. "And I hardly ever have the phone off. I don't think I remembered to turn it on after I got home. I just had a cuppa and went to bed."

"That's good," said Gibbons encouragingly. "So the next morning, when you got up—did you ring anybody then?"

She had stopped crying now and, so far as he could tell, was making an honest effort to recollect what she had done.

"Wednesday morning . . ." she said. "Oh, yes, of course, I woke rather late. I remember now. The girls were already up and watching the telly, and I was hurrying to get them breakfast when Diane rang me. Oh! Oh, dear."

"What?" demanded Gibbons impatiently.

"I think it must have been Mandy," she said, her tone tinged with pride at her eldest's accomplishment. "Because when Diane rang, I had to fetch the phone from the sitting room—and I know I didn't go in there the night before. Mrs. Carlson was in the kitchen when I came in, and I went straight there and had a cuppa with her before she left. Then I went in to bed. Mandy must have got the phone out of my bag when she woke up in the morning and turned it on. And that's how I missed your message."

She beamed at him as if she had been very clever.

"Splendid," said Gibbons, trying to sound encouraging rather than sour, which was how he felt. "So that just leaves what you were doing on Tuesday night and why it's such a secret."

"Well . . ." she said uneasily. "It's just that . . . well, it's just a spot of bother, really."

Gibbons interpreted this as meaning that she was in trouble.

"What bother?" he asked.

"Well . . . you won't tell Aunt Margery, will you?" she asked anxiously.

"No," promised Gibbons, and when she still hesitated, "Good heavens, Dawn, I don't tell my mum everything."

"No, no, of course not." She took a deep breath. "Well, it's just that Danny owed a bit of money."

Danny, as Gibbons recollected, was her ex-husband.

"Right," he said.

"It was a little bit more than I thought," she admitted.

Gibbons raised a brow. "So?" he said. "You're divorced now, and as I recollect, all his debts were settled when you sold the house." In fact, he was guessing at that; his mother had told him all about it at the time, but Gibbons had not really been listening.

Dawn shifted uncomfortably and her eyes fell away from his face.

"Danny's had a hard time of it," she said.

Gibbons remembered his mother's earlier comment on the phone. "Oh," he said. "Were you meeting Danny that night?"

"It was just for a minute," she said earnestly. "And I didn't give him much."

"I see," said Gibbons, the light dawning at last. "By all rights, he should be giving you money, and you didn't want anyone in the family to know it was going the other way. But then why the devil did you ring me? You couldn't have thought I was going to approve of the transaction."

"I'm not quite such a fool as that," retorted Dawn, with the first sign of spirit Gibbons had seen in her. "I didn't mean to tell you anything about it. I just thought if I could get you to go with me, then Danny wouldn't have a chance to ask for any money. He wouldn't, you know, in front of you."

This was such a poor solution to her problem that Gibbons was left speechless. He thought about it for a moment, decided being shot meant he didn't have to bother about it, and said, "There's a pad and a pencil on the table there. Write down Danny's current phone number and address."

Dawn obliged, once again extracting a promise from him that he would not tell his mother of her indiscretion. Gibbons personally thought a good dose of common sense from his mother would do the woman a world of good, but gave his promise anyway; he took note, however, that she was shortsighted enough not to include her own mother in the ban.

Then he sent her off to fetch the others back. Left in solitude for the moment, he curled himself round the pain in his abdomen as best he could in the chair. He had been holding himself together so tightly in order to get himself through the interview that giving into the pain was almost a relief. A tear oozed silently down his cheeks.

"You've overdone it, haven't you?"

Nurse Pipp's voice was soft.

"Could be," grunted Gibbons from his bent-over position.

"I think we'd best get you back into bed," she said.

Gibbons did not think he could move, but she eased the chair over close to the bed after lowering it so he would barely have to stand to make the switch. Then, with a gentle hand and an arm of steel for him to lean on, she maneuvered him out of the chair and into the bed. It hurt less than Gibbons could credit.

"Cheers," he gasped once he was settled.

She drew the blankets up over him and smoothed the pillow.

"You lie still for a bit," she said. "Have you dosed yourself? Good. I'll be back to check on you in a little while."

Gibbons nodded soundlessly while she left the room, closing the door behind her.

When he woke again an hour later, he felt as though he were swimming up toward consciousness from the bottom of a very murky pond. Even once he had opened his eyes, he lay very still, blinking, for some minutes before he remembered what he had been about and that he really ought to ring Carmichael.

But his belly still throbbed and he did not think he had the strength of mind to force himself up again. And then he realized that the object he was blinking at was the phone, sitting within reach on the tray table; Nurse Pipp must have placed it there. Cautiously, he worked an arm out from under the blankets, and in the interest of moving as little as possible, he tugged at the cord until the receiver pulled out of the cradle and landed on the bed by his knee. He was smiling faintly as he picked it up and dialed Carmichael's mobile.

As the day wore on, various officers dropped by to contribute what they could to the translation of Gibbons's notebook. At one point in the afternoon, Carmichael's office became quite crowded with people trying to help and mostly getting in the way. Inspector Davies was the one person who had really had anything illuminating to say; he had been able to explain several things on the pages that dealt with the jewels themselves.

Not that Carmichael really cared much, although he tried to

hide that. Gibbons, he was sure, had not been shot on account of the technical details of the stones and their settings.

So he was almost annoyed when at last he had managed to clear everyone but himself, Lemmy, and Davies out, and the three of them were just settling in to work on Gibbons's notes of his interview with the Colemans, only to be interrupted by the ringing of Carmichael's mobile.

"Bugger it," he muttered under his breath, grabbing it and checking the caller ID. But the exasperation vanished at once when he saw the University College Hospital number, and he answered the call at once. He was relieved to hear Gibbons's voice, however weak he sounded.

"How are you, lad?" he asked, full of concern.

"I'm fine, sir," answered Gibbons. "I spoke with my cousin this afternoon, and wanted to let you know what she said."

"Ah!" said Carmichael, pushing himself back from the desk. "Did she talk to you? Or did she just cry?"

"There was crying," admitted Gibbons. "But she came across with the story eventually, and I believe she was telling me the truth."

He related Dawn's story to Carmichael, who grunted and said, "She's the most feather-brained female I've ever met. I hope you don't mind my saying that, Gibbons."

"Not at all, sir," answered Gibbons. "I've spent most of the day thanking God that most of my relatives aren't like that, and wondering why Dawn has to be the one that lives closest to me."

Carmichael grinned. "It's often that way with relatives, isn't it?" he said sympathetically. "Here, give me this Danny's address and I'll run round and see him this afternoon."

Gibbons read the information off, and then added, "He doesn't seem to have a job, or at least not one he was willing to tell Dawn about, so his home information is all I've got."

"It'll do," replied Carmichael. "You've done brilliantly to get that much out of her. Now, tell me: why do you think you rang her back when you did?"

"I've been thinking about that," said Gibbons slowly. "It's odd that I rang her first if I was about to ring you, and I've been trying to work out how that happened. But since I left a message on your office phone rather than your mobile, I probably scrolled through my incoming calls to find the number. And of course, the one at the top of the list would have been Dawn's."

"Yes, I see," said Carmichael. "And you were only leaving me a message, not planning to speak to me, so you rang her while it was at the front of your mind."

"Right," said Gibbons. "But what that also means is, whatever I was doing in Walworth—I'd finished it. Perhaps I was only following the other bloke to see where he went, or who he met. But I would never have rung Dawn while I was still in the middle of something, not even if I had been waiting for a suspect to reappear and had reason to believe it would take some time. I might have left you a message in that case, but I would have waited to ring Dawn till later."

"Of course," breathed Carmichael. "I never thought of it that way, but I'd have done the same thing if it had been me. Well, Sergeant, you've put in a solid day's work for someone on the sick list."

"Thank you, sir," said Gibbons, clearly pleased with this praise.

"I'll go ferret out this Danny once I'm done here," continued Carmichael, "and then I'll stop by the hospital and let you know how it went."

"I'd appreciate that very much," said Gibbons.

Carmichael hesitated, but then said good-bye without telling Gibbons about the notebook facsimile. It was becoming evident that he would have no choice but to give it to Gibbons, but he was still unsure how to prepare the sergeant for what he would be looking at. It was, he decided, something that was probably best done in person.

After talking with Carmichael, Gibbons pulled out the copies of his own reports as well as the one from O'Leary, and began reading through them. He had done this countless times before, but then he had been concentrating on the effort to jog his memory. He had never, he realized now, looked at them with his investigator's eye, merely as data in a case, and not as the outline of what he could not remember.

It took him some effort to get everything arranged exactly: the reports in an easily readable place, with one of the notebooks Bethancourt had brought him balanced open on the bed beside his thigh where he could write in it without having to move any part of his torso.

He was well into it when his father appeared.

"Well," he said, smiling as he came into the room, "you don't look so bad. Your mum and I were a bit worried earlier, when Nurse Pipp wouldn't let us in."

"I just needed some rest," said Gibbons reassuringly. "I'd had my physio, and then that chat with Dawn, and I was done in."

His father nodded, unzipping his jacket and easing his bulk into a chair.

"What's all this, then?" he asked, nodding to the papers and notebook arranged over the bed.

"Some of the reports about my case," answered Gibbons. "I'm trying to think how I would go about solving it if it were just any case, and nothing to do with me."

His father looked a little surprised at that, and took a moment to think it over.

"Well, yes," he said at last. "I can see where that might be a help. Are you getting anywhere with it?"

"I might be," answered Gibbons, squinting down at his notes thoughtfully. "It's really too early to say yet. But," he added, "it's better than trying to remember things I can't."

"I'd imagine almost anything would be better than that," said his father sympathetically.

"So where's Mum?" asked Gibbons.

"She'll be along in a bit," answered his father. "She took Dawn off shopping after we left here. I think she wanted to get out of her what she'd been telling you."

Gibbons smiled faintly. "And I'll bet she manages it," he said.

"That's not a bet I'll be taking," said his father, grinning. "Your mum's a powerful force when she's got her mind set on something."

"So what have you been doing all afternoon?" asked Gibbons.

"Oh, I've been at the museum," replied his father complacently.

"I've been spending a lot of time there. It's right handy here, and it'd take more time than I've got to see it all. Today I was looking at the Sutton Hoo exhibit—amazing stuff it is."

"It is," agreed Gibbons, who had, over the years, spent a fair amount of time at the British Museum himself.

But his father had moved on from the glories of Sutton Hoo. He was looking down at his hands in his lap and frowning a little.

"They still have no idea who shot you, do they?" he asked.

"No, but it's early days yet," answered Gibbons, trying to be reassuring. "It hasn't even been a week—we'll nail it down in the end. We'll have more trouble with it if it turns out to be a random crime, but somehow I don't think it is. I didn't have much on me, but a thief would have taken whatever he could get, even my Oyster card."

His father was silent a moment.

"You do know, Jack," he said, looking up from his clasped hands, "if this career isn't turning out how you thought it would, there's always a place for you at home. The shop'll have to go to your brother in the end, but we could take you on there for a bit if you needed it."

This was so far from anything Gibbons had considered that he was at first merely confused, at a loss for what his father was talking about. Then the penny dropped.

"No, Dad," he said, not even having to think about his answer. "I love this job—really I do. It's a good career, and I like the work. Getting shot—well, that was an anomaly."

His father met his eyes, as if reading the truth from them. Which, Gibbons reflected, his father was well accustomed to do from his childhood.

"If you're sure, Jack," he said earnestly. "And mind, you can think it over, decide later if you like. Hell, it'll always be there for you, son—I hope you know that."

"I do—and I appreciate it," said Gibbons. "But this hasn't put me off being a detective, Dad."

"Well"—his father rubbed his head—"I don't know. It's not the kind of thing that's ever happened to anyone in the family before. Your brothers seemed to think you might be traumatized."

"I don't think so," said Gibbons, turning this idea over. "At least,

I don't feel traumatized. Maybe it would be worse if I could remember anything about it, but I don't. It's more disturbing having lost a whole day than having been shot. That's almost like being in a traffic accident."

"So long as you're sure," said his father. "Your mother, I don't mind telling you, wants you out of London altogether."

Gibbons laughed at this, though he was careful not to let the laughter penetrate to his belly; he was always wary now of provoking more pain.

"Talk her out of that, would you, Dad?" he said. "I don't want to leave London. It's my home now."

But he was gratified nonetheless by this show of familial support. Later, after his parents had gone off for dinner and a film, he considered his father's offer, but he still had not the slightest inclination for it. He tried to imagine what it would be like, when he was better again, and once more out on the streets, tracking down murderers, but no matter how he thought of it, it did not seem frightening. It seemed right.

17

Gibbons's Notebook

At dinner, Gibbons was given a bowl of cream soup, which represented a step up from the clear liquids he had been getting. He was not sure how he felt about it. He sat in the bed, propped up by lots of pillows, and stared down at the pale, bland surface of the soup. The faint scent that rose up from it did not smell terribly appetizing, and he could not make up his mind whether he felt nauseated or hungry. It had, he realized, been a very long time since he had been hungry.

Cautiously, he dipped the spoon into the soup and gingerly brought it to his lips. It did not taste like much of anything, and it felt a little odd going down, as if his esophagus had forgotten what real swallowing was like. He tried a slightly fuller spoonful and was pleased to discover that it provoked no further nauseous sensations. On the other hand, it was not very satisfying either. Beggars, he decided, could not be choosers.

He had not quite finished the soup when he heard the sound of Cerberus's toenails in the hall and in a moment the dog appeared with his master.

"Oh, look," said Bethancourt, his face lighting up, "they've given you some soup. That's encouraging, don't you think?"

"I do," said Gibbons. "Although I could have wished it tasted a little better."

"Really?" Bethancourt ventured nearer and then stopped abruptly, his face breaking into a broad smile. "Jack!" he said. "They've taken away the tube."

Gibbons grinned back. "I know," he said. "My throat is sore as hell, but I feel ever so much better without it."

"Well, apparently I've missed a lot," said Bethancourt, dragging one of the chairs round and dropping down into it. "Tell all."

"You first," said Gibbons, reaching out to pet Cerberus. "You've been up to something or you would have come round earlier."

"I've been doing my best to help," admitted Bethancourt. "Unfortunately, it doesn't seem to have come to much in the end."

Succinctly, he described his theories and his various conversations. When he finished, Gibbons was smiling at him.

"It's nothing to smile about," he said. "Not unless you think sweet old Nicky Burdall hiked over the fields with her great-grandchildren to commit a felony."

"No, I don't," answered Gibbons, "but I think you thoroughly enjoyed finding out she didn't. If it had been me, I should be feeling quite annoyed and frustrated, but it's obvious you had a perfectly delightful time."

"Ah, well, they were nice people," said Bethancourt. "And old Grenshaw was a wonderfully preserved specimen from my grandfather's time. But you seem to be doing very well yourself today—and I didn't think I'd be saying that anytime soon."

"I think I do feel better," said Gibbons, sounding almost surprised. "It still hurts like bloody hell, but I think my head is a bit clearer. At any rate, I managed to do something."

Bethancourt raised his brows in query, his hazel eyes behind his glasses looking hopeful.

"It wasn't very much," Gibbons told him. "I told you about Dawn and the phone calls."

Bethancourt nodded. "You seemed to think it didn't amount to much," he said, "although if you ask me it was decidedly odd."

"Not if you know Dawn," said Gibbons, making a face. "In any case, Carmichael had her down at the Yard yesterday to get it sorted out."

"And?"

Gibbons grinned. "She cried."

Bethancourt hesitated, unsure how to respond to words and expression so at odds with each other. In the end, he fell back on polite formula.

"I'm sorry to hear it," he said. "Did she have an explanation?"

"You don't understand," said Gibbons, still smiling. "Crying was all she did. Carmichael couldn't get her to stop."

"You're joking," said Bethancourt, incredulous.

"Well, to give him credit, I don't know how hard he tried," admitted Gibbons. "He knew he had another way in. But apparently she put on quite a show. So I had her here this afternoon to find out what she was hiding."

Bethancourt, observing Gibbons's good humor, had already concluded that whatever it was, it had nothing to do with his friend being shot.

"Did she cry?" he asked.

"Copiously," confirmed Gibbons. "But I told her I wasn't having any of it and threatened her with my mother."

"I see," said Bethancourt, smiling. "So the threat of Scotland Yard pales beside the threat of her aunt Margery."

"Pretty much," agreed Gibbons. "It was all terribly silly, really. She'd snuck out to meet her ex-husband and lend him money and she's petrified lest that come out and somebody tries to talk some sense into her. She doesn't actually want to lend him money, so she rang to see if she could hoodwink me into going with her, since she reckoned he wouldn't ask for money in front of a third party."

Bethancourt was frowning. "But how would that help?" he asked. "It's just putting off the evil day."

"Exactly," said Gibbons. "Hence the tears."

"Ah. When in doubt, cry?"

"That seems to be her philosophy," agreed Gibbons.

"Well," sighed Bethancourt, "I suppose it's one point cleared up."

"Yes—is that someone else coming?"

Bethancourt twisted round to look and saw Carmichael appear in the doorway, peering in cautiously to see if he was interrupting anything.

"Come in, sir," called Gibbons. "It's good to see you."

Carmichael came into the room slowly, greeting both young men and pausing a moment to give Cerberus's ears a rub before settling himself in the second armchair, holding his briefcase in his lap. But his shrewd blue eyes were on Gibbons, assessing his condition.

"You look better, lad," he said to Gibbons.

"It's the tube being out," said Gibbons. "I can't tell you what a relief it is."

"And he's had soup for dinner," put in Bethancourt, sounding like a proud parent.

"Good, good," said Carmichael. "That's a step forward, eh?"

His tone was pleased, but Gibbons had worked with him for years and could tell he was distracted.

"What is it?" he asked simply. "Is there bad news?"

"No, no," Carmichael hastened to reassure him. "No, not bad news. In fact, Hodges over at forensics has worked his usual miracle."

Gibbons's eyes lit up. "My notebook?" he asked eagerly. "Did you bring me a copy?"

"That's right," said Carmichael, still making no move to open the briefcase on his lap.

"I can excuse myself, sir," said Bethancourt, already half out of his chair. "I don't mind in the least."

"Because Gibbons here will just tell you everything afterward," retorted Carmichael. "No, Bethancourt, keep your seat. It's not you I'm hesitating about."

Bethancourt dropped back into the chair obediently, shooting a puzzled glance at Gibbons.

Gibbons did not notice. He was eyeing Carmichael, trying to work out what the problem was.

"Sir," he said, "I'm full of morphine and I have trouble staying awake for more than an hour altogether. Could you just tell me what's wrong?"

Carmichael sighed. "I'm sorry," he said. "I didn't mean to be mysterious. I just don't know what to say." He shook his head as if to clear it. "Here's the situation," he said. "I've gone through the part of the notebook that deals with the Haverford burglary, and I'll need your help to read it and decipher any clues that might be there."

Gibbons was impatient. "Yes, of course," he said. "I won't overtire myself, if that's what you're on about. I promise."

Carmichael looked faintly guilty. "I hadn't thought of that," he muttered. He glanced at Bethancourt.

"I wouldn't worry," advised Bethancourt. "He can barely keep awake as it is."

Gibbons glared at him and Bethancourt's heart leaped. He had not been properly glared at in days.

"The problem," continued Carmichael, "is that some of the facsimiles are, well, a little disturbing to look at."

Bethancourt looked perplexed while Gibbons merely stared at his superior incredulously.

"I've already seen my notebook," he said. "I've seen it lots of times—I wrote whatever's in it, for God's sake."

"It doesn't look the way you remember," said Carmichael gently.

Gibbons raised a dubious brow, but that was enough to make the light dawn for Bethancourt.

"Oh," he said. "I see."

"You do?" demanded Gibbons.

"Yes. The notebook's got your blood all over it now."

Carmichael winced at the baldness of this statement, but Gibbons's eyes merely widened in comprehension, and he leaned back against his pillows for a moment. Then, his face blank, he turned to Carmichael.

"Give it to me," he said.

And Carmichael obeyed silently, fumbling open the briefcase and removing a large envelope, which he handed to Gibbons.

"That's a complete copy," he said. "I mean, it's got all the earlier pages, too."

Gibbons merely nodded; he was already busy pulling the pages out of the envelope and sorting through them. He put aside the top half dozen or so sheets that did not relate to the Haverford case and bent his head over the first of the Haverford pages.

Even from where he sat, Bethancourt could see the deep coloring of the photographs, though a good deal of it looked more like chemical stain than blood. But Gibbons did not seem disturbed by it, and to Bethancourt the large, glossy sheets bore such little resemblance to the notebook he had so often seen Gibbons scribbling in that the impact of the images was negligible.

He leaned forward to get a better view of the page, though he knew he wouldn't be able to read any of it; he had encountered Gibbons's version of shorthand before.

Carmichael, having got over the difficult bit of his visit, relaxed in his chair, setting his briefcase aside on the floor and crossing his legs, while he watched Gibbons with a concerned eye.

But Gibbons did not seem any more bothered by this evidence of the violence done to him than was Bethancourt. His eyes moved rapidly down the first page and as he laid it aside, he said, "These are just the notes I took at the scene on Monday—I remember that part. Oh, and this next page and I believe the next two—yes, two more— are my notes while I was swotting up on gemstones."

"That was on Monday as well?" asked Bethancourt, and Gibbons nodded, never lifting his eyes from the page.

"That's right," he said. "Davies and I went out to the scene and met James and the Colemans there. Then we came back and he went over some of the basics with me. I made some notes then, but most of these are from the research I did once I got home. Ah, here we are: this looks like the notes I took at Grenshaw's office on Tuesday morning."

He fell silent while he read and the others were quiet, too, lest they disturb his concentration.

"Well," he said after a time, "I don't know that there's much here—most of it seems to be in the report I wrote. You can tell from this"—and he laid a finger on the page—"that I was surprised to find out there was virtually nothing left of the estate except the jewels themselves. And I've made a notation here that says *old*. I'm not sure what I meant by that." He looked up, as if inviting suggestions.

"Possibly," suggested Bethancourt, "that everyone connected with

Miranda Haverford—with the exception of the Colemans—was exceedingly elderly. It does rather explain why they were her heirs."

Gibbons nodded. "Very likely," he agreed, returning his attention to the next page of the facsimile. "This must be the interview with the Colemans," he said in a moment. "Here, just let me read through it."

On the verge of proposing that he read it aloud, Bethancourt bit his lip and managed to remain silent. He glanced at Carmichael, but that gentleman seemed well content with the way things were proceeding. He was slouched comfortably in the chair, holding some papers in his lap, which he glanced down at occasionally, though most of his attention remained on Gibbons.

Gibbons skimmed through his notes, carefully laying aside the pages as he finished with them. When at last he looked up again, Carmichael said, "There's a lot there we couldn't make out, particularly all the notations in the margins."

"Oh, I often do that," said Gibbons, reassembling the pages. "I note down the salient points in an interview—the stuff I'm going to put in the report—and then in the margins I make notes about what I'm thinking about it all. Like just here"—he searched for a moment for the place on the page—"here, where I've written £££! next to the note that says the Colemans had only recently moved to England."

"Yes," said Carmichael dryly. "That was one of the things we couldn't make out."

Gibbons looked surprised. "I thought that one was clear enough," he said. "I obviously thought they had come in order to ensure their inheritance."

"If that's true," pointed out Bethancourt, "then your impression of them was less favorable than was conveyed in your report."

Gibbons shrugged. "Probably. You don't put your feelings into a report."

"So," said Carmichael, firmly pulling them back to the subject, "you thought it likely that the Colemans' motive in coming here was to ensure Miss Haverford did not change her will. Does that mean you had some intimation that she might?"

"Not that I know of, and I think I would have made a note of something like that," answered Gibbons. He was silent for a moment, looking down at what he had written. "I think," he said at last, "that the £ sign refers to my estimation of their character. It's hard to tell," he said, looking up, "since I only remember meeting them briefly on Monday afternoon."

"What the hell do the triangles mean?" asked Carmichael. "Nobody could make that out."

"Triangles?" Gibbons looked down at the sheet before him as if surprised to see that there were any triangles contained in it. "Oh, that. It's the symbol for change in chemistry—I use it as an abbreviation."

Carmichael muttered something and made a note. "What about the rest of the annotations?" he asked.

"Well," said Gibbons, referring back to the facsimile, "I think all this here"—and he held up the sheet, pointing to some scrawling down the right side of the margin—"must be questions I had about the jewelry. You can see in the body of the notes that we were discussing the various pieces, and the Colemans and James were probably using terms I didn't know. And there are question marks next all these jottings—I usually do that when there's something I have to look up."

Carmichael was nodding and looking down at the papers he held. "You seem to have discussed the details of the jewelry pretty thoroughly," he said.

"There's a lot about it here," admitted Gibbons. "But I probably would have made more extensive notes about that, since the jewelry was the thing I knew least about."

"Of course," murmured Carmichael.

"But in that case," said Bethancourt, "there might be things you spoke about which you wouldn't have made note of at all."

Both detectives looked at him.

"Well, of course," said Gibbons. "I'm not a stenographer—I jot down pertinent facts or anything that strikes me. Half this stuff I probably wrote after the fact."

"Oh," said Bethancourt, a little crestfallen.

"It's always like that," Carmichael told him. "I did the same when I was a sergeant. Did you think that every word would be in there?"

Bethancourt grinned sheepishly. "I suppose I didn't really think at all," he said.

Carmichael smiled at him sympathetically while Gibbons snorted.

"To get on," he said, "we also went over the timing of the burglary—that's this bit here—and when it might have happened, if there had been anyone suspicious about, the usual stuff."

"We reconstructed most of that," said Carmichael. "It was all in your report in any case."

"Mmm," said Gibbons, who was reading again. "Now here," he said, "at the bottom of this page, I think these must be notes from my lunch with James. Yes, and on this next page, too."

"We read that as more information about jewels and jewel thieves," put in Carmichael. "Inspector Davies was a great help there—I couldn't make head nor tail of the stuff."

"I'm having rather a difficult time of it myself," admitted Gibbons. "Since I can't remember what the notes refer to, it's hard to make out my own abbreviations."

"Most of them seemed to make sense to Davies," said Carmichael, glancing down at the papers in his lap.

"Is that what you were able to work out from Jack's notes?" asked Bethancourt, craning to get a look.

"That's right," said Carmichael. "All typed out in ordinary English by Constable Lemmy, who has a real future in word processing if you ask me."

Bethancourt laughed, but Gibbons was more intrigued with the translation Carmichael had managed to make. He winced as he leaned forward in an effort to read it upside-down, but Carmichael immediately covered it with one hand.

"No, no," he said. "Some of this may be quite wrong, and I'm not having you influenced by it until you've told me what you think it all means."

"Oh," said Gibbons, who had been forced to abandon his inspection in any case by the pain in his belly. He was rather pale as he leaned back against the pillows again. "I suppose," he said grudgingly, "that only makes sense."

"It most certainly does," said Carmichael firmly, ending further discussion of this point. "So," he continued, "do you think you stopped somewhere to make notes of what you had discussed over lunch with James, or were these all taken at the lunch itself?"

Gibbons frowned and studied the pages in front of him again.

"There's too much here," he said at last. "I wouldn't have written all of it down in the middle of lunch. Did I leave the restaurant with James? I can't remember what Davies told me."

"I believe you left together," replied Carmichael.

"Then I probably stopped at a caff to make these notes," said Gibbons. "I'm sure I was alone when I made them, because they're too elaborate. Like here, where it looks like I'm drawing parallels between theft and murder investigations. I wouldn't have written that down while I was talking to James."

"Where?" asked Carmichael. "I don't think I have that."

Gibbons turned the facsimile sheet so they could see it.

"Here," he said, pointing to a passage that read:

3: Info CS—where? → transport.
Benefits? Motive? Emo.

"And what does that mean when it's at home?" demanded Bethancourt.

"Three ways to come at theft: info gathered from crime scene, ultimate destination of the goods, and how it gets there. Like murder, who benefits? Motives very different; not emotional," Gibbons read. "You see? That's a reminder to myself not to think like a homicide detective, that the two kinds of investigations are different in very specific ways."

"Yes, I see." Carmichael nodded, making a note of his own. "You were still trying to change gears, so to speak."

"Right." Gibbons had moved on to the next page and was frowning over it. "I'm not sure what this next bit is," he said slowly.

Bethancourt could restrain himself no longer.

"Do you mind awfully if I come and look?" he asked.

Gibbons looked contrite. "Of course not," he said. "I should have said."

Bethancourt rose and positioned himself so that he could see over Gibbons's shoulder, being careful not to jar the bed. As he had expected, the writing was just so much gibberish to his eyes, but one marginal notation did jump out at him.

"That 'MH-NC,'" he said. "Couldn't that be a reference to Miranda Haverford?"

"Very likely," agreed Gibbons. "I wonder what I meant by 'NC,' though. I must have thought it important—I've underscored it heavily."

"And you've got exclamation points by '4 mos!!!,'" pointed out Bethancourt.

"I've no idea what I meant by that either," said Gibbons. "Or by 'Bs—j fake.' What's a 'B,' for heaven's sake?"

"Book," supplied Bethancourt readily. "Banger, box, birth, binge—"

"Or," interrupted Carmichael, stemming this flow, "Bethancourt."

The two younger men looked at each other.

"But I hadn't spoken to you," said Gibbons. "I hadn't even left that message for you yet."

"We talked on Sunday," said Bethancourt. "But I don't think you said anything about the Haverford case then."

"Well, I wouldn't have, would I?" said Gibbons. "I didn't know about it then. We didn't get called out to it until Monday afternoon."

"Oh, right," said Bethancourt. "I'd forgotten. But look here," he added as another thought came to him, "if I were making a note about you, I wouldn't use the initial 'G.' I'd use 'J' for 'Jack.'"

"Oh," said Gibbons, struck by this. "That's absolutely true. If I'd been referring to you, I would have put down 'P.'"

"We don't have your afternoon completely filled in yet," said Carmichael. "It could be that these are notes you made later, somewhere else."

"And about something else," said Gibbons gloomily.

"Well," said Bethancourt, endeavoring to look on the bright side, "these notes are pretty brief—not much there, really."

"But they could be important," said Gibbons. "In fact, if we're right about their referring to something I did or thought in the time that's still missing, they're important by default."

Bethancourt had to admit that this was true.

"We'll look for the café where you stopped," said Carmichael. "Perhaps we can get a line on where you went from there."

"Right," said Gibbons, a little gloomily. It had not occurred to him before that his notes might be obscure to him, although it seemed obvious now. By definition, notes were made to jog one's memory; if one had no memory, the notes would be meaningless.

"Well, let's get on," said Bethancourt, sensing his friend's despondency and making his tone determinedly cheerful in consequence. "What does 'WC' mean, or is that just a reminder to fix your loo at home?"

Gibbons frowned at it. "Is it 'WC,' or is it 'NC'?"

"It's 'W,' " said Bethancourt firmly.

"I took it as a 'W,' " said Carmichael, once again referring to his notes. "I had rather discounted it, to be truthful. There are quite a few notes which obviously have nothing to do with work. That first page has a grocery list on it."

"Well, it's natural enough to write things down where I'm used to writing them," said Gibbons defensively. "It's not as though I was expecting to have other people going through my notebook."

"Of course not," said Carmichael soothingly. "I only meant that I assumed 'WC' stood for 'water closet' and referred to something you meant to pick up for your bathroom."

"Well, it can't have been that," declared Gibbons. "There's nothing wrong with my bathroom."

"Maybe something went wrong with it that afternoon," suggested Bethancourt, but Gibbons only gave him a scornful look.

"Don't be silly," he said. "I wouldn't have stopped at home after lunch when I meant to head back to the Yard. And my landlady didn't ring to say there was a problem, because there would have been a record of the call on my mobile."

"That's true," agreed Carmichael thoughtfully. "And the notation stands alone just there—it's not as if it's part of a shopping list or anything. Perhaps it has to do with the case after all."

"I think it must do," said Gibbons. "I'm damned if I know what, though."

"Well, let's take the thing as a whole," said Bethancourt, adjusting his glasses and peering down at the page on Gibbons's lap. "We've got 'Bs—j fake, 4 mos!!!, WC,' and whatever this is here."

Gibbons squinted at it. "It's hard to make out," he said.

"I think that might be another B," said Bethancourt, pointing.

"And it's connected to something with a tail," said Gibbons. "It might be a note to do a background check on somebody or something."

"On WC?" asked Bethancourt.

"It could be. It seems to be grouped with that note. But this is the worst part of the page—I think it might say 'Bgr-US.' "

"So you were going to do a background check on someone with the initials 'WC' in the United States," said Bethancourt.

"I suppose," said Gibbons doubtfully. "At least, I could have been."

"That," said Carmichael dryly, "is hardly a resounding endorsement."

"Well, really, it could say almost anything," apologized Gibbons.

"On the other hand," said Bethancourt, "it doesn't seem to have anything to do with details of the jewelry. There's a lot of that in the rest of it."

"That's true," said Gibbons, looking back at the page. "If you're right and 'MH' stands for Miranda Haverford, then it almost seems like these were thoughts I had about the situation the jewelry was in. Perhaps I was trying to draw a connection between Miss Haverford's friends and relations and the burglary."

"Or at least trying to rule it out," said Carmichael. "Unlike murder, these crimes are usually committed by professional thieves, or so Davies gives me to understand."

Gibbons nodded. "Yes, I remember discussing that with him when I first got assigned to him. Oh!"

Both Bethancourt and Carmichael were instantly alert, but Gibbons's exclamation stemmed from a mental surprise, not a physical pain.

"That's what this on the next page means," he said, laying aside the current sheet in favor of the one beneath it.

Bethancourt stooped to look at the stained picture of a mostly blank sheet of paper with two columns in Gibbons's cramped writing at the top.

MURDER	THEFT
Plan	Plan
Kill	Steal
Hide	Fen/despo
	Acquire £
	hide

Under that, after two blank lines, was "*Imps? Con? C-prfl,*" and after that, "*Fun., 2-fence.*"

"What does which mean, exactly?" said Bethancourt.

"Well, in the chart here," said Gibbons, running his finger down the list, "I seem to be further delineating the differences between investigating a murder and investigating a burglary. This is basically saying that after the initial crime, for a murderer the end goal has been accomplished—the only thing left to do is try not to get caught. But for a thief, the initial crime is just that, the first of several steps to the end result of money in hand. I think I was trying to find the right angle to come at the whole thing from. That would be very like me."

"Would it," murmured Carmichael, somewhat bemused by this.

Bethancourt was nodding. "Yes, of course," he said. "I see what you mean. You're saying murder is the end of a chain of events; burglary is the start of the chain. Yes, that makes perfect sense."

Carmichael supposed that it did, but it didn't seem to be getting them anywhere.

"So where are we, then?" he asked. "I can't see myself that any of this tells us what you were doing in Walworth getting yourself shot. Who could you have been following?"

Gibbons suddenly looked tired.

"I don't know," he answered, a little hopelessly.

"Well," said Bethancourt, returning to his chair and settling into it comfortably, resting his elbows on the arms and folding his hands across his chest, "let's see. We've got a better idea of what you were thinking. And one of those last notes must have been the one you made in the pub—you know," he added as Gibbons looked blank, "the one the bartender told O'Leary he saw you make after O'Leary left."

"Oh, right," said Gibbons. "I can't believe I forgot that."

"You're not yourself," said Bethancourt kindly, which provoked a rather wan glare from his friend. "So we believe you were thinking about the Haverford case, and you seem to have had an idea, or at least some thought as to how to approach the whole thing, right?"

Gibbons nodded. "That's a fair assumption," he said.

"So," continued Bethancourt, "we know you didn't return to the Yard, and we know you didn't start for home."

Carmichael raised a bushy eyebrow at that. "We do?" he asked.

"Well, I thought so," said Bethancourt. "It's a straight shot on the District line from St. James to Hammersmith. Even if one of the thieves was tramping about London leaving a trail of alexandrite gemstones behind him, why on earth should he be on that particular part of the District line at just the time Jack was heading home? It beggars belief."

Carmichael was amused. "When put like that," he said, "it does rather. All right, go on with your theorizing."

Bethancourt sat up a little and cleared his throat, wishing for a cigarette. He was suddenly self-conscious.

"I was only thinking," he said, "that given Jack didn't show up in Walworth until two hours later, he must have gone somewhere to either speak to someone, or possibly to look at the Haverford house again. Somewhere, at any rate, where he could encounter someone who said something suspicious, or see someone where they shouldn't be."

"If I was all the way up in Southgate," said Gibbons, "it would explain why it took me two hours to get to Walworth."

"But of course we don't know how or when you picked up our mystery bloke's trail," said Carmichael. "I do wish that second cabbie would come forward."

"That's the working theory, then?" asked Bethancourt. "That whoever Jack was following was the one who shot him?"

Carmichael shrugged a little. "Not necessarily," he replied. "I can think of other scenarios. But I think if he didn't do it himself, he bloody well knows who did."

"So then," said Bethancourt, "you believe what happened to Jack is connected to the Haverford case after all."

Carmichael narrowed his eyes in thought. "I always had that feeling," he said in a moment. "Perhaps I've been relying too much on that—God knows I can't be said to be very objective in this case."

Gibbons grinned faintly from his bed. "I'm glad of that, sir."

Carmichael smiled sheepishly back at him. "So am I, lad, so am I." He cleared his throat, clearly discomfited by this display of emotion.

"Although," added Gibbons thoughtfully, "it's odd that I rang you instead of Davies later. If it was to do with his case, I can't imagine why I wouldn't have left him a message instead."

"That's the one thing that's made me doubt my instincts," admitted Carmichael.

"You would have rung the chief inspector here if you thought Davies was up to some funny business," said Bethancourt.

Both policemen turned to stare at him, clearly taken aback by this suggestion.

"I don't know the man well," said Carmichael, exchanging dubious looks with Gibbons, "but he has an excellent reputation. Really, it would be most unusual for a detective to turn coats—it's the sort of thing that only happens in telly programs."

"I really can't imagine," said Gibbons, looking rather shocked, "that Inspector Davies would shoot me."

Carmichael burst into laughter. "Well, now," he said. "That's a solution to Constable Lemmy I hadn't thought of."

The two younger men joined in his laughter.

"In any case," said Bethancourt, "it might not be Davies who shot you. He could have accomplices—and it certainly wasn't Davies you were following that night."

"No," agreed Carmichael, "our witness said it was a young man." He ran a hand over his head. "I expect it's something to consider," he said, but not as though he were convinced of it.

"It does explain why I rang you," said Gibbons, but he, too, sounded doubtful. "And," he added reluctantly, "it would also account for the fact that I made an appointment to speak with you the next morning, instead of ringing you directly."

"True," said Carmichael. "I've been thinking that was an indication that, whatever you wanted, it wasn't urgent. But it could equally well have been discretion on your part."

They looked at each other a little blankly.

"It's not the only possibility," interposed Bethancourt, feeling as if he had set the cat among the pigeons. "Let's go back to what you might have done when you left the pub."

"I can't have gone to see Davies," said Gibbons, frowning. "I would have gone back to the Yard to look for him, and we know I didn't do that."

"And you can't have tried to see Grenshaw," said Bethancourt. "It was half-six—he would have left his office before that."

"I could have gone back to check something at the Haverford house," said Gibbons. "Although none of these notes seem to refer to the scene of the crime."

"You might have wanted to ask the Colemans something," suggested Bethancourt. "Or Colin James—he doesn't strike me as the type who leaves the office promptly at five."

"Either of those is a good guess," agreed Gibbons. "But for all we know, I could have met someone on my way from the pub to the tube and gone off with them to have some dinner."

"Well, yes," said Bethancourt, feeling discouraged.

"But in that case," said Carmichael, "you have to think about how seeing someone from the case at a restaurant would have struck you as suspicious. You did follow someone, after all."

"Or," said Bethancourt, "it could be what you told the cabbie was true: you knew the chap in the other taxi and the two of you simply didn't want to arrive in the same car. In that case, the man you were following was an acquaintance with whom you had just dined."

Carmichael looked at him, slightly exasperated by this explanation.

"Is there no instance you can't spin a story for?" he demanded.

"Sorry, sir," said Bethancourt. "I'll try to stick to the most likely scenarios."

"In any case," said Gibbons, raising his voice slightly to assure he had their attention, "if that were true, it wouldn't help us any. It would mean I had gone to Walworth with a friend and presumably been attacked by a random mugger."

"Who shoots his victims from a distance before robbing them?" asked Carmichael scornfully. "It's hardly a very successful strategy, is it?"

"It doesn't seem very likely," admitted Bethancourt with a smile.

"So let's return to the more plausible," said Carmichael. "You went off to check on something about the case. If we're all very lucky, you did not surprise Inspector Davies in the act of retrieving the stolen jewels—hold on a minute."

Carmichael, struck by a sudden thought, fell silent, a speculative look in his eyes. In a moment his focus slid sideways toward Bethancourt, who met his gaze, his own eyes alight with curiosity.

"You suggested Gibbons might have gone to speak with the Colemans or with Colin James."

"Yes, sir," acknowledged Bethancourt. "They were the first two names that popped into my head."

"And I believe," said Carmichael slowly, as if he were still thinking the idea over, "that Davies and Colin James are quite friendly."

"Oh!" said Gibbons. His mouth remained open for a moment, as if he were going to add something, but then he closed it without speaking, looking rather stunned.

"If the two of them colluded to steal the jewelry," said Bethancourt, "they must also have a third accomplice: the man Jack was following on Tuesday night. Does James have a younger boyfriend?"

None of them knew.

"It's only a hypothesis," said Carmichael firmly, relegating this flight of fancy to its proper sphere. "It's even more likely that Gibbons went back to the Haverford house and found someone—a professional thief, perhaps—there before him, someone he then proceeded to follow."

"But then why did I ring you instead of Davies?" demanded Gibbons.

And none of them had an answer to that, either.

But Carmichael made up his mind that first thing tomorrow he would set about discovering where Davies had been on Tuesday evening.

Bethancourt, leaving the hospital deep in thought, walked aimlessly down Gower Street before realizing he had left the car in the other direction. As he turned back, it dawned on him that it was late, likely much later than he had intended to leave. He pushed back his coat cuff and yelped as he saw the time.

"Come along, Cerberus," he said, quickening his pace. "I'm awfully late—it's a wonder Marla hasn't rung—oh, dear Lord."

This exclamation came as he remembered he had switched off his mobile phone upon entering the hospital. Anxiously, he fished it out of his pocket and turned it back on, swearing again as it announced to him that he had messages from three missed calls.

"Oh dear, oh dear," he muttered as he listened to Marla's increasingly irate messages. Glancing down at himself, he reflected that he could not possibly fulfill their evening engagements without first going home to change. "Well, at least I've got the car," he told the dog. "It's a pity the shops are shut," he added as he dialed Marla's number. "I could have just bought some things—it would have been faster."

"Where on earth have you been?" she demanded. "We're going to be horribly late for dinner."

"I'm terribly sorry," he apologized. "Jack and I got to talking and I lost track of time."

"Oh, how is he?" she asked.

"I think he might be a bit better," he told her. "At least, he seemed more alert and he stayed awake for longer. That's why I'm so late."

"I'm glad he's getting better," she said, but she sounded distracted and he knew he had not entirely diverted her from his tardiness.

"Look here," he said, "how would it be if I met you at the restaurant?"

"Deirdre and I are nearly at the restaurant now," she snarled and he winced.

"Ah, yes," he said. "Well, I'll be right along, then. It won't take me a minute."

"Well, do hurry up, Phillip," she replied. "Remember, we've got David's party to go on to, so we can't spend all night at dinner."

"Right," he said. "I'll be there in no time."

He sighed as he rang off and looked forlornly at Cerberus.

"She's going to murder me," he said.

David's birthday party had been a huge success. The champagne had flowed, and had been accompanied by mini chocolate tortes and strawberry tarts instead of the usual hors d'oeuvres, an inspired innovation. It was no doubt the unusual combination, thought Bethancourt, that had him awake at 6:00 A.M., a scant two hours after he had fallen asleep, with a decidedly acid stomach.

He was not a man who normally had much trouble that way, and he lay awake for several moments, listening to the rain against the windows, before tracing the complaint to its source.

"Bother," he muttered.

Marla beside him was very still, burrowed beneath the duvet, apparently without digestive difficulties. This made his own discomfort all the more irritating. Sighing, he rolled over on his side, hitching his head a little farther up on the pillow, and wondered if he could go back to sleep or if he would be forced to rise and seek a remedy.

The rain was coming down steadily outside, a peaceful drone that spoke of sleep. Bethancourt closed his eyes and tried to concentrate on it, but his brain refused to cooperate. Pleasant scenes from the recent party drifted through his mind, which he then found himself contrasting with the equally pleasant—if wildly different— scene of high tea with three generations of Burdalls.

And that suddenly brought him wide awake, his eyes flying open in the darkness. Gibbons had not remembered the Burdalls, which meant he had not gone to interview them on Monday when he and Davies had been at the scene. It was possible, of course, that Inspector Davies had followed up with the Burdalls on Tuesday, but

Bethancourt thought it unlikely; he had spent enough time around police investigations to know that an errand like that was usually given to a subordinate, not carried out by the officer in charge. Which in turn meant it was quite likely that when Nicky Burdall said her family had been interviewed by Scotland Yard, it was to Gibbons she was referring, and—since Gibbons had no memory of them—that the interview had taken place on Tuesday.

In fact, thought Bethancourt, there was even that mysterious initial "B" in Gibbons's notebook. It could well refer to the Burdalls, and if so, there was part of Gibbons's time accounted for. Since that particular note was placed toward the end of what Gibbons had written that day, it was even possible that his interview with the Burdalls had taken place after his pint with O'Leary—the crucial missing time period.

Between acid indigestion and detective excitement, sleep had become impossible. Reluctantly, Bethancourt slipped out of the bed without waking Marla, wrapped himself in his dressing gown, and sought out the kitchen. Milky tea and toast—his childhood nanny's solution to upset stomachs—would probably do as well as anything to settle his innards and let him get back to sleep.

18

Cautious Distrust

Carmichael saw his wife off to church on Sunday morning before leaving for the Yard. Ordinarily, he would have accompanied her unless events in a case were particularly pressing, but he was too worried about Davies's possible malfeasance to do anything but go to work. During the night, the likelihood of Davies's culpability had seemed to loom over him, seeming almost certain, and preventing his getting much sleep. But this morning over his first cuppa he had had another, more cheerful thought. If Colin James might have colluded with Davies to steal the jewels, it followed that another possibility was that James had stolen them himself, and might not have involved Davies at all other than to take advantage of the inspector's trust.

Carmichael liked this scenario so much better than the one that painted Davies as the criminal mastermind that he was, at heart, rather doubtful of it. Still, both possibilities would have to be looked into and it was going to take a great deal of tact to find out the truth without alarming (or, if innocent, insulting) either party.

The end result of which was that Carmichael did not think he could possibly sit piously in church while an internal police investigation hung over him like Damocles's sword.

The day was gray, but not rainy, and it looked as though it might be clearing. Carmichael, who was heartily sick of the November weather, reflected that having the sun peep out—if it happened—could be taken as a good omen for his investigation.

When he reached the Yard, Constable Lemmy was not in evidence, which Carmichael took as another good omen, though he found it nonetheless irritating. He got himself a coffee and settled in at his desk, taking a cigar from the drawer where he kept them and placing it above his blotter, like the promise of a reward. Then, with a knot in his stomach, he picked up the phone and dialed Inspector Davies's mobile.

Davies answered at once, as might be expected of a detective inspector involved in an ongoing investigation.

Carmichael identified himself and then continued, "There's just a detail I wanted to clear up, Inspector. Could Gibbons have got hold of you on Tuesday night if he had tried?"

"Yes, of course," replied Davies, sounding rather surprised at this question. "I spent the evening at home, but I had my mobile close at hand—I was hoping to hear from one of my contacts, in fact, but he didn't ring until the next day. I understood, sir," he added, "that we had the sergeant's phone records. If he had tried to ring me, wouldn't it have shown up there?"

"Oh, yes," said Carmichael. "I was simply trying to reconstruct Gibbons's thinking. I'm still rather perplexed that he rang me instead of you that night."

"I've always assumed, sir," said Davies, "that there was a personal reason behind that. After all, the two of you have worked together for years and presumably he would turn to you if he felt the need of an older man's advice."

"True enough," responded Carmichael cheerfully. He did not point out that Gibbons had a perfectly serviceable father with whom he was on good terms and whom he could consult if need be. Or that young men in their twenties seldom felt the need for such advice at all. "In any case, I just wanted to make sure he could have spoken to you if something about the Haverford burglary had come up."

"I see," said Davies, sounding distracted. "Excuse me, sir, but here's my call from South Africa coming through—I must take it."

"Certainly, certainly," said Carmichael, and rang off.

He replaced the receiver and frowned at the cigar. Davies, it seemed, had no alibi, unless one wanted to count his wife, and Carmichael didn't. He had not realized how much he had been hoping that the inspector would produce an ironclad alibi, but he felt the disappointment keenly now. The knot in his stomach tightened another notch.

"Damn it all," he muttered under his breath, and leaned back in his chair to consider. Was the fact that Davies had immediately, without waiting to be asked, related his whereabouts that evening a suspicious occurrence or the opposite? Did it indicate a lie already prepared, or complete innocence? One could go round and round with that question, like a hamster on its wheel.

"Let's move on," he said to himself. Next up was Colin James, and he was going to be a more difficult nut to crack; Carmichael had no ready-made excuse to ask him about his movements on Tuesday night. He didn't fancy ringing James up in any case—not having encountered him previously, he preferred a face-to-face meeting so he might make his own assessment of the man. Perhaps, he decided, inspiration was best left to the moment.

Accordingly, he pawed through the case file until he found James's address and then donned his overcoat again before venturing out to beard the lion in its den. If, that was, the lion worked on Sundays.

Carmichael had not expected the offices of a private investigator to be well appointed. He was used to the offices of those who collected evidence of adultery or who traced the biological parents of adopted children, and although he had known that an insurance investigator was of a different stripe, he was unprepared for the hushed atmosphere that spoke of exquisite taste backed by solid wealth.

He was also surprised to find that not only was James working on a Sunday, so apparently was his secretary. She was a slender young woman installed at an antique desk in the anteroom, dressed in the last word of fashionable elegance. She received him graciously, in a cool, husky voice and ushered him into an overstuffed leather armchair to wait while she inquired when Mr. James would be available. Carmichael watched the sway of her hips appreciatively as she walked back across the room and entered the inner sanctum.

She was gone for some five or ten minutes, during which Carmichael took stock of his surroundings and decided that insurance investigation paid better than he had realized. Either that, or Colin James was as crooked as they came which, considering Carmichael's errand, was an interesting thought.

The secretary returned, smiling pleasantly, and informed him that Mr. James would see him now. Feeling rather as if he were being admitted to an exclusive club, Carmichael followed her into James's office.

The inner sanctum was as beautifully outfitted as the anteroom to Carmichael's eye, with the addition of what even he could recognize as very expensive touches. James waited for him behind a highly polished partner desk, a tall, fit-looking man with shrewd gray eyes, dressed casually in a gray cashmere turtleneck and a pair of exquisitely pressed flannels.

"It's very good to meet you, Chief Inspector," said James, coming round the desk to shake hands. "Do be seated—can we get you anything? There's coffee or tea, or I believe there's some orange juice in the refrigerator."

Carmichael accepted coffee and sat down in another overstuffed leather armchair, one of two positioned opposite James's desk.

"And how is Sergeant Gibbons doing?" asked James, resuming his own seat.

"He's improving," replied Carmichael. "I visited him yesterday evening, and he seemed considerably more alert than he has been before."

"I'm glad to hear it," said James. "I was very impressed with the sergeant in the short time we worked together. It would have been a great pity if he had not been able to make a full recovery."

"Certainly it would," agreed Carmichael wholeheartedly. "But I'm happy to say he seems well on the way, although I understand there will be a substantial recovery period."

"Of course, of course," said James. "Ah, here's your coffee. Thank you, Vivian, that's very nice."

The elegant secretary had reappeared bearing a salver on which rested a small French press coffeepot, a jug of cream, a bowl of sugar, a cup and saucer, and a sterling silver spoon. Carmichael gazed at it all bemusedly as she set it down on the little piecrust table at his elbow, nodded at his thanks, and then disappeared silently.

"I hope that suits?" asked James.

"Yes, certainly," answered Carmichael, pouring out for himself and adding cream. "Delicious," he added after taking a sip, and he meant it. The coffee was truly excellent.

"I like coffee," said James, a little complacently. "Now then, Chief Inspector, what can I do for you? If you've come for an update on the Haverford case, I'm afraid I've nothing new to report, more's the pity. The damn jewels seem to have disappeared into thin air."

"No doubt you and Davies will find them in the end," said Carmichael genially. "No, I've come about Sergeant Gibbons. We're still trying to piece together his movements on Tuesday, and I wanted to hear from you what the two of you had talked about over lunch."

"Looking for a different perspective?" said James, nodding. "That makes sense. Well, as I told Grant Davies, I'm afraid I did most of the talking. Sergeant Gibbons is an intelligent young man, but he knows nothing about gemstones or heritage jewelry. He was trying to bone up and I was more than happy to help him."

It had not occurred to Carmichael until that moment, but despite his interest and expertise in the subject, James wore no jewelry of any kind. James seemed to notice his inspection because he grinned and said, "I own several pairs of very nice cuff links, but men's jewelry is generally not to my taste. Nor to yours, I see."

"Well, no," said Carmichael, smiling inwardly at what his wife might say if he was to buy himself jewelry instead of her.

"I don't remember the details of the conversation at this point," said James, returning to the original topic. "But I don't imagine a lot of minutiae about jewelry would be much help to you in any case."

"No," agreed Carmichael. "But if perhaps you could remember anything personal that was said? Or any question Gibbons asked which might have a personal connection for him?"

James raised an eyebrow. "Personal?" he repeated. "Well, he didn't ask me how to pick out an engagement ring or anything of that sort, if that's what you mean."

"Not exactly," answered Carmichael, "although it might make things easier if he had. No, it's more a matter of trying to make out Gibbons's train of thought that day. I would like very much to be able to determine if he was going about his own business when he was shot, or if he was following up something to do with the case. There's evidence on both sides, you see."

"I don't think I'm going to be much help with that," said James. "Our discussion over lunch was purely shop talk. Gibbons told me something of his background as a detective and we swapped a couple of stories about particular cases, but that's as personal as it got. Certainly the neighborhood of Walworth never came up."

Carmichael nodded acknowledgment of this. "I also wanted to know," he said, "if Gibbons had had a question for you that night, could he have got hold of you? Do you think he would have ventured to ring you out of business hours?"

James shrugged. "You know him better than I," he said. "I certainly gave him my mobile number and urged him to ring if he had questions. Whether he would have done so, I can't say."

"Well . . ." Carmichael rubbed his chin. "I rather gathered the two of you had got on well, so in that case he might have done. I'm just wondering about what resources he might have felt he had."

"I was at his disposal," said James. "In fact, I was here that night until ten, so even if he hadn't wanted to bother me after business hours and had rung here instead, he would have got me."

That was just what Carmichael had wanted to know, but he concealed his satisfaction. "It's a puzzle," he said, shaking his head. "If Gibbons was investigating the Haverford burglary that night, I really can't make out why he rang me when both you and Davies were available."

He expected James, like Davies, to conclude at once that Gibbons had not in that case been engaged in police business, but James surprised him. He cocked his head, lifting one brow, and said, "He rang you that night? I didn't know that."

"Oh, yes," said Carmichael. "He rang my office line just a few minutes before he was attacked. Unfortunately, he only left a message asking to see me the next morning."

But James's focus had turned inward. He folded his hands with the index fingers extended and tapped his chin slowly. "So he rang you from his mobile while he was on the street somewhere in Walworth?" he asked.

"That's right," said Carmichael.

"But then isn't the answer obvious?" said James, his eyes turning back to his guest. "He rang you because he'd found there was murder involved."

Carmichael stared at him for a moment, taken aback by the unexpectedness of this reply. It was an explanation that had never occurred to him.

"There may be something in that," he said, recovering himself.

James shrugged. "Perhaps not," he said. "It's your bailiwick, after all, and if it wasn't obvious to you, well then."

"Ah, well, we all overlook the obvious at times," said Carmichael. Having got what he had come for, he rather wanted to get away and turn over this new idea at his leisure. "Thank you for your time, Mr. James. I do appreciate it."

"Not at all, not at all," said James, rising to see him out. "I liked Sergeant Gibbons and I'd like to see his attacker caught. Please don't hesitate to call on me again if I can be of any further help."

They parted on amicable terms, and Carmichael made his way outside thoughtfully. James had not been quite what he had expected, and he had the feeling the man knew exactly why he had come and was not disturbed by the suspicion in the least. Whether that was because James had great faith in his own abilities, or because he was truly innocent, remained to be seen.

James did not immediately return to his office once Carmichael had gone. Instead he plunged his hands deep into his pockets and strolled over to stare aimlessly out of the window. Vivian, working at the computer at her desk, eyed him, but said nothing. The silence stretched between them, broken only by the soft clack of the computer keyboard.

James swung away from the window abruptly, turning on the balls of his feet, and wandered back across the room, his lips pursed in a soundless whistle, his eyes apparently fixed on the ceiling molding. At the desk, Vivian cast him a single sardonic look before returning her gaze to her monitor. She continued to steadily ignore him as he turned again and came to stand at the edge of her desk, staring down at her. She worked on for a few moments, and then asked, without looking up, "Was there something you wanted?"

James shook his head in the manner of a parent sadly disappointed in his offspring. "Ah, Viv," he said. "Wouldn't you be upset to see me sent to prison?"

"I would certainly find it inconvenient," she replied, swiveling away from the computer to turn her attention to the printer. "Did you expect to be arrested anytime soon?"

"You're heartless," declared James. "Couldn't you see that the good chief inspector thinks I may have made off with the Haverford jewels and shot poor Sergeant Gibbons into the bargain?"

"It did seem a likely reason for him to have come," Vivian replied, unperturbed.

While James watched, she took the printed pages from their tray, inspected them briefly, and then swiveled back to meet his eyes at last.

"Here are the reports you wanted from Ukraine," she said, holding out the papers.

"Oh, very well," said James, snatching the papers from her. "I'll stop being dramatic and go back to work. But, mind, I'm no longer saving that Golconda diamond brooch for you."

A smile just touched the corner of Vivian's lips. "Just as well," she said as he strode back into his office. "It's the Colombian emeralds I really fancy."

When he returned to the Yard, Carmichael was annoyed to find Constable Lemmy still absent. If it had been Gibbons—or, really, any of his more recent assistants—who was so late, he would have been ringing around to find out what had happened to them, but as it was Lemmy, he simply assumed the boy had slept in on a Sunday.

So he was greatly surprised, as he settled at his desk to run a background check on Colin James, to see Lemmy appear in the doorway, looking as if he had been at his desk all along.

"Hullo, sir," he said. "I thought you'd want to know: I've found the footage of Sergeant Gibbons at Waterloo."

Carmichael immediately felt both guilty and irritated. Guilty, because he had done the constable an injustice, and irritated because he had been inveigled into misjudging Lemmy by the young man's own past performance. It was all, however, superseded by the constable's news.

"That's very good, lad," he said, managing to put some real warmth in his tone.

"I've got it all queued up for you downstairs," continued Lemmy. "I thought you'd want to see for yourself."

That, thought Carmichael, was a massive understatement.

"So I do," he said, rising. "Have you sorted out who he was following?"

"No, sir, not yet," replied Lemmy, leading the way down the hall. "I did just have a look, but I couldn't make it out right away and I thought you'd want to know at once."

Carmichael certainly could not fault this logic, and he gave Lemmy a sharp glance, wondering if his incompetent constable had somehow been magically transformed during the night.

The CCTV footage was, as always, blurry and hard to make out, at least for Carmichael. To the Yard's video analyst, it appeared as clear as day, or so he seemed to indicate.

"There's our lad," he said, setting the video in motion.

Carmichael squinted. Several people were emerging from the station doors and heading off in various directions. Among those who moved out of the camera frame to the left was a young man, well wrapped up against the cold with a thick scarf and heavy coat, who strode along in a purposeful manner, his hands buried in his pockets. Carmichael recognized him more by his stride than anything else.

"And then here," said Lemmy, moving over to a second screen, "here he is getting into the taxi."

The angle of the camera at the taxi queue was not as good, but Gibbons could be made out entering the frame, bending to speak to the driver, and then climbing into the taxi.

"So who was in the first taxi in the queue?" asked Carmichael.

"It's hard to make out," said Lemmy, fiddling with the controls. "There's not a clear shot. Here, see that bloke in the pea jacket and cap? You can just see him here—" He ran the film forward in slow motion, showing a dark figure, visible briefly between a pillar and the other pedestrians. "And then here he is again, getting into the taxi, but he came from the other direction, so there's no shot of his face."

"Once we trace Sergeant Gibbons's path back through the station," put in the video analyst, "we'll probably have a better picture of the fellow. After all, he should be in almost every shot the sergeant is in—can't be that hard to pick him out."

Carmichael was to remember those words later with grim humor.

19

Tea with the Burdalls

*G*ibbons was surprised when he woke on Sunday to feel—
for the first time since he had been shot—the faint stir-
rings of hunger. He had not previously considered
whether he was hungry or not, and it only now occurred to him that
with nothing to eat since Tuesday lunch, it was odd he had not been
hungry before. But he was actually eager for the chicken soup they
brought him, though he was rather annoyed to discover coffee was
not part of a liquid diet, as defined by the hospital nutritionist.

"I'd kill for a coffee," he confided to John, the young man who
brought the soup.

"Sorry," he replied. "I can't give you any."

"Why not?" demanded Gibbons. "Coffee is a liquid, after all.
And I'm on a liquid diet."

"It's not an approved liquid," he said. "I can only give you what's
on the list, and coffee's not there."

Gibbons could clearly see John was bent on being obdurate.

"What about tea?" Gibbons asked. "Much nicer than coffee, really. Soothing."

The young man shook his head. "No caffeine," he said firmly.
"I'm sorry, mate, but that's how it has to be."

And with that, he departed.

"It's un-British," Gibbons complained later to Nurse Pipp. "Tea is the national beverage of England."

"Is it?" she asked dryly. "I thought that was beer. And you can't have any of that, either."

Nor would she agree to bring him any interim liquids when he asked for something about midmorning.

"We've got to reintroduce your system slowly to the idea of digestion," she explained. "If we go too fast, well, you'd be amazed at how sick you can be."

"I can't see that a mug of broth could hurt anything," he answered.

"Well, I can," she replied. "You leave the nursing to me and concentrate on your detective work."

But Gibbons was tired of the detective work. He had spent all morning pouring over the facsimile of his notebook, but had not managed to elucidate anything further from it and he was in consequence feeling frustrated.

"You're getting fretful," said Nurse Pipp. "You probably need a bit of a rest—you've been up all morning."

That made Gibbons determined to stay awake, but after she had left he did indeed drop off. He was awakened by the arrival of lunch, which turned out to be a cup of fruit juice and a container of custard.

"That'll stick to your ribs," said John, which Gibbons took as his idea of a joke.

But he was eager for anything to eat at that point, which was why he found it so unaccountable that the custard seemed to repulse him. He was puzzling over this phenomenon when Bethancourt and Cerberus appeared.

"Hullo," said Bethancourt cheerfully. "How are you? Nurse Pipp seems to think you're progressing very nicely."

"I suppose," said Gibbons, still dubiously regarding the custard.

"What the devil is that?" asked Bethancourt, peering down into the plastic cup.

"It's custard," replied Gibbons. "Anybody could see that it's custard."

Bethancourt picked up the plastic spoon and poked at the mixture dubiously.

"This?" he said, watching it resist gravity as he lifted the spoon and the fat globule of custard persisted in clinging to it. "I don't know what it is, but believe me, it's not custard. I'm not entirely sure it's edible."

Although Gibbons had loathed the stuff, he was perversely annoyed by this criticism of it.

"Of course it's custard," he snapped. "Nurse Pipp would hardly have lied to me about that. There would be no point."

"There would if she were trying to poison you," retorted Bethancourt, dropping the spoon. "If they want you to eat custard, I will go and fetch some for you. Hell, I'll make it myself—it's not that difficult."

Gibbons, with his mouth open to snap back, paused, somehow touched by the idea of Bethancourt actually taking the trouble to cook for him.

"Can you really make custard?" he asked.

Bethancourt looked indignant. "Of course I can," he replied. "I'm not a gourmet chef, but I can do the basics."

"Well," admitted Gibbons, "this stuff isn't very appetizing. In fact, I don't feel hungry at all now."

"I'll bring you back some proper custard tonight," promised Bethancourt.

"Thanks," said Gibbons. "So what are you up to today?"

"Ah, you made me forget with all your talk about custard," said Bethancourt, slapping his forehead. "I've found out where you went after lunch on Tuesday!"

Gibbons stared at him. "You have?" he demanded. "Phillip, that's wonderful! How did—I mean, where—oh, bother, I can't think where to start."

Bethancourt beamed at him. "You went up to see the Burdalls," he announced. "I thought of it last night and rang them this morning to confirm. They couldn't remember your name right off, but they described you well enough, and said you turned up at about three and spoke to them for about half an hour."

"Then these notes here must refer to the conversation I had with them," said Gibbons excitedly, pushing aside the hated custard and pulling the facsimile sheets back onto his lap. "Here—this bit. 'Bs' must mean 'Burdalls,' don't you think?"

"It would make sense," agreed Bethancourt. "The previous notes were made after your lunch with James, weren't they?"

"That's right." Gibbons frowned down at the page. "This, where I've written *j fake*—I thought earlier today that might have meant the jewelry was fake. But that doesn't make sense."

Something he had read came back to Bethancourt as he peered over his friend's shoulder. "There was some fake jewelry," he said. "At least, there was at one time."

Gibbons looked up at him. "What do you mean?" he asked.

"I came across it when James took me to see the Haverford house," said Bethancourt. "I was looking at some of the old account books from Evony St. Michel's time, and there was an entry in one of them for a payment made to have replicas made of some of her jewelry. I don't know why the Burdalls would have brought it up, though. If they even knew."

"They might have known," said Gibbons, considering. "Nicky Burdall was close to Miranda Haverford."

"I can ask," said Bethancourt. "What about the rest of this?"

"Well, the only thing I've come up with this morning is the fact that I normally use 'NC' to mean 'natural causes,'" said Gibbons, "which is certainly what Miranda Haverford died of. It even makes some sense in the context of the rest of the notes—I was clearly trying not to let my mind revert back into the old homicide investigation channels."

"It does make sense," agreed Bethancourt. "But you've underscored it rather emphatically. Doesn't that rather suggest that there was something that made you think of murder?"

"Well, on this other page—" Gibbons paused, searching it out from the pile. "Yes, here—we took this to mean that I thought the Colemans were here principally for the inheritance, rather than from any family feeling. And if there had been any suspicious circumstances regarding Miranda Haverford's death, well, they would look a bit fishy, wouldn't they?"

"But there weren't any, correct?" asked Bethancourt. "Suspicious circumstances, I mean."

Gibbons shook his head. "No, it was definitely natural causes. A heart attack in her sleep, I believe."

"Still," said Bethancourt thoughtfully, picking up the previous page and studying it, "if the Burdalls had said anything against the Colemans, it might have made you think of how convenient Miranda's death was for them. Which in turn might have made you write a note like this, to remind yourself in no uncertain terms that they couldn't have murdered her because she died of old age."

He looked up to see how this logic sat with Gibbons, and found his friend nodding his head.

"You may be right," he said. "Did the Burdalls say anything to you about the Colemans?"

Bethancourt thought back. "Nothing very much," he said. "Only that they weren't sure if the Colemans had turned up when they did because Miranda wanted to have a look at them or if they had come off their own bat."

"Well, there's something I hadn't thought of," said Gibbons. "I was assuming they had come on their own."

"They say not," said Bethancourt. "Rob Coleman claimed Miranda had written to him, asking him to visit. No doubt she was curious as to who her heirs were. I mean, if I had a fortune in jewelry and proposed leaving it to distant relatives I'd never met, well, I'd want to see who it was going to."

"Curiosity is only human nature," agreed Gibbons. "Let me see that page again."

Bethancourt handed it over, remarking, "There's still a bit of it we haven't figured out yet."

"I know," sighed Gibbons. "WC, for example. Or who I wanted to run a background check on. And I really don't think it was some man named Wilbur Carson in the States."

"I never said his name was Wilbur Carson," said Bethancourt with dignity.

Gibbons only grinned at him. Which made Bethancourt grin back, elated that Gibbons was feeling well enough to jest. He had never consciously thought of what life would be like without his friend, but the relief that washed over him now proved that his subconscious at least had dreaded it.

"I'll remember that," he said, "and ask the Burdalls about it. They're trying to remember exactly what they said to you—I told them I'd be by shortly."

"Carmichael's going to want to talk to them, too," Gibbons warned him.

"Oh," said Bethancourt, who had not thought of this. "Of course he will. Er, you don't mind if I go along now, do you? No harm in it, really, since I've already spoken to them. Or do you think the chief inspector will be cross with me?"

"He probably will be, but he'll get over it," said Gibbons. "You found the Burdalls, after all. Go on—go now before I ring him."

"Thanks, Jack," said Bethancourt, collecting his dog. "I rather want to follow this up. And," he added as he headed for the door, "I won't forget the custard. I'll make some up directly I've talked with the Burdalls."

It was Bethancourt that deserved the thanks, reflected Gibbons, watching his friend disappear out the door. It was quite a feat, having filled in part of his missing day.

Nicky and Dylan were just arriving home when Bethancourt arrived at the house in Southgate. They both looked delighted to see him.

"You're back," said Nicky. "I didn't expect that—you're the first one that's come back."

"You must like Gran's tea," observed Dylan. "You've shown up at teatime twice now."

"Have I?" said Bethancourt, checking his watch. "So I have. Well, I do like your grandmother's tea. And not only have I come back, but shortly you'll be able to add to your collection, Nicky."

She cocked an eyebrow. "I will? Who's coming next?"

"A detective chief inspector from Scotland Yard," Bethancourt told her, and smiled when her eyes lit up.

"Oh, that's a good one," she said. "The other one was only a sergeant. But," she added, "he was awfully nice."

"I liked him," put in Dylan firmly. "He wasn't half as stuffy as the regular police."

"No," agreed Bethancourt. "Jack's not stuffy at all."

"Well, come along in," said Nicky, leading the way toward the front door. "We'll let Grandma Nicky know you've come. She'll be glad you've brought Cerberus again."

The elderly lady was indeed pleased. She buried her frail hands in the borzoi's fur while Bethancourt again took the seat to her left and watched the reenactment of the teatime ritual.

The Burdalls were excited to learn they were being of actual help in the case, and did their best to remember exactly what had been said in their conversation with Gibbons. Here Nicky and Dylan were of great help, prompting their elders.

"We might have mentioned the fake jewelry," said Mrs. Burdall, looking to her son for confirmation.

"You did, Gran," said Nicky. "Sergeant Gibbons asked if we had ever seen any of the jewelry."

"Oh, yes, I remember now," said Mrs. Burdall. "And of course, both Neil and I have been to some of the exhibitions, and I even remember Miranda wearing some of it a very long time ago. But we haven't seen any of the pieces in some time now, although Miranda did occasionally wear some of the faux pearls."

"There were other costume pieces as well," put in Neil. "There was a copy of the amethyst and diamond brooch, and another of an emerald and diamond necklace."

"And the earrings," said Nicky. "Don't forget the ruby earrings." She sighed. "Aunt Miranda said I could have those when I grew up."

"I'm sorry, Nicky," said her grandfather.

Bethancourt was surprised. "She left the ruby earrings to you?" he asked.

Mrs. Burdall laughed. "Not the real ones—those went with the rest of the collection. But Miranda had promised some of the copy pieces to a few of her friends."

"I take it," said Bethancourt, "that the copies vanished along with the real jewels?"

"So we were given to understand," said Neil. "At least, there's been no sign of them, and the police did search the rest of the house."

"I imagine," said Mrs. Burdall, "that Miranda probably kept all the jewelry together, both the genuine and the copies. A thief wouldn't bother sorting them out—if he even knew that some of the pieces weren't real."

"You couldn't tell at a glance," agreed Neil.

"Do have another biscuit, Mr. Bethancourt," said Mrs. Burdall. "Dylan, pass the plate, please."

"Thank you," said Bethancourt, taking another piece of shortbread. "What else did you talk about with Sergeant Gibbons?"

They had gone into some depth about the events of the past months: the Colemans' arrival, Rose's death, followed by Miranda's passing, and then the burglary.

"He asked a lot about the Colemans," offered Dylan.

"That's right," said Nicky. "He didn't know they hadn't been here that long."

"Of course," breathed Bethancourt. "Four months—that's what he meant."

The Burdalls looked curious.

"He had that written in his notebook," explained Bethancourt, "but we couldn't make out what it meant. I should have known— Colin James told me the first day that the Colemans had only come to England this past summer. I'd forgotten it, actually."

Neil shrugged. "I can't see why it's important," he said. "Miranda didn't seem to think much of Rob Coleman, but she had no plans to change her will."

"It may not be important per se, but since Sergeant Gibbons made a note of it, he must have felt it was significant in some way. This is all," Bethancourt added, "in aid of trying to map his train of thought that day."

"What else was in his notes?" asked Mrs. Burdall.

Bethancourt consulted his memory. "The initials 'WC,'" he said. "Not," he added, as both Nicky and Dylan giggled, "meaning the usual abbreviation. We think—although this isn't at all certain—that the initials refer to a person."

"Coleman begins with a 'C,'" volunteered Dylan.

"But their first names don't begin with a 'W,'" Nicky corrected him.

"They could have relatives," argued Dylan, and that remark turned on the light for his great-grandmother.

"Oh, I wonder if it could be William Coleman," she said. "I'm sure I mentioned him to Sergeant Gibbons—he was asking how the Colemans were related to Miranda."

"Oh, good Lord," said Bethancourt, irritated with himself.

Mrs. Burdall stopped speaking and raised a white brow.

"Mr. Bethancourt?" she said.

"Sorry," apologized Bethancourt. "It's just that I asked Mr. Grenshaw the same thing yesterday, and he told me all about William Coleman, and how he married one of Evony's nieces. I can't believe I didn't think of it before."

"But who was William Coleman?" asked Nicky curiously.

"He was Rob Coleman's ancestor," replied Mrs. Burdall. "He married one of Evony's nieces, as Mr. Bethancourt said, but William died young and his wife and son returned to the Ukraine. That's how Rob comes to have an English last name, even though he comes from the Ukrainian side of the family."

"But can we think of any other explanation?" asked Neil. "It seems unusual that a police detective would be interested in that kind of genealogy."

They all thought for several minutes, but no one could come up with anyone or anything else with the initials "WC" that related to the Haverfords or their jewels.

"Maybe," said Dylan after a few moments, "it means Sergeant Gibbons thought Miss Haverford hid her jewelry in the toilet tank."

Nicky hooted at this, rolling her eyes, and received a punch in the arm from her brother for this impropriety. Even the two elders smiled.

"I don't think," said Mrs. Burdall gently, "Miss Haverford was quite that eccentric."

"Though," put in Bethancourt, who rather felt for the boy, "odder things have been known, and my police acquaintances have found some very strange things in toilet tanks over the years. But I'm afraid it's not likely in this case—the police searched the house, you see."

Dylan nodded, apparently gratified to have his remark taken seriously.

From outside the room, the sound of the door chimes rang out clearly, interrupting the conversation. Nicky jumped up at once.

"I'll get it," she said. "It's probably the chief inspector."

"I'm coming, too," called Dylan, running after his sister, who was already across the room.

The two older Burdalls looked merely confused.

"I'm sorry," said Bethancourt. "I should have said—now you've confirmed Sergeant Gibbons was here that day, his superior naturally wants to come and talk to you. I probably should have left it to him altogether," he added deprecatingly, "but, well, it was my idea and I wanted to follow it up."

Mrs. Burdall smiled, apparently finding humor in the situation.

"The more the merrier," she said. "Neil, would you tell Molly to put on some more tea? And perhaps bring out another plate of biscuits? I'm afraid the children have pretty well decimated this one."

In a few moments, Carmichael appeared with a child on either side. Both youngsters were beaming, and Carmichael wore a genial smile, but Bethancourt detected a distinct bristling of his bushy eyebrows when the chief inspector's eyes lit on him. Bethancourt rose politely at his entrance, but before he could effect introductions, Dylan burst out, "Look, Grandma Nicky! This Mr. Carmichael—he's a detective chief inspector from Scotland Yard!"

"It's *Chief Inspector* Carmichael, not Mr.," corrected his sister, apparently a bit put out that Dylan had beaten her to the announcement of Carmichael's identity.

Dylan paid no attention to this criticism, concentrating on guiding Carmichael to his grandmother's side, where Cerberus, detecting a familiar scent, wagged his tail in greeting.

Mrs. Burdall smiled and held out a hand. "I hope you don't mind the enthusiasm of our welcoming committee," she said.

"Quite the contrary," replied Carmichael, grinning at the children. "I found the welcome charming, which is not always the case with a policeman."

"Thank you," said Mrs. Burdall, "do sit down."

This occasioned a flurry of activity in which Nicky and Dylan brought up another chair, Neil arrived back from his errand to Molly, bearing a tray, and Carmichael was got settled with tea and biscuits. The detective at first tried to put off all the fuss by saying he did not care for anything, but gave up his protests almost at once, realizing they would have no effect.

But once they had fulfilled their responsibilities as hosts, the Burdalls were content to let Carmichael take over the reins and direct the conversation where he would. Bethancourt, sitting silent, was very pleased to find the chief inspector going over much the same ground as he himself had covered. He did it far more efficiently, without letting his witnesses meander off on various digressions, but Bethancourt did not think there was much of import said that he had not already been told. And, he admitted to himself, he had quite enjoyed the digressions.

Unlike himself, Carmichael could and did demand to speak to the middle generation of Burdalls, and was duly conducted upstairs by Nicky and Dylan to meet their parents. Ordinarily, Bethancourt might have been invited along to observe, but it was clear Carmichael was annoyed with him for going along to the Burdalls without police supervision.

In view of this, Bethancourt decided it would be prudent to take his leave whilst Carmichael was occupied upstairs. Neil saw him to the door.

"Do you think," he asked, "you'll ever sort it all out?"

"I hope so," replied Bethancourt. "There's been a few new things that've come up in the last few days, so at least we haven't reached a dead end."

"Well," said Neil, "I'd appreciate it—and so would my mother— if you wouldn't mind stopping by to tell us how it all ends up."

Bethancourt felt quite flattered. "Of course I will," he said.

"Although I imagine it will make the papers once the case is solved. But I'll come along and tell you whatever I know."

And he made a mental note to himself not to forget this promise; he had taken a definite liking to the Burdalls.

"There you are, my man," murmured Markham.

There was an edge of relief in his tone; for what seemed like an age, he had been tracing the train Gibbons had taken to Waterloo back through station after station. He had been beginning to think he must have missed the sergeant somewhere along the line, but now, at last, he'd found him.

Markham tweaked his controls, bringing the picture on his screen into clearer focus and enlarging slightly the section that showed Gibbons. Then he turned to Constable Lemmy, who was working on the footage from the stations south of Waterloo.

"I've got him, Constable," he said. "The sergeant got on the train at Camden Town."

"Oh, let's see," said Lemmy, swiveling his chair round. His eyes found Gibbons on the screen and he smiled. "That's him all right," he said happily. "I'll switch over to the Camden footage, too, shall I? And we can look to see if the sergeant was following anyone."

Markham had rather thought the idea that Gibbons had followed anyone to Waterloo had already been dismissed, since they had traced the path of the peacoated man back through Waterloo station and proved conclusively that he had come off the 9:06 train from Reading. But Markham agreed to the constable's suggestion anyway, that being the easiest course.

"Gibbons can't have transferred at Camden," he remarked, turning back to his screens. "There's no connection there. So he must have been somewhere in the neighborhood. Have you heard of any connection with Camden in the case, Constable?"

"No," answered Lemmy, who did not seem very curious. "Perhaps Sergeant Gibbons has friends up there."

Markham shot him a puzzled look. "If he'd been visiting friends, wouldn't they have come forward by now?"

"Oh, right," said Lemmy, whose attention was fastened on his screen. "Still, he can't have been up in Southgate—he'd get the Piccadilly line from there, not the Northern."

This was undeniably true, but Markham nonetheless found Lemmy's lack of curiosity distinctly odd in a newly made detective. However, he shrugged it away and returned to his work; after all, Lemmy's career was no business of his.

20

On Hampstead Heath

n old Counting Crows CD was playing over the stereo and Bethancourt was warbling along to it absentmindedly as he carefully set the custard to bake in the oven. He associated that particular band with domestic activity, it having been a favorite of an old cook his family had employed in his youth. He surveyed the debris his efforts had left scattered across the counters; he rather enjoyed cooking from time to time, but he was not very keen on clearing up afterward. He considered tackling the job briefly, but ended up, as he usually did, just shifting it all into the sink to await his charwoman's ministrations in the morning.

That matter disposed of, he lit a cigarette and was just pouring himself a fresh cup of coffee when the phone rang. Bethancourt raised a brow when he saw the number listed on the caller ID and he reached to answer the call immediately.

"Phillip?" said Colin James. "It's a glorious day—excellent weather for dog-walking on the Heath. Would you care to venture out with Churchill and me?"

"Thanks very much," answered Bethancourt. "I was just thinking about taking Cerberus out, in fact. I've got something in the oven just at the moment, but I could be up there by four."

"That suits perfectly," said James. "I don't mean to imply I have great news, by the way. I'm only after an exchange of thoughts."

"Always beneficial," said Bethancourt, who would have gone to meet James for any reason at all, given his latest suspicions. "I'll see you there, then."

He gazed thoughtfully at the phone after he rang off, wondering greatly what had prompted James to make the call. After all, if the investigator wanted information about the police investigation, he already had a good working relationship with Inspector Davies who would know all about it. But Bethancourt was more likely to be privy to the inner workings of Gibbons's mind.

"Of course," he said to Cerberus, "if James is innocent, he might still want to know what Jack's been thinking. I would, in his place."

Cerberus lifted his head, but when no food was forthcoming, he laid his muzzle back on his paws and ignored his master's conversation.

"In any case," Bethancourt continued, "it ought not to be too difficult to find out if James has a younger boyfriend. I wonder if I could get myself invited back to his house."

Still turning the possibilities over in his mind, he went to change while the custard finished baking.

Nurse Pipp looked dubiously at the custard Bethancourt presented to her.

"I'm not sure," she said. "It looks very rich."

"I thought of that," said Bethancourt, very proud of himself. "I didn't use cream—only milk. Here, taste it."

Nurse Pipp seemed more agreeable to this suggestion and allowed Bethancourt to feed her a spoonful.

"Mmm," she said. "That's very good."

"I kept it nice and bland," said Bethancourt. "It's only flavored with vanilla."

Nurse Pipp reached for the spoon and Bethancourt handed it over readily. She took another spoonful, savoring the taste on her tongue while Bethancourt watched anxiously.

"The eggs," he added persuasively, "were quite fresh."

Nurse Pipp laughed at him.

"Very well," she decided. "You can give him some. I'll take the rest and put it in the refrigerator and dole it out at the appropriate times."

Bethancourt beamed at her and trotted off to Gibbons's room with his prize.

He found his friend frowning over the fresh notebook Bethancourt had brought him.

"Your custard, sir," announced Bethancourt with a flourish as he entered, and Gibbons looked up and smiled. "It has been Nurse Pipp-approved."

"Thanks, Phillip," said Gibbons, reaching for the dish eagerly. "God, that smells much better than the rest of the muck they've been trying to feed me."

"Taste it," urged Bethancourt.

Gibbons was already digging into it, and he smiled beatifically as he savored his first spoonful.

"That's wonderful," he said, dipping the spoon back in. "Is there any more?"

"Lots," said Bethancourt. "Nurse Pipp has got it and will be doling it out in medically appropriate amounts." He was smiling while he watched the success of his culinary creation, much pleased. "I can't stay long," he added in a moment. "Colin James rang to invite me to walk dogs on Hampstead Heath and I've got to meet him there by four."

Gibbons looked up. "Did he give a reason for this invitation?" he asked.

"He said he was after an exchange of ideas," replied Bethancourt. "I'm going to try to find out if he has a younger boyfriend possibly matching the description of the man you were following last Tuesday night."

"It needn't necessarily be a boyfriend," said Gibbons. "It could be any trusted associate."

"Yes, but I've got to start somewhere," said Bethancourt.

"I expect so," said Gibbons, his attention on scraping the last remnants of the custard out of the bowl. "Do you know, I was just thinking about James and Davies when you came in."

"Oh?" asked Bethancourt. "Any fruitful thoughts?"

"Not exactly. I was only thinking that they both fit the description James himself gave me of the kind of people who commit jewelry thefts. They both are great appreciators of art and beauty, they both know a great deal about gemstones and their history, and they both have a taste for the finer things in life."

"True enough," agreed Bethancourt. "Though actually a lot of that applies to me as well."

"Jewelry is not one of your hobbies," said Gibbons dryly. "You only know about gemstones because you date the kind of women who expect them as presents."

"Well, I can't deny it," said Bethancourt good-humoredly. "I really must run, Jack. I'll stop on my way back and let you know if I found out anything."

"Do," said Gibbons. "Go on now—and ta very much for the custard."

Bethancourt waved the thanks away as he led his dog out the door.

The sun hung just above the bare branches of the trees as Bethancourt let Cerberus out of the Jaguar and led his pet into Hampstead Heath. The air was crisp, but blessedly dry, and the darkening sky above remained clear. Bethancourt headed for the area where he had last encountered James and was shortly rewarded by the sight of an English bulldog lumbering toward Cerberus, tongue lolling happily.

"There you go, lad," murmured Bethancourt, slipping the great dog from his lead. He pushed his glasses up onto the bridge of his nose and scanned the area until he spotted the tall figure of Colin James. He waved and began to make his way in that direction, keeping one eye on the frolicking dogs.

"Hullo!" said James. "Nice change from the wet, isn't it? It seems like it's been weeks since I didn't get soaked walking Churchill."

Bethancourt agreed. "The rain's been pretty constant," he said. "Do you always take Churchill out yourself?"

"Not always," admitted James, his eyes following the dogs. "I have an arrangement with an obliging neighbor. But I like to take him myself as often as I can—he gets left alone too much, poor chap."

"Cerberus goes most places with me," said Bethancourt, turning his back to the wind in order to light a cigarette.

"Ah, well, there's no denying he's a better behaved dog than Churchill," said James, somewhat sheepishly. "My own fault—I'm no good at discipline."

Bethancourt considered this as they strolled after the dogs.

"I'm pretty awful at self-discipline," he offered.

James laughed. "So am I," he said, "so am I. What fun is it, after all?"

"None," said Bethancourt with a grin.

Ahead of them, Cerberus and Churchill had paused to inspect a clump of rather shriveled bushes, judiciously choosing the best spot to mark on.

"Well," said James, "pleasant as this is, I expect I had better deliver the bad news."

Bethancourt was immediately alert. "Bad news?" he asked.

"Bad enough," answered James. "The prospect of recovering the Haverford jewels anytime soon is looking rather bleak."

Bethancourt absorbed this in silence for a moment. If James had stolen the gems, he would naturally be certain to introduce this idea sooner or later, but Bethancourt could not help but wonder why he had been chosen as the recipient of this information. Surely Carmichael—or Davies, if he was innocent—were more important people to convince of this point.

"Not good," he said at last. "Why have you come to the conclusion it's hopeless?"

"I didn't say *hopeless*," said James, who seemed to resent the term. "I just said the prospects were poor. There's not a whiff of the benighted jewelry anywhere. Inspector Davies is waiting on some further inquiries he's put out to some of his contacts in Hawaii, but it's unlikely anything will come of them. And I've drawn a blank on every level. The closest I've come is an old friend in Amsterdam who once, several years ago, saw a diamond similar to the one in the Haverford brooch."

"How nice for him," said Bethancourt dryly, and James snorted.

"He seemed to think so," he said. "He went on about it for an unconscionably long time. Anyway, the point is that when things are this quiet after a big job like this, there's usually only one reason, and it's never good for our side."

"What reason?" asked Bethancourt.

"It usually means it was a custom job, undertaken for a specific client," answered James. He was frowning, as if in distaste for the very notion. "Even then, there are normally rumors circulating because one or more of the thieves can't keep from hinting about their big coup. But sometimes—not often, mind—the thieves are loyal to their employer, possibly even regular business partners of his, and they keep mum."

"So what you're saying," said Bethancourt, "is that the jewels have most likely gone into a private collection, from whence they will never be recovered."

James's frown deepened into a scowl. "Never is a long time," he said, with a hard edge in his tone. "I've pulled off a few recoveries of that sort. But," he added, almost apologetically, "such things can take years, unless one is extraordinarily lucky."

Bethancourt took a last puff of his cigarette and exhaled slowly, watching the thin stream of smoke whisked away by the wind. He suspected that if the private collection in question was James's, there was every likelihood that collector and thief were one and the same. But, he reminded himself, what if the private collection belonged instead to Davies? Was it possible James had let friendship blind him? Bethancourt glanced at him sidelong; James was watching the dogs, the trace of a fond smile on his lips.

Cerberus was chasing Churchill in a wide arc across the meadow; the race was a very uneven one, but both dogs seemed to be enjoying it. Cerberus kept catching his prey up, at which point they tousled briefly, and then Churchill would trundle off again while Cerberus lay panting happily, watching his friend's progress until he judged him far enough away. At which point the borzoi would regain his feet and sprint off in pursuit.

"Well," said Bethancourt as they strolled on toward the trees, following the path of the dogs, "I hope if you do recover them some years on, you'll remember me. I had rather been looking forward to viewing the alexandrite necklace."

James sighed. "Weren't we all," he said.

"And," continued Bethancourt, "it may be that the Haverford case has nothing to do with the attack on Jack. In any case—"

He broke off at the sound of a sharp report.

"What was that?" asked James.

For a split second, Bethancourt could not place the sound, though he knew he recognized it. In the next instant, realization dawned and he shouted out even as he reached for James and a second shot rang out.

Oddly enough, Bethancourt's first thought was for the safety of his dog, and in his first stunned moment, all he could think was that it was not possible to mistake Cerberus for a deer despite his size.

"Cerberus!" he bellowed. "Down!"

Even as the words left his lips, he had seized James's arm and was dragging the larger man down into the bleached grass.

They fell heavily into the soggy ground.

"Christ!" swore James.

"Roll!" ordered Bethancourt, shoving at the other man's shoulder. "Roll for the bush there."

Swearing mightily, James rolled while a third shot echoed across the Heath.

People were screaming now and Bethancourt wondered if he had just badly overreacted to an attack on someone else.

"Dear God," said James. They had reached the scant cover of the bush the dogs had earlier shown such interest in, and James was squirming in an effort to see through the sparse foliage. "Churchill! Where's Churchill?"

Bethancourt was just as worried about his own dog, but was hoping Cerberus had obeyed his command. He dug in his pocket for his mobile, hoping he had not damaged the device by rolling on it. It had certainly bruised his ribs nicely.

He had lost his glasses along the way and had to squint at the phone's screen to make out the right number. He hit the "call" button and pressed the phone to his ear in a hand that, he suddenly noticed, was shaking.

Some of the tension seeped out of him at the sound of Carmichael's raspy voice.

"Bethancourt?" he said. "Is something up?"

"Yes, sir," replied Bethancourt. "I'm on Hampstead Heath with Colin James and someone is shooting at us. Or," he amended hastily, thinking that sounded too dramatic, "at least shooting at *someone.*"

"Have you been hurt?" asked Carmichael, his voice anxious. "Are either of you shot?"

"I don't think so," replied Bethancourt, suddenly unsure. "Nothing hurts at any rate, and I don't see any blood. Are you all right, Colin?"

James simply stared at him incredulously.

"Have you got shelter?" demanded Carmichael. "Where on the Heath are you?"

"By the ponds," answered Bethancourt. "We haven't exactly got shelter—we're behind a bush—but actually I think maybe the shooting has stopped." He had only just become conscious of this last, realizing that though his body was braced for the sound of more gunshots, it had now been silent for several seconds.

"For God's sake don't assume that," ordered Carmichael, sounding alarmed. "They might just be waiting for you to stick your nose out. Stay down, do you hear me, Bethancourt?"

"Yes, sir," said Bethancourt, who was being distracted by James shouting for his dog.

"Unless there's a safer place nearby," Carmichael amended himself. "Concrete would be preferable."

"We're in the middle of a meadow in November," said Bethancourt. "Concrete is not an option. If you want the truth, sir, I was pretty happy there was a bush."

"Yes, of course. I'm on my way, Bethancourt. Just hold on."

Bethancourt rang off just in time to see Churchill pounding up and bounding into James's outstretched arms. Now even more concerned about Cerberus, Bethancourt risked sitting up and peering around the bush.

"I can't see," he said, his voice a little panicky. "Colin, can you see Cerberus? I've lost my glasses."

James extricated himself from under his bulldog and propped himself up to look round the other side of the bush.

"He's there," he said. "I don't know if he's hurt—he's lying down, but his head is up and his ears are pricked."

It was more than Bethancourt could stand. Heedless of Carmichael's warning, he got up and ran toward his pet, who remained quite still. As Bethancourt approached, Cerberus lifted his chin but did not rise and it dawned on Bethancourt that the borzoi had indeed obeyed his command to lie down and in fact was still obeying it.

"Good lad," said Bethancourt, coming up. "Good lad, Cerberus. Come."

And the great dog leaped to his feet, tail wagging energetically, and then reared up to place his front paws on his master's shoulders. Bethancourt, braced for this, flung his arms around his pet and hugged him.

"Thank God," he murmured. "Come along, lad."

It was clear Cerberus understood that something had happened, but having been praised by his master, he seemed content to settle down at Bethancourt's side.

"Here," said James, coming up. "I've found your glasses. I'm afraid one of the lenses is cracked."

"Cheers," said Bethancourt, taking them and settling them on his nose despite this defect. At least he could see clearly out of one eye.

"Do you mind getting out of here now?" said James, glancing around nervously. "I don't know about you, but I'm suddenly feeling very exposed."

Bethancourt had to agree. The meadow was deserted now, everyone having fled, and the shadows under the trees had become menacing. In the distance there was the wail of sirens.

"By all means," he said.

They broke into a jog as they made for the car park, only to be brought up short just before they reached it by dark figures holding powerful torches.

"Police," announced a voice, and the light struck their eyes, blinding them.

"Splendid," James greeted them.

"You coming off the green where the shooting occurred, sir?" asked the policeman.

"That's right," answered Bethancourt. "We were giving the dogs a run."

Other policemen came up and they were led into the car park where a number of other people were being interviewed. Bethancourt and James were ushered over to wait their turn.

It all seemed vaguely unreal to Bethancourt, and he was aware of reaction setting in now that the danger was over. His knees were definitely feeling weak and he wanted very much to find someplace to sit down. Instead he lit a cigarette and brushed fruitlessly at the mud and bits of grass that seemed to be ground into the fabric of his coat.

A paramedic approached and asked if they were hurt at all.

"No," answered Bethancourt.

"Not unless I come down with pneumonia from standing about in the cold," said James, but his heart wasn't in it and his tone reflected that.

The paramedic wandered off again.

"It is cold," agreed Bethancourt.

"It's being all wet and muddy," said James, adding sadly, "I'm afraid this coat is done for."

A uniformed constable with a notebook came over next.

"Do either of you have a motor vehicle here?" he asked.

"A gray Jaguar," answered Bethancourt. "That's it, over there."

The constable looked and wrote something in the notebook.

"Might I see your license and registration documents, sir?"

Silently, Bethancourt produced his wallet and hunted through it until he found his license.

"The documents are in the car glove box," he said, handing the license over.

The constable nodded and began to copy down Bethancourt's license information. He was still working at it when Carmichael arrived, trailing detectives in his wake. He brushed the constable aside like a horse swishing its tail at a fly and took charge of Bethancourt and James.

"Give your car keys to Constable Lemmy," he told Bethancourt, who did so, too spent to even inquire why. "You look pale, lad. Sure you're all right?"

"I'm all right."

"I think we had best get you both out of the cold," said Carmichael. "How on earth did you come to get so wet?"

"It's been raining for a fortnight," replied Bethancourt. "You try rolling about on the ground up there."

"If I might," said James, "my house is very near here and I have plenty of warm drinks available."

"Excellent, thank you very much," said Carmichael at once, almost pouncing on this offer, which seemed to make James smile faintly. "We'll drive, if you don't mind. Constable, take down Mr. James's address and bring Mr. Bethancourt's car round when they're done with it here. And," he added, on the verge of turning away, "be sure you tell Inspector Hollings and Sergeant O'Leary where we've gone." He paused a moment, as if running down a list in his head, and then nodded and ushered his two stray lambs into the police Rover.

Bethancourt was exceedingly glad to sit down. It was a rather tight fit, with himself and James and both dogs, but he would not have cared if he had had to ride with Cerberus in his lap so long as he could relax for a moment or two.

And a moment or two was all it took; James had not lied when he claimed to live nearby. The house was a beautiful early Georgian one, just the sort of place Bethancourt would have imagined James lived in.

James shed his soiled coat almost as soon as he had crossed the threshold, dropping the garment in a heap on the polished floorboards. Bethancourt added his to the pile and then joined James on the antique hall tree bench to pull off his Wellies while Carmichael waited patiently.

"Sitting room's through here," said James, motioning toward a square archway. "Just let me get the light—there. Tea all round?" he added, almost perfunctorily.

"I'd love a cuppa," said Bethancourt feelingly.

James nodded. "I'll be back directly," he said, and left his guests alone in the exquisite room.

"Run over it for me while he's gone," said Carmichael quietly when the sound of James's footsteps had faded. "Were you actually with James when the shooting started?"

Bethancourt nodded wearily. "We hadn't been walking long," he said, trying to remember exactly what had been said before the shots. He recapped it as best he could for Carmichael.

"So you never saw the gunman?" asked Carmichael.

"No. I think the shots came from the general area of the trees, but I didn't notice anyone there before I heard the first shot."

A shiver ran through him and he shook himself impatiently.

"Did you think the shots were aimed at you?" asked Carmichael.

"I don't know." Bethancourt ran a hand through his hair, pushing the heavy fair locks off his forehead. "I didn't think at all, really. I just yelled for Cerberus to get down and pulled James down on the ground with me."

"It's lucky you reacted that way," said Carmichael, and the praise was clearly heartfelt.

Bethancourt shrugged. "I've been in enough shooting parties," he said. "As soon as I realized it was a rifle shot, the reaction was automatic."

"A rifle shot," repeated Carmichael. "You're sure it was a rifle? Not a handgun?"

Bethancourt paused, thinking it through. "I don't know," he said at last. "It sounded to me just like a hunting rifle. But now I come to think of it, I don't know that I've ever heard any other guns fired. Perhaps they all sound the same."

"Well, we'll have the answer to that shortly," said Carmichael. "Ah, here's our tea. Thank you very much, sir."

Bethancourt noticed that James looked tired, and once he had set the tea tray down he collapsed with a groan on the sofa.

"Do help yourselves," he said. "It's very odd, but I'm quite done in. I expect it's the aftermath of the adrenaline rush. I don't think I've ever been shot at before."

Carmichael smiled at this and moved to pour out.

"I'd like to know what you remember of the incident, Mr. James," he said, handing his host a mug of tea.

"Thank you," said James automatically, taking the mug while he gazed into the distance and tried to put together an account. Then he sighed and looked slightly ashamed. "I'm afraid I didn't notice anything," he said. "We were walking along, watching the dogs and chatting about the Haverford jewels when I heard a loud bang. I didn't even recognize it as a gunshot."

"Did you notice the direction the bang came from?" asked Carmichael.

"Oh, yes," answered James. "It came from the trees up ahead. I looked in that direction just as Phillip here knocked me over and I thought I saw someone there. But I didn't see him clearly enough to identify, or even to say for certain it was a man."

Carmichael nodded and began to ask another question when his mobile rang.

"Excuse me," he said, rising to answer it and moving back out into the hallway to take the call.

Bethancourt and James sat silently for a moment, sipping their tea. Then James's phone began to ring, and after glancing at the screen, he exclaimed, "Good Lord, it's Vivian. I have no idea how that woman manages to know everything the moment it's happened. It's positively eerie."

He answered the call and Bethancourt was left to sit quietly by himself in the comfortable corner of James's sofa and sip his tea in peace. He was grateful for this; he was finding the tea quite reviving, but was not yet ready to take an active part in affairs. But then his own mobile started ringing; when he saw it was Marla, he had a moment, like James, of wondering how on earth she knew what had happened.

"Hullo," he said.

"Hullo," she answered. "I'm thinking of going to dinner and having an early night—I've got that morning shoot tomorrow. Do you want to meet me at the restaurant?"

And Bethancourt could do nothing but laugh.

21

The End of a Long Day

Gibbons knew nothing of all the excitement, though he was rather wondering when Bethancourt would return. As the evening wore on with no sign of his friend, he assumed things were going well and that Bethancourt and James had gone to dinner together. Impatient as he was to hear what Bethancourt would have to say, he was pleased that he apparently was ingratiating himself successfully.

Nurse Pipp looked in before she left for the night.

"Still up, are you?" she asked with a smile.

Gibbons was at first surprised, then struck by this remark.

"It's true, isn't it?" he said. "I'm usually asleep when you leave. I don't know you're gone till the night nurse comes in later."

She nodded. "But you're looking better tonight," she said. "There's finally some color back in your cheeks."

"I feel better," declared Gibbons. "The pain's still there, but it's not as bad as before. And I don't feel so muzzy-headed."

"Well, I don't mind telling you the doctor's very pleased with your progress," she said. "I think when he sees you tomorrow, he might even set a date for your release."

Gibbons's eyes got very bright. "Really?" he said. "Oh, God, that would be heaven."

"We'll see. Don't get your hopes too far up," she warned him. "I said 'set a date' not 'let you go home tomorrow.'"

Gibbons grinned at her. "I know," he answered. "And you mustn't think I'm not grateful for all your ministrations. But it's not really awfully comfortable here."

Nurse Pipp laughed. "I know," she said. "I've had enough patients tell me so. Well, I must get on—have a good night."

Gibbons let her go, leaning back contentedly on his pillows and dwelling happily on the prospect of going home.

He had dozed off by the time Bethancourt finally appeared, but woke at once at the sound of Cerberus's nails on the tile.

"There you are," he said, blinking sleepily. "Did it—what happened to you?"

Bethancourt, who looked very tired and very dirty, sank into one of the armchairs and stretched out his legs while Cerberus lay down beside him with a great *whoof.*

"There was an incident," he replied. "Someone let loose with a hunting rifle on Hampstead Heath. It rather looks like they were aiming at James and I."

Gibbons gaped at him. "What?" he demanded.

"You heard me," said Bethancourt, taking off his glasses and rubbing at his eyes. "I've been holed up at Colin's house with Carmichael for the past four hours. Thank God they agreed to let us order in some food."

"Was anybody hurt?" asked Gibbons, running his eyes over his friend's lanky frame, but finding no sign of anything more serious than possibly some bruises.

"No, amazingly enough," replied Bethancourt, replacing his glasses and blinking. "Damn, but it's aggravating only being able to see properly out of one eye."

"I thought it looked like one of your lenses was cracked," said Gibbons sympathetically. "And it looks as if you've been rolling around on the ground."

"So I have," said Bethancourt dispiritedly. "I don't recommend it."

"No, of course not," said Gibbons. "Do tell me what happened, Phillip—I'm bursting here."

"I did tell you," retorted Bethancourt. "Someone—as yet unidentified—took a couple of shots at me with a rifle on Hampstead Heath. Why, I have no idea. I wasn't doing anything, and neither was James. We were just walking along while James told me he doubted the Haverford jewels would ever be seen again and I wondered if that was because he'd stolen them when some idiot started in with the rifle. I fell flat, taking James with me, and we got behind the nearest bush. Then the shooting stopped, we got up, collected the dogs, and went off to meet the police."

"I see," said Gibbons, trying to contain his impatience. "How did you end up at James's house with Carmichael?"

"That was Carmichael's doing," answered Bethancourt. "He turned up and took us off—and I was damned grateful for it, by the way. I was bloody well freezing to death in a soaking overcoat in a car park in November."

"I'm sure it was very uncomfortable," agreed Gibbons impatiently. "What did the police find out? Carmichael must have told you something."

Bethancourt thought for a moment. "They found the rifle," he offered. "Oh, and apparently several people had noticed the chap because he was carrying a cello case. Or maybe it was a double bass, I can't remember. I think a bass seems more likely—most rifles are longer than a cello now I come to think of it."

"Finding the rifle would be important," said Gibbons dryly. "I take it you're trying to tell me the shooter concealed the gun inside a double bass case? And presumably the police found both items where he left them when he fled?"

"Well of course," said Bethancourt irritably. "Why on earth should I be going on about musical instruments otherwise?"

Gibbons regarded him silently for a moment

"I don't think," he said, "that being shot at agrees with you very well."

"That's the understatement of the year," agreed Bethancourt with feeling. "To be perfectly frank, I loathed it."

"At least you didn't get hit," retorted Gibbons. "Some of us haven't been so lucky."

"Just because it could have been worse doesn't mean I have to approve of the way it was," said Bethancourt, and Gibbons had to pause to work out exactly what he meant.

"Oh, really," he said, once he had it. "You are in a mood, aren't you? Never mind—let's get back to what happened. How many shots were there?"

"I thought there were dozens," said Bethancourt, "but in fact there were only three. The police found the casings, and then dragged James and I back up to the Heath so we could show them where we were standing when we heard the first shot. Then we had to wait around while they traced the trajectory. They found the first bullet—or at least *a* bullet—in a tree on the other side of the meadow and the SOCKO chap said it looked very much as if our man had been aiming for me or James. I'm exceedingly glad he was a lousy shot."

"So am I," said Gibbons. "You didn't see the gunman yourself, then?"

Bethancourt shook his head. "There were several people about," he said, "but I didn't see anyone carting a double bass around."

"Still, you said there were other witnesses," said Gibbons thoughtfully.

"But not much of a description yet," said Bethancourt. "Just a young man of average height in a dark coat and cap. What people noticed was the bass case."

"Could be the chap I was following on Tuesday night," said Gibbons, and Bethancourt nodded.

"Could be," he said.

Gibbons was silent a moment, turning it all over in his mind.

"So what do you think, Phillip?" he asked at last. "Do you think this was a setup by James to avert suspicion from himself?"

Bethancourt shrugged. "It could have been," he said. "Particularly as no one was actually harmed. Frankly, I can't imagine why anyone would want to shoot either of us otherwise. James was telling me that the jewelry seems to have disappeared altogether, and Lord knows I don't have an idea in the world that would incriminate anybody. On the other hand, Carmichael and the others seemed very sure they'd find the man in short order."

"There is that," said Gibbons. "He must be all over the CCTV footage, and it won't be hard to pick out a man running about Hampstead Heath with a bass case." He thought a moment. "If I were going to try to bring something like that off," he said, "I'd be out of the country by now—it would be the only way to avoid getting caught."

"James would realize that, of course," said Bethancourt. "Well, I suppose we'll know soon enough, one way or the other. Either they'll catch the bloke in the next day or two, or they won't."

"Even if they don't," warned Gibbons, "it doesn't mean Colin James *is* guilty, only that he might be."

"And even if he is guilty, it doesn't necessarily follow that Davies is his accomplice," said Bethancourt. "I know, I know. I'm feeling very discouraged by the whole thing." He yawned.

"Reaction, I expect," said Gibbons. "You go home and tuck yourself up in bed with a drink and a nice book and you'll feel right as rain in the morning."

"I think I will," said Bethancourt, a little apologetically. "I'm done in, I'm afraid. Besides, I need to smoke—I haven't had nearly enough cigarettes in the past four hours."

"Take yourself off then," said Gibbons. "I'll probably fall asleep again soon anyhow. Ring me when you wake up in the morning."

"Will do," said Bethancourt, regaining his feet with an effort. "Come along, Cerberus. Good night, Jack."

But Gibbons did not fall asleep once Bethancourt had gone, though he turned off the light and arranged himself as comfortably as possible. Instead he lay staring out into the darkness, watching the pattern the streetlights outside made on the wall, and thinking over everything.

As Bethancourt and Gibbons wished each other a good night, Carmichael was standing in a chill wind on Hampstead Heath. The SOCKOs had brought out powerful flood lamps and were busy examining the ground beneath the trees where the rifleman had stood. Others were shooting laser beams through the darkness to estimate the trajectory of the bullets. They had dug two of them out of the trees on the farther side, but the third was proving elusive. The two trajectories they had thus far traced, however, went more or less through the spot where Bethancourt and James had been standing, leaving little doubt as to the shooter's target.

Why, was a harder question. Both James and Bethancourt claimed to know nothing that could possibly give anyone a motive for doing away with them. And if James was innocent of stealing the Haverford jewels, it was difficult to see a motive. On the other hand, if James were in possession of the jewels it was a very different story. Carmichael's eyes narrowed as he contemplated this possibility.

His mobile rang and he answered it quickly.

"Public relations has got their statement ready for the ten o'clock news," reported Inspector Davies. "And the communications center has already brought the fellow up on CCTV. Nothing good enough for an ID yet, but they're working on it."

"Good work," said Carmichael. "We ought to get something out of that. What about the rifle?"

"It's registered to a Gerald McSweeney," answered Davies. "Address in Mayfair. Sergeant O'Leary has gone off with a couple of uniforms to make inquiries."

"It'll be a miracle if we can clear it up that quickly," said Carmichael.

Davies agreed. "I'm afraid so," he said, "but it had to be followed up."

"Yes, of course," said Carmichael. "Well, I'm nearly finished up here, as soon as they come up with the third damn bullet. There's no doubt who our lad was shooting at."

"I didn't think there would be," responded Davies glumly. "I've never seen such a case, sir. I keep wondering what we'll have next: Bombs? Perhaps a grenade launcher?"

"At least no one got hurt this time," said Carmichael. "All right, Inspector. Ring me if you find out anything more."

"Will do, sir," said Davies, and rang off.

Davies was right, of course, reflected Carmichael. It was incredible to have a crime committed with an untraceable handgun, and then to have the culprit commit a second crime with a registered hunting rifle.

"Chief Inspector," someone called, and Carmichael turned to see Vivian Entwhistle, Colin James's secretary, coming toward him across the green. She had arrived at James's house earlier, at about the same time as O'Leary and Lemmy had turned up with the witness statements, and had at once begun to shower James with silent criticism. Carmichael had quite liked her.

"Yes, Miss Entwhistle?" he said once she came up beside him. "Do you have something for me?"

"I believe I do," she answered, proffering a large manila envelope. "In there," she continued, "are several threatening letters Mr. James has been receiving over the past few months. The first one I opened and handled, but the rest I have worn gloves while inspecting, and have placed them into individual plastic bags at once."

Carmichael frowned as he took the envelope and peeked into it. "This should have been reported at once," he said.

"I know," Vivian replied. "Mr. James refused to let me contact the police on the grounds that the letters were merely cranks. I disagreed with him, but I am in his employ and did not feel I could override his decision. So I merely kept the letters. When you read them, I think you'll see why I was alarmed."

"Do they threaten anything specific?" asked Carmichael.

"No." Vivian shook her head. "They accuse Mr. James of harming the letter writer's loved ones, and two of them accuse him of murder. They promise retribution, but do not specify what form it will take."

Carmichael nodded, and tucked the envelope securely under his arm. "Thank you for coming to me with this, Miss Entwhistle," he said. "I'll read them as soon as I'm done here, and then give them to the forensics team to work on. This may prove very helpful indeed."

"You're welcome," Vivian replied, and then, wishing him a good night, she retreated back the way she had come while Carmichael watched her go and wondered, if this was all a plot of James's, whether she was in on it or not.

"Got it, sir," called one of the SOCKOs, and Carmichael turned in that direction. The officer was crouching down on the ground some ten or fifteen yards beyond the bush Bethancourt and James had taken shelter behind. Carmichael moved to join him.

"This one came pretty close," he said as Carmichael came up. He nodded at the bush. "It must have been the last shot he fired. If he hadn't been letting the barrel jerk up as he squeezed the trigger, he might have got them."

Carmichael shuddered at the idea.

"Not very used to rifles, then, you think?" he asked.

"Oh, he'd probably been shooting before," replied the SOCKO. "Either he's just really rotten at it, or he'd never used this particular gun before. At least, that's my guess right now."

Carmichael nodded, thanked the man, and began to trudge back to the car park. It was going to be a long night, and he didn't see any chance of illumination at the end of it.

Upon arriving back at his flat, Bethancourt went at once to turn on the taps in the bath and then poured himself a whisky to drink while he waited for the tub to fill up. It was absolute luxury to lower himself into the steaming water and feel the cold and dirt seep away. He very nearly fell asleep on the spot.

He felt much better when he emerged nearly an hour later wrapped in a warm dressing gown and feeling distinctly peckish. Rummaging in the refrigerator he found some cold mutton and cheese, which he wolfed down on the spot. Then he made himself a fresh cup of coffee, added a healthy dollop of Irish whisky to it, and toddled off to bed with a book.

And yet even once he was all settled in, his mind kept reverting to the events of the day. Something James had said nagged at the back of his tired mind, but he could not quite bring it into focus.

"There's really no point in thinking about it now," he told himself firmly. "You're in no shape to devise any kind of reasonable theory."

That settled, he fixed his focus firmly on his book, which he had chosen specifically for its mindless entertainment value. But somehow the adventures of Captain Alatriste failed to capture his attention, partially because the glasses perched on the bridge of his nose were his second pair, and not quite as comfortable as the damaged ones, but mostly because his mind refused to let go of the problem at hand.

The thing about the original burglary that bothered him now was the timing. He had always assumed that Miranda Haverford's obituary had been the precipitating factor in the robbery—someone had seen it and taken advantage of the empty house. But an unscrupulous private collector would already have known of the jewels; any collector, unscrupulous or not, would have. So why had he waited to have them stolen? There was not, really, that much difference between an empty house and one tenanted by two very elderly women.

"I suppose," said Bethancourt dubiously, "that even criminals have their finer feelings. Perhaps this one didn't want to deprive Miranda of the pleasure of her jewels and thoughtfully waited until after she was dead to take them."

It did not seem a very likely explanation. Which left him with Colin James as the culprit.

"And he's already in Carmichael's sights," he told himself, "and the chief inspector hardly needs your help nailing a criminal."

He returned firmly to Captain Alatriste. But he found himself reading the same paragraph over and over again while his brain toyed with other explanations, most of them too fantastic to waste time thinking about. And then the remark James had made about the Golconda diamond brooch at last came back to him.

And suddenly a new possibility opened up. Bethancourt dropped his book and sat bolt upright in astonishment at the simplicity of this idea.

"Why, of course," he murmured. "That would explain everything—but how to confirm it?"

He dropped back on the bed and reached for his cigarettes. If his theory was right, there was someone out there who knew the truth, but he had no idea of how to find them. Mr. Grenshaw, the solicitor, would have been the logical person to have included in the secret, but Bethancourt was certain he knew nothing more than he had already told them. Was there anyone else Miranda Haverford might have trusted? What about the elderly gentleman whom she had named executor of her estate?

"He's worth a try," said Bethancourt. "I can't think of anyone else there could be. And even if he knows nothing, maybe he'll have more suggestions. I'll talk to him in the morning."

And with that settled, he stabbed out his cigarette and fell asleep almost at once.

22

A Place For Lemmy

Carmichael was back at the Yard by half six the next morning, in time to receive the first responses to the morning news. They had pulled a good likeness of their rifleman from the CCTV footage the night before, but it had been too late to get the image out to the public. It had also been too late to do much about finding Gerald McSweeney, the owner of the rifle. There had been no one at home at his London house, and his neighbors had only known that the McSweeneys had gone away for the weekend to visit family "somewhere up north."

The shooting on Hampstead Heath had engendered a general public outcry, and the Yard's public relations department was swamped with calls not only from concerned Londoners, but also from Whitehall. The first message Carmichael received was that he was expected to appear in Detective Superintendent Lumsden's office at nine o'clock to provide an explanation of events. Carmichael really did not know what he could say; he would be pleased to get an explanation himself.

"I think I've found the McSweeneys," O'Leary reported at about eight. "The family owns a hunting lodge up in Scotland, and most of the family still lives up there in the area. Shall I contact the local police up there to go have a word with them?"

"Good work, Sergeant," said Carmichael. "Yes, get on to them, would you? I don't expect," he added forlornly with a glance at the clock, "they'll be likely to be back to us before nine."

"No, sir," said O'Leary sympathetically. "But you can always say we've got inquiries pending."

Carmichael sighed. "I'll have to, won't I?" he growled.

Before O'Leary could reply, the phone rang and Carmichael reached to answer it, motioning O'Leary to stay.

"Is that Detective Chief Inspector Carmichael?" asked a male voice with a distinct north London accent. "My mates said to ring you. I'm Herbert Cannon."

The name did not register with Carmichael, and his brows rose. "Did they now?" he said.

"That's right," the man answered. "Everyone's saying you want to know about a fare I had last Tuesday night."

The light dawned. "You're the second taxi driver!" exclaimed Carmichael, feeling rather as if he had just hit the jackpot. His grip on the telephone receiver tightened. "Yes, I do very much want to talk to you. Can you come by Scotland Yard?"

"I can as soon as I get my rig out," answered Cannon. "It'll take me forty-five minutes or so. What do I do once I get there?"

"Just ask for me," replied Carmichael. "I'll come straight down and meet you. Thank you very much, Mr. Cannon, for coming forward."

He met O'Leary's eyes as he rang off.

"The taxi driver who had the man Gibbons was following?" asked O'Leary eagerly.

Carmichael nodded. "If we're very, very lucky," he said softly, "he'll have a description of the fellow. Here, go make your call to Scotland, O'Leary. Then come back here and we'll talk to Mr. Cannon together."

O'Leary rose with alacrity. "I'll be right back," he said. "Thank you, sir," he added, pausing as he turned for the door. "I do appreciate your including me."

Carmichael waved him away, brushing away the thanks.

In the end, he summoned Lemmy back from the video room as well, armed with several different and yet uniformly poor pictures of the man who had taken the cab in front of Gibbons's.

Herbert Cannon, when he appeared, was a solid citizen with a prominent nose who clearly wanted to get this business over with.

"I've looked up the fare in my logbook," he said, "and written down the details for you here. See? I picked up this young fellow in the queue at Waterloo station and let him off at East Street and Walworth."

"Excellent," said Carmichael, taking the paper the driver offered. "Very organized of you, Mr. Cannon. Do you remember the young man at all?"

"Well, I been thinking about that," said Cannon, "and I think I do, for all it was a week ago. I remember the Tuesday night well enough, and I'm thinking the fare I took to Waterloo in the first place was that very disagreeable gentleman who wanted me to hurry so he didn't miss his train, but then barely gave me any money above the fare. Because I remember being worried that there'd already be too many taxis in the queue there, and thinking it was a lot of trouble to go through for a bloke as didn't appreciate it. But the queue wasn't crowded as it turned out."

It was rather a pity, thought Carmichael, that they weren't interested in the disagreeable gentleman—there was no doubt Cannon remembered all about that fare. But he smiled, held onto his hopes with both hands, and asked, "And that was where you picked up the young man I want to know about?"

"That's right," said Cannon. "Pleasant fellow, as I recall. Was asking me about the Walworth neighborhood, about the shops and the kinds of fares I picked up there. Gave me a decent tip for the ride, though nothing special. Still, it was a short run."

"Did he say anything about a friend in the taxi behind yours? That the friend would be following you?"

Cannon frowned. "No," he answered. "But this young fellow, he didn't have any luggage or such—there was plenty of room for a friend if he'd had one with him."

"I see," said Carmichael neutrally. "Now, do remember anything about his appearance? You've said he was a young man."

"Oh, yes." Cannon nodded. "He wasn't above thirty—I'd put him in his mid-twenties, myself. Not too tall, and solid-built. He had short hair—brown, it was. And he had a dark jacket on—a nice warm one it looked. I'm not sure what else he was wearing. Oh, and I think he had some freckles."

Carmichael and O'Leary exchanged disbelieving looks. They were staggered by the detail of this description—it was far better than they had ever dared to hope for.

Unexpectedly, Lemmy spoke up.

"Was he wearing a cap?" he asked.

Cannon scowled at him. "Of course not," he said. "How could I see he wore his hair short if he'd had a cap on?"

Lemmy shook his head.

"It's not our bloke, sir," he said to Carmichael, crushing all Carmichael's elation in a single sentence. "Here, you can see in this picture. The man was definitely wearing a cap."

He passed the photo over, and Cannon craned his neck to see it.

"There he is, right there," he said indignantly, stabbing his finger down on the photograph. "Not a bloody cap in sight."

He glared at Lemmy.

"Oh, my God," said Carmichael, staring down at the picture.

"But that's Jack, isn't it?" said O'Leary, peering over his shoulder.

Lemmy looked confused.

"Is this one here your taxi, sir?" asked Carmichael, turning the picture round on his desk so Cannon could view it more easily.

"That's right," said Cannon. "The second one in line, that's my rig. And right there's my passenger, just bending to tell me where he wants to go."

"Oh," said Lemmy, enlightened. "Sergeant Gibbons was in your taxi, not the other driver's."

Carmichael turned to O'Leary. "Go find that other driver," he ordered.

O'Leary, already out of his seat, nodded silently and was out the door in an instant.

Lemmy was shuffling through the other photographs he had brought along.

"Sir," he said, "I'm pretty sure there's some good footage of the taxi behind Mr. Cannon's, but not in this batch. If I could just go back to the video room, I'm sure I could have it for you shortly."

"Go, go," said Carmichael, and then he turned back to his witness.

"Mr. Cannon," he said, "I can't thank you enough for coming forward. Your evidence has been of the utmost help—in fact, without it I dare say we might not have solved the case at all."

Cannon looked gratified. "Just doing my duty," he said gruffly.

"Now then," continued Carmichael, "if you could recall any of the particulars of your conversation with this passenger . . ."

After days of digging and coming up with nothing, the flood gates had opened and information was pouring down on Carmichael from every possible source. He was late getting to the superintendent's office, but at least the sudden influx of evidence made the interview a mercifully brief one. And his various subordinates were lined up waiting for him when he emerged, all holding a different piece of the puzzle.

Out of the hundreds of calls that had come in response to their appeal to the public for information about the Hampstead Shooter, a tentative identification of the man had been made. He was believed to be one Richard Denby and a bulletin had been put out with orders for his immediate detainment if and when he was spotted. A couple of uniformed policemen had been sent to the address on Denby's driver's license, but no one was at home there.

"And who the hell is this Denby?" demanded Carmichael. "He's not a jewel thief, is he?"

"Not that we know of," said Inspector Hollings. "We haven't got much on him, though. I'm working on his employment record right now."

O'Leary had tracked down Bradley Johnson, and he was on his way in from his home in Enfield.

"And I've found Tom Gerrard, the witness who saw Gibbons that night," added O'Leary. "He's off work today, and said he'd come round."

"That's good," said Carmichael. "With the two cabbies and Gerrard, we should get this sorted. I don't know, to be honest, how we came to make such a mistake."

"Well, sir," said O'Leary, "when you hear that one man was trailing another, it's only natural to assume the chap doing the following is the policeman. I know I would have."

"I suppose so," said Carmichael, still displeased with himself. "You realize what this means, of course?"

O'Leary nodded. "Yes, sir. Since we now know he wasn't following anyone, it means we still don't know why Gibbons went to Walworth that night in the first place."

"Right enough," said Carmichael, scowling. Then he shook off the expression and sighed. "Well," he said, "one thing at a time. Let's have all our ducks in a row on this go-round. Have we got a picture of Gibbons to show this lot? A good one, I mean, not the awful stuff from the CCTV footage."

"I should be able to dig one up out of files," said O'Leary. "I'll just run have a look—oh, and I'm still waiting to hear back from the lads in Scotland."

Carmichael nodded and let him go, turning to Lemmy, who stood waiting his turn.

"We've found the fellow who was following the sergeant, sir," he reported. "We've got him entering the Camden Town tube station a few seconds behind Sergeant Gibbons, so he must have followed him from there. The pictures aren't the best—the blighter was obviously trying to avoid the cameras—but there are a couple of good possibilities. Markham's working on cleaning them up right now."

"Good, good," said Carmichael. "Bring the photos up to my office as soon as you've got them, will you, Constable? I want to know if it's this Denby character."

"Oh, it's not him, sir," answered Lemmy. "The shots are blurry, but I would have recognized Denby."

Carmichael, poised to go, frowned and paused. "How can you be so sure?" he asked.

"I have a photographic memory, sir," answered Lemmy, his voice tinged with pride. "It's why I thought I might be good at detective work. I didn't recognize Denby because I've never seen him before, but if the man following Sergeant Gibbons is anyone with a picture in the case file, I'll be able to pick him out."

For a long moment, Carmichael simply stared at him, torn between astonishment and exasperation. Then he began to laugh.

Lemmy shifted uncomfortably, not certain of the source of this humor.

"Go on, lad," said Carmichael at last, overcoming his mirth. His tone was probably the kindest Lemmy had yet heard from him. "You're doing brilliantly—just get those photos clear for me, and I'll see you shortly."

Lemmy nodded and moved off while Carmichael shook his head bemusedly, at last enlightened as to the reason for the constable's presence in the detective division.

"He'll do well enough in the CCTV surveillance department," he said to himself as he turned back toward his office. "I must speak to Evans about it."

But the thought of CCTV footage brought him back to the business at hand, and he frowned over Lemmy's declaration that Denby was not the one who had followed Gibbons to Walworth on Tuesday night. He wondered if there was any hope that Gibbons might recognize his pursuer once they had a decent photograph of the man. He would have to go round to the hospital, Carmichael decided, once he was done here; indeed, he felt an urge to talk all the new developments over with his sergeant. But it would have to wait until Lemmy and Markham had finished their work, and in the meantime he had best concentrate on finding out what connection Denby had with the case.

Upon reaching his office, he picked up the telephone and dialed James's office number. Vivian answered the telephone in her smooth contralto voice, and remembering her levelheadedness the night before, Carmichael decided on the moment to question her first.

"Denby?" she repeated thoughtfully. "It is a familiar name, sir. If I could just—oh!"

"Oh?" asked Carmichael.

"But it can't be," she said, and he heard the clack of her computer keys in the background. "I'm certain he was sent up for at least twenty years. Yes, here it is: Carl Denby, sentenced to thirty years for armed robbery and assault with a deadly weapon. That was only three years ago, Chief Inspector—he can't be out yet."

"Probably not," agreed Carmichael. "This bloke's name is Richard Denby. Does Carl have any relations?"

Vivian began to reply, but then broke off and Carmichael heard the resonant tones of James in the background.

"Excuse me a moment, sir," said Vivian. "Mr. James apparently has something to say that won't wait."

Carmichael did not mind the interruption in the least, as he was already turning to his own computer and bringing up Carl Denby's police record.

"Damn," he murmured when he saw it. "Miss Entwhistle?" he said, and then repeated the name more forcefully.

"Yes, Chief Inspector, I'm here," she said at last, though he could still hear James talking in the background.

"Miss Entwhistle, those anonymous letters you gave me last night—do you remember when you received the first of them?"

"I believe it was about three months ago," Vivian replied. "I can look up the exact date for you—"

"No, no," said Carmichael, staring at his computer screen. "Never mind. I think it's pretty clear what happened, though of course I won't know until we track this Denby down."

"Vivian," James bellowed so loudly that Carmichael could hear him clearly, "let me speak to the chief inspector, damn it all. Anybody would think you were the one who got shot at."

"Chief Inspector?" said Vivian. "Mr. James wants a word if you'll speak to him."

Her tone conveyed clearly that she thought this would be a monumental mistake on Carmichael's part, and he grinned.

"Certainly, Miss Entwhistle," he said, "I'd be very happy to speak to Mr. James."

"Chief Inspector?" came James's voice, once again perfectly under control. "Vivian seems to think you suspect Carl Denby of shooting at me last night? I really don't think that's possible."

"Neither do I," Carmichael assured him. "Carl Denby is dead."

There was a stunned silence.

"Dead?" asked James. "Not in prison?"

"He was in prison," said Carmichael. "He apparently died about three and half months ago of a congenital heart defect, previously undiagnosed."

"Well, that's a corker," said James.

"According to my records, however," continued Carmichael, "Carl had a younger brother with whom he was very close."

"Oh, yes, the puppy," said James. "I remember now—well, of course you do, Viv, he was slobbering all over you at the trial."

"The puppy," said Carmichael, raising his voice to attract James's attention, "is likely the one who shot at you last night, and also the author of the threatening letters you've been receiving. As I remember, they accused you of harm to a loved one."

"Did they?" asked James, sounding surprised. "Wait a moment— how did you get them? *Vivian . . .*"

"Miss Entwhistle gave them into evidence last night," said Carmichael. "As was quite proper, Mr. James. You didn't even mention them."

"Well, why would I have?" demanded James. "I thought they were pure bunk. I still can't quite believe . . . Oh, all right, Vivian, have the damn phone."

"Chief Inspector?" came Vivian's voice. "I'd like to thank you very much on Mr. James's behalf for clearing this matter up so quickly."

"It's not cleared up altogether," warned Carmichael. "We haven't got Denby yet, and until we do we can't be sure this explanation is the right one. It certainly seems to fit all the facts, but other explanations might do that as well."

"You've still accomplished a remarkable amount in such a short time," said Vivian. "We'd appreciate it very much if you could let us know once Richard Denby has been captured."

"Of course," said Carmichael. "Thank you for your information about Mr. Denby. You've been most helpful, Miss Entwhistle."

And with these mutual compliments, they rang off.

Carmichael sat with his chin sunk on his breast for several minutes after he had replaced the receiver in its cradle. It was all very neat, and on the face of it seemed a straightforward case. If it had not been for James's involvement with the other matter, Carmichael would have felt relatively sure he had the case wrapped up. But as it was . . .

Colin James was a very clever man, and Carmichael did not put it past him to have arranged this distraction, with or without his secretary's complicity. Until he had Richard Denby's confession in his hands, Carmichael was taking nothing for granted.

23

The Executor

In the morning, Bethancourt's inspiration of the night before seemed less brilliant, but he determined to follow it up anyway, the more so as he could think of nothing else he could do. If Colin James was guilty, Carmichael would have him to rights soon enough.

He was almost sure he had written down the name of the nursing home Ned Winterbottom lived in, so while he had his morning coffee he went through the bits and pieces of paper he regularly turned out of his pockets at night and piled on the dresser. Eventually he discovered it scrawled on the back of a torn receipt: Southgate Beaumont.

The day was bright but chilly as Bethancourt negotiated the Monday traffic on his way north. Southgate Beaumont proved to be a lovely old manor house off Cannon Hill, hidden from the road by a belt of trees. Bethancourt sat for a moment after he had parked the Jaguar, just admiring it.

"It wouldn't be a bad place to be when we get old and feeble, eh, Cerberus?" he said. "Well, let's have a look at the inside."

The entry was as grand as the outside with classical murals, a beautifully painted ceiling, and fine antique furnishings. Bethancourt asked for Ned Winterbottom, gave the receptionist his card with the message "Re: Haverford Estate" written on it, and was asked to wait.

Eventually an aide appeared to escort him to Winterbottom's apartment. They chatted amiably about the architecture of the manor house as she guided him up the staircase and down a long gallery until they reached a door bearing a discreet brass plaque that read "Mr. Edward Winterbottom."

The aide knocked briskly and then opened the door without further ceremony.

"Mr. Winterbottom?" she said. "Here's Mr. Bethancourt for you."

Ned Winterbottom was a wizened old man with a fringe of pure white hair running around the edges of his otherwise bald pate and clothes that hung loosely on his emaciated frame. He wore large-framed glasses through which he peered up at Bethancourt.

"Hmph," he said.

"It's very good of you to see me, sir," said Bethancourt.

"I'll leave you to it, then, shall I?" said the aide, a little over-brightly. "Just ring if you want anything."

Winterbottom waited until she had shut the door behind her before speaking.

"So what have you got to do with Miranda's estate?" he demanded, somewhat querulously. "You're not a solicitor or a policeman."

"No," admitted Bethancourt. "I'm a private citizen. I've only come into it at all because a friend of mine who was investigating the robbery was shot."

"I heard about that," said Winterbottom in a less confrontational tone. "I hope the young man is recovering well?"

"Yes, very well, thanks," said Bethancourt.

"Hmph," said Winterbottom again. "Well, sit down, can't you? It's putting a crick in my neck looking up at you."

Bethancourt sat down obediently in a second armchair. He was not entirely sure what to make of Winterbottom, or what approach to take with the old man.

"I assume," said Bethancourt, "that Mr. Grenshaw has been keeping you abreast of matters related to the case?"

"He's been popping in and out of here like a jack-in-the-box, bleating at me as if I'd stolen the bloody jewels myself, if that's what you mean," said Winterbottom. "God knows what he expects me to do about it." He narrowed his eyes. "Or what you expect, either," he added.

"I only wanted to ask you a question," said Bethancourt, keeping his tone pleasant. "As I understand it, you and Miss Haverford were very close."

"Yes, we were," snapped Winterbottom. "You could have asked that over the phone. I may be old, but I do know how to use a telephone."

"So do I," replied Bethancourt. "But I wanted to see you. And that was by way of being a prelude, not the question I came to ask."

"Thank God," muttered Winterbottom. "Maybe you're not such an idiot after all."

Bethancourt eyed him, wondering if he had been wildly mistaken in thinking Winterbottom might know anything, if perhaps he had in fact been quite mistaken about everything. But then he caught a gleam in the old man's eye, which made him ask simply, "When did Miss Haverford sell the last of her jewels, do you know?"

And Winterbottom broke into a delighted cackle, rocking back and forth and clapping his hands. He looked back at Bethancourt with an entirely different expression in his rheumy eyes.

"I was wondering if anyone would ever figure it out," he said. "I was beginning to think not. Did you come up with it yourself? Or was it your policeman friend who sent you round?"

"It was an idea I had last night," said Bethancourt. "I was talking to the insurance investigator on the case, and he happened to mention that one of his contacts recollected seeing a stone very like the Golconda diamond from the Haverford brooch, only that had been a number of years ago. Why did you not tell Grenshaw?"

Winterbottom scowled. "That ass? Why should I have? It was much more entertaining watching him scurry about like a rat in a maze. At my age," he added loftily, "there's not so very much entertainment to be had out of life. You have to take what you can get."

Bethancourt laughed. "And you weren't going to tell me anything, either, were you?" he said. "You had your crotchety old gentleman persona firmly in place when I came in—what made you change your mind?"

"Oh, I was never going to lie about it," answered Winterbottom. "If anyone had bothered to ask me what I knew about the jewels, I would have told them. I just didn't see any reason to volunteer the information."

Waiting, thought Bethancourt, for someone to treat him as a serious participant. And in the meantime thoroughly enjoying the irony in the fact that the answer to the mystery was so easily available, if only anyone had thought to ask an elderly man for it.

"Will you tell me about it now?" asked Bethancourt.

Winterbottom shrugged. "Not much to tell," he said. "It should have been obvious to any idiot from the condition of the property that Miranda was very hard up indeed. Where else was she going to get money?"

"But how did you come to know of it?" asked Bethancourt. "Did Miss Haverford confide in you at the time?"

"Well, naturally," said Winterbottom. "She hadn't the least notion how to go about selling the stuff on the quiet, she needed my help. I did try to persuade her," he added, "to put it all up for auction. I explained that she would make double, maybe even triple the money that way, but she wasn't having any." He sighed. "She was always stubborn. And proud—that was the problem, you see. She couldn't bear that anyone should know that the Haverford fortune was gone."

"So no one knew but you?" asked Bethancourt.

"Rose, her housekeeper, knew," replied Winterbottom. "I don't think anyone else did. And it didn't all go at once, you know. At first she thought she'd get by with just selling off some of the less spectacular pieces. 'After all,' she told me, 'I'm old—I won't last much longer.'" He laughed. "That was some ten or fifteen years before she died. You never know what span the Lord has in store for you, and so I told her. But she wouldn't listen."

"So how did you sell them?" asked Bethancourt.

"Mostly to private collectors," said Winterbottom. "I expect you already know about my spot of bother?"

Bethancourt shook his head. "No," he said. "No one's mentioned anything to me."

"Ah." Winterbottom looked a little embarrassed. "Well, I suppose you had better know. I once did a stint in prison for embezzlement. It was after the war," he added, rather apologetically, in explanation, "when my family's finances had pretty much gone south, and my brother—well, never mind about that. Anyway, I met many unsavory characters in jail, some of whom I kept in contact with afterward. One of them was a dealer in stolen jewelry, and he was happy to supply me with buyers for Miranda's jewels for a commission."

"I see," said Bethancourt. He paused for a moment in thought. "What about the Colemans?" he said. "Did she tell them? It was rather their business, after all."

Winterbottom sighed. "She was going to," he said. "She began to feel guilty, you see, as the collection shrank. She'd put off selling the last of it for years, but finally there was nothing else left to do. The alexandrite necklace was the last to go—she somehow thought if she could just pass that on, not having the rest wouldn't make so much difference. But after that went, she had to face the fact that there would be nothing for the Colemans to inherit."

"Is that why she asked them to come?" said Bethancourt. "To break the news in person?"

"More or less. Less, really," said Winterbottom. "To tell the truth, I'm not sure exactly what she had in mind. She was a bit odd in this last year—I'm not certain but what she had some idea of their helping her out. She and Rose were really getting past it, and if it weren't for the Burdalls, the whole place would have been falling down around their ears. But it was all irrelevant once the Colemans actually showed up."

Bethancourt raised his brows. "It was?"

"Haven't you met them?" asked Winterbottom, surprised.

"Yes. Once."

"Once should have been enough," said Winterbottom scornfully. "Rob Coleman is a money-grubbing lowlife who's out for whatever he can get. Miranda saw that immediately—she began to think that having to sell her jewels was God's way of making sure Rob Coleman didn't get his hands on them. In the end, she rather enjoyed playing him for the fool, although I think she felt badly about his wife. She and Lia began to quite like each other before the end, I believe."

"You know, of course," said Bethancourt, "that they're in line for the insurance money—or would be, if you hadn't decided to talk to me."

Winterbottom shrugged. "What's the insurance company to me?" he asked. "I dare say they've refused to pay out on enough occasions when they should have that this could be considered payback. It all evens out in the end."

"Well, I suppose it does at that," said Bethancourt, willing to be magnanimous on this point. "Just as a matter of curiosity—do you know where the alexandrite necklace ended up? I'd rather have liked to see it."

Winterbottom shook his head regretfully. "It was worth seeing," he said. "But I'm afraid I don't know. Old Pennycook handled all that end of the business, you see."

And Bethancourt, stunned that this connection had not occurred to him, was momentarily speechless.

"Bloody hell," he said at last.

Gibbons leaned back in the armchair, very pleasantly surprised. He had just been returned to his room after his morning bout with physical therapy and for the first time he was not in absolute agony. True, it had not been a comfortable process, and it remained an activity he would do almost anything to avoid, but not wanting to scream in pain was a vast improvement.

He reached for his notebook—another action only recently possible—and flipped it open to the page he had been scribbling in before the therapist arrived. The news that he had taken the tube from the Camden Town station had disturbed him as being further evidence of James's possible guilt; Camden was only two stops from the Hampstead station. He had consoled himself with the fact that James had been in his office in the City at the time, but then he remembered that information rested on James's word alone and had not been corroborated.

So now he was reviewing the profile James had given him of the kinds of people who committed arts thefts, and there was no doubt both James and Davies fit it. But, he reminded himself, there was also no doubt that neither of them had been the man he had followed to Walworth.

His train of thought was interrupted by the telephone, which, again, he had to reach for. It still hurt, but the motion no longer left him gasping for breath, and he was quite pleased with the firmness of his voice as he answered.

"We've been utter idiots," said Bethancourt. "Well, I have, at any rate—you've been under the weather."

His friend sounded both excited and distraught, and Gibbons's first instinct was to calm him down in order to get some sense out of him.

"It won't have been the first time," he said soothingly. "What have we been idiots about?"

"It was obvious from the start they were connected," went on Bethancourt, clearly unsoothed. "I thought so at the time—I just couldn't see how. And, Jack, God help us all if we don't remember to show the elderly some respect."

"What?" said Gibbons, utterly confused. "What elderly are you talking about?"

"All of them," answered Bethancourt. "I've just come from talking with Ned Winterbottom, and if I'd just thought to do that a week ago, we'd have known exactly what happened. But no, he was off in a nursing home, so I didn't bother. Disrespectful is the only word for it."

"I'm sure it is," said Gibbons, beginning to be irritated. "Who the devil is Ned Winterbottom?"

"See?" said Bethancourt. "You didn't even know his name. That's exactly what I'm talking about."

"You're talking a lot of nonsense is what you're doing," said Gibbons. "Are you trying to tell me you know who shot me? Because if so, I wish you'd come out with it."

"Not exactly," replied Bethancourt. "Although, now you mention it, I suppose it follows that—oh, damn. There's a traffic jam up ahead. Hold on, I've got to change down."

But after a moment in which there was the sound of several loud clanks, the line went dead.

"Bother," muttered Gibbons, quite annoyed. He tried to ring Bethancourt back, but his friend was apparently passing through a no-service zone. "Bugger it," said Gibbons, ringing off again. "He'd damn well better be on his way here."

Bethancourt was. Although it seemed like æons to Gibbons, in fact Bethancourt and Cerberus appeared at the doorway in scarcely ten minutes.

"I'm abjectly sorry," said Bethancourt, unzipping his jacket as he came in. "I would have rung back, but I really had to pay attention to the road—the traffic was wild. Dear God, Jack, can you believe it?"

He flung himself into the second armchair with the air of a man who is flabbergasted by the unexpected course of events.

"I'd have an easier time believing it if you would tell me what it was," answered Gibbons testily. "All you've said to the point so far is that something is connected and you've spoken to some elderly gentleman I've never heard of before."

Bethancourt had the grace to look ashamed. "I do apologize, Jack," he said. "I didn't realize I'd been so incoherent—it's just that it came at me out of nowhere."

"Could you please," said Gibbons between clenched teeth, "just start at the beginning?"

"Yes, yes, of course," said Bethancourt hastily, sitting up and making an effort to marshal his thoughts. "The beginning, right. Well, last night—before we got shot at—James told me that one of his contacts had mentioned there being a diamond very like the Golconda one from the Haverford collection for sale several years ago. He also told me that as far as he could tell, the Haverford jewels had vanished into thin air. At the time, I thought he might be covering his own tracks, but later it occurred to me that perhaps the diamond James's friend had seen all those years ago *was* the Haverford one."

"I see," said Gibbons, his interest piqued. "It does make sense, Phillip—the house could certainly have used some upkeep, and in my report Grenshaw said there wasn't really anything left of the estate."

"Exactly," said Bethancourt. "If you're old and getting desperately hard up and are sitting on a million pounds' worth of jewelry, well, the answer to your problems is pretty obvious really."

"I take it this Winterbottom fellow confirmed this?" asked Gibbons. "Who in blazes is he, anyhow?"

"An old friend of Miranda Haverford's, whom she named executor of her will," replied Bethancourt. "You can't remember your interview with Grenshaw, and Winterbottom didn't make it into your report, so you wouldn't know. But I should have seen him earlier—before the Burdalls, actually. He was the executor, after all."

Gibbons ignored this reintroduction into the conversation of Bethancourt's new Respect for Our Elders cause. "So that means the whole thing has been an insurance scam from the beginning," he said, thinking it through. "No doubt the Colemans got into the safe early on—possibly even before Miss Haverford died—and realized their inheritance was gone. So they staged the robbery in order to collect the insurance money. It makes perfect sense." He frowned. "I still can't see why Coleman would have shot me, though. I expect I—oh, wait."

Bethancourt, who had been on the verge of interrupting, paused. "What?" he asked.

"I forgot," said Gibbons. "They've traced my movements back that night and apparently I got on the tube at Camden Town."

"But that's where the Colemans live," said Bethancourt excitedly. "You must have gone to see them that night."

"It looks like it, doesn't it?" said Gibbons, grinning broadly. There was something immensely satisfying in knowing where he had been, even if he could not remember it.

"And then Coleman shot you because you'd caught on to his involvement with the Pennycook murder," said Bethancourt. "I thought it must be that, since—"

"What?" demanded Gibbons. "How do you make that out? I swear, Phillip, you're enough to try a saint's patience sometimes. What had Pennycook to do with any of it?"

"It's what Winterbottom told me," said Bethancourt. "I was just getting to it. It was he, you see, who arranged for the sale of Miss Haverford's jewels through an old connection of his—a fence named Pennycook."

Gibbons's eyes went very wide. "No," he breathed. "And Penny-cook liked to indulge in a spot of blackmail."

Bethancourt nodded. "That's how Winterbottom and I figured it," he said. "When Miranda's obituary appeared and mentioned the jewels, Pennycook would have known it was pure bunk. It may even have been he who informed the Colemans that there were no jewels, and suggested the faked robbery in return for a share of the insurance money. But instead of giving him a nice juicy cut of the loot, Coleman gave him a whack over the head."

"Dear God," said Gibbons.

"I don't know how you twigged it," continued Bethancourt, "but you'd just finished hearing all about the Pennycook case from O'Leary before you went up to speak to the Colemans. Perhaps you made a reference to it, or perhaps Coleman did."

"I've got to ring Carmichael," said Gibbons, reaching for the phone. "Unless," he added, pausing, "you've already told him?"

Bethancourt looked indignant. "Of course I haven't," he said. "I always tell you everything first, even when you haven't been shot."

"Right," said Gibbons, picking up the phone and dialing.

But Carmichael, when he picked up, sounded surprised.

"Gibbons?" he said. "I'm just on my way up to see you, lad. There's been some developments."

"There's been some here, too," answered Gibbons. "But it can wait till you're out of the elevator—if you're literally on your way up?"

"I am," answered Carmichael. "I'll be with you in two ticks."

Gibbons rang off.

"He's here?" asked Bethancourt happily. "Great minds think alike."

Carmichael, when he came in a few seconds later, was armed with a photograph.

"There you are, sir," said Gibbons. "Phillip's solved the whole thing—"

"Just a moment," said Carmichael, holding up a hand. "I want to know one thing first: do either of you recognize this man?"

And he held out the photo.

Gibbons frowned at it. "Yes, I've seen him somewhere."

"It's Rob Coleman," said Bethancourt.

"Of course!" said Gibbons. "I remember now—yes, that's him."

Bethancourt raised his eyes from the photograph to meet Carmichael's gaze. "How did you know, sir?"

Carmichael cocked his head.

"Know what?" he asked.

"That Coleman was the one who shot Jack," said Bethancourt, and Carmichael frowned.

"I still don't know it for certain," he answered. "This photograph is of the man who followed Gibbons to Walworth on Tuesday night. Constable Lemmy identified him as Coleman, but I hadn't got as far as pinning the shooting on him. How did the two of you come up with that?"

"Stop a bit," said Gibbons. "*He* followed *me?* Not the other way round?"

"That's right," said Carmichael. "I told you there had been developments."

"Here, sir," said Bethancourt. "Do take my chair—I'll be perfectly comfortable on the bed—and then we can all share our stories. It seems to have been an eventful day."

"That it has," said Carmichael, settling himself gratefully in the chair. "Now, tell me exactly how you came to the conclusion that Rob Coleman shot Gibbons here."

They explained, the words tumbling over each other in their haste to fill the chief inspector in on all they had learned. Carmichael, leaning back in his chair and sipping thoughtfully at the coffee he had brought with him, sorted out the jumble of words with the ease of long experience, letting the two younger men go on without any interruption beyond the astonished reaction of his bushy eyebrows.

"Good Lord," he muttered when they seemed to have run dry. "That's a remarkable piece of detective work."

Bethancourt beamed.

Carmichael sat silent for a moment, turning it all over in his mind while the others watched him respectfully. Then a wolfish smile spread slowly over the chief inspector's face.

"Well," he said, pulling his mobile out of his pocket, "I think I'd best have a bit of a chat with our Mr. Coleman."

"I wish I could be there," said Gibbons, looking frustrated.

"Don't worry, lad, I'll do you proud," promised Carmichael. "O'Leary," he said into the phone, "is that you? Yes, Gibbons and Bethancourt both recognized him—it's Rob Coleman, the Haverford heir. Run out and pick him up, will you? Take Davies if you can—and you'd better bring the wife along, too, but don't put them in the same room. . . . No, there's more, but I'll fill you in when I get back. I won't be long, I'll probably be there before you. . . . Good man, I'll see you there."

"But you're not leaving at once, are you, sir?" asked Gibbons when Carmichael had rung off. "I'd still like to know how you found out I was being followed instead of doing the following."

"So would I," chimed in Bethancourt.

"It was getting all the witnesses together that did it," answered Carmichael. "The second taxi driver came forward this morning, and it became obvious in short order that the man he'd had in his cab that night was you, Gibbons, and not somebody you were following. Which meant that the first driver's fare—who had instructed him to follow the taxi in front of them—must have been tailing Gibbons, and not the other way around."

"I see," said Bethancourt. "And then Lemmy identified Coleman."

"I didn't realize he'd ever seen the Colemans," said Gibbons. "I didn't think you'd been to talk to them, sir."

"I haven't," said Carmichael. He was smiling ruefully. "It turns out our Lemmy has a photographic memory—he recognized Coleman from the photo in the Haverford case file. It's the entire reason he decided to become a detective."

"A photographic memory would certainly come in handy," said Gibbons, a little dubiously, "but, well, it's not much to build a career on, really."

Carmichael sighed. "A great deal more is needed to make a good detective," he agreed. "On the other hand, the lad is to be commended for wanting to use his rather unique ability for the greater good. I'm going to stick Superintendent Evans with him."

Gibbons grinned. "That ought to suit."

"Superintendent Evans?" asked Bethancourt.

"He's in charge of CCTV footage," explained Gibbons.

"Oh, I see," said Bethancourt, nodding wisely despite never having had to deal with incompetent subordinates. "Then the one thing that's still a mystery," he said, going on, "is why Coleman popped off at me and James last night. I don't know about James, but I certainly had not the least suspicion of the man."

"And the answer to that," said Carmichael, smiling a little, "is that he didn't."

"Excuse me?" asked Bethancourt politely. "Who didn't what?"

"Coleman didn't shoot at you," replied Carmichael. "I did think at the time it was damned odd that a fellow who possessed a perfectly good handgun would go to the trouble of packing up a rifle in a bass case and toting it around the Heath."

"It is odd, now you mention it," said Gibbons.

"But if it wasn't Coleman, who did shoot at us?" demanded Bethancourt.

"A man with a grudge against Colin James," Carmichael told him. "The idiot was actually aiming for the dogs, but that's by the way. He's in custody now and busy pouring out his soul at the Hampstead nick."

"That was quick work, sir," said Gibbons.

Carmichael shrugged. "All according to the book," he said.

"Was it his own rifle?" asked Bethancourt.

"No," answered Carmichael. "Denby—that's the fellow's name—mostly makes a living from doing odd jobs for those wealthier than he, including a fair amount of house-sitting and dog-walking. The McSweeneys had hired him to look after their place while they were away, and Denby found a rifle in one of the closets. Pure luck, really—he'd been wanting to attack James for months, but just hadn't had the means."

"Well, thank heavens it hadn't anything to do with me," said Bethancourt. "Do you know, I was feeling quite alarmed by the idea that someone thought it worth their while to shoot me."

"Natural enough," said Carmichael, but he was smiling broadly.

"I quite often want to shoot you," offered Gibbons.

"But you obviously haven't thought it worth your while," pointed out Bethancourt, "as you've never done it."

"I usually don't have a firearm handy," explained Gibbons. "And the urge passes after a bit."

Carmichael rose, smiling at them.

"I'll leave you to it," he said. "I've got a suspect to question."

"You'll ring when you're done, won't you?" asked Gibbons anxiously.

"I certainly will," promised Carmichael. "Perhaps I'll even stop by if I leave the Yard early enough. But I'll let you know what happens one way or the other."

"Thank you, sir," said Gibbons. "I do appreciate it."

After he had gone, they sat silently for a few minutes, each contemplating all they had learned. At last Gibbons stirred, shifting uncomfortably, and eyed his bed.

"Do you think," he asked, "you could help me over there? Suddenly I'm quite done in."

"I'm feeling much the same myself," admitted Bethancourt, rising to give his friend a hand. "Here we go—you're feeling better, aren't you?"

Gibbons merely grunted in reply, having used most of his breath in getting up from the chair.

"I can tell," went on Bethancourt, "because you're really doing all the work yourself."

Gibbons eased himself down onto the bed and sighed.

"I'm a lot better," he said in a moment. "The doctor says I can go home soon if I keep on this way."

Bethancourt dropped back into his chair and shook his head.

"It's incredible," he said. "And it's only a week since I was standing here, thinking you were dying. God knows you looked like it."

Gibbons grinned at him. "I'm not so easy to kill," he boasted. He shifted against the pillows and then sighed again. "That's better," he said. "I hate to be rude, Phillip, but I'm feeling awfully drowsy—I may drop off."

"Have your nap and don't worry about me," said Bethancourt.

"I'm going to take myself home, just as soon as I can summon the energy to get up."

But the energy was apparently lacking, for when Nurse Pipp looked in some ten minutes later, she found both of them fast asleep.

Inspector Davies was waiting for him when Carmichael returned to the Yard.

"We've got Rob Coleman in an interview room," he reported. "O'Leary says you think he was the one who shot Sergeant Gibbons?"

His tone was incredulous, and Carmichael didn't blame him.

"The sergeant and his friend," he said, "have been doing some detective work of their own, and it's proved damned useful. Here, let me just give you a quick explanation before I tackle Coleman. Where have you put Mrs. Coleman, by the way?"

"She wasn't there," answered Davies. "In fact, Coleman didn't seem to know where she was—he claimed she had left him last night. I had a discreet look around, and a good portion of the closet in the bedroom has been cleared out, so maybe he means it."

"Dear God," said Carmichael. "Every time I turn around in this damn case, something else crops up. Well, see if you can track her down while I'm talking to Coleman. Let's get a cup of coffee while I go over what we've found out with you."

But by the end of Monday, no sign of Lia Coleman had been found.

Epilogue

*I*t was raining again on Hampstead Heath, a steady winter drizzle.

"How on earth," asked James, "do you cope with all that wet fur?"

Bethancourt sighed. "I have towels in the car boot," he said. "Lots of them."

James shuddered. In another moment he asked, "Do you think they've had enough? Because, to be frank, I certainly have."

"So have I," agreed Bethancourt. "It's getting too dark to see, anyway."

They called the dogs back, and turned in the direction of the pub where they could shed their wet overcoats and warm themselves with some very fine single malt whisky. On a chilly Tuesday evening, they had the place almost to themselves, which was fortunate as there was a distinct odor of wet dog coming from their vicinity.

"Ah," said Bethancourt, leaning back and lighting a cigarette. "That's very much better, I must say."

"Indeed," said James, raising his glass.

They sat in contented silence for a moment.

"I've been doing a bit of research," said James. "Vivian's about to murder me for spending time on it when I should be working." He grinned, and Bethancourt chuckled. "Once you know," he continued, "that the jewelry was sold piece by piece some years ago, it's not so difficult to find traces of it. I've already happened on one gentleman in South Africa who was quite astonished to find out exactly where his wife's ruby earrings came from and very pleased to have a proper provenance for them. There may be others like that, and I've been talking with one of the curators at the V&A who would quite like to do an exhibit, particularly if we can find the alexandrite necklace."

"Any luck on that score?" asked Bethancourt.

James shook his head. "Not yet," he said. "It's such a unique piece, I imagine it went into the collection of someone very shady. But even someone like that might be amenable to owning up to having it if I made it clear that the sale was perfectly legal, and offered a provenance. I have hopes."

"Hope," said Bethancourt, "is a great thing to have in life."

James laughed and raised his glass. "To hope."

"To hope," echoed Bethancourt, and they drank.

"Inspector Davies stopped by the hospital today," said Bethancourt. "The reports from the Swiss police make fascinating reading."

"Do they?" said James. "Grant mentioned it to me, but all I gathered was that our Coleman had been a very naughty boy."

"That's right," said Bethancourt. "They now believe he was involved in an armed robbery in Lausanne that took place about a month before he left for England. But they've also heard from the Ukrainian police, where apparently he has quite a record. He ran several pyramid schemes there, and then got involved with a gang stealing high-end art and jewelry. He fled the country after their last job, when a security guard was killed. The Ukrainians have never managed to catch all the gang members, but the couple they did get claim that Coleman was the killer in that instance."

James let out a low whistle. "And he seemed like such a nice chap," he said, and Bethancourt laughed.

"There's been nothing on Lia Coleman, though," he added. "Apart from the fact that she flew to Paris on Sunday night and then disappeared."

"I actually have a bit more there," said James, turning to rummage in the pockets of his overcoat. "It's why I rang you, in fact—I thought you'd like to see it. I gave the original to the police, of course, but I made copies first. It came in the mail this afternoon, postmarked from Paris."

He handed Bethancourt a photocopy of a letter, printed on a single page with a clearly written signature at the bottom: Lia Coleman.

Bethancourt raised his brows, startled, and James grinned at him.

"I thought you'd be surprised," he said. "Here, I'll fetch us another round while you read it."

"Cheers," said Bethancourt, turning his attention to the letter.

Dear Mr. James,

I am writing to you rather than the police because, to be frank, I have not always been on the best terms with law enforcement, but also because you struck me as a very astute man.

By the time you read this, I will have left England with the little I have been able to garnish from this misadventure. But I did not feel it right to leave without letting someone know I believe my husband is a murderer.

I now realize that my husband staged the robbery of Miranda's jewels in order to collect the insurance money. I admit I had begun to suspect that was the case sometime before, but was not entirely convinced I was right. But last Tuesday night, Sergeant Gibbons came to visit us at about seven o'clock. He was most genial (may I say here that I very much liked the sergeant and hope he makes a full recovery?), but despite his easygoing tone I noticed my husband seemed on edge, and I believe the sergeant noticed it, too. I do not remember now how the topic arose, but the sergeant happened to mention the murder of a onetime fence named Pennycook. I had heard of this before, as Rob had mentioned it to me one morning while he was reading the newspaper, and I remarked on that. Sergeant Gibbons seemed to find this very interesting, and Rob suddenly began to talk about the weather in England, which had nothing to do with our previous conversation, and which was a decided non sequitur.

I might not have thought overmuch about this, except that my husband made an excuse to go out after Sergeant Gibbons left, and was gone rather longer than I had expected. We heard the next morning that Sergeant Gibbons had been shot. After that, I looked up the article in the paper which had mentioned the Pennycook murder, and discovered that it had occurred on the night my husband had gone out without me to meet an old friend.

I then remembered that Miranda had kept an old German Luger which someone had given her as a souvenir from the war. The next time I went to the house, I looked for it and found it was gone.

I have no proof, but I believe this Pennycook tried to blackmail my husband over his scheme to cheat the insurance company and that my husband killed him in consequence. Fearful that Sergeant Gibbons was about to discover this, he followed him that night and shot him with the intention of killing him as well. I do not know what he did with the gun, but on reflection I think it most likely he simply threw it in the bin that night, as our pickup comes on Wednesday mornings, and he was most particular about taking out the trash that night.

I should, of course, have come forward with all this long ago, and I certainly should never have agreed to back up my husband's story that we had not seen Sergeant Gibbons that night. In my defense, I can only say that I had great difficulty accepting the fact that the man I had married was a murderer.

I trust you, Mr. James, to see that this letter gets into the right hands.

Yours truly,
Lia Coleman

James had returned with the whiskies by the time Bethancourt had finished reading. Bethancourt set down the page, picked up his drink, and took a large swallow of it.

"That," he said, "is a most remarkable letter."

"Isn't it?" said James. "You can have that copy, by the way. I asked Davies if they had traced her from Paris and he said no, but that it hadn't been a priority as they had nothing to charge her with except conspiring to defraud the insurance company, and he doesn't think they really have a very good case even for that. So, since I was curious, I rang an old friend of mine in Switzerland, who did a background check for me."

"Oh, this ought to be good," said Bethancourt, watching the gleam in James's eyes.

"Interesting, very interesting," said James. "The record of her marriage to Coleman is quite aboveboard, and lists her maiden name as Emilia Rossi, from Locarno. The only difficulty with that comes when you take a look at the records in Locarno and discover that Emilia Rossi died in an automobile accident when she was eight."

"My," said Bethancourt, his eyes dancing. "I'm beginning to be quite impressed with our Mrs. Coleman."

"Then you may also be interested to know," said James, smiling broadly, "that I stopped by the Haverford house on my way home this evening. The couple of pieces of sterling that were left are now gone, as is the set of Fenimore Cooper that you were going on about the other day."

Bethancourt burst into laughter. "Mr. Grenshaw will be so disappointed," he said. "Will they bother trying to track her down for that?"

"I can't see why they should," replied James with a snort. "After all, she's legitimately married to Coleman, and he's legitimately Miranda Haverford's heir. She may have jumped the gun by not waiting for probate to finish, but the stuff is ultimately hers."

"So it is," said Bethancourt, amused.

"I swear to God," said James, "if it hadn't been for her wretch of a husband, the woman would have pulled off her insurance scam. I'm not sure I ever would have figured it out."

"Then you think she's lying in her letter when she says the faked robbery was all Coleman's doing?" asked Bethancourt.

"I'm sure of it," said James. "Frankly, my estimation of Lia Coleman is that she's a professional con woman who married Coleman for his inheritance. The faked robbery may even have been her idea. But I do think she's telling the truth when she says she knew nothing about the Pennycook murder or the attack on Gibbons. If I read her right, she'd be far more likely to simply have paid up to keep Pennycook quiet."

Bethancourt nodded his acceptance of this theory. "I've never met a con artist before," he said. "I rather wish I had followed up the acquaintance—although perhaps I shouldn't say that. I might have been a poorer man by the end of it."

James laughed. "You might at that," he agreed. "Well, it's been a very interesting case. I don't regret it, despite having lost money on it—I get paid for recovering jewels, not for finding out they've never been stolen in the first place."

Bethancourt chuckled. "Do let me know," he said, "if you ever find the necklace and get that exhibit put on at the V&A. I'd very much like to see it."

"I will," promised James. "Oh, and I meant to ask Davies, only I forgot—how is Sergeant Gibbons doing?"

"Quite well," replied Bethancourt. "In fact, they say they're going to let him go home tomorrow."

"Oh, good show," said James. "I'm very glad to hear it. Well, here's to his convalescence."

"Hear, hear," said Bethancourt, raising his glass to James's.

Gibbons sat in the armchair, feeling better than he had in some time. He had been given eggs for breakfast that morning and he was certain they were the most satisfying eggs he had ever tasted. And afterward Nurse Pipp had helped him dress in his own clothes, brought round earlier by his mother. He was just waiting now for all the paperwork to be finished. He rather wished he was going home to his own flat in Hammersmith rather than to his parents' house, but getting dressed this morning had proved that he was not fit to be on his own yet. Not, he admitted, that his mother had had any doubts on that score.

He heard footsteps in the hallway outside, and in a moment Bethancourt appeared.

"Sorry to be late," he said. "I've got your new phone for you, all registered and ready to go. The voice mail," he added, handing it over, "lit up as soon as I turned it on."

"It's probably been collecting messages for days," said Gibbons, admiring his new acquisition; it, like his street clothes, was yet another proof that he had a life beyond the hospital walls.

"I'll go through them later." He looked up at his friend. "You look a little under the weather this morning," he said. "Were you out with Marla last night?"

"No, James and I were celebrating the successful end to the case," replied Bethancourt, perching on the bed. "We celebrated a little too much. I had to get a taxi home."

Gibbons laughed at him.

"I've got something else for you, by the way," said Bethancourt, pulling a package out of his overcoat pocket. "I'd nearly forgotten I'd ordered it in all the excitement. Here you go."

Gibbons took it, curious, and pulled the leather notebook cover, embossed with his initials, out of the bag. He stared down at it in silence for a moment, very touched by this evidence of Bethancourt's affection.

"Thanks, Phillip," he said. "I appreciate it very much—you know how fond I was of the old one you gave me."

"Which is why it seemed a shame it got ruined," said Bethancourt. "I reckoned it was bad enough getting shot—you didn't need to lose something you liked on top of it all."

"I've got my notebook right here," said Gibbons, pulling it out of his pocket and fitting it into the cover.

Bethancourt raised a brow. "You've written quite a lot in that one," he said. "Is it the one I bought you after you were shot?"

"That's right." Gibbons paused, laying the notebook in his lap and looking down at it for a moment. "Over the last couple of days," he said, "I've been writing down what happened the day I was shot, trying to fill in all the holes."

"I thought we'd pretty much covered that," said Bethancourt. "The last gap was what you did that night after O'Leary left you at the pub, and we know now that you went back to see the Colemans."

"Yes, that letter of Mrs. Coleman's was quite helpful," agreed Gibbons. "But what I've been writing down is not just where I was and what I did, I've also been trying to reconstruct my thoughts. It's quite uncomfortable, not remembering a whole day in your life."

"I dare say it is," said Bethancourt. "How are you coming with it?"

"I think I've got most everything now," answered Gibbons, glancing back down at the notebook. "I'm actually very grateful to Lia Coleman for writing that letter because it finally told me why I had gone to Walworth in the first place. I really couldn't make that out until I read her letter."

"I still can't make it out," admitted Bethancourt. "Why did you?"

"Because talking to the Colemans would have given me my first idea that the two cases might be connected," said Gibbons. "I think the note I made in the pub was the one about the kinds of people who commit arts theft—you can see from my earlier notes that both the Colemans exhibited a fairly thorough knowledge of gemstones when James and I were interviewing them."

"I see," said Bethancourt. "So you went back to see them just to sort them out in your mind."

"Right," said Gibbons. "And then while I was there, the mention of Pennycook would have provided the clue about the cases being connected. I think I still didn't have much notion how, but my first instinct would be to go and have a look at the scene of the crime, just to get a feel for it. I wouldn't have bothered O'Leary for that, though I might have rung him in the morning if I hadn't been attacked."

Bethancourt nodded. "It makes sense," he said. "And I suppose it also explains why Coleman shot you—he couldn't risk your putting the two cases together. I take it he's still not talking, by the way?"

"Not a peep out of him," confirmed Gibbons. "Not that it matters—we've got him bang to rights, and I think he knows it. Carmichael says his solicitor has been hinting about a plea deal."

There was a knock on the doorjamb and a smiling orderly came in pushing a wheelchair.

"You're okay to go," he said. "Your people will be along in a minute, but I just thought we'd get you into the chair while we were waiting for them."

"By all means," said Gibbons eagerly.

Bethancourt looked around. "Where's Nurse Pipp?" he asked. "I ought to say good-bye to her."

"She was in earlier to say good-bye," answered Gibbons, grunting as he levered himself up out of the chair. "Did you know that the night nurse is now dating my police guard?"

"No, really?" said Bethancourt. "Which one?"

"Jeffries—the tall one with dark hair," said Gibbons. "No, I'm all right," he added to the orderly, "it's a bit difficult getting back down, that's all. There I am."

"And here I am," said his mother from the doorway. "Your father has gone to bring the car round and we're all set."

She looked, thought Bethancourt, very relieved and happy to be getting her son back.

He accompanied them out and helped load Gibbons into the car. The orderly wheeled the chair away, and Bethancourt stood back to let the car start off, waving at his friend as the vehicle pulled away from the curb. He was going to miss not having Gibbons around in the coming weeks.

FIC
Chan

Chan, Cassandra.

Trick of the mind.

$24.95